WOULD SHE BE HONORED AS A PATRIOT...OR SHOT AS A SPY?

Janine Mercer, the beautiful adopted daughter of a prominent Philadelphia physician, had sworn to remain neutral—now she gave herself wholly to America's cause. As Washington's rag-tag army faced starvation, as New York burned and the Cradle of Liberty rocked in defeat, she learned firsthand the horrors of war.

Thrust into the white-hot center of conflict, she would be at the mercy of the mysterious soldier who invaded her life, commanded her heart—and ordered her shot as a spy! Swept up heart and soul in America's struggle, she would stop at nothing to serve the glorious fight for freedom, to fulfill the rapturous promise of love.

Freedom's Flame

DEE STUART

A DELL BOOK

Published by
Dell Publishing Co., Inc.
1 Dag Hammarskjold Plaza
New York, New York 10017

Dell ® TM 681510, Dell Publishing Co., Inc.

ISBN: 0-440-12532-4

Printed in the United States of America

First printing—April 1980

For Bruce

Freedom's Flame

Chapter 1

On a warm April evening in 1775 five ladies entered
the elegant Palladian drawing room at Gunston Hall
on the Potomac River and sat down to wait for the
gentlemen in the dining room to join them. Although
the political leaders of the Virginia colony and their
wives often gathered in Mr. Mason's home, this was
an occasion of some tension and anxiety. While the
ladies were exchanging pleasantries, they were all well
aware that the men were engaged in a matter of grave
importance. Otherwise Mr. Mason would not have
summoned them so summarily to Gunston Hall.

Janine's gaze swept the room, gathering swift im-
pressions of the flickering candles in the crystal chandelier as they shed a golden glow upon the beige
walls, the finely carved Doric pilasters flanking the
windows, the colorful Oriental carpet, the bas relief
figures adorning the fireplace, and the portrait of Mr.
Mason's late wife, Anne, which graced the mantel.
Mrs. Mason's dark eyes bored into her, seeming to
warn her against the deception she was about to per-
petrate. Aunt Ellen, seated not too far away, was, as
usual, belittling the French.

Janine clasped her hands. Looking up, she saw Ellen
watching her, her lips a fine line, turned down slightly
at the corners. Janine flushed and was immediately
angry with herself. She mustn't let her aunt upset her.
Not if she expected to get away alone. She straightened
up, arranged her shoulders in an attentive position,
and wrinkled her normally smooth brow slightly. If

she expected to have a headache in ten minutes, she must start preparing now.

Across the room Mrs. Jefferson pulled her shawl around her shoulders, though the night was warm. Janine thought that she, too, was forcing herself to be attentive.

Ellen's authoritative voice resumed her dissertation. "It's disgraceful—this worship of the French!"

"That's a bit strong, don't you think, Mrs. Burke?" asked Mrs. Washington. "It's only that the French will be our natural allies if the unspeakable should come to pass."

Janine's lips curved in a knowing smile. No observation condemning the French would be too strong for Aunt Ellen.

"God forbid!" Ellen waved her fan in dismissal of the French. "There never has been a reliable Frenchman." She frowned, intentionally avoiding looking at Janine, and added, "And the women are even worse."

Hot anger flashed through Janine. Her eyelids stung. *Don't let her see. Don't be angry. Don't jeopardize your chance to see Jonathan,* she kept repeating to herself. She stopped listening to the hurtful words and waited for a lull in the chatter. When it came, she rose, and, apologizing to Anne Cockburn, pleaded a headache and begged to be excused. Janine could feel her aunt's disapproval as she crossed the room and left, closing the door firmly after her.

Janine fled through the entrance hall, past the wide staircase, out the door, and across the octagonal river porch. Picking up her skirts, she ran down the steps and through the formal gardens, leaving Gunston Hall behind.

Wispy clouds hung in a sky bright with stars as she hurried on, keeping well in the shadow of the towering boxwood hedges, whose tangy scent floated on the warm spring air. Janine shivered as a dark cloud crossed the moon, shrouding the gardens in darkness. Beyond the box walk she sped through the rose garden to the latticed summerhouse. Inside the doorway she paused, her breath coming in short, quick gasps, eyes straining to see through the darkness.

"Jonathan?" she whispered.

Silence closed around her. The summerhouse was deserted. She tried to still the trembling inside and sank down on a bench beside the window to wait. In her mind's eye she pictured Jonathan fidgeting at the table, a captive audience for George Mason and his guests lingering over pipes and Madeira in the dining room. Surely they must be discussing more than tariffs and tobacco crops, for they had gathered in response to an urgent summons from Mr. Mason. She frowned, thinking of those who had come, as though it would explain the reason for their presence.

Martin Cockburn was Mr. Mason's cousin. His wife, Anne, frequently served as hostess. The Washingtons, of course, were neighbors. So was Uncle John. Janine often accompanied her uncle, Aunt Ellen, Jonathan, and Adam from her home at Heritage Hall. But what about Mr. Jefferson? Why had he brought his fragile wife, Martha, all the way from Monticello? And Peyton Randolph had come from Williamsburg with his nephew Edmund. Certainly this was no ordinary political discussion. And then, just before the ladies had retired to the drawing room, Mr. Lee and James Madison had arrived. Even Aunt Ellen had been surprised! Once again Janine marveled that her aunt could hang on Mr. Madison's every word only to speak of him later in such sarcastic tones. The purpose of this hastily assembled gathering remained a mystery— at least to Janine. She shrugged. Politics, no doubt. No matter. She was grateful for the stroke of good fortune that would give her a few precious moments alone with Jonathan for the first time in almost three weeks.

Anxiously she tapped her carved ivory fan on the bench. Had he been unable to excuse himself after all? She couldn't bear the disappointment. It was incredible that they could live under the same roof yet never have a moment alone. He had to come! Taking a deep breath to compose herself, she tucked in a strand of hair that had fallen over one of her shoulders. She tugged at the bodice and smoothed the folds of her yellow silk gown. She had taken good care of it, for it was her only fancy gown, one her father had bought for her two years ago, before he'd sent her to live in Virginia with his sister, Ellen, and Uncle John.

Janine sighed deeply. It seemed impossible that almost two years had passed since she had come to live at Heritage Hall. At first she had thought she would die of homesickness, for Dr. Robert Mercer had been both father and mother to her since her mother's death during a smallpox epidemic when Janine was four.

Janine's only clear memory of her mother was of being rocked in her lap while Mama sang gay French tunes in a clear, lilting voice. Zoë, a robust, gap-toothed, coffee-skinned woman from Santo Domingo who came to help out, stayed on to care for her and Papa.

As Janine had grown from baby to young girl, she took over the running of the household and attended Miss Cavendish's School for Girls. Though Papa's medical practice caused him to be gone much of the time, Janine was generally happy—until the fateful spring day Dr. Mercer told her, "You've grown up, *ma petite poulette*. You need the gentle guidance of a lady. I'm afraid I must send you to live with your Aunt Ellen at Heritage Hall."

"But, Papa, I'm happy here!" Janine's dark blue eyes brimmed with tears. "I don't want to go away to live with Aunt Ellen."

Dr. Mercer steeled himself against the tearful protests of his merry, lovable, and stubborn daughter. "No more than I wish to give you up." He sighed heavily. "But we'll write to each other and I'll come to see you. . . ."

"No! No! I won't go, Papa. I won't leave you."

"I don't want you to go, my angel, but we must do what's best for you. You'll love Aunt Ellen and Uncle John, and they'll love you. They have no daughters, only sons, Jonathan and Adam. Ellen has always longed for a daughter. She'll teach you to be a lady and be like a mother to you."

How wrong he had been. . . .

The memory of their first meeting seared her mind. She would never forget Aunt Ellen standing in the doorway of the red brick Georgian mansion, tall and austere in her stiff brown bengaline dress, her ash-brown hair pulled back and twisted into a coil atop her head. Her thin lips were forced into a grimace of a smile. Her eyes, black and bright as an adder's—and as cold—swept Janine from head to toe in stern disapproval.

Smiling, Janine stepped from the carriage and ran to her, arms outstretched, impulsively embracing her new mother.

Ellen's arms hung at her sides, fingers curled into fists. "So you are Janine." Ellen pursed her lips, frowning. After a moment's silence she said, "You are the image of Nicole." Her tone was accusing, her words a condemnation.

Janine's smile froze. Papa had always said how fortunate it was for him and for her that she resembled Mama. She backed away, and the warm words of greeting she'd intended to speak stuck in her throat. All she could manage was a hoarse whisper. "Yes."

Aunt Ellen leaned over and gave her a peck on the forehead. "Come along, then." She turned and led the way inside the entrance hall. "We have no room for you on the second floor. There are only four bedrooms. One is Mister Burke's and mine; one is Jonathan's, one Adam's and the fourth is for guests. I've had a room prepared for you on the third floor, with furnishings from storage that belonged to Mister Burke's mother—heirlooms. She made the sampler and also the quilt."

She beckoned to a young servant girl. "Esther will show you the way."

Taken aback, overwhelmed with disappointment, Janine's knees were weak and shaking. But she stiffened her spine and mutely followed the girl up the curving stair.

The room was small and dim. The feeble sunlight filtering through a single dormer window failed to warm the cold, whitewashed walls. Janine gazed around the room at the scarred washstand, the straight wooden chair beside the narrow bed which was covered with a frayed quilt, and the tattered sampler on the wall overhead. Her spirits sank to her toes.

For a long time Janine was unutterably miserable. Aunt Ellen's conception of tasks a lady should learn to perform were far removed from her expectations. Polishing silver, making soap, dipping candles, spinning cotton and wool.

"Even if you have servants," Aunt Ellen insisted in a voice that implied this was highly unlikely, "you must know how to do these things properly." There were also lessons in dancing and deportment, as well as endless needlework and embroidery that bored Janine nearly to distraction.

The isolation of life on the vast sprawling plantation was unbearably lonely compared to her life in the cozy little house she had shared with Papa amid the excitement and bustle of Philadelphia. From Heritage Hall the nearest city, Alexandria, was ten miles distant.

She was unaccustomed to boys, and her cousins were a revelation. Jonathan, two years her senior, teased her unceasingly, delighting in her outrage and spirited attempts to defend herself. She was awed by Adam. little older than she, who kept to himself and ignored her as much as possible.

Janine sighed deeply. She never could bring herself to write her kind and gentle Papa how miserable she was at Heritage Hall, for he was happy in the knowledge that he was doing what was best for her, and his increasingly demanding practice never allowed him time to make the five-day journey to Alexandria to see how she fared. And even if he had come, he wouldn't have known, for Aunt Ellen was sweeter than butter when others were about.

Eventually Jonathan took pity on Janine and taught her to ride Beauty, a chestnut gelding. Day after day they rode over the plantation, Janine mounted on Beauty, with Jonathan at her side astride his stallion Brandy. There was something sure and free and vibrant about Jonathan that gave Janine a sense of security and brought back her optimism. She was happier than she had been in a long while. Now, she thought, smiling to herself, there was a good reason for wishing to remain at Heritage Hall.

The vague sound of footsteps along the path interrupted her from her thoughts, and she strained her ears to listen. All she heard were the call of the whippoorwills and the lonely hoot of an owl. The moon slipped from behind the clouds and flooded the summerhouse with a thin, clear light. She gazed across the long sloping grounds to the bluff that overlooked the Potomac, its rippled surface gilded silver by the moonlight.

She heard no sound the moment before she felt strong arms encircle her waist from behind, as Jonathan pulled her to her feet, pressing against her, sending a delightful shiver through her body. His lips brushed her ear.

"Jonathan!" she cried, joy pulsing through her.

"I thought I'd never get away!" he murmured in the deep, slow drawl she had come to love. "Damned statesmen and their philosophical politics!"

Janine turned in his arms and placed her hands on his shoulders, staring at him, devouring him with her eyes. How handsome he was tonight in his dark blue coat and breeches cut to perfection, showing to best advantage his tall, lean, muscular body. Moonlight silvered his thick blond hair, accentuating his tanned face, the strong line of his jaw, and the slight cleft in his chin. His eyes were shining with love and anticipation, and he drew her to him, kissing her gently at first, then eagerly, forcing her lips apart, demanding.

She flung her arms around his neck, responding fervently, pressing her body against his, warm with desire. They had kissed before, but never with such passion and abandon. Their enforced separation had only served to strengthen their awareness of their need for each other, and every sense and emotion had heightened to an almost painful intensity. Jonathan's hands caressed her back and moved upward to unhook her gown.

A deep instinct warned her that there could be only one conclusion to such ardent embraces. Fearful of the consequences, she pulled her lips from his, twisting her head away.

"Jonathan, no. You mustn't."

His mouth found hers. "Janine, I love you, I want you. . . ."

She wrenched away from him. "No!" she cried. "Let me go!"

"Janine!" He stared at her in pain and bewilderment.

"You go too far. . . ."

"I'm sorry, sweetheart. We've been apart so long— you're not angry with me?"

She shook her head, troubled and utterly miserable. Jonathan stood, hands on his hips and feet spread, looking down at her, his face unhappy and upset.

"Janine," he pleaded, "don't turn me away. Have you forgotten all the good times we've shared together?"

"Well, I remember, Jonathan." Her lips curved in a wistful smile.

"Are you no longer my devoted little sister?"

She wheeled around, afraid to face him, afraid she would fling herself into his arms again. "The trouble is our fondness for each other has gone beyond the devotion of brother and sister."

Jonathan grinned. "Thank God you're *not* my sister, when it comes to that. Anyway, what's the harm in my loving you?"

Janine flushed. "Jonathan, I'm trying to tell you. We'll come to no good end because . . . I want you as much as you want me. Soon everyone will know . . . about us. The servants must already know. And I'm sure your mother suspects." With a feeling of distress, she recalled Aunt Ellen's cold and accusing eyes upon her the last few times she had returned to the hall after riding with Jonathan.

"Nonsense. You're imagining things." Jonathan's hands reached out for her, but she stepped backward out of his grasp.

Frowning, she shook her head. "Haven't you questioned why we've seen so little of each other of late?"

Jonathan threw up his arms in an impatient gesture. "I've told you. I've had to see to the unloading of provisions at the wharf, the shearing of the sheep, the planting of crops—"

Janine interrupted him. "You mistake my meaning, Jonathan. It is *I* who no longer have a moment to call my own. Aunt Ellen invents endless tasks for me to do so that I can no longer ride with you. She's doing everything she can to keep us apart."

Jonathan grasped her arms firmly and drew her down beside him on the bench. "That's ridiculous, Janine. Spring is always a busy time on a plantation, sweetheart. Stop fretting. We're together now. And as for loving each other, there's nothing wrong in that. I want you. I need you. All I want is to be with you, day and night. And didn't you just admit you feel the same?"

Head bowed, Janine nodded. "But, Jonathan, that cannot be—there's no hope for us." She raised her head and gazed at him, her eyes filled with longing and despair. Heritage Hall and her life here had suddenly become intolerable.

"Of course there's hope for us!" Jonathan burst out. His jaw set in a determined line, as though reinforcing a sudden decision. "We'll be wed."

Janine stared at him, eyes wide with surprise and disbelief. "Jonathan, you've taken leave of your senses. You're crazed."

A frown furrowed his brow. "You've no wish to marry me?"

For a moment hope made her heart flutter wildly in her breast. "You know I have. But—"

"No excuses, my sweet." He put an arm around her shoulders, holding her close. With his free hand he tilted her face up to his and kissed her tenderly on the brow, then on each eyelid.

"Jonathan, Jonathan," Janine murmured, her lips hot against his cheek. "How I wish it could be so, but we can never marry."

His eyebrows lifted in astonishment. "Why, in the name of—"

Janine placed her fingers on his lips. "Though it grieves me to say it, Aunt Ellen—your mother—dislikes me so. No, much more than that. She hates me!"

"Nonsense." Jonathan smiled indulgently. "Would she have taken you into our home if she'd hated you?"

Janine nodded. "Because her own brother asked her to—as a favor to him. She'd do anything for Papa." To Janine, it was strange indeed that Jonathan had never perceived the depths of his mother's devotion to her younger brother. Early on, Aunt Ellen had told her that Robert had been born to their mother late in life. "And after the slow fever took our parents, I reared that child as though he'd been born to me." Fine lines of bitterness radiated from Aunt Ellen's pinched mouth. "It was my dream for him to become a physician, to study medicine in Philadelphia and to come home to Virginia"—she paused, staring directly into Janine's eyes—"not to study in Edinburgh and then go running off to Paris!" She turned away and clamped her lips shut, as though to keep from saying something she would later regret. It wasn't until much later that Janine had realized the significance of Aunt Ellen's shared confidence.

"Your mother didn't know me then," Janine went on. "She thought me a child to do her bidding like a slave."

A look of annoyance crossed Jonathan's face. "She loves you, Janine. She's always been a strict disciplinarian. It's for your own good. You must know that." He smiled as though to reassure her. "If she's tired of the responsibility, that's my good fortune. She can turn you over to me."

"But, Jonathan—"

He silenced her protests with his lips, kissing her mouth, the hollow below her throat, the soft valley between her gently rounded breasts. A sensation she'd never felt before stirred within her. Her desire mounted, matching his. She cradled Jonathan's head against her bosom, resting her cheek on his thick blond hair. She caught her breath as he began loosening the bodice that imprisoned her breasts. She was beginning to feel a little uncertain.

"No, Jonathan. Please!"

The yellow gown slipped off her right shoulder. Why not let him have his way with her? She wanted it as much as he, and after all, they were going to be married. She clasped his face between her palms and tried to raise his head, to make him look at her.

He resisted. "Janine! Janine, don't!" he cried.

If she didn't stop him now, it would be too late. Her mind reeled. She didn't want him this way, she wanted to go to her husband a virgin. Yet she didn't want him to stop. A delicious languor was sweeping through her body. Tormented with longing for him, weakness overcame her and she knew she hadn't the strength or will to resist him much longer.

Above the sound of Janine's soft, tremulous breathing, they heard footfalls approaching along the path from the garden. Then Adam's voice, sharp, peremptory.

"Jonathan? Jonathan, are you there?"

Janine jumped to her feet and ran to a dark corner of the summerhouse and hid in the shadows. It would never do to let Adam know she'd stolen out to meet Jonathan. Adam was so proper, so circumspect. She couldn't be sure he wouldn't tell his mother, and if he should, it would go hard with her. She trembled at the thought of Aunt Ellen's wrath. With shaking fingers she rearranged her gown and pinned stray locks of hair into place.

Jonathan went to the doorway and stood blocking Adam's view. "I'm coming, Adam. Go back to the house. I'll join you directly."

Janine peeked through the wooden lattice of the summerhouse at Adam. His gray satin coat and breeches blended with the darkness. Only his white ruffled stock and pallid face stood out, giving him the appearance of a ghost. She could barely see his faded blue eyes, his mouse-colored hair, powdered and drawn into a queue, tied with a ribbon in the current fashion. He was shorter than Jonathan and slight like his mother. And he carried himself with an air of authority that he no doubt thought befitted a young man reading law with Mr. Simms in Alexandria. His attitude always unnerved her; she never knew what he was thinking. Now she fervently hoped he would think that Jonathan was courting one of the serving maids at Gunston Hall.

Adam stood silent for a moment as though considering his reply. Finally he said, "You'd best hurry. You've already been missed. Father is ready to leave and Mother has sent a servant to fetch Janine." Without waiting for an answer, he strode away in the darkness.

Jonathan took Janine's hand. "Hurry, sweet, before the guests leave. We'll tell them our good news."

His arm encircled her waist and he pressed her close to his side as they made their way through the rose garden and along the shadows of the high boxwood hedge that hid them from view of anyone scanning the gardens from the river porch.

A feeling of foreboding that would not be stilled began to creep through her. "Jonathan, please. Wait till we return to Heritage Hall to announce our betrothal."

"Why, in the name of heaven? Now is a fine time, here at Mister Mason's, with friends and neighbors to celebrate."

Jonathan was so happy and confident, she hated to dim his joy, but she plunged on. "We should tell your parents first." She paused, groping for the right words. "They may need time to become used to the idea. . . ."

Jonathan gave her a quick hug. "My little Janine, such a worrywart. Not at all like you. What's come over you?"

She held tightly to his hand encircling her waist, as though drawing strength from him. "I'm fearful something will happen. . . ."

"Don't be afraid." His lips brushed her temple. "I'll take care of you. And if it comforts you to wait until we return to Heritage Hall to announce our betrothal, we shall. They'll be delighted, believe me."

Janine took a deep breath to calm the fluttering inside. "Yes, Jonathan." The strength of his lean body firm against her side as they hurried back to the house and his hearty confidence that all would be well gave her courage and, for the moment, allayed her apprehension.

When they left the shelter of the boxwood hedge to cross the wide expanse of moonswept lawn, they parted. Jonathan strode toward the octagonal river porch and Janine picked up her skirts and hastened toward the north end of the house. She knew there was another entrance, for she recalled seeing a caged mockingbird standing near a door.

She ran up the steps and grasped the handle. Locked! The bird inside trilled maddeningly. She shook the handle and twisted it back and forth to no avail. Turning, she ran down the steps and hurried around the house to the front entrance. Her breath was coming in great gasps, and a stitch in her side knifed through her. Lights blossomed from the lamps on the carriages lined up in the driveway circling past the small porch that sheltered the entrance. As she reached the door it opened suddenly upon Martin and Anne Cockburn bidding Mr. Mason goodnight. With vast relief she saw that the entrance hall was crowded with departing guests. She stepped inside, hoping to slip unnoticed past Mr. Cockburn's ample back.

"Janine!"

Aunt Ellen's rasping voice sliced through the loud chatter in the hall like the lash of a whip. Janine's cheeks burned with embarrassment as she saw her aunt pushing and shoving her way toward her. Finally she stood facing Janine, her eyes hard and bright with anger. She caught her niece's elbow in a tight grip.

"Wherever have you been?" she demanded in a low, sharp voice. "The parlor maid couldn't find you anywhere!"

Janine raised her chin defiantly, meeting Aunt Ellen's hard eyes head on. "I thought I'd feel better for a bit of fresh air."

Aunt Ellen's eyes narrowed. "A physician's daughter should know that night air is bad for you."

"Walking is healthful," Janine said defensively. "I went for a stroll."

"Alone? In the dark?" she screeched.

"The coachmen were about. . . ."

Aunt Ellen wasn't listening. "Just look at you!" she ranted. "The hem of your gown is soiled, your hair is disheveled. I don't know what I'm to do with you. You're imposs—"

At that moment Uncle John, a short, robust, agreeable man with a round face, apple cheeks, and puffy white hair, strode up, smiled, and gave them a courtly bow. He radiated the optimistic air of a man who always looks on the bright side of things.

"Well, here are my ladies. Ellen, I see you've found our Janine."

"Found her!" Ellen hissed. "She came traipsing in here like a stray cat!"

Janine's face flamed with humiliation.

Ignoring his wife's outburst, Uncle John continued smiling affably. "Come, my dears, our carriage is waiting." He beckoned over the heads of the guests to Jonathan and Adam, and taking Ellen and Janine each firmly by the elbow, ushered them out the door and handed them into their carriage.

Ellen spread her crisp taffeta skirts halfway across the seat and patted the space beside her. "Sit here, John."

On their way to Gunston Hall the three men had sat on one seat, leaving the seat opposite the ladies to give them room to spread their voluminous skirts. Janine bit back a sharp remark at her aunt's childish behavior and sat squeezed uncomfortably between Jonathan and Adam.

Before the carriage had reached the end of the lane leading away from Gunston Hall, Aunt Ellen turned to her husband and asked in a petulant voice, "Whatever kept you so long in the dining room, Mister Burke? I was ready to take our leave an hour ago."

Uncle John heaved a sigh. "Politics, my dear. What else?"

"And what was so urgent? Why Mister Mason's hasty summons? Has he perhaps penned additional Fairfax Resolves? Or another letter to the king protesting British tyranny?"

"No, my dear. We were trying to persuade our reluctant statesman to serve again in the House of Burgesses."

Adam leaned forward as if to see his father's face more clearly in the pale gleam of moonlight. "How do you think the Virginia Assembly will react to the fighting in Massachusetts?"

Aunt Ellen's bony body jerked upright on the edge of the seat. "Fighting in Massachusetts? Pray tell me, Mister Burke, have you been keeping something from me?"

Uncle John's voice was elaborately casual, a ploy Janine noticed he used on occasions when he wished to keep something of importance from arousing "m'lady's ire," as he put it.

"I had no wish to alarm you, my dear. Mister Mason called us together to discuss the news brought him by courier the day before yesterday."

"Well, go on! Don't keep me waiting."

"It appears that seven hundred British regulars coming ashore to confiscate cannon and gunpowder exchanged fire with a small group of Minutemen in Lexington."

Adam interrupted. "It was rumored that Samuel Adams and John Hancock would be arrested."

"Rabble-rousers!" Aunt Ellen hissed. "Ridiculous to oppose British soldiers!"

Uncle John cleared his throat. "Actually the British continued their march to Concord and the militia, a ragged band of farmers and merchants, gaining supporters along the way, fought them at Concord Bridge." He turned to Aunt Ellen with a mild look of reproof. "And they chased the British all the way back to Boston!"

"Incredible!" she retorted, tapping her fan on her wrist with an agitated motion.

"Incredible, but true nonetheless," her husband replied.

"Surely the problems of Massachusetts have naught to do with us." Aunt Ellen expressed this sentiment not as a question, but as words carved in granite.

"Their problems are our problems, my dear," Uncle John replied. "In fact, the Virginia Assembly has already elected delegates to the Second Continental Congress at Philadelphia next month."

"Faugh! What's the good of men gathering together and talking?" She sniffed in disdain.

Jonathan spoke up. "They are determined to convince King George that we will no longer be put upon."

Adam leaned forward again, his pale face intense, eyes alight. "No, Jonathan, they've tried and failed. The king continues to ignore their petitions. I'm very much afraid, Mother, that the only solution is rebellion."

Uncle John sighed again. "That's the exuberance of youth, my lad."

Janine, vexed at Adam's air of authority, burst out, "I'm certain that only a minority feels that the solution lies in revolution. Most colonists believe that a compromise can still be reached. As between friends every affront is not worth a duel, between nations every injury is not worth a war."

"Janine," Aunt Ellen snapped, "it is unseemly for young ladies to enter into political discussions, and furthermore, no one is interested in your opinion."

Janine felt the redness creep up her neck and into her face, but on this issue she would not be put down. "That is not only my opinion, Aunt Ellen. I was quoting Mister Benjamin Franklin from a newspaper Papa sent me. Mister Franklin's opinion is well thought of in Philadelphia."

Uncle John cleared his throat loudly, forestalling further argument. "I quite agree with your Mister Franklin, Janine, but the time for compromise is past. The battle is joined."

"Politics! Grievances, petitions, rights, rebellion!" Aunt Ellen ranted from her citadel in the corner of the rocking carriage. "Will they never end? I wish to hear no more!"

The rest of the ride home was long and silent, the air heavy with tension; Aunt Ellen dour, nursing her ill humor; Janine smarting under her aunt's reprimand; and the men keeping their own counsel.

Once, when Uncle John made a feeble attempt at conversation, his wife snapped, "Do be quiet, Mister Burke. You're babbling!"

Her husband made no reply. Soon his head dropped forward and he dozed off, nodding with the rhythm of the carriage. Jonathan reached over and squeezed Janine's hand, but from this she took small comfort. For once his presence failed to warm her. Shivering with apprehension, she drew her cloak more tightly around her. The night air blowing up from the river had turned cool, and the birds were still. The only sound was the creak and groan of the carriage clattering down the dark, rock-strewn road. Occasionally a shaft of moonlight passed over Ellen's face, revealing her thin lips set in a determined slash across her grim countenance. Clearly she was reveling in self-righteous anger. Janine need not be told who the culprit was. She could almost hear Aunt Ellen formulating the tongue-lashing she was preparing to give her as soon as they reached Heritage Hall.

Janine smiled to herself, savoring her secret. When Aunt Ellen learned that she and Jonathan were to be married, she would hold her tongue. Surely she would have no desire to be at loggerheads with her eldest son. And Ellen would be forced to treat her, as Jonathan's wife, with due respect.

All too soon the carriage was rumbling down the narrow lane leading to Heritage Hall. Leaves brushed the roof as they jolted under slender oak trees whose branches met in a canopy overhead. At the end of the lane the sloping roof and dormer windows of the red brick Georgian mansion rose dark against the sky, the chimneys at each end silhouetted against the moon.

In frigid silence they alighted from the carriage. The only sound was the rustle of Aunt Ellen's taffeta skirts swishing about her legs as she strode inside. In the entrance hall Ellen turned to Janine, looming

over her, her aunt's eyes boring into her like fire
irons.

"Janine, come into the sitting room. I wish to speak
with you privately."

Janine stiffened. Now that she was betrothed, she
had finished with being treated like a recalcitrant
child. She opened her mouth to speak, but before she
could reply, Jonathan came to her side.

"Mother, I wish to speak to everyone." His glance
took in his father and Adam. "If you please, we'll all
retire to the sitting room."

Aunt Ellen glared at her son with cold condescension, but it was lost on Jonathan. He wheeled around
and, taking Janine's arm, led her through the sitting
room where they stood before the marble fireplace,
waiting for the family to be seated. Nervously Janine
let her gaze wander about the room. She loved this
room, especially in the warm glow of candlelight as it
was now. Gold brocade draperies softened ivory walls
and green paneling, and a deep red Oriental carpet
graced the gleaming oak floor. On one side of the
room stood a gold brocade couch, and on the opposite
side two Chippendale chairs flanked an intricately
carved lowboy. Books lined the shelves in the corner
cupboard to the right of the fireplace.

Uncle John lighted his clay pipe with a match from
the fire crackling on the hearth and eased into a green
brocade wing chair. He leaned back and began blowing small white puffs of smoke toward the ceiling.

Adam stood in the center of the room, facing them,
balancing his weight on the balls of his feet, rocking
on his heels, his hands folded behind his back in an
attitude of attentive anticipation.

Ellen sat ramrod-straight on a Chippendale chair
beside a tilt-top table. A determined stiffness seemed
to freeze her features as she gazed past Jonathan and
Janine at the ormolu clock on the mantel, as though
at a predetermined time she could take her leave.

Jonathan gave them his most engaging smile, and in

his slow, deep drawl he said, "It gives me great pleasure to tell you that I have asked Janine to become my
wife and she has done me the honor of accepting. We
are betrothed." He slipped his arm around Janine's
waist in a possessive gesture.

Uncle John, his face wreathed in smiles, set his pipe
down on a tray and rose from his chair, hands outstretched. "Wonderful news, my boy," he said, pumping Jonathan's hand. "I was beginning to wonder if
you were ever going to indulge in holy matrimony."
He clasped Janine's moist, trembling hands in his.
"I've always wished for a daughter, my dear. It's welcome news indeed that you are to marry into the Burke
family."

Janine stepped forward and kissed him lightly on
the cheek. "Thank you, Uncle John." Her heart lifted
at the sight of Uncle John's obvious pleasure at their
announcement. Now he sank back in his chair and
took up his pipe, at peace with the world.

Adam stepped forward as though he were addressing
a jury, his expression grave and serious. "I'm most
happy for you, Jonathan. And you, Janine. I wish you
both great happiness."

Janine stifled a giggle. Adam, always so formal, always an enigma hiding behind his manners and reserve. Maybe now she would learn to know him, to
know the person hiding inside that bland exterior.
Her spirits rose considerably. First Uncle John, and
now Adam accepted their betrothal with good grace.
This was not nearly so difficult as she had feared. She
glanced up at Jonathan, and her eyes met his, sparkling with happiness.

Gradually Janine became aware that a heavy silence
had descended upon the room. A terrible coldness
seemed to emanate from Aunt Ellen, sitting regal and
tight-lipped like an enraged monarch on her Chippendale throne.

Jonathan gazed at her expectantly. "Mother, have
you nothing to say?"

Her piercing black eyes challenged him and her color darkened as she rose to face him, her expression one of barely controlled fury. "What you are suggesting is out of the question. I absolutely forbid this match."

Janine gasped. She couldn't believe the words she'd heard with her own ears. A palpable tension in the air gripped them, holding them motionless for a long moment, and Janine's skin prickled with a sudden chill.

Aunt Ellen stood and turned as if to leave the room. "I shall forget you made such a witless proposal," she said, starting toward the door.

"Mother!" The word was a command of a sharpness that brought Ellen up in midstride. She turned to face Jonathan, eyes narrowed, full of hate.

He addressed her in patient, measured tones. "We're not asking your permission. Janine and I are going to be married. We'd like your approval."

His words unleashed a torrent of feeling barely held in check.

"Approval!" she shrieked. "May I remind you, Jonathan Burke, that someday you'll inherit Heritage Hall? Managing an estate of a thousand acres is a tremendous responsibility. To succeed you must have a wife who is capable of running a plantation—one to the manner born." Ellen's black eyes touched on Janine and dismissed her with contempt.

Jonathan's jaw tightened and his eyes turned to flint. "I'm not certain I entirely understand your meaning."

Ellen, suddenly conscious of the effect of her tirade, abruptly altered her tactics. "The time is out of joint. You heard the news tonight at Gunston Hall. Both your father and Adam have told us what the future holds. Not idle talk, but the opinions and conclusions of political leaders, statesmen who will mold the future of the colonies. Rebellion is imminent." Her voice turned soft and pleading. "Surely you'd not leave a young widow to take on the responsibility of Heritage Hall!"

Uncle John leaped to his feet, puffing agitatedly on his pipe. "Hold on, my dear! You've got the boy killed in a hypothetical battle! Surely you don't know what you're saying!"

Ellen Burke whirled on her husband, eyes blazing. "I know whereof I speak! Must I spell it out for you? Jonathan's and Janine's backgrounds are entirely different. The girl's mother was a Frenchwoman!" She spat out the word like an epithet, glaring with cold condemnation at Janine. "And we've no idea *who* her natural father was. . . ."

Janine flew at her in a rage, hands clenched at her sides, eyes stinging with tears. "What you imply is not true, Madame! My father was a physician at the court of King Louis!" She choked, gasping for breath, and plunged on. "Your own brother knew him well—before he came to love my mother—and me!"

Ellen's eyelids flickered, hooding her sharp eyes. "To my dear brother's great misfortune!"

"And after my father's death it was *your brother's* wish to marry my mother and bring us to live in this accursed country!"

Ellen's lips curved in a small, malicious smile. "But then who could foresee that your frail mother would die and my brother would foist her brat upon me!"

"Your accusation is unjust, Madame!" Janine exclaimed, trying to control her anger. And before she could blurt out anything further to alienate her aunt, she dashed to the door, jerked it open, and fled upstairs.

Chapter 2

Once in her room she slammed the door and leaned her back against it, breathing heavily as she blinked back tears of outrage and disappointment. She stumbled across the moonlit room, sank down on the window seat, and flung open the window. Leaning her head against the frame, she let the cool April breeze wash over her.

As she gazed out the window beyond the sloping lawns and gardens, the dark Potomac flowing past seemed to sweep all her hopes and dreams along with it. The newly budding trees, black in the moonlight, reached up like skeleton hands clawing at the full moon. Her heart beat heavily with failure.

Despite Aunt Ellen's cool initial reception, Janine had hoped she could win her over. She had earnestly tried, but everything she turned her hand to displeased her aunt. She'd hoped that she and Aunt Ellen would become close friends—that Ellen would replace the mother she'd longed for. But tonight proved the ultimate failure. She knew there was no atonement she could make to placate Ellen, for Janine had come to understand that her mother had committed the unforgivable sin: marrying Robert. Her own sin was her mirror image to her mother. Clearly it was through Janine that Ellen would wreak revenge upon Nicole.

Biting her lip to hold back the tears, she jumped up and crossed the room to her bed. She reached under the pillow and drew forth the brooch that Papa had given her, a miniature of her mother, and then returned to the window. Moonlight illuminated a pale oval face, rose-tinted cheeks, gleaming black hair, a soft, full mouth curved in a gentle smile, and eyes that seemed to speak to her. Janine closed her eyes and tried to conjure up her mother.

During her childhood Papa had kept Nicole's image alive for her as best he could. In the evening he would draw her up in his lap in the big wing chair before a crackling fire, and she would beg him to tell her stories about Mama.

Janine never tired of hearing how Robert Mercer had gone to Edinburgh to study medicine and on to the Sorbonne. There he had met her parents, François Le Maître and his beautiful wife Nicole, who had befriended him. He told Janine of the good times—picnics in the Bois de Boulogne, boating on the Seine, evenings at the opera. And the bad times. . . .

"One foggy fall evening on our way home from the opera, we were overtaken by a pair of runaway horses pulling a carriage. Your father tried to stop them, lunging for the reins, and the carriage overturned, crushing him underneath. He saved the lives of the ladies in the carriage at the cost of his own. A tragic accident." Dr. Mercer's warm brown eyes misted and he gave Janine a hug.

"At first your mother was inconsolable. I tried to comfort her, to take care of you both. Though I kept it from her and refused to admit it even to myself, I loved your mother with all my heart. And *ma petite* Janine as well."

He kissed her lightly on the top of her head. "Gradually your mama came to love me. Not the romantic way she had loved your father, of course, but a deep, abiding love. . . ." He paused, gazing at a miniature of Nicole on the table, and went on. "I finished my studies at the Sorbonne, and when the time came for me to return to Philadelphia, your mother and I knew we'd never be happy apart. And so we were married in Saint Étienne." Her father smiled down at her. "I won a wife and a little girl as well."

"Go on, Papa," Janine would coax. "Tell the rest!"

"We decided to move back here where I had a position waiting for me teaching medicine at the College of Philadelphia. We made a new life together here and were happy, you and your mama and I." He stroked Janine's silken black hair. "You are so like her, *ma petite*. I am indeed a fortunate man."

The sound of a door creaking open, then footsteps on the porch below, startled Janine from her reverie. She smelled a whiff of smoke, the spicy aroma of Uncle John's pipe tobacco, and heard voices drift upward through the darkness. She heard Aunt Ellen's voice, strident and indignant. ". . . a most unsuitable match for Jonathan. I had in mind one of the Carlyle girls, someone from his own station in life. One must be practical, John. Furthermore, uniting the Burke and Carlyle families would be the coup of the Virginia colony."

"You underestimate Janine, my dear. She's most capable and intelligent. How many young ladies do we know who can read and write?"

"Faugh! John, don't be a dunce. I grant you, if the girl used her reading and writing properly, they would be a great asset. Unfortunately she wiles away the day reading novels and playing the spinet. So you see, her schooling and her father's spoiling have only made her bold and obnoxious. Every time Mister Worthington comes to tutor the boys, she sneaks into the schoolroom and listens." Aunt Ellen emitted a snort of disgust. "Totally unnecessary and unladylike."

"In my presence she's always been a perfect lady." Uncle John's voice was calm and reasonable, but the more calm and reasonable he was, the more agitated Ellen became. Her voice rose sharp and insistent.

"In *your* presence, of course, my dear. But you've no idea what goes on behind our backs."

Janine drew in her breath sharply. She and Jonathan had done nothing wrong. How could Aunt Ellen abuse her so?

"She's a wild and headstrong baggage, I tell you! One of the servants told me she goes riding with Jonathan when he's supposed to be carrying out his duties on the plantation. And all the while I thought she was riding alone."

"Seems harmless," Uncle John said mildly.

"Harmless! She dons a pair of Jonathan's old breeches in the stable, and then, to make matters worse, she rides astride, galloping over the countryside, through the fields and woods like an Indian. The girl has absolutely no sense of propriety. If you think I'm going to stand quietly by and allow our son to marry the irresponsible daughter of a French adventuress, you are quite mistaken. She's a disgrace—a most unsuitable match for a Virginia gentleman."

Janine's face burned with anger and resentment, and she bit her lip to keep from crying out.

"Come, come, Ellen. What you're telling me simply proves Janine's courage and determination. It appears to me, my dear, that if these qualities were directed into the proper channels, they would become attributes. Courage and dermination are certainly required of the mistress of a great plantation."

Ellen's voice rose in rage. "You are siding with that vixen?"

"Of course not, my dear. But I cannot take such a dim view of this marriage—"

Ellen interrupted him, assuming a martyred air. "My brother told me she was fearless and impulsive, always rushing out to meet life. Hardly ladylike qualities, John. The very reason Robert asked me to take her in hand was because he felt she needed gentling, to learn self-discipline, self-control, to become a lady." She whined as though in pain. "I've tried, John, Lord knows how I've tried, for two ghastly years. And I've failed miserably."

"I wouldn't say that, my dear," John replied a shade

too heartily. "I think she's turned out uncommon well!"

"Mister Burke!" Ellen's voice was hard and challenging. "I will not tolerate this marriage. Are you with me or against me?"

Janine held her breath, the pulse at the base of her throat throbbed painfully. "Dear Lord, make him take my part!" she whispered.

There was a long moment of silence. Then she heard a sharp rapping sound, which she recognized. Uncle John was knocking the tobacco from his pipe on the porch railing. A delaying tactic Janine had observed him use before when under duress from his domineering wife. At last he let loose a long, loud sigh.

"I'm always with you, my dear—right or wrong."

Janine could bear to hear no more. She jumped up, ran to her bed, and flung herself down, burying her head in the pillow, sobbing wildly. Without Uncle John's support her cause was hopeless. How could he have deserted her if he were truly as fond of her as he implied? Aunt Ellen's condemnation was so unjust. Janine had suffered few disappointments in life, and this one was shattering indeed, plunging her to the depths of despair.

Bitterness against Aunt Ellen and Uncle John rose like gorge in her throat, choking her. Yet, in her verbal duel with Aunt Ellen, Uncle John had tried to defend her. She had to give him credit for that. And of course he had to *live* with Aunt Ellen. She shouldn't fault him for wishing to preserve the peace.

She heaved a convulsive sigh and rolled over on her back to stare at the square of yellow moonlight etched on the ceiling. She would have to forgive Uncle John, for she knew only too well how miserable Aunt Ellen could make the life of anyone who opposed her or incurred her displeasure.

A soft tapping sound interrupted her thoughts. Janine raised her head from the pillow. There it was again, a gentle tapping upon her door. She rose and opened it a crack, peering into the dimly lighted hallway.

Jonathan stepped inside, quickly closing the door after him, and drew her into his arms. She clung to him, letting him hold her in a close embrace, taking refuge in the protection of his arms around her, warm and comforting, burying her face in the curve of his shoulder.

"Jonathan, it's hopeless," she cried. "I heard Uncle John and Aunt Ellen talking on the porch below. They'll never give their approval. Never!"

He kissed her tenderly on the forehead. "I know, my sweet. I know. For the past thirty minutes I've set forth every argument I can think of—all useless. You'd have thought they were both stone-deaf. At the last I told them that I'd forefeit my property rights as eldest son—let Adam take over Heritage Hall—and that I would read for the law. They wouldn't hear of it."

"Oh, Jonathan, what are we to do?" Tears brimmed in her eyes and slid down her cheeks.

"Don't worry, sweetheart. I'll think of something." He stroked her hair, smoothing a few soft black tendrils away from her forehead until she grew calm.

At last she drew away from him and, as though putting distance between them would strengthen her resolve, she went to the window and stared out at the river flowing ever onward on its relentless course. Her voice was low and even in the darkness. "I'm going away, Jonathan."

Swiftly he crossed the room and stood behind her, his arms encircling her waist. "Janine! You can't! I won't hear of it!"

She steeled herself against his charm and the warmth of his embrace. "How can I stay here?" She sighed in weary resignation. "Your mother hates me. And now living under the same roof with her will be intolerable."

"Don't be so hasty, sweetheart. She'd react this way

to any woman I would choose to marry, don't you see? All she needs is time. Give her time to get used to the idea of our being together. Be patient. She'll come around. Believe me."

Janine shook her head. "It won't work, Jonathan— you and I wanting each other the way we do—"

Jonathan bent his head, burying his face in her thick, silken hair. His lips, warm and moist, found the tip of her ear and traveled down the slender curve of her neck. Janine closed her eyes and stiffened her body, willing herself not to respond, standing as though she were carved from wood.

"I'll write to Papa and tell him the truth: that I can remain here no longer. He'll have to let me come home to Philadelphia."

"Nonsense." Jonathan grasped Janine's shoulders and turned her around to face him. "Listen to me, Janine. I said we'll be married, and so we shall. To-morrow night we'll go to the ball honoring George Washington."

Numbly Janine nodded. This was nothing new. For weeks she'd been looking forward to attending the ball at City Tavern in Alexandria.

"And at the opportune time we'll slip away from the tavern and find the circuit rider—"

Puzzled, Janine looked up into his face. His blue eyes under full, straight brows were pleading and earnest.

"The circuit rider will marry us."

Janine gasped. Wide-eyed, she stared into his face. "Surely you've taken leave of your senses!"

Jonathan began pacing the room, hands clasped behind his back, afire with his idea. When the moonlight touched his face, Janine saw his jubilant smile and his eyes reflecting a peculiar light. His voice contained daring mingled with excitement.

"Not at all, sweet. It's quite the most sensible plan."

Janine ran to him, catching his arm midstride. "No, Jonathan. What you propose is pure folly. It would only make matters worse. It will turn your parents against us forever. And what's more, they'll refuse to recognize our marriage unless we're wed in Christ Church."

His handsome face broke into an appealing smile. "Janine, you're thinking like a child. After we're married, what anyone else thinks is of no importance."

Married! Her heart pounded so hard that the sound seemed to echo in her ears. She leaned her cheek against Jonathan's shoulder and put her arms around him, clasping him to her as if to assure herself that this moment was really happening. A betrothal with a proper marriage in the distant future was one thing. An elopement now was quite another.

At first she had hoped their betrothal would soften Aunt Ellen's hatred and resentment of her; and later, when she had mellowed a bit, would be time enough to marry. Now, after tonight's fiasco, Janine knew that nothing could redeem her in Aunt Ellen's eyes. Clearly it would be just the reverse. Reason and common sense overcame her reckless urge to elope with Jonathan.

"No, Jonathan. Our marriage now will only serve to bring down your mother's wrath upon both our heads. She'll never forgive you, never!"

He seized her shoulders and rocked her gently, as though to shake some sense into her head. "Goose! We won't stay here in Virginia! Come away with me, Janine!"

"Run away?" she whispered, eyes wide in surprise. She hesitated, mulling it over. Thoughts of Aunt Ellen and the countless subtle cruelties she could and would inflict upon her if she had to stay here, now that Ellen knew Jonathan loved her, went swiftly through her mind. Escape from Aunt Ellen and her torments loomed before her with all the promise of entry through the heavenly gates.

Taking her silence for consent, Jonathan swept on, carried away by the bold inventiveness of his plan.

"We'll ride to Philadelphia and stay with your father until we find lodging. . . ."

Janine nodded. The very outrageousness of Jonathan's proposal began to intrigue her.

Encouraged, he rushed on, persuasive, pleading. "We won't be a burden to him, I promise you. I'm well versed in letters. I'll find work—in Mister Franklin's print shop—if not his, there are others."

Janine rose on tiptoe, studying Jonathan's face. "Jonathan," she commanded, "look me straight in the eye. You'll lose your birthright, your home, your lands. Your parents will disown you. Am I worth Heritage Hall and all that goes with it?"

His strong hands on her back crushed her to him as he murmured against her hair, "All that and more, my sweet!"

When she started to speak, his lips on hers, silencing her doubts and fears, were first gentle, then demanding. Her body responded, molding to his, aflame with desire, hungry for fulfillment of passions as yet unsated, as she felt his body press against her own.

Lost in Jonathan's embrace, she began to think his preposterous, harebrained scheme was possible. Why did she hesitate? He was so ardent, so devoted. He truly loved her, and she him. Why then this reservation? Yet something held her back. In her heart she knew it was wrong. If she agreed, Aunt Ellen would have all the proof she'd ever need that she was the wild and headstrong baggage she made her out to be.

Janine drew back, peering into Jonathan's face. "If I should decide to come away with you—"

He tipped her chin upward and stood looking down at her in the thin moonlight, his face alight with anticipation and happiness.

"You'll come away with me, sweetheart. You'll come!"

Chapter 3

The following evening Janine stood before the mirror above the washstand in her room, her hands shaking as she tried to dress her hair for the ball. For once she was grateful that Aunt Ellen forbade the serving maid to assist her. Besides, she loathed the high towering creations, carefully powdered hair-do's worn by ladies of fashion, and preferred to dress her own hair.

She parted the shining black tresses down the center and combed a soft wave above each temple, framing her forehead. Gathering the silken mass in her hands, she drew it back behind her ears and fashioned it into a bun, which she fastened high on the back of her head. To the right of her part she tucked a nosegay of yellow primroses that Jonathan had given her. She straightened the fine lace ruffle edging the neck and sleeves of her yellow silk gown. Then, leaning toward the mirror, she peered at her face, searching for any sign of nervousness or anxiety that would betray her guilt.

Innocence shone forth from the deep blue eyes gazing back at her. How astonishing, she thought, that outwardly she appeared calm and serene while inside her nerves crackled with the realization of what she was about to do. Her breath quickened with excitement, and her gaze dropped to the gently rounded curves of her breasts rising and falling above the lace trimming on her gown. No longer a child, but a woman about to be married!

She smiled at her reflection, then her cheeks reddened as she recalled more than one occasion when Papa had come upon her gazing at herself in the pier glass in the hall at home, despairing at her image—a thin, bony scarecrow of a child—and Papa's gentle admonition as he turned her away. "Come, *ma petite*, stop admiring yourself. It's not seemly. Ladies are not vain." He had succeeded in making her feel beautiful even though she was not. Dear Papa.

She was more worried than she cared to admit to Jonathan as to how Papa would receive them. After all, as far as he knew, Aunt Ellen had not only taken her into her home, but had proved a kind and loving mother. She feared he would not look with favor upon her defying Aunt Ellen and Uncle John and running away with their son. Far from giving his blessing to her marriage, he might consider that she had ill used the Burke family. She couldn't bear to fail Papa. She heaved a sigh. It was still not too late to refuse to go along with Jonathan's preposterous plan.

Turning from the mirror, she gave a final glance around the small room she might never see again— the hard, narrow bed under a frayed quilted coverlet; the washstand holding a white bowl and pitcher; the straight spindle-backed chair; the rag rug, an oasis of color on the bare wood floor; the wardrobe full of Aunt Ellen's cast-off clothes. Had she forgotten anything? Earlier in the day she'd wrapped in her green linsey-woolsey dress a small bundle of possessions she wished to take with her and smuggled it to Jonathan.

Flinging her cloak around her shoulders, she tried to still the nervous fluttering inside her breast as she hurried downstairs and outside where Jonathan was waiting beside the carriage.

Aunt Ellen was already inside, sitting next to Uncle John, her black and white taffeta skirt all but hiding his legs. As Jonathan handed Janine into the opposite seat next to Adam and eased in beside her, Aunt Ellen gave a loud, irritable sniff.

"You've kept us all waiting, Janine."

"I'm sorry, Aunt Ellen."

All day Aunt Ellen had maintained a cool composure, acting as though the terrible events of the previous evening had never happened. But Janine felt wretched. Her emotions pulled her in two ways, desire in one, loyalty to Papa in another.

Aunt Ellen's critical eyes swept over Janine as she arranged her skirts about her. "And you're wearing that tattered yellow gown? Why aren't you wearing one of the ones I gave you?"

Through stiff lips Janine replied, "They're too tight, Aunt Ellen."

"Hmm." Her taffeta skirt rustled disdainfully. "Too much reading and sitting at the spinet tends to make one plump. We'll have to find more active pursuits to keep you busy, my dear."

Janine made no reply. Despite her nervous apprehension, a small smile curved her lips at the irony of Aunt Ellen's words, "active pursuit," which were far more apt than she dreamed.

They lurched along in the carriage under the clear, star-hung sky in a strained silence. At last in an effort to lighten their mood Uncle John said, "Janine, have you ever heard the story they tell around Market Square about Mister Mason when he was running for the Virginia Assembly?"

"No, Uncle."

Ellen gave an exasperated sigh. "John, please. You've told that story a thousand times."

John chuckled. "Then don't listen, my dear." He leaned toward Janine. "When his opponent charged that he was losing his mind, Mister Mason retorted that if his adversary's mind should be lost, nobody would notice it."

Janine forced a nervous little laugh. "How comical, Uncle John. Mister Mason has a quick wit indeed."

Adam related a dry, humorless event that had occurred that day in Mr. Simms's law office. Janine wasn't listening. Her mind was in turmoil, her damp hands opening and closing her fan in an agony of indecision.

At last the horses clattered down Royal Street and drew up before the tavern, an imposing red brick building ablaze with lights. The street was congested with carriages driving up and discharging passengers. Linkboys carrying lanterns lighted their way to the door.

Inside, the Burke family threaded their way through the crowded tavern room past a roaring fire, pausing to greet the Ramsays, Carlyles, and Dr. Craik. They nodded to the innkeeper dispensing ale behind the bar and climbed the narrow stairs to the ballroom. Candlelight gleamed from a shining brass chandelier and wall sconces shed a soft radiance upon the guests. The ladies had seized the opportunity to wear the colorful silks and velvets they had so carefully laid away in favor of homespuns and muslins after the First Continental Congress had decreed that no more British goods were to be imported into America. Gentlemen were no less brightly attired, strutting like cocks in brocade waistcoats, richly embroidered satin coats, and knee breeches showing off well-turned legs. Few of the men still wore powdered wigs, lately gone out of fashion. Janine caught sight of Mr. Washington, a head taller than most of the men, his hair drawn back in a queue, powdered and tied with a bow—the center of attention in a circle of laughing, chatting friends.

Janine's gaze lifted to a small white balcony where musicians were tuning up their instruments. Moments later the first notes of the violins rose above the noise of the crowd.

Janine stood facing Jonathan, outwardly calm, though her heart was pounding so hard, she felt it would surely fail. Gentlemen bowed, ladies curtsied, and Janine's feet moved mechanically through the slow, stately steps of a minuet. Shortly after the dance

ended, couples formed for a quadrille, Uncle John and
Aunt Ellen among them.

Jonathan whispered in Janine's ear, "Now, Janine!
Hurry—upstairs—first room on your right. I've left
your clothes in the pine chest. Change and leave by
the back stairs. I'll be waiting outside in the alley."

Janine froze. Her throat was dry and her body was
gripped by a paralyzing fear. "Jonathan, I can't. . . ."

He seized her elbow in a firm, hard grasp and ushered her across the room, through the doorway. "I
bribed the stableboy to bring up Brandy and Beauty.
He can't hold them in the alley all night. Now hurry!"

Shaking like an aspen, Janine lifted her skirts and
mounted the stairs. She found the first door on her
right unlocked and entered the small, sparsley fur-
nished room. Raising the lid of the pine chest, she
pulled out a bundle wrapped in Jonathan's old brown
woolen cloak. Inside were the riding clothes she'd
kept hidden in the stable: jacket, shirt, knee breeches,
stockings, and riding boots. Her hands were trembling
so, she could hardly unhook her dress. Thank heaven
she'd had the foresight not to lace herself into stays
tonight.

She stepped swiftly out of her petticoats, pulled the
rough garments on over her chemise, donning the
cloak and drawing the hood well over her head. Reluctantly she stuffed her yellow gown and petticoats
inside the chest and closed the lid. Taking a deep
breath, she opened the door a crack and peered into
the hallway. She saw no one. Laughter, loud voices,
and shouts of revelry floated up the staircase from the
first-floor tavern room, and strains of music issued
faintly from the ballroom. The lengthy quadrille was
still in progress.

Summoning her courage, Janine ran lightly down
the stairs. On the last step she froze, hardly daring to
breathe. In the narrow hallway outside the ballroom
stood Aunt Ellen engaged in conversation with Mr.
Cockburn. Though Ellen's back was turned, she and

Mr. Cockburn were blocking Janine's passage down the back stairs. Fighting down panic, she lowered her head, hoping her cloak would hide her face, and shoving Aunt Ellen roughly aside, bolted between them and raced toward the stairs.

Angrily Aunt Ellen and her companion spun around. "Hold on, you young jackanapes!" Martin Cockburn cried.

Heedlessly Janine fled down the stairs and out the door into the protective darkness of the alley. Someone grabbed her around the waist and clapped a hand across her mouth, stifling the scream that bubbled up in her throat.

"Janine, it's me, Jonathan. Hurry. I'll give you a leg up." He bent down and laced his fingers together to form a stirrup. As her eyes adjusted to the darkness she saw Beauty standing quietly beside him. Quickly she set her foot in Jonathan's hands and sprang lightly onto Beauty's back.

"Jonathan," she gasped, "your mother and Mister Cockburn saw me leaving. She may have recognized me!"

Jonathan swore softly. "We'll hope to heaven that she took you for a linkboy. Unless they took you for a cutpurse, I doubt they'll sound an alarm."

Jonathan mounted Brandy and led the horses at a walk around the rear of the tavern, picking his way through mud and overgrown weeds along a circuitous route toward Cameron Street.

Janine's teeth were chattering and her legs were shaking so that she wove her fingers in Beauty's mane lest she slide from her back. "Jonathan," she said in a harsh whisper, "can't we hurry?"

He turned his head toward her. "I want to keep clear of the coachmen," he said in a low voice. "We look like a pair of horse thieves. It would surely arouse suspicion if we galloped through the streets, and I've no wish to be stopped and questioned."

Janine nodded and followed Brandy down a dirt

lane onto Cameron Street where the clip-clop of the horses' hooves struck loudly against the cobbles. Janine held her breath. If they were being pursued, their whereabouts were certainly no secret.

On her right she recognized Colonel Washington's white clapboard townhouse, and further along, the home of Lord Fairfax. At the next corner Jonathan turned and urged Brandy into a fast trot. At the sight of the spire atop Christ Church rising above the trees, Janine felt a pang of regret that she was not to be married within its hallowed walls.

"Jonathan," she cried, drawing abreast of Brandy, "hold up! Where's the circuit rider who's to marry us?"

Without slowing his pace, Jonathan called over his shoulder, "The innkeeper told me he's ridden on to Pohick Church. We'll find another along the way. Don't worry!"

A wave of disappointment and anxiety swept through her, but nothing could be done to alleviate it. Jonathan spurred Brandy to a canter and Janine, gripping Beauty's reins with white-knuckled hands, forced her body to match the rocking motion of the animal's rhythmic gait. "Are you sure you know the way?" she shouted.

"We're taking the King's Highway. Look at the stars. We're heading due north."

Janine looked up at the sky, a clear, dark vault studded with stars that seemed unusually brilliant. The moon, a bright disc hanging in the sky, shone like a beacon spotlighting their headlong flight.

When they had left the town well behind, Janine began to breathe more freely. Still her heart pounded with fear and apprehension when she thought of the enormity of what they had done. Aunt Ellen would never forgive them. What would she do when she discovered they were gone? The answer struck her like a blow.

"Jonathan," Janine shouted, "do you think Aunt Ellen and Uncle John will send someone to apprehend us?"

Jonathan looked at her with a jubilant grin. "They'll send someone after us right enough. It's just a matter of time—whether Mother decides we've eloped and is determined to bring us back—or Father figures someone has stolen Beauty and Brandy and is determined to recover his horses. Either way I'm certain we'll be pursued. First they'll search the tavern courtyard and the rooms. They won't know for certain that we're gone until the ball ends—and Colonel Washington's been known to dance until three in the morning! Since the ball is in his honor, no one should leave until he does, which gives us several hours on our pursuers. Stop worrying, sweetheart."

Jonathan's cheerful certainty regarding their escape did nothing to bolster her confidence. She pushed far back in her mind the thought of what would happen if they were caught and concentrated on keeping pace with Jonathan.

Oak and pine trees grew thickly along the rock-strewn road. Occasionally she caught a glimpse of the river. Her hood had fallen to her shoulders; her hair had come loose, streaming out behind her like a banner. A stiff breeze blowing up from the river stirred the leaves on the trees. She breathed in the tangy scent of leaf mold with the night air. Crickets chirped and once a small animal, frightened from its hiding place, scampered across their path. They settled down to a steady gait and Beauty's and Brandy's hooves pounded the muddy, rutted road in time with her thudding heart.

After a while the air turned cold and a heavy mist settled upon them, seeping into Janine's bones. Her hands grew stiff and her legs ached from gripping Beauty's sides.

"Jonathan, how far is Philadelphia?"

He turned his head and smiled. "Oh, a hundred and forty or fifty miles."

She made no reply. It wasn't until the ferryman had plied them across the Potomac that she felt free from pursuit.

Chapter 4

After a time the flat marshy woodland gave way to higher ground, and the horses labored up a steep hillside, emerging from the pocket of mist into a thinly wooded area. A mottled moon shed a pale watery light through hickory, oaks, and pines. Above the dull thudding of the horses' hooves Janine heard the sound of water trickling over rocks.

"Hold up," called Jonathan over his shoulder. "We'll rest and water the horses."

When they reached the stream, Jonathan swung down from Brandy's back and helped Janine dismount. Numb from hours of riding, her legs shook as she stumbled to the water's edge. She knelt beside Jonathan among the ferns on the mossy bank and cupped her hands, scooping up the cold, clear water, gulping it down, then splashing it on her face until her skin tingled. She dried her face and hands on her sleeve, and gathering her long hair into a coil, pinned it high on her head. A short distance away Beauty and Brandy stood, forelegs deep in water, snuffling noisily.

Jonathan fetched beef jerky, biscuits, and a flask of rum from his knapsack and sat down beside her on the bank. While they devoured their meal, he wrapped his arm around her shoulders, pulling her close to his side. Janine, shivering more with apprehension than cold, snuggled against him, grateful for the warmth of his body.

As though sensing her anxiety, Jonathan brought her to him and kissed her gently on the forehead. "Another hour should put a safe enough distance between us and Heritage Hall, sweet. And there's an inn ahead where we can stay the night."

Janine nodded, pushing down her fear, pushing down the thought that this was indeed a foolhardy, harebrained scheme, longing only for the comfort of a bed on which to rest her bone-tired body.

They remounted and started off at a fast, steady trot, the horses' hooves thudding along the hard-packed ground cushioned with pine needles. The April wind freshened, stirring the trees with a soft rushing sound; the stars paled in the cloud-shredded sky. Abruptly the land flattened out, the trail widened, and they entered a small, rock-strewn clearing in the forest. Janine urged Beauty forward abreast of Brandy and took a deep breath, letting the tangy air fill her lungs to clear the fatigue from her brain. The horses' ears twitched nervously. Beauty tossed her head and slowed the steady rhythm of her pace, holding back.

At the far edge of the clearing the forest loomed darkly ahead and shadows obscured the trail. Janine tensed. Had the shadows moved? She strained her eyes, concentrating. It was the wind brushing the stunted pines, setting them bending, swaying, that was all. Her exhausted mind was playing tricks on her.

At that moment two blurry shapes detached themselves from the shelter of the trees and stood blocking their way.

"Stop, or I'll put a ball through you!" ordered a harsh voice.

A tall, lanky man with a pockmarked face and a rough black beard stepped forward into the moonlight. Stringy black hair escaped the red kerchief tied around his head. His companion, a burly, bug-eyed man who looked slow and a little thick-witted, gave them a wet-lipped sneer. Both wore ragged breeches and jackets and gave off an odor of rum and sweat that turned Janine's stomach. Moonlight glinted on pistols held at the ready.

"God's death!" yelled Jonathan, pulling up on Brandy. "Get out of our way. You're scaring our mounts!"

Beauty, startled by Brandy's sudden stop, flattened her ears and shied away to the left. With trembling hands Janine jerked the reins sharply in an effort to bring the animal under control.

"Hold up there," the tall man snarled. "All we want is your horses and your money."

"Brigands!" Jonathan yelled. "You'll get nothing from us. You're crazy drunk. Be off with you before you get hurt!"

Fighting down panic, Janine reined in her agitated mare beside Brandy's left flank and tried to hold her steady.

"Easy, girl, easy," she murmured in Beauty's ear.

The small click of a pistol exploded in the stillness of the clearing. Jonathan wheeled Brandy swiftly around, exposing the horse's left side to the ruffians. Using Brandy as a shield, he leaned down and whacked Beauty smartly on the rump.

The frightened mare reared on her hind legs, forelegs slashing the air. Frantically Janine clutched the horse's mane and flattened her body against its neck.

The cock fell, the powder flashed, the gun exploded, and the ball hissed past Janine's ear. Beauty let out a terrified whinny. At the same time Jonathan struck her another stinging blow on the rump, shouting. "Hi-yah, Beauty, go!"

Clinging to the rearing horse, Janine saw the burly man bolt toward Jonathan and screamed a warning. The man lunged for Brandy's reins. Jonathan jerked upright and his leg shot out in a vicious kick, catching the man full in the chest, knocking the gun from his hand. The man stumbled backward, lost his balance, and fell, mouthing a stream of curses.

Enraged, the bearded man darted around Brandy and leaped upon Jonathan from behind, grabbing his collar with both hands, yanking him off Brandy's back.

They crashed to the ground, locked in a vicious embrace, grunting, straining, rolling over the rocky ground. The short man ran to Janine and clutched the hem of her cloak, trying to tug her from her mount.

"Go, Beauty!" came a muffled shout from Jonathan.

Beauty snorted and pranced, waiting for Brandy to lead. Suddenly the catch on Janine's cloak broke, and the man tumbled to the ground, floundering under its folds. Jonathan threw off his attacker and scrambled to his feet, shouting. "Janine, fly for God's sake!" and struck Beauty another whack on the rump.

At the same time Janine dug her heels hard into Beauty's ribs, and the horse bolted, down the trail. Desperately she clung to Beauty's mane, her bottom bumping hard on the horse's back, her cheek pressed against its powerful neck.

"Easy, Beauty, easy," she gasped.

With all her strength Janine gripped Beauty's shoulders with her knees and tried to match the rhythm of the frightened animal's breakneck gallop. Sky and ground dipped crazily and trees sped past in a blur. If only she could hang on till Beauty ran down! She tightened her hold on Beauty's mane with one hand and with the other groped for the reins. With a stab of horror she discovered that the reins were dragging on the ground. Yet she dared not loosen her grip to try to retrieve them. Fighting against her fear of falling, frantically she prayed the reins wouldn't become tangled in the horse's legs, tripping the flashing hooves, and breaking both their necks. The wind roared in her ears. Her eyes began to water, and tears streaked down her cheeks. Breathlessly she clung to Beauty, hearing the pounding hooves throwing rocks up, scattering mud, and praying for Beauty's labored breathing to slow. She could feel the mare's sides heaving under her thighs. Her face was wet with the pungent sweat lathering Beauty's neck.

Suddenly the leafless branch of a long-dead tree stretched out like a gnarled arm before her face,

threatening to sweep her off Beauty's back. She flung
an arm over her eyes and ducked low as the branch
snagged her hair, pulled, then let go.

"Easy, Beauty, easy," panted Janine again and again
as the animal continued its heedless flight.

Abruptly they rounded a sharp bend in the track.
Neither Janine nor Beauty saw the slab of rock jutting
up through the muddy ground. The mare's hooves
slipped and slid on the smooth worn boulder, and she
lurched forward, buckling at the knees, head down.
For a terrifying moment the earth tilted under them
and Janine saw herself flying over Beauty's head to be
trampled under the flailing hooves. She flung her arms
around the massive neck, clinging like a cocklebur. At
the last instant Beauty surged upward, righting herself.

Thrown off her breakneck stride, gulping air with
deep, harsh breaths, the horse slowed to a trot and
Janine brought her to a walk. Leaning forward, she
seized the reins and pulled Beauty to a halt. Her heart
was thudding, and the muscles in her arms and legs
cried out in pain. She drew a deep breath in an effort
to steady her shattered nerves.

At first she didn't recognize the source of the violent
explosion that ripped through the silence of the forest. But before the echo had died away, she knew.

"Oh, dear God," she cried, "they've shot him!"

She thought she heard faint shouts on the wind.
Jonathan's voice? She couldn't tell. With a violent
motion Janine jerked Beauty around and spurred the
tired horse to a canter down the trail toward the clearing. Her mind seethed with fear. They couldn't have
killed Jonathan. Maybe Jonathan had wrested a gun
from one of his captors—had killed him even. She
urged Beauty on to a gallop.

As they approached the curve where the treacherous
rock jutted upward in their path, Janine slowed
Beauty to a walk, and then she heard a sound that
made her knees go weak. Somewhere ahead drummed

the steady beat of a horse's hooves. Someone was riding toward her, hard and fast. Jonathan? She almost shouted his name, and then the chilling thought struck her. *What if it isn't Jonathan?* For a moment she sat motionless, paralyzed with fear.

Abruptly she turned Beauty off the trail, urging her through the thick underbrush, scraping past briers, pushing aside spindly saplings, hoping the cushion of pine needles would deaden the sound of her flight. Slowly threading her way among oaks and feathery pines, she wanted to scream with impatience at her plodding mount, but she dared not urge the mare to go faster, lest the rustling underbrush betray their presence. Darkness, broken by occasional patches of moonlight, closed in around them, and for this she was grateful.

The sound of the hooves grew nearer, and she pulled Beauty up behind three young pine trees. Though they were not tall enough to conceal Janine and Beauty should anyone come searching for them, the trees hid them from sight of anyone on the trail. She slid to the ground and looped the reins over a sapling. The exhausted horse stood motionless with lowered head, and Janine pressed her body against the mare's shoulder, straining her eyes to see the path. Though she was shrouded in darkness, the rough track, carved wide enough for a stagecoach to pass, was visible in the murky moonlight.

It has to be Jonathan. "Please God," she prayed, "let it be Jonathan!"

She stood on tiptoe, craning her neck, peering between the pines, holding her breath as the horse drew nearer. Her heart turned over. It was Brandy carrying two figures astride his broad back. One, short and stocky, slouched forward. The man mounted behind him sat as tall as Jonathan in the saddle. Hope flared within her, but she held back, staring at the passing figures. Had Jonathan taken the burly renegade prisoner?

She opened her mouth to cry out, but as Brandy rounded the bend in the trail, they cantered from the shadows and a shaft of moonlight highlighted the figures. On Brandy's back rode the burly, bug-eyed brigand and behind him she saw the bearded, pock-marked face of his companion. Janine's hand flew to her mouth, smothering a cry. Into her mind flashed a vision of Jonathan lying dead in the rock-strewn clearing, and a voice in her head screamed, "Jonathan, Jonathan!" Just as quickly her mind rejected the image. Jonathan couldn't be dead!

At that moment Beauty raised her head and, catching sight of Brandy galloping away, lurched forward and gave a long, shrill whinny. The sound seemed to echo and reecho through the stillness of the night.

Janine felt as though the blood had stopped flowing through her veins. She closed her eyes, straining her ears to hear. Had the hoofbeats stopped? They seemed to slow for an endless moment then continue on. Her breath left her body in a rush, and she sank down on her knees, listening intently for the sound of Brandy's hoofbeats receding in the distance.

Gradually she became aware that the drumming sound, far from receding, was growing louder. She heard Brandy's even canter slow to a trot. Swiftly Janine rose to her feet and cradled Beauty's head in her arms, clamping her hand over the horse's soft muzzle to stifle the sound of her plaintive whinny summoning Brandy. Trembling with fear, Janine peered through the pines. Around the curve trotted Brandy bearing the two ruffians, one leaning to the right, the other to the left, staring down at the trail.

"Pull up," ordered a rough voice. "Here's hoof-prints, right here." He paused and added in a bewildered tone, "They give out. . . ."

Janine saw the stocky man leap from Brandy's back and run into the woods on the far side of the trail. She didn't wait to see more, but turned and fled through the forest like a rabbit pursued by dogs, running, stumbling blindly through thickets and briers, seeking refuge. Thank God the fat dolt had gone off the far side of the track to look for her. She would have a few more precious minutes to widen the distance between them.

Above the pounding of her heart she could hear them thrashing about through the underbrush as she plunged on through the dark woods, hands outstretched before her, shielding her head against tree trunks that loomed before her, against low-hanging branches raking her face.

Suddenly she heard Beauty's familiar whinny, and gooseflesh rose on the back of her neck. Had they found the mare? If not, thought Janine in despair, they would surely find her now!

She never felt the sensation of falling. She seemed to float gently to earth, as though it were happening to someone else. Her fingers clutched the bare root snaking above the ground that tripped her, knocking the breath out of her. Dimly she heard her pursuers scuffling through the woods, closer now. *Oh, God,* thought Janine, *they're searching this side of the trail.* Weak and trembling, she rose to her knees and crawled toward a thicket of laurel. If she could bury herself under the thick, leafy branches, maybe the men would miss her in the darkness.

Slowly, painfully, she scrabbled toward the stand of laurel and crept between two massive clumps, crouching under the leaves on the dank earth, her face buried in her hands.

"And where might you be going?" whined a high-pitched voice somewhere over her head.

Janine's throat closed and her tongue stuck to the roof of her mouth. She heard the rustle of underbrush, and the leaves above her parted. Slowly she raised her head and forced her eyes to focus. Peering through the ghostly light, she saw two mud-caked, booted feet planted solidly on the ground on the far side of the bushes where she'd taken refuge. Her breath caught in her throat, then burst in a choked gasp.

The man chuckled. "Ain't saying, are ye? Well, yer going with me, is where yer going."

Thrusting a long arm through the shiny leaves, the man's fingers found the coil of hair on her head and yanked her to her feet, pulling her roughly toward him through the laurel branches. Holding her by the hair as he'd hold a trapped rabbit by the ears, he looked her over.

Her scalp stung with pain. "Let go!" she shrieked.

"Damme, if it ain't a wench!" He let go of her hair and grasped her arms. "Why you got up in them britches, woman?"

With a sudden movement she flung her hands against his chest and gave a mighty shove. Taken by surprise, he reeled backward, uttering an oath. Janine spun away from him and broke into a run. She'd taken only three steps when he grabbed her loosened coil of hair and gave it a violent jerk that snapped her head back painfully. Her scream echoed through the silent forest. Startled, the man released her hair and gripped her right arm, twisting it upward behind her back.

"Got him, Lige!" he yelled to his companion. "He's a female!" With his free hand he grabbed her shoulder, pushing, shoving her ahead of him through the woods to the trail.

Lige, a slack grin on his wet lips, stood in the middle of the trail holding Beauty's and Brandy's reins. He spat on the ground at her feet.

"Too bad there ain't no bounty on them woods creatures, Jake."

"Makes no never mind, Lige. She's gonna make it up to me, ain't ye, sweetheart?"

"Let me go," pleaded Janine. "Take the horses, but let me go, please!" If only she could get back to Jonathan. That was all that mattered.

As though reading her mind, Jake said, "That fancy

gentleman ye was traveling with ain't gonna be no use to ye now."

Her terror and rage at whatever they had done to Jonathan erupted, and her foot shot out in a savage kick, catching Jake a heavy blow on the knee; at the same time she tried to wrench from his grasp.

"Damn ye!" His hand came up and dealt her a stinging blow on the cheek. His other hand tightened like a steel band around her wrist; a searing pain shot through her arm and she went limp in his grasp.

Lige snorted gleefully. "A dead man ain't no fun, but she got some life in her, that one."

"You killed him," screamed Janine, flinging herself at Lige, pounding his chest with her fists in rage and horror.

Cursing loudly, Jake whipped the filthy red kerchief from his head and bound her wrists tightly together. He grabbed her around the waist and flung her up across Brandy's back, then leaped up behind her. Roughly he set her upright and spread her legs astride the horse.

"Now ye set up there nice, or I'm gonna scalp ye faster'n an Indian!"

She said nothing, but sat stiffly erect, numb with shock. Jonathan couldn't be dead. She couldn't believe it, wouldn't believe it. Her mind refused to accept what they'd told her.

Jake bent his head close to hers, and his right hand slid up from Brandy's neck, inside her jacket, squeezing her breast.

"We're gonna have a little fun, ye and me."

Janine shuddered, jerking away from him. "Get your filthy paws off me!"

"Oh, this ain't nothin'," he whispered, nibbling the tip of her ear. "Yer soon gonna be enjoyin' delights ye ain't never had before."

The stench of his filthy, sour-smelling clothes and his rum-laden breath sickened her. She pressed her lips together, swallowing hard, fighting down the sour taste that rose in her throat.

"And I'm gonna show ye more," said Lige, licking his blubbery lips in anticipation. "Ain't that right, Jake?"

Janine could feel Lige's bulgy eyes raking her body as he leaped on Beauty's back, and she thought she would die if he so much as touched her.

"I reckon she's up to two stout fellas like us," said Jake. "I like a wench what's got spirit, and she got right much spirit. Ain't that right, sweetheart?" he asked, leaning forward so that his beard scratched her neck.

She shivered in revulsion, but said nothing, for she perceived that the more she resisted, the better they enjoyed their sport—tormenting her. They spurred the horses into a canter, and she huddled miserably over Brandy's neck, her numb fingers clutching his mane. For a wild moment she considered heaving herself off Brandy's back, but she knew the attempt would be foolish and futile, imprisoned as she was between Jake's muscular arms, his hands tight on the reins.

Weary with exhaustion, lulled by the rocking motion of Brandy's smooth stride, Janine sank into a stupor, sagging over Brandy's neck, only to be jerked upright by the foul-smelling Jake.

"Lean back against me, sweetheart, and rest yerself. Don't want ye to be all tuckered out. We still got a long night ahead."

Janine stiffened and Jake flung an arm across her breasts and hugged her to him. She shut her eyes and wished she would die.

Chapter 5

To Janine it seemed they had ridden for hours, pounding and jolting through the darkness on the rough trail. Despite her determination to stay awake, she found her head dropping time and again as she lapsed into a fitful doze, only to awake with a start when Jake jerked her upright.

When at last they emerged from the forest, Jake and Lige paused to reconnoiter. The land ahead sloped gently into a wide, flat valley, which had been cleared for farming. On the rise beyond, Janine thought she saw a flicker of light through the trees, and hope fluttered inside her. Here someone would be about, and when they passed by, she would scream loud enough to summon help. If Jake and Lige had seen the gleam of light, they gave no sign.

They pushed on, down the gentle slope past moon-drenched fields and orchards guarded by silent stone farmhouses, up the rise, into a thick wood. Janine breathed deeply, bracing herself to cry out for help. But when they gained the crest of the hill, her hopes died. The flickering light had disappeared. They continued on, and as they cantered around a sharp curve in the track, a yellow beam shone through a window of a two-story stone structure, illuminating a faded sign: Boar's Head Tavern.

The men reined in the horses and Janine slumped over Brandy's neck, unmoving, feigning exhaustion. Jake shook her roughly by the shoulder.

"Look smart, wench!"

The men slid to the ground and tied up the horses. Jake turned to Janine and dragged her from Brandy's back. She closed her eyes and swayed on her feet, allowing Jake to support her weight against him, his arm around her shoulders. He stuck his bearded face close to hers.

"I'm gonna leave ye loose now," he said, untying the kerchief that bound her wrists. "When we get inside, don't ye say nothing to nobody, or it'll be yer last word. Got that straight?"

Janine said nothing and began rubbing her chafed wrists. Lige reached out and pinched her cheek hard. Clenching her teeth, she stifled a cry.

"Got that?" he snarled.

Janine nodded.

Jake grabbed her mane of black hair and, twisting it into a rope, stuffed it down her back inside her jacket. Then gripping her arms, he half-walked, half-dragged her between them inside the tavern.

A dozen or more men sprawled at rough wooden tables, quaffing mugs of ale and talking, their loud, coarse voices interrupted by bursts of laughter. Before a blazing fire sat a dark, thin, squint-eyed man bouncing a yellow-haired, rosy-cheeked barmaid on his knee. Swiftly Janine's gaze traveled to the bar in the corner of the room where the beefy, red-faced tavern keeper was polishing tumblers behind a high counter. The man's jowls hung in folds over his soiled shirt, and his eyebrows lifted as they dragged Janine toward him.

She opened her mouth to cry out. Faster than lightning, Jake, standing behind her, clamped his filthy kerchief over her mouth and flung an arm across her breast, clutching her hard to his chest. At the same instant Lige bent down, grabbed her ankles, and lifted her feet from the floor. She sagged between them like a hammock, writhing, mumbling unintelligible sounds.

Jake gave a hopeless shrug, and Lige erupted in laughter. The tavern keeper eyed them skeptically, a puzzled expression spreading across his fat red face. "Taken a fit, has he?"

Jake grinned, shaking his head in mock despair. "The boy couldn't wait till we got here. He been swilling his own brew all the way. We got to have somewheres to bed him down for the night."

Janine shook her head violently, arching her back, twisting and straining her body in an effort to wrench free of her captors. The innkeeper gazed at her in amusement.

"He be fightin' drunk, this one. Wants to fight ever'-body," said Lige. "Takes the two of us to hold him down."

The innkeeper let out a hearty laugh. "You're in luck, boys. Got a bed with only one sleeping in it, so far, and he ain't ready yet." He winked and nodded at the squint-eyed man fondling the barmaid and slid a key across the counter. "Second door on your left."

The last thing Janine heard as they hauled her up the steps was the laughing voice of the innkeeper, "No, the lad's not daft. He's only a stripling what thinks he's an oak," followed by a raucous burst of laughter.

Lige kicked open the door. In the faint light of a candle set on a rude pine chest of drawers, Janine glimpsed a window, a straight-backed chair, and a washstand holding a white bowl and pitcher. On her left stood a rough wooden bed with a lumpy mattress.

They tossed her on the bed where she lay stiff with fear, her heart hammering painfully. Lige threw down her bundle, slammed the door, and turned the key in the lock. The chair creaked as he sat down heavily and began pulling off his boots. Through slitted eyes Janine saw Jake light another candle and set it on the washstand along with his pistol. He turned to face her, his hands on his hips, feet spread, his pitted face accentuated in the candlelight.

"Now we're gonna have some fun."

He took off his tattered coat and shirt and dropped them on the floor. Leaning against the washstand, he brought a knee up and tugged at his boot. Janine closed her eyes and lay rigid, filled with a terror so overwhelming that she could hardly breathe. She heard the thump of a boot striking the floor, then another. The sounds of boisterous laughter and coarse voices drifted up from the taproom below. If she screamed, no one would hear her. She felt a finger jab her sharply in the ribs.

"Hear me? I said we're gonna have some fun. Get them clothes off!"

She lay still. She would die before she would submit to these swine. Determined to fight to the death, she braced herself for what she knew was to come.

Jake lunged toward her. Quickly she rolled away from him across the mattress to the far side of the bed and leaped to her feet. Lige jumped up from the chair by the window and clutched her shoulder, spinning her around to face him. Her knee shot out, dealing him a sharp blow in the groin. With a grunt of pain Lige doubled over and backed heavily onto the chair.

She was halfway to the door before Jake came up behind her. His hands clutched the shoulders of her jacket, tugging it off her back, down her arms. She tried to run, but he pinned her to him, his arm about her waist in a bone-crushing grip. With his free hand he caught the back of her collar and gave it a vicious yank, ripping the fabric from neck to hem.

Lige leaped from the chair, his eyes gleaming with lust. He lurched toward her and pulled her shirt from her body. Jake's rough hands moved upward from her waist, fondling her breasts in a bruising caress. Terror and revulsion such as she'd never known came over her. She tried to scream, but her throat closed on a strangled cry. Jake's fetid breath filled her nostrils, and a wave of nausea swept through her.

"We got to have our reward for bringing ye to this nice place," said Jake, his pockmarked face twisted in a leering grin.

She screamed like a mad woman as he dragged her backward toward the bed, his sinewy arms locked about her waist. She jerked forward, momentarily regaining her footing, and with all her strength, she brought the heel of her boot down on Jake's toes. He shouted in pain and flung her down onto the mattress, cursing loudly.

Panting with fear, her hair streaming wildly over her shoulders, she rose to her hands and knees and scrambled across the bed. She gained the floor and dashed to the window. Through her terror she was conscious of someone screaming, without recognizing the sound issuing from her own throat. If that stupid oaf caught her again, she would die before he got his hands on her.

"Come back here, ye little bitch!" Lige roared. He rounded the foot of the bed, his fat arms reaching out toward her. She seized his hand, brought it to her mouth, and, bending her head, sank her teeth into the plump flesh between his thumb and forefinger.

With an enraged howl Lige jerked his hand to his mouth, staggering backward. Jake rushed forward and swung, his balled fist striking a blow to her head that sent her reeling across the room. She slammed into the door and slid down to her knees. Lige lumbered across the room, wound a fistful of her long black hair around his hand, and yanked her to her feet. Her hands flew to his face, her nails clawing savagely at his glittering pig eyes.

Suddenly the door behind her rattled, shaking under a violent pounding that she'd thought was in her head. Jake seized her hands and spun her around, twisting her arms cruelly behind her back, and her shrieks filled the room.

The door burst open. For a fraction of a second they

stood frozen in a silent tableau. Filling the doorway stood a tall, dark-haired man, his olive-tinted face flushed with anger, his thick crescent brows drawn together in a scowl. He wore snuff-colored breeches, and above them his broad torso was covered with a triangular mat of curly black hair.

Janine saw his dark eyes sweep over her tangled hair, which tumbled over her shoulders, barely covering her nakedness. Her clothes were strewn on the floor. He stared at the two enraged men, sweat streaming down their faces; Lige's eyes wary; Jake's bearded jaw thrust forward in defiance and outrage. The stranger rocked back on his heels, hands on his hips.

"What the devil is going on here?" he bellowed.

Taken by surprise, Jake's grip on Janine's hands loosened. She wrenched free and ran to the man and seized his arms, shrieking, "These renegades have killed my fiancé, stolen our horses, and abducted me!"

Jake stepped forward. "She's mad!" he shouted. "She's my woman, and I'll do with 'er as I want!" His chin jutted out belligerently.

The stranger's dark eyes gleamed like wet coal. "That's not what she says."

Lige stood behind Jake, his expression that of a snarling pug. "We don't care what she says."

"You woke me from a sound sleep," the man said angrily. "What in God's name are you doing with her?"

Jake laughed uneasily. "Having ourselves a little fun, is all."

The tall stranger's eyes mirrored suspicion and contempt. "All right, you've had your fun. Now I'll take her with me."

"The devil you will!" Jake shouted.

The man's smile was patronizing, but his voice held a note of authority. "I outrank you, gentlemen. I'm Lieutenant Furneaux, First Pennsylvania Militia. What I say goes."

"Not with me, it don't," Jake snarled. He moved toward the lieutenant in a fighting crouch, his pitted face twisted with rage. Though he was taller than the lieutenant, the lieutenant's well-muscled shoulders and torso bespoke the power of a bull gathering in to charge.

The lieutenant's attention was distracted by a movement behind Jake. Lige held his pistol leveled at his adversary's head. The cock fell. The tendons in his wrist shortened as he began to apply pressure to the trigger. For one dreadful moment the candlelight flickered on the pistol barrel pointed directly at the lieutenant's forehead. The lieutenant dived to the left and rolled across the bed. At the same instant Jake lunged, going for his adversary's throat.

The lieutenant checked Jake's attack with his forearm, and Jake followed with a vicious blow across his wrist. Jake swung from the bed and snatched up his gun from the washstand. Before he could fire, a sharp crack filled the room. Janine saw a spurt of flame, and the smell of powder seared her nostrils.

Lige's bullet spun across the room and demolished the wooden bedpost above the lieutenant's head. Startled by the sudden disintegration of wood, Jake's arm wavered. For an instant Lige's eyes swiveled to Jake. The lieutenant hurled himself across the bed, jumping Lige from behind. His powerful arm went around Lige's neck, snapping his head back, and Janine heard something crack like a walnut shell.

Lieutenant Furneaux held the sagging Lige before him as a shield, pivoting as Jake stalked him trying for a clear shot. With a roar of rage, Jake attacked, swinging at the lieutenant's head with his pistol. The man wrenched his head out of the way but Jake beat at the side of his head with the butt of his weapon. One dizzying blow, then another, accompanied by blasphemous curses. Stunned, the lieutenant staggered backward. At the same time he heaved Lige's heavy body at his attacker. Under the impact Jake stumbled and dropped his pistol.

Regaining his footing, Jake sprang toward the dazed lieutenant, who fell back on the bed and drew up his knees, aimed his feet at Jake's chest, and gave a powerful thrust that sent him spinning across the room. A crash of shattering glass erupted. Jake sat framed by the broken glass of the window. Swearing violently, he struggled to get clear of the window.

The lieutenant's fist shot out. Jake's body twisted and jerked. As he fell forward a broken triangle of glass pierced his unprotected neck. With a hoarse cry he tumbled to the floor and rolled onto his stomach. Blood spurted from his wound, spattering the floor at Janine's feet.

Lige sat up, holding Jake's pistol, his gaze fixed on the bloody floor. He seemed frozen. Events had moved too swiftly for him. He stared at his unconscious companion. With the side of his hand the lieutenant cracked the man's fat wrist. He grunted in pain and dropped the pistol. The fight had gone out of him. He stared wildly around the room, looking for a way out. He stood up and started toward the door, but the sight of the lieutenant stopped him. He turned toward the window and ran, scrabbling over the sill, dropping out of sight in the darkness.

Lieutenant Furneaux strode to the window and leaned out.

"Is he gone?" asked Janine in a choked voice.

Lieutenant Furneaux turned to face her. "Like a regiment of Redcoats were after him," he said, grinning.

He stepped over Jake, picked up her bundle from the bed, and scooped up her clothes from the floor. Then with an easy motion he swept her up in his arms, flung her over his shoulder, and strode from the room, down the dark hall.

They entered a small room much like the one they

had left, lighted by the glow of a single candle. He dumped Janine on the bed and, stepping back, smiled, and made her a courtly bow.

"Lieutenant Mark Furneaux at your service."

Chapter 6

Janine sat on the bed, her hands clasped tightly around her knees, her head resting on her arms. Her heart was still thumping wildly and a tremor shook her, just thinking about the events of the night. In retrospect, the whole terrifying experience was far worse than any nightmare she'd ever endured. She let out a long sigh of relief at her narrow escape, trying not to think of what would have happened to her had this handsome, dark-eyed lieutenant not come to her rescue. She heard the lock on the door click into place and footsteps coming toward her. She sat up, turning to look at him, and noticed where his gaze had wandered. Suddenly aware of her nakedness, she blushed furiously and crossed her arms over her bosom.

Mark Furneaux sat down on the edge of the bed. Golden flecks danced in his dark eyes, his strong white teeth gleamed in the candlelight, and his full lips curved in a comforting smile.

"I can't thank you enough for coming to my rescue," said Janine in a voice that trembled with gratitude.

"Good. You can start now." His expression was one of cheerful expectation.

Janine could hardly believe her ears. "Start now?" she repeated, perplexed.

"You can start thanking me now," said Mark, smiling.

Startled, Janine stared up into his face, her blue eyes wide in surprise. Surely he didn't mean what was implied.

He reached out and placed his fingertips under her chin, lifting her face up to his. Swiftly she leaped from the bed and snatched her shirt from the chair, pulling it on over her arms and shoulders.

"What the—" exploded the lieutenant. He swung down from the bed and in two strides crossed the room to Janine. He gripped her forearm tightly and jerked his head toward the bed.

"Get in!"

The relief she had felt at escaping her abductors drained away, and all the terror of the last few hours flooded back through her. The blood pounded in her head and she felt sick and weak with fright. She must not let him see her fear. She lifted her chin and summoned a haughty air.

"I'm afraid you mistake me, sir."

Relentlessly he shook his head. "No mistake. I know a wanton baggage when I see one."

Aghast, she stared at him. His black hair curled like devil's horns atop his head, and his tanned face split in a grin that would shame Satan himself. With a sudden twist she wrenched from his grasp and flew toward the door. The lieutenant was quicker. She felt his big hands close on her shoulders, halting her in midflight. He scooped her up in his arms and flung her onto the bed.

She rose to her knees, sitting back on her heels, her breath coming in short gasps, her hands outstretched imploringly. "Listen to me, please. You're wrong! I am Janine Mercer of Heritage Hall Planta—"

Mark knelt on the bed on one knee, leaning toward her, and placed a hand firmly on each of her shoulders. "And I'm George the Third, come to subdue the rebels, little darling."

His face was so close to hers that she could feel his warm breath on her cheeks and smell the spicy scent of soap on his skin, the masculine odor of horses, and sweaty leather. Before she could move, his lips came down on hers, hard and demanding.

She twisted from his grasp, crying out wildly, "No! No, you don't understand. I'm not what you think. I'm betrothed—spoken for. I belong to someone!"

His arms came around her, and she felt his strong hands on her back as she strained away from him.

"Nonsense," he said fiercely. "Don't hand me that twaddle! I saved you from those renegades. You belong to me. I'm claiming my reward."

He pulled her to him in a passionate embrace. Looking up into his flushed face, she saw desire that would not be denied, and her heart raced with terror. His hands slid up her back, found her collar, and pulled her torn shirt from her body. She heard a sharp intake of breath, and an anguished cry escaped her as his hands went to her waist, tugging at her breeches. Her own hands shot up against his chest, and she shoved as hard as she could, thrusting him away from her. Caught off balance, he was forced to slacken his hold on her momentarily. In an instant she leaped from the bed, ran to the washstand, and lifted the stoneware pitcher high over her head.

"Maybe this will cool your ardor!" shouted Janine and hurled it at his head.

The pitcher arced through the air. Water spewed across the floor, over the bed, the bulk of it striking him full in the face. He dodged an instant before the flying pitcher sailed over his head and shattered harmlessly on the wall behind him.

Janine dashed toward the door, but before she reached it, Mark Furneaux stood with his back against it, arms folded across his chest, his wet face gleaming in the candlelight. His black eyes blazed with barely controlled fury.

She stood petrified, staring up at him, her eyes wide with terror. Watching her through narrowed lids, he wiped the dripping water from his face with his forearm. Something about her lightning change from an avenging fury to the terrified creature rooted before him struck him as comical, and his anger suddenly dissolved in a shout of laughter.

"Cool my ardor, little darling? On the contrary, I find cold water quite refreshing."

For a moment Janine was almost overcome by her hatred of the man. Now his insolent, nonchalant attitude toward her infuriated her.

His dark brown eyes picked up the dancing flame of the candlelight. "Come now, I'm not going to hurt you."

She stood her ground, determined to march out the door. "Get away from me, you blackguard," spat Janine.

Before she realized his intent, he leaned down, grasped the top of her breeches, and with a quick motion yanked them down to her feet. Shrieking at the top of her lungs, she struck out at him with her fists.

Disregarding her feeble blows, his hands spanned her waist and he lifted her off the floor, then holding her out before him like a plucked chicken, he strode to the bed. She clawed at his hands about her waist, kicking violently at his shins. Together they crashed down on the bed. The breath rushed from her lungs.

"Stop! Let me go!" she gasped, pounding his hard shoulders and back till her hands ached. His mouth crushed her own, silencing her screams. At last she wrenched her head away.

"Listen, please listen!"

"You little cheat!" he snarled. "This is no way to show your gratitude. Is there no honor among whores?"

Sputtering, she tried to raise up on her elbows. With one hand he caught her wrists and held them above her head. With his free hand he struggled out of his breeches and then began to explore her body, firmly imprisoned under his, his fingers tracing its curves in a tender caress. Again his mouth found hers. In agonizing silence she writhed and twisted, trying to escape the torture of the warm, demanding body pressing down on her own.

Strange sensations she'd never felt before rippled through her, confusing pleasure with pain, threatening to overwhelm her. Still she fought him with every ounce of strength in her. But after a time, her strength drained away, leaving her empty and defenseless. She went limp and lay like a corpse under the warm, muscular length of him. Never in all of her most desperate days at Heritage Hall had she felt so humiliated, so brought down. Fervently she prayed she would die at this moment. But now there was no escape from the unspeakable thing that was happening to her. Clenching her teeth, she forced her mind to go blank, hoping the Lord would strike her dead.

Suddenly she became aware of the absence of feeling—his warm, sensuous mouth no longer seeking, his hands no longer roaming her body, searing her flesh with his touch.

With an oath, the man thrust her roughly from him. She sat up, drawing her feet up under her, poised to run. He gave her another shove, and she sprang from the bed and stumbled blindly across the room, taking refuge behind a rush-bottomed chair. She clung to the back of the chair, breathing hard.

"I'll not force myself on any woman!" he shouted, glaring at her.

The contempt she read in his eyes sparked her anger. "I'm not what you think!" Her eyes blazed with fury and outrage, made all the greater by the proud and disdainful look of him and his stubborn refusal to believe her.

"A likely story," said Mark, his voice filled with scorn.

"Furthermore," said Janine heatedly, "I'm not accustomed to having my word doubted!"

He laughed derisively. "You needn't have troubled to make excuses. There's many a wench who'd beg me to bed her. Anyway, I've no taste for custard pudding!"

Speechless with rage and humiliation, she turned her back to him and, with shaking hands, swept up her bundle of clothes from the floor. She found her shift and slipped it on over her head. With canny intuition she perceived she'd wounded him in a way far deeper than the futile blows of her fists on his body. Rejecting him, making it plain that he repelled her, she'd dealt a mortal blow to his pride. She glanced at him from the corner of her eye.

"Rescuing me does not give you the right to bed me," she said unsteadily.

She watched him wipe the sweat from his forehead with the back of his hand. His gaze traveled appreciatively over her shining black hair and her high, full breasts as she stood defenseless before him in her thin white shift.

"I've a good mind to leave you to your bearded friend down the hall," he snapped. "He should be ready for a bit of sport by now." He swung down from the bed and started toward her.

With both hands she seized the rush-bottomed chair and upended it, thrusting the legs toward him, jabbing the air as though warding off a lion about to spring.

The lieutenant snorted in disdain, bent down, retrieved his breeches from the floor and, turning his back to her, pulled them on over long, lean, muscular flanks.

Color flooded her face, and she stood uncertainly, the chair wavering in her hands, still not sure he didn't intend to carry out his threat to leave her to Jake.

"Surely a lieutenant of the Pennsylvania Militia wouldn't abandon a lady in distress!" Her tone was challenging.

"Lady!" Mark whirled to face her, hands on his hips, rocking back on his heels, his brows raised in a mocking stare. "Do you think I doubt the evidence of my own eyes? No *lady* would be found dressed in a man's garb, carousing around in a tavern in the middle of the night with two brigands!"

Janine swallowed hard. Her eyes were wide and uncertain, and her mouth quivered.

Abruptly his expression changed, as though a revelation had burst upon him. "Unless, of course, she's thrown in with them in a scheme to trick unsuspecting travelers into stopping along the road to aid a lady in distress—and then rob them blind. That's your game, isn't it? Suddenly it's all quite clear. Oh, yes, you were willing enough to share your companions' spoils, but when you refused to share their bed, it was a different kettle of fish!"

Janine slammed the chair down on the floor with a bang. "That's not true!" she fumed. "Go on, believe what you want to believe, but I *am* Janine Mercer of Heritage Hall on the Potomac near Alexandria. . . ." She paused to catch her breath, and a thought struck her with the force of a blow.

Until now she'd taken no thought of the future, but speaking of Heritage Hall sparked the painful reminder that she was fleeing her past. Now it occurred to her that Jake and Lige were not the only brigands on the road to Philadelphia. Bands of ruffians and robbers plagued the countryside. If only she could convince this man that she was a lady and not to be trifled with, she could very well do worse than to have his company on her journey. Nervously she ran her tongue over her lips.

"I can prove the truth of my claim—if you wish to ride home with me." She let the words trail off.

Lieutenant Furneaux gave a derisive snort. "I care nothing for your past, Mistress Mercer. Nor your future. Anyway, I'm not bound for Alexandria. I'm heading north, to Philadelphia."

Janine forced a tremulous smile. "Oh, but that's where I'm going. My father lives in Philadelphia. We were going to stay with him, Jonathan—my fiancé—and I. If Jonathan survived—" She halted abruptly, pushing down the unthinkable thought. That's where Jonathan will go to look for me."

Mark leaned against the bedpost, smiling sardonically, his arms folded across his chest. "My, aren't you inventive? A story to fit every occasion."

"Please, it's true," cried Janine, her eyes wide and imploring. "Please, please take me with you!"

She hated herself for groveling before this arrogant stranger, hated him more because she was compelled to depend upon him for her safety.

"Take the stage." His dark eyes mocked her. "It's much safer, though not nearly as profitable, of course."

With great effort Janine controlled an impulse to lash out at him. "I'm in a great hurry, Lieutenant Furneaux. Who knows when the stage will come through!"

"The tavern keeper," said Mark shortly. "There's a schedule hanging on the wall beside the bar."

Janine's lip quivered. Her eyes were wide and appealing. "Please . . . I won't be any trouble to you."

He stared at her speculatively, appraising her. Then he shook his head and sank down on the bed, throwing up his hands in a helpless gesture.

"My horse is going lame. He can't possibly carry two. . . ."

"I have a horse—two horses," said Janine eagerly.

Mark hesitated; temptation showed on his face.

Thinking to push her advantage, Janine rummaged through her bundle of clothing and withdrew a small purse, opened it, and shook out several coins. She held out her hand. The silver coins lay on her palm, gleaming in the candlelight.

"Look. I have money. I'll pay you whatever you ask."

"I don't want your money!" Mark bellowed. "Put it away for a time you'll need it." He shot her a scornful glance. "You certainly won't win any favors from anyone for your sweet and gentle nature."

She blinked back swift and unbidden tears of indignation and anger. "Swine!" she spat venomously. She turned her back on him in frustration. There was no use talking to this bold, arrogant scoundrel.

He threw back his head and roared with laughter. But the sight of her standing stiff-backed, small and defenseless, in a shift that did nothing to hide the softly rounded contours of her buttocks seemed to set him on fire. He rose from the bed and threw open the window. The cool April breeze invaded the room, raising gooseflesh on her skin.

"It's cold," said Janine, shivering. "Close the window—please."

"I think we need some fresh air in here," said Mark cheerfully.

Annoyed, Janine pressed her lips tightly together to keep from saying anything further to incur his wrath. She dropped the coins back in her purse and stuffed it inside her bundle on the seat of the chair.

Mark Furneaux stretched out on the bed and pulled the bedclothes snugly about him, watching her with an amused grin.

"Are you going to cower behind that chair all night?"

Her chin rose defiantly and before she could stop herself, she snapped, "If you were a gentleman, you'd give me the bed."

Again she seemed to amuse him. "I make no claim to being a gentleman, little darling. But I will give you exactly one half the bed. Take it or leave it." He folded his hands behind his head and yawned.

Janine's blue eyes blazed with indignation. She would freeze to death before she'd crawl into his bed. She stamped out from behind the chair, grabbed up Jonathan's old jacket and spread it on the floor. She lay down on her side, her back to Mark Furneaux, resting her head on her bundle. Suddenly something swooshed through the air and fell gently on top of her, smothering her. Frantically, arms and legs churning, she fought to be free of it. A burst of laughter exploded in the room.

"It's only a sheet," came Mark's deep voice. "Wouldn't want you to catch cold."

She bit back a sharp retort and clutched the sheet around her shoulders. She heard a short expulsion of breath and the candle flame died, leaving the room in darkness; then a crunching sound as Mark Furneaux rolled over on the cornhusk mattress.

Janine lay curled in a ball on the hard floor, shivering, seething with anger at this ruffian who was gentleman enough to rescue her from her attackers, yet tried to bed her; who, she supposed, was too much of a gentleman to force himself upon her, yet was not gentleman enough to treat her like a lady. She was glad she was too angry to sleep. She didn't trust Mark Furneaux any farther than she could throw a bull, and she was determined not to drift off till she was certain he was sleeping soundly. In spite of her resolve she dozed, plagued by visions of Jonathan lying dead in the rock-strewn clearing.

The April night turned cold, and chill and dampness blew in through the window. She drew the jacket about her, but her limbs were stiff and she longed for the warmth of the bed. Freezing was not much fun. She clenched her teeth to keep them from chattering, and every muscle in her body tensed to keep from trembling. Through the darkness came a low growl. Alarmed, she rose up on her elbows and glanced at the bed, washed in moonlight. Mark Furneaux was sleeping soundly on the far side of the bed, the bedclothes tumbled about his waist, his chest rising and falling in rhythm with a gentle snore. The empty space beside him looked soft and inviting. The floor was hard and cold. Why should she let that arrogant blackguard hog the bed?

Quietly she rose and crept to the side of the bed, easing her hips onto the mattress. The cornhusks rustled faintly. Cautiously she stretched out her legs and lay down, pulling the blanket up around her neck. She held her breath and listened to Mark's deep, even breathing. Good! He hadn't awakened. She smothered a sigh of relief, closed her eyes, and relaxed.

"Good night!" came Mark Furneaux's deep voice from the far side of the bed.

Chapter 7

Janine stirred and opened her eyes, peering through the gloomy gray light that filled the room. Morning already! Thank goodness she'd wakened before dawn so she could steal back to her jacket on the floor. She had no wish to give the arrogant fool lying beside her any mistaken ideas. She cast a sidelong glance over her shoulder. The space beside her was empty. She sat up quickly, her eyes searching the room. The window was closed. Mark's fringed shirt and jacket, which he'd slung over the pine chest, were gone. Even his boots were gone!

He's gone—ridden off without me, she thought miserably. Her heart beat frantically as she ran to the window overlooking the yard at the rear of the tavern and peered out at the weathered wooden shed where the stableboy had tethered the horses. Eight or ten horses stood placidly under the shelter, munching hay, Beauty and Brandy among them. Whether Mark's horse was missing, she had no way of knowing, but the tall, dark-haired lieutenant was nowhere to be seen. Of course he hadn't said she could ride with him, she recalled uneasily. In fact he'd said she couldn't. But she was sure she could persuade him; and if she couldn't, she'd just follow a safe distance behind. Now he'd tricked her, sneaking off in the night!

Tears of anger and disappointment rose unbidden to her eyes. Impatiently she brushed them away. This was no time for tears. If she hurried, maybe she could overtake him. Driven by desperation, she climbed into her breeches, flung on her torn shirt and jacket, and pulled on her boots. She was stuffing her shift into her bundle when the door creaked open.

"Is the bird flying the coop?" asked a deep, amused voice.

She whirled around to face Mark Furneaux as he stepped into the room and closed the door behind him.

"I—I thought you'd gone," stammered Janine, hoping he hadn't noticed her tearstained cheeks.

His thick crescent-shaped brows rose at her obvious distress over his supposed departure, and he jerked his head toward the rear of the inn. "The necessary is behind the stable. If you're riding with me, you'd best hurry."

Her face broke into a radiant smile.

"I'll hurry!" cried Janine, and snatching her bundle, she dashed from the room.

When they were well on their way, pelting down the woodland trail astride Brandy and Beauty, Mark told her that he had checked his mare, and, as he feared, her ankle was swollen and tender to his touch. Janine said nothing. He went on, scowling.

"The animal is in no shape for a long, hard ride, and it's imperative that I reach Philadelphia without delay. My business in Charleston took longer than I'd figured, and my superior will be hopping around like a hen on a hot griddle waiting for my return."

It was on the tip of her tongue to ask the nature of his business, but she checked the impulse. Mark turned his head and looked at her. One eyebrow rose, and a corner of his mouth went down. "I'm a fool to take you with me. But contrary to what you may think, I'm too much a gentleman to take your horse and bolt."

She bit back a sharp retort, and they rode on in silence in the cold, gray morning light.

They had been riding several hours when light flakes began drifting down from the molten gray sky and a bitter wind whipped cruelly about them.

Janine's cheeks stung. Her hands were red and her fingers stiff with cold as she clutched the reins. She could feel the strength of Beauty under her. The mare's legs stretched in long, easy strides, and her breath exploded in short puffs of steam on the frosty air.

They rode hard, stopping only to rest the horses and to eat the cold mutton and biscuits Mark had bought at the tavern, washing their meal down with rum from his canteen. Though he had agreed at the last moment to let her accompany him, Janine still had the feeling that it was with a grudging sort of gallantry that might be withdrawn at any moment. Whenever they stopped, she set out to make herself as pleasant a companion as she possibly could, entertaining him with stories of her childhood and life on the plantation in Virginia.

He listened politely, his handsome, olive-tinted face impassive. At last he said, "So you are a fleur-de-lis, a transplanted lily of France, blooming in the wilderness." He gazed at her quizzically with a smile that was half-mocking, half-challenging, so that she wondered whether he believed her even now. She retreated into silence, waiting for him to volunteer something about himself.

Instead he gathered up the remains of their meal and stashed it away in his blanket roll. "If you're finished, we'd best be going."

They emerged from the woodland, and Janine breathed deeply of the sweet scent of hickory smoke curling up from the chimney of a stone farmhouse set among the fields. Cows huddled together against the cold and a lone hawk circled above the chicken house in the farmyard. They met no other travelers except those on the stage from Philadelphia. They heard it before they saw it, creaking, jolting toward them, and they pulled up at the side of the track. As the coach rumbled past and the passengers leaned from the window, waving and shouting, Mark and Janine waved back and galloped on.

By four in the afternoon the light, powdery snow had frosted the trees and ground, blanketing the trail. Even though these unseasonable early spring snows never lasted, Janine sighed with relief when the Black Horse Tavern loomed up through the swirling flakes and they drew up their mounts.

Inside the rustic, candlelit tavern room, they sat facing each other, devouring a supper of meat pie and ale. A long, uncomfortable silence stretched between them, and Janine's curiosity finally got the better of her. She blurted out, "What business were you in before you joined the militia, Lieutenant Furneaux?"

One black eyebrow rose and the corner of his mouth went down. "You may call me Mark."

"Mark," she repeated, stifling her annoyance. "What business were you in before—"

"Shipping." He lifted his tankard of ale and drank deeply.

"In Philadelphia?"

"Um-hum."

"What kind of shipping?"

He set down the tankard and speared a chunk of meat on his fork. "Import, export. Bring in goods from Málaga, the Indies. . . ." His voice trailed off.

"Are you with John Drinker's company, then?"

Mark shook his head, and as he lifted the tankard again it seemed to Janine his face took on a guarded expression. She saw no reason why she shouldn't show an interest in his work and plunged on.

"Who, then?"

"It's my ship. I own it," said Mark shortly.

"Oh!" said Janine, her eyes wide in astonishment. "What sort of ship?"

"A merchant ship—the *Adventure*, a brig of two hundred tons—big as a man needs." He set the tankard down sharply on the table, as if to close the subject.

"And when you're gone?"

"An agent handles the cargo." His dark eyes met

hers in a direct, level gaze. "That's all there is to know."

Janine pressed her lips together in a thin, tight line, not daring to question him further, and they finished their meal in silence. At last he stood up and gazed out the window, a thoughtful expression on his face.

"Have you arranged for our rooms with the inn-keeper?" asked Janine, stressing the word "rooms."

Mark turned from the window and in a voice that brooked no argument said, "We're pushing on. It's too early to stop for the night."

By the time they left the tavern, the snow had stopped, and they cantered on through a ghostly forest whose stillness was broken only by the chattering of squirrels, an occasional rabbit darting across their path, or a startled deer plunging through the trees. Dusk blended with the somber sky and the world about them became a monochrome, black and gray etched against the stark white of the snow-covered ground.

The wind rose, stinging Janine's eyes so that tears ran down her cheeks. Her nose kept running and her fingers were numb with cold. Suddenly Mark drew up before an ancient oak—to rest the horses, thought Janine.

"How much farther is the inn?" she asked.

He looked at her strangely. "We passed the inn at suppertime."

Annoyed at his deliberate obtuseness, she asked wearily, "Where are we staying the night?"

"Follow me." His eyes glinted in amusement. "I'll show you."

He turned from the trail and, urging Brandy a short distance through the woods, emerged in a grassy glade. He halted before two massive pine trees, their thickly furred boughs creating a canopy overhead. He swung down from his horse and with his hat, cleared a space in the light, crisp snow, laying bare a thick cushion of bronze pine needles. He extended his arm in a sweeping bow, as though he were ushering her into an elegant suite.

"Soft, clean, fragrant, what more could you ask?"

"Here!" exclaimed Janine in a loud, incredulous tone. "You're going to sleep here?"

"*We* are going to sleep here," said Mark pleasantly. He strode a short distance away and tethered Brandy to a sapling, then loosened the straps at the rear of his saddle, took down his blanket roll and returned to her side. He threw down two blankets and spread them on the ground.

"I'll be glad to share my blankets," said Mark, deliberately avoiding her gaze.

"Thank you. I'd prefer to sleep alone."

"Perhaps you'd prefer to freeze to death," he said cheerfully. "Suit yourself."

Fuming, she sat astride Beauty, staring at the blankets, weighing the advantages of crawling into a nice warm bedroll against lying huddled on the ground with no more protection than Jonathan's old jacket. She'd had more than enough of freezing to death last night at the inn. Tonight, outside, would be worse. Painfully aware of the absurdity of her position, her face flamed. Was it only last night that this arrogant stranger had told her that there were women begging to share his bed? She forced herself to speak, though she almost choked on the words.

"I'll accept your offer," said Janine haughtily, "but only if you promise to keep to yourself."

He looked up at her, his eyes gleaming with distaste. "You need have no fear on that score."

His tone was so condescending and superior, she could have struck him.

He patted the blankets confidently. "I well know how to lie still when there's a viper in my bedroll."

Stung to the quick, Janine leaped from Beauty's back and stood facing him, arms akimbo, her blue eyes flashing fire.

"Viper, am I? You're a fine one to be calling me a viper, you—you womanizer!" She drew in her breath sharply and rushed on. "But indeed, that's all one can expect from a rough-hewn, ill-bred seaman, or a militiaman who does nothing but ride over the countryside, living off the fat of the land, hoping for a war so he can reap a profit from the misfortunes of others!" Even as she spoke the words, she wanted to bite her tongue, but she did not seem to be able to stop.

He jumped up and stepped forward to face her, meeting her angry glare head on. With exaggerated politeness, he said, "May I remind you that I'm doing you a service, allowing you to accompany me on this journey!"

His eyes glinted dangerously in the moonlight, warning her not to try his patience too far, and she resolved to hold her tongue no matter how much he infuriated her.

"Not to mention," he went on, his voice heavy with sarcasm, "that I make it a rule never to make love to children, only women."

"Women!" cried Janine despite her resolve. "That's all you think about, isn't it?" Anger and indignation boiled up inside her. "And all you want of a woman is one thing. You're no better than—than an animal!"

A quirk tugged at the corner of his mouth as though he were trying not to laugh. "My, my, such an unlady-like display of temper. . . ." His dark brows lifted questioningly.

"Oh!" shrieked Janine, "you're detestable!"

Before he could reply, she seized Beauty's reins and stamped over to the sapling where he'd tied Brandy. She tethered Beauty and marched back to her bed under the pines, as Mark sat pulling off his boots.

Without looking at him, Janine slid down between the blankets and lay on her side, her back to him, as far away from the center as she could. Moments later she felt him slide in beside her, and she bit her lip to keep from asking if he had to be that close. She could feel his chest against her shoulder blades, his thighs against hers, his knees touching the calves of her legs. The heat of his body filled the bedroll, and a comforting warmth flooded through her own shivering body. She lay stiff as a ramrod, not daring to move.

"You may as well relax," Mark whispered, his lips brushing her ear, sending a tremor down her spine.

"Stop that!" she snapped.

"What?"

"Whispering . . . that way."

"Oh, for God's sake," he said, exasperated, and rolled over on his other side.

Janine lay silent, rigid with anger and indignation. She stared upward through the spreading branches of the pines and watched the wind chasing gauzy clouds past a full moon that hung like a golden sovereign in the sky. Her resistance began to ebb away, and a feeling of warmth and comfort stole over her. Why she should feel so safe, bedded down with such a rogue, was beyond all reason. She snuggled down further under the rough blanket and pulled it up over her head.

A rush of cold air creeping along her spine awoke her the next morning. Rolling over on her back she saw Mark kneeling a short distance away, scrubbing his face and neck with handfuls of snow, rubbing his dark skin to a ruddy glow. She lay quietly, watching him as he dried his face on his sleeve. She couldn't help thinking how handsome he was, though he was certainly no gentleman.

As though sensing her eyes upon him, he jumped up and strode swiftly to her side. He stood towering over her, arms akimbo, feet spread wide, his thick brows furrowed in a wrathful glare, his mouth a thin, angry line.

She flinched under his furious gaze. What could she have done wrong now?

"Your horse is gone!" His voice was like a whiplash,

and he looked at her as though she had driven Beauty off in the night.

Janine jerked bolt upright. "Beauty, gone?" she cried, aghast. "She can't be!"

"Gone!" he repeated, his voice hard with anger, his eyes boring into her accusingly. "You didn't tie her up right."

"I did!" cried Janine. "I know I did!" She jumped up and ran to the sapling where she'd tied the mare. Brandy stood quietly, head down, snuffling the ground. Beauty was nowhere in sight.

"Beauty!" she shouted wildly. "Beauty, where are you?"

She cocked her head, listening intently for an answering whinny. All she heard was the scolding of a squirrel scrambling along a branch overhead and the early morning twittering of birds.

"Beauty!" she shouted again, running farther into the woods. "Beauty . . . Beauty. . . ."

She heard no sound of hooves shuffling through the underbrush, no answering whinny.

"Come back here!" Mark bellowed.

Pretending not to hear him, she strode deeper among the hickory and oaks, pushing past dogwood, unmindful of briers clawing at her clothes. All at once she heard a thrashing through the woods behind her and whirled around. Mark was striding toward her, his face as red and angry as a turkey gobbler's.

"I said come back here, before you get lost!" he said through clenched teeth. Suddenly he shook her, shook her until her black hair tumbled down about her shoulders, shook her as if in a mad rage at her and at himself. She tried to speak and choked on the words, a stricken look on her face.

"There's no use looking for her now," said Mark harshly. "She's probably been running around loose for hours."

Janine bit her lip in despair. "I know I tied her se-

curely. Someone must have stolen her while we slept
. . . some brigand. . . ."

Mark snorted derisively. "Don't be ridiculous. A
brigand is not going to make off with only one horse
when two are there for the taking!"

Guilt swept through her, and her face flamed as she
realized that this pompous cad was right. A hint of
tears glistened at the corners of her eyes.

"I can't leave her wandering around lost in the
wilderness," cried Janine in despair. Abruptly she
tried to pull from his grasp, but he held her arm in a
tight grip.

"Do you think it would be better for *both* of you
to be lost?" asked Mark sarcastically.

She said nothing, but stood looking up at him, a
silent plea shining in her dark blue eyes.

His mouth turned down in a determined grimace.
"I can't waste the day searching for a lost horse. If you
want to stay here, stay!" He released her arm, and
walked back to the blankets. Janine followed him
silently.

He knelt down and rolled up the blankets, then
strode to Brandy and strapped the bedroll to the saddle. He loosened the reins, leaped onto the horse's
back and rode up beside her, extending his hand
toward her.

"Jump up."

Quickly she stepped back and tossed her head,
flinging her black curtain of hair over her shoulder,
reminding Mark of a yearling biting the bit. He urged
the horse a few steps nearer to the stubborn, stiff-
backed wench. Swiftly he leaned down, and before she
realized his intent, he flung an arm about her waist
and hauled her up before him, facedown across
Brandy's wide withers.

"Put me down!" she shrieked, her arms and legs
flailing the air on either side of Brandy's powerful
shoulders. "What do you think you're doing?"

"I'm performing an action above and beyond the call of duty!" shouted Mark.

She shrieked and shrieked again, kicking and striking out at him. In a swift reflex action his hand flashed downward and struck the rounded bottom a stinging blow as it squirmed before him.

From Janine's throat came a screech that chilled his blood. Startled, Brandy reared up, prancing on his hind legs, slamming Janine hard against Mark's chest. He reeled backward, gripping the reins in one hand, clutching Janine tightly to him with the other. Janine shut her eyes. For one dreadful moment she thought they would topple from Brandy's back and crash to the ground. At the last instant Mark gave a mighty lunge forward and reined in tightly in an effort to control the prancing, snorting animal.

"Damn it!" he yelled. "Shut up and sit astride this damn animal!"

With Mark's arm securely about her waist, Janine struggled to a sitting position and wound her fingers in Brandy's mane just as the horse took off in a wild, reckless canter. Crashing through the forest, they dodged low-hanging tree limbs and saplings that seemed to spring up in their path, as Mark guided the frightened steed back onto the uneven road that led toward Philadelphia.

A pale sun crept slowly up the sky, melting the mantle of snow that dripped from shining leaves, glistening on bare boughs, as though to wash away the last vestiges of winter. The day passed much as the day before. They rode hard, stopping only to rest the horse and eat a strip of salted cod or beef jerky and biscuits, washing it down with rum from Mark's canteen, or water from a gurgling stream.

Janine didn't know which pained her more: her wounded pride, or Mark's stinging blow on her bottom. Whichever it was, she felt even more deeply grieved and angered at being forced to abandon Beauty. Fervently she prayed that someone would find her, that she wouldn't wander lost and forlorn through the forest and eventually starve to death. If she did, thought Janine venomously, it would be that black-guard's fault for insisting that they go on without her. She clenched her teeth to keep from calling him all the terrible names she could think of. Oh, how she longed to be rid of this detestable clod! She rode before him in tight-lipped silence, her narrow back rigid, resisting every stride of the great mahogany steed.

As the day wore on, dark clouds, like billowing smoke, blotted out the sun, and at about three in the afternoon a fine misting rain began to fall, settling into a steady drizzle. The sky darkened until they could see no farther than a horse's length ahead. They didn't see the shrouded figure trotting toward them through the slanting gray rain until he was almost upon them.

The rider jerked his mount to a halt. They drew alongside him, and he smiled and tipped his hat in greeting. He was a thin, wiry little man with a curly black beard and intense blue eyes that peered at them curiously from under shaggy black brows. His cheeks were sunken in a lined, leathery face, and water dripped from the end of his nose.

"John Fleming, circuit rider, traveling to Williamsburg. Can you tell me how far the inn might be?"

Mark Furneaux greeted him as though he were never so glad to see anyone in his entire life. He told the man where the inn was, then quickly launched into an explanation of Janine's plight, ending with a plea for him to take her with him as far as Alexandria.

The little preacher nodded sympathetically. "I'm acquainted with John Burke. . . ."

Janine's heart quickened. He must know Jonathan, then! The Reverend John Fleming was no doubt the man who was to have married them. Surely he'd be willing to help her search for Jonathan—and Beauty too.

The circuit rider was stroking his beard, shaking his

head regretfully. "I'm days behind schedule now." He patted his bony horse's head. "My horse is old and feeble. He can't accommodate two—"

"Don't worry," Mark interrupted. "Mistress Mercer has a horse not too far ahead. A fine, strong mare. Surely someone will have found her by now and taken her to the inn."

Janine stared at Mark in open-mouthed astonishment.

He ranted on. "I'm certain you'll find her in the stable there. You both can ride Beauty . . . give your own mount a rest. . . ."

Janine frowned in annoyance. Lieutenant Furneaux was succeeding far too well in persuading the itinerant preacher to take her with him, and he gave her pause to think things through more carefully. If Jonathan were alive, she was sure he'd make for Philadelphia. For him to return to Heritage Hall after their headlong flight would be pure folly. If Jonathan were dead —and she refused to believe he was—it would serve no purpose for her to return. To return to the plantation alone was unthinkable.

"Well . . ." said the little preacher in a doubtful tone, "I suppose we can make it as far as the inn. If her horse isn't there, she can wait for the stage. . . ."

Janine turned her head to face Mark, her gaze hard and implacable. "I'm not going back with Mister Fleming."

The lieutenant's mouth dropped open and his thick brows drew together in a scowl that would have frightened the devil himself. "You *must* go. . . ."

"No!" said Janine vehemently. She turned back to the Reverend Fleming. "Thank you, but I must go on to Philadelphia."

His patience at an end, Mark thundered, "Now look here, Mistress Mercer, I've done all I can for you!"

He put his hands around her waist and started to lift her from Brandy's back. She threw her arms around the horse's neck, clamped her knees around his shoulders, and clung with all the strength that was in her. Mark tightened his hold in a bone-crushing grip that made her cry out, yanked her free, and swung her to the ground. He slid down beside her, propelling her firmly toward Mr. Fleming. She looked up into Mark's face, her eyes burning with an unholy light. Suddenly she hated him with a strength that overpowered her reason.

"All right," she said furiously. "I'll go!" Suddenly her reason came back with a rush. "But you must give Brandy back to me now. He *is* my horse, and I've no wish to slow Mister Fleming further."

Mark's hand dropped from her waist as though he'd held a branding iron. His face flamed crimson, the muscles in his jaw tightened. His fists, hanging at his sides, clenched and unclenched as they stood glaring fiercely at each other in the cold, gray rain. For a moment she thought he would shove her aside, leap astride Brandy, and gallop away.

At last he heaved an exasperated sigh. Turning to the Reverend Fleming, he gave him a mock salute and bid him a safe journey.

Suppressing a small, victorious smile, Janine scrambled up on Brandy's back. Thank heaven she'd had the courage to stand up to the officious lieutenant. Mark sprang up behind her. Furiously he dug in his heels, spurring the horse to a gallop.

Not long after, the sky opened up and the rain lashed down upon them like showers of steel needles. Without speaking, Mark drew rein. He yanked a gray blanket from his bedroll and flung it over his shoulders, tucking the ends around Janine's neck so that it enveloped the two of them like a cocoon. She felt his arms close around her, his thighs pressed against her own and a warm tide of feeling, bewildering, frightening, swept over her. She started to cry out in protest at being imprisoned in such an intimate manner, but she knew he would only laugh and make some insulting remark. She held her tongue and clutched the blanket around her, grateful for its cozy warmth.

Thunder boomed across the dark sky, pierced by crackling shards of lightning that made Janine wince. Despite the protection of the blanket she was soon drenched through, her shirt and breeches clinging tightly to her skin. A harsh, driving wind rose, swaying the trees, turning the leaves inside out, hurling twigs and broken limbs in their path. But Janine was aware only of the warmth of Mark's body shielding her own as Brandy stumbled and splashed along the trail, kicking up mud and stones behind him. Weariness overcame her, and though she tried to sit erect, her body betrayed her. Again and again she sagged against Mark, his warm, muscular body pressing into her back with each stride, as Brandy drove on through the slashing wind and rain.

It was well past dark when they drew up under the swaying sign of the Red Lion Inn. Janine was numb with cold, chilled to the marrow, and too weak and exhausted to protest when Mark lifted her in his arms and carried her inside. She dreaded to think what Papa and Aunt Ellen would say about her staying at an inn, but she had no other recourse. Dimly she was aware of Mark lowering her gently on the bed, and as though from a great distance, she heard his voice.

"We may have to share the bed with other travelers," he warned her. "All the rooms are filled." No need to mention he'd slipped the innkeeper an extra pound to insure their privacy.

She was too tired to care. Whitewashed walls tilted crazily about her, and the bright red and yellow flames blazing merrily on the hearth seemed to be licking at the foot of the poster bed. She closed her eyes, feeling as though she were on a ship tossed by a storm at sea.

"I've ordered food sent up," Mark said, unbuttoning his shirt.

She said nothing, but lay quietly, eyes closed, hoping the dizziness would pass.

"You'd best get out of those wet clothes." It was an order.

Janine opened her eyes and saw Mark standing before the fireplace, peeling off his sodden breeches, firelight gleaming on his broad back. Her eyes closed. She heard him walk across the room, and moments later something landed lightly on her chest.

"There's your shift. Put it on."

She rolled from the bed and stood up. Her knees wobbled, threatening to fold under her, and she clutched the bedpost for support, shivering uncontrollably.

Mark had donned dry breeches and stood watching her, arms folded across his chest, waiting for her to do his bidding. Her long wet hair lay like seaweed streaming over her shoulders, and her white linen shirt clung to her body, accentuating her curves. A tremor shook her, and small peaks rose under the cloth. She swayed, then steadied herself, and gazed directly into his warm brown eyes.

"Close your eyes."

A grin tugged at the corners of his mouth as he turned his back and began to drape his wet clothes over a ladderback chair.

Janine's arms felt like lead, and it seemed to take all her strength to draw off the wet garments plastered to her skin. She let them fall in a heap on the floor and pulled on her shift, then sank down on her knees before the hearth, her head bent, her graceful hands spreading, fanning strands of silken black hair to dry in the warmth of the leaping fire. She felt Mark's steady gaze upon her and she tensed, wondering what deviltry he could be planning now. A sudden thumping on the door interrupted her thoughts. Wearily she got to her feet, staggered to the bed, and climbed in. She sat up, leaning against the pillows, and pulled the bedclothes up around her shoulders.

Mark opened the door to admit a gangling, sallow-faced boy carrying a tray bearing two plates heaped with mutton and potatoes, and two steaming tankards of rum.

After the door had closed behind him, Mark sat on the side of the bed and set the tray down between them. Eagerly they quaffed the hot rum, and Janine was grateful for the quick warmth that flowed through her, driving the chill away. Her eyes met Mark's over the rims of the pewter tankards. His gaze was impersonal, inscrutable.

She knew he was still angry with her over losing Beauty and even more annoyed that she had bested him in his attempt to foist her off on Preacher Fleming. She dropped her gaze to the food cooling on her plate, and the sight of it made her stomach turn over.

She managed two bites of mutton, but the stringy meat was tough and it hurt her throat to swallow. She ate several bites of potatoes before she set down her knife and fork.

"Aren't you going to finish?" Mark asked.

She shook her head and lay back on the pillow.

"Eat up," he said sharply. "You'll need your strength for tomorrow."

Ignoring him, she closed her eyes.

He shook her shoulder roughly. "Sit up now and eat!"

She lay like the dead, deep in the sleep of exhaustion, her thick dark lashes brushing her cheeks.

"The devil take you!" Mark muttered. He rose from the bed, picked up her crumpled clothes from the floor, and hung them from the mantel to dry. Then he stirred the glowing coals with a poker and stood staring into the fire.

Chapter 8

When Janine awoke the next morning, her throat felt as though someone had been hacking through it with a saw, and her head felt stuffed with wool. Though the fire on the grate had died in the night, chilling the room, her skin was hot to the touch.

She glanced at Mark sleeping soundly beside her and slipped from the bed, shivering as her bare feet struck the cold floorboards. She poured water from a pitcher into the bowl on the washstand and, cupping her hands, sloshed the icy water over her burning forehead, cheeks, and neck, drawing in her breath sharply when the water trickled down between her breasts. She doused her arms, letting the water drip back into the bowl.

"God!" groaned a voice from the bed. "Don't tell me it's still raining!"

Janine turned and glanced out the window. "No. The sky's turning pink. It's going to be a fine day." She reached for a towel from the rack on the washstand and rubbed her face, neck, and arms vigorously.

With easy grace Mark swung from the bed, strode to her side, and placed a large, gentle hand on her forehead.

She stepped back quickly, flapping the towel at him. "Get away from me!"

Rebuffed, he stood looking down at her, his lips pressed into a grim line.

"You have a fever." His voice was matter-of-fact,

brooking no argument. "You can't go on. You'll have to stay here till you're well."

"I do not have a fever," cried Janine, her blue eyes sparkling with indignation. "I was roasting like a chicken in that bed last night, with you giving off heat like Mister Franklin's stove. If I'm flushed, it's from the toweling!"

His eyes mocked her and his lips twisted in a grin, but he said nothing. Annoyed, she turned away from him, flung the towel on the rack, and, stepping to the mantel, snatched down her clothes.

"You're ill," he went on reasonably. "It would be foolish for you to go on. Tomorrow you'll feel better and you can take the stage. . . ."

Ignoring him, Janine stepped into her breeches, tugging them up under her shift. Then drawing her shift high around her waist, she slid her shirt on over her arms and shoulders. Mark turned away and pulled on his fringed shirt and ran his hand over his head, smoothing his thick black hair. Taking her silence for consent, he said, "It's settled then. After breakfast I'll ride on."

She whirled to face him, writhing in helpless rage at being dependent upon this rogue for her safety.

"When you ride on, you'd best make jolly well sure it's not Brandy under you!" Her voice shook with the effort of challenging him. "Horse-thievery, I believe, is a hanging offense."

His face reddened with anger, erupting in an outraged roar. "Damn, if you're not a bullheaded hellcat!" He stamped to the window and stared out, as though there were something to see besides the road through the forest.

Janine bit her lips, trying not to laugh at the image a bullheaded hellcat conjured up, and tucked her shift inside his blanket roll. She donned her jacket, and when he turned from the window, she stood before him, her chin raised, determination and defiance shining from her indigo eyes.

"I'm ready to ride."

The sun climbed high above pillowy white clouds in a china-blue sky, and Janine was grateful for its comforting warmth on her back. She inclined her head, breathing deeply the fresh, clean scent of the April wind, trying to ignore her aching limbs, the tightness in her chest, the rawness in her throat when she swallowed.

In contrast to the golden brilliance of the day, Mark sat behind her, dour and ill-humored, astride the mahogany steed.

Ignoring Mark's punishing silence, Janine concentrated on the beauty of the countryside they were passing through. In shadowy woodlands dappled with sunlight, ferns shot up from the damp scented earth; she saw clusters of bluebells, anemones, lilies of the valley, and parchment dogwood blossoms that seemed to bow and wave among trees sprouting tender young leaves. Brandy scrambled down steep ravines, dislodging rocks and dirt that tumbled after them in small landslides.

When they halted to rest, Janine plucked several bluebells and tucked them in the thick coil of her hair, then, turning to Mark, she grinned and wove another in the fringe of his hunting shirt. He eyed her sternly, unsmiling, refusing to be placated or cajoled into enjoying the day.

As the day wore on the ache in her bones grew worse, and she clenched her teeth to keep from crying out at every bump and jolt as the galloping horse pelted down the rutted road. Her head, her eyes, even her teeth ached. Her merry, frivolous mood gave way to silence as she slumped over Brandy's neck. As though sensing her misery, Mark's arm went around her shoulders, pulling her back against him, and his hand on her cheek pressed her head down on his shoulder. And there she stayed. Though she longed desperately for a bed on which to rest her weary body, she murmured a silent prayer that they wouldn't come upon an inn—for fear he would abandon her to the mercies of the innkeeper.

They heard the Green Dragon before they saw it, and when Mark drew rein before the old stone tavern, boisterous laughter and shouts greeted them from the small knot of men who stood outside joking, arguing, swearing, lurching about the yard. Mark dismounted, lifted Janine from the horse, and carried her toward the door, her long black hair spilling over his arm. As he stepped onto the porch a sotted frontiersman in ragged homespun called out, "Gather 'round, boys! Here's a good man brought us a wench to warm our beds!"

A shout of laughter went up from the men, and lust gleamed in their eyes. One of them reached out and chucked Janine under her chin, and she went rigid in Mark's arms. He shot them a look that would freeze the devil.

"My wife has a fever," he said sharply. "Get out of the way!"

"Fever!" the man shouted. Curses and murmurs of putrid fever raced like fire through the small knot of men. Quickly they fell back. Mark strode inside and glanced hastily about the low-ceilinged room murky with smoke from the fireplace. Behind the bar stood a short buxom woman of about fifty. She wore a soiled white apron, and tangled brown curls escaped from her mobcap. Her pointed nose and glittering dark eyes under eyebrows that formed a V gave her the look of an owl. Hands on her broad hips, she stared at them malevolently.

"Where's the innkeeper?" Mark demanded. "Quickly, I must have a room."

"I'm the innkeeper—Widow Green." Her voice was strident and harsh with anger as she jerked her head at Janine. "I heard the commotion out there! You get her out of here, before she brings the pox down on all of us."

"It's not the pox, I swear it!"

Her bright eyes, gleaming with suspicion, sized him up. He could see her greed for his money fighting her fear of the dread disease. She wiped her hands on her dirty white apron and took a key from a hook on the wall. "I'll take a look at 'er," said the woman grudgingly. "Come along." Taking a candlestick from the bar, she led the way upstairs to a small dingy room into which were crowded a bed, chest, chair and gate-leg table. No rugs graced the scarred floor, and the fire in the fireplace had long since died.

Mark lowered Janine to the bed, and the Widow Green, reeking of ale, waddled to her side. Quickly she stripped off Janine's clothes and looked her over carefully. Too weak to protest, Janine lay like a lamb waiting for slaughter, staring at the sweat stains ringing the underarms of Widow Green's homespun gown.

"It's not the pox," said the widow, clearly relieved. "She's got no red spots on her chest and belly, but she's took bad." She shook her head at Janine, her expression of grudging tolerance changing to one of sympathetic concern.

"Yes, I realize that," said Mark solemnly. "In fact she's much too ill to continue our journey." He bent his most engaging smile upon Widow Green. "I'd be most grateful if you'd look after her. . . ."

The buxom widow backed away, shaking her head. "No, sir, not me," she said emphatically. "I got no time to look after the sick. It's more'n I can do to keep the taproom below. I'm shorthanded now. I ain't be taking on no invalid."

"But look here, I'll pay you well!" Mark drew some money from his pocket and waved it under her beak-like nose.

For an instant her bright eyes lighted with avarice. Then, as if to keep herself from snatching the money from his hand, she backed toward the door, shaking her head, her face showing genuine regret. In the doorway she paused, gazing at Janine, and said, not unkindly, "What she needs is a good soaking. Steam

the poison outta her. And a mustard plaster on her
chest. I'll see you get a flannel and a tub, but *you* got
to see to her!" With that, she waddled away down the
hall.

Mark tucked a green woolen blanket around
Janine's still form, then set about tossing pine-knots
in the fireplace and lighting a fire. Soon a servant appeared lugging a wooden tub, followed by another
toting buckets of water.

When Mark lifted Janine from the bed, she opened
her eyes and looked at him with a dazed, helpless expression. A strangled cough escaped her, and pain
knifed through her chest. Though it hurt her throat
to speak, she asked in a harsh whisper, "Where are
we going? Put me down!"

"Easy now," said Mark softly. "I'm taking care of
you." He lowered her gently into the water and
draped her arms over the side of the tub. She moaned
softly as the hot water engulfed her burning flesh.

"Hang on to the edge of the tub and try to sit up,"
he commanded. Beads of sweat formed on his brow
and rolled down his face.

Janine sank lower into the tub, her head lolled
back, and the water lapped about her shoulders.
Kneeling on the floor, Mark lifted her silken mass
of black hair out of the way, draping it over the rim
of the tub. Suddenly her limp body slid further down
into the water and Mark slipped one arm beneath her
shoulders and held her firmly against his chest. Awkwardly he sponged her face, neck, and shoulders, her
throat and chest.

Mark's big, gentle hands were comforting, the hot
water soft and soothing. She felt a lethargy steal over
her, a delicious warmth creep through her body, and
she let out a long, tremulous sigh. She knew she should
feel embarrassed, but she truly felt only gratitude toward Mark Furneaux.

In the gleam of the firelight her skin glowed golden
beneath the shimmering water, and she heard Mark

draw in his breath sharply. His hand shook as he continued to scoop up water and let it flow over her shoulders until it grew tepid. Then, lifting her dripping from the tub, he placed her on the bed and patted her dry with a sheet.

He tucked the green blanket around her neck, took more blankets from his bedroll, and spread them over her.

"Mark, no!" she said weakly. "I'm burning up!"

"You'll keep them on!" he commanded. Then more gently he said, "Once at sea I saw a fever burn itself out in an afflicted seaman. The men piled blankets atop him, holding him down all the while he was fighting to throw off the bedclothes." He grinned down at her. "Thank God you're not up to fighting me now!"

There came a sharp knock on the door, and the Widow Green entered carrying a mustard plaster. Wordlessly the woman waddled across the room and without preamble ripped the covers from Janine and placed the flannel, spread with a dark, evil-smelling paste, on her chest and wrapped her up again.

"Good for what ails her—drives out the humors," said the Widow Green flatly, wiping her hands on her apron. Turning to leave, she said, "I'll send the girl up with your supper," and trundled out, closing the door behind her.

Through drooping lids, Janine saw Mark sink down in a chair and wipe his forehead with the back of his hand. She smiled to herself. Obviously he was unused to bathing ladies, tending ailing females. Yet she had never felt so well cared for, so comforted, and her heart warmed toward him in a way she had never thought possible.

The serving maid entered the room with his supper, and he pulled a chair up before the scarred gateleg table. Covertly she watched while he devoured his meal, frequently glancing over at her still form on the bed. When he finished, he picked up a copy of the

Pennsylvania Gazette from his supper tray and began to read.

Janine's eyes closed, and when she opened them again, the candle had burned down to a stub. As though sensing Janine's eyes upon him, Mark looked up from the paper.

"Hungry?"

She shook her head. Her throat felt coated with sawdust. Shivering, she ran her tongue over parched lips. "May I have a pot of tea, please. I'm freezing!"

Mark went to the bed, placed his hand on her forehead, and quickly withdrew it. His dark brows furrowed in a frown, and Janine shrank back into the pillow. Clearly he was fed up to the teeth with her, and much as she detested him, she could not blame him. Oh, why did this wretched ailment strike now when she was within a day's ride of Philadelphia? she thought furiously.

Mark strode to the door and barked an order down the stairs. When the serving maid brought the tea, he set the tray on the table and carried a cup of the steaming brew to Janine. An aroma of sassafras assailed her nostrils, and she tried to sit up, but fell weakly back onto the pillow. He set the cup on the night table and slipped his hand around her shoulders, cradling her in the curve of his arm. He held the cup to her lips and she sipped the hot tea, letting it trickle down her throat.

Suddenly his hand jerked and some of the tea spilled on the blanket. Awkwardly he dabbed at her bosom.

"I'm no damn good at this sort of thing," he muttered, not looking at her. Her lips curved in silent amusement, but she said nothing. Even though he was a clumsy, arrogant cad, he made her feel safe and secure. When at last she finished the tea, she drifted off to sleep.

Sometime during the dark night Janine awoke with a chill. She burrowed deeper under the covers and felt a warm bearlike figure lying beside her. Mark had undressed and stretched out under the bedclothes next to her! Drowsily she thought, *I should wake him and order him out of my bed at once!* Then she rolled over on her side and snuggled up against him, savoring his warmth.

The next morning a draft of cold air woke her. Mark had left the bed and was dousing his face and hands with water from the pitcher on the washstand.

"Good morning," said Janine in a voice like the croak of a frog.

Mark turned to face her, and she shifted uneasily under his intense scrutiny. She felt feverish and she knew that her face was too flushed, her eyes too bright.

"Feeling better?"

"Much better," lied Janine. She started to thank him for taking such good care of her yesterday, but the image of him bathing her fevered body in the tub rose in her mind, and her cheeks burned with mortification. She said nothing.

He strode to the bedside and placed his hand over her small, slender one. "Cold as a fish from the Schuylkill!"

His dark eyes were filled with concern, and he wasn't urging her to hurry as he had when they'd started out. The suspicion crossed her mind that he was going to ride on without her.

"Is it time to be on our way?" She gazed up at him with trusting eyes and saw a quick flash of guilt pass over his face that confirmed her fear.

Mark hesitated. "I'll bring us something to eat first."

He left the room, and as soon as the door closed behind him, Janine crawled from beneath the bedclothes and shed her blanket and mustard plaster. Her limbs felt leaden and she shook all over. Her legs almost gave way as she crossed the room to retrieve her clothes. She slid onto the chair and pulled them on.

She was buttoning her jacket when Mark returned carrying a tray laden with food.

The heavy aroma of ham turned her stomach, and despite his urging, she could eat nothing. While Mark devoured the ham and cornmeal mush, she sipped a steaming cup of sassafras tea. The hot liquid seeping through her body gave her strength, and she sat up straight, stiffening her spine, bracing herself for the long ride ahead.

When Mark finished his meal, she rose from the table and took up her small bundle of possessions. "I'm ready when you are."

"Now look, Janine," he said sternly, "you'd be much better off to stay here. You can pound on the floor or shout for the Widow Green if you need anything and—"

Janine's chin lifted in a stubborn tilt, and a steely look of determination flashed in her blue eyes. "If you try to leave without me, I'll shout for the Widow Green all right! She'll come on the run, and she won't let you abandon me!"

Mark gazed at her speculatively, as though weighing her threat. Then, with a heavy sigh of defeat, he stood up. "Let's go."

The late afternoon sun was slipping behind John Chad's two-story fieldstone house, and the tall pine standing beside it cast a long shadow by the time they forded Brandywine Creek.

"We're no further than Chad's Ford!" fumed Mark, and Janine, slumped wearily against him, felt his body stiffen with anger and irritation. Brandy slowed his pace as they passed the Baptist church, whose gold-streaked windows looked sightlessly over a lovely quiet valley. "We should stop and rest," said Mark irritably, "but I'm determined to reach Rose Tree Tavern tonight. Even at that, we're fifteen miles from Philadelphia. We spent five nights on the road!" He drove the horse relentlessly and under his breath Janine heard him cursing himself round the bend.

It was well after midnight when they reached Rose Tree. Janine, weak with fever and fatigue, was barely conscious of Mark carrying her inside and putting her to bed.

The next morning her cough was worse, and though she tried hard to suppress it, pain knifed through her chest every time she inhaled. One moment her body burned with fever, and the next her teeth chattered with chills. She felt weak as a jelly fish, but she'd never admit it to Mark Furneaux. She had the feeling that he was not deceived, for while she dressed, he paced their room, his face drawn with worry. At last he threw up his hands in a helpless gesture.

"You're no better. If anything, you're worse. I'm going to find a doctor!" He started toward the door.

"No, Mark, please!" cried Janine. "We'll be in Philadelphia before the day is out. Papa will take care of me."

He stopped short in surprise, wheeling to face her. "I'd forgotten your father is a doctor."

She knew by the look on his face that he had dismissed it from his mind that night along with the rest of the incredible tale she'd told him when he'd rescued her from the ruffians at the Boar's Head. Oh, why wouldn't he believe her!

"Papa *is* a physician!" cried Janine. "Oh, please, let's go on!"

Mark eyed her doubtfully. "It's against my better judgment," he said in a resigned voice, "but have it your way, little darling."

Darkness had long since fallen by the time the boatman had ferried them across the Schuylkill, and they clattered through the streets of the sleeping town, through pools of faint light shed by the streetlamps. As they passed the State House yard, the nightwatch emerged from his octagonal box, bawling in his thick German accent, "Basht ten o'clock und all isht vell."

Janine's heart hammered with joy and anticipation.

She was almost home! "Turn right at the next corner," she told Mark breathlessly.

They rounded the corner onto Second Street, past Mr. Smith's City Tavern, past darkened shops, past the Golden Fleece Tavern, past Cadwalader's brick mansion.

"There's our house—with the Hand-in-Hand fire mark over the door!" cried Janine.

Mark reined in before the three-and-a-half story red brick house, shouldered between others like it, fronting upon the brick pavement that bordered the street. No glimmer of light showed from inside.

Mark slid to the ground, looped Brandy's reins over a cedar post, and, grasping Janine around the waist, swung her down beside him. He led her up the marble steps and knocked sharply on the white wooden door.

Janine could have screamed with impatience, until at last the door opened a crack. Zoë dressed in a red flannel night rail with a red turban round her head, peered cautiously through the crack, the dark irises of her eyes rimmed in white. She raised a candle high above her head, shining a circle of light full on their faces.

"Everybody sleeping round here," she snapped, annoyed. "Doctor Mercer ain't seeing nobody tonight." Before Janine could answer, the door slammed shut in their faces.

Chapter 9

Janine gasped in shocked surprise. "Zoë didn't even recognize me," she said, abashed. "Surely I haven't changed that much in two years!"

She saw a glint of amusement in Mark's eyes as his gaze traveled down her figure, taking in her tangled hair drawn back and tied with a tattered ribbon, her smudged face, her bedraggled jacket and breeches. She realized she must look like a street urchin.

"You can hardly blame her," said Mark, raising an eyebrow and grinning. He pounded on the door again.

Again the door opened and Zoë's frightened face appeared in the crack. In a high-pitched, excited voice she cried, "You go 'long with you. Doctor Mercer ain't be seeing no patients this time of night. He plumb wore out. . . ."

"Zoë!" cried Janine, pushing against the door. "It's me, Janine. Let me in!"

"What's all the fuss down there, Zoë?" came a loud, authoritative voice from the hallway beyond. "Has a plague struck the town, that I'm to be disturbed from my sleep, routed from my bed?" Abruptly the door was flung wide and Dr. Mercer appeared on the threshold, red-faced and indignant. Dr. Mercer, a man of forty-odd years, his black hair graying at the temples, stood bundled in a brown night-robe. His shoulders were slightly stooped from the exertion of trying to cram thirty hours into a twenty-four-hour day. Few acquaintances suspected that his choleric exterior hid a charming old gentleman with an iron will and

strong backbone. Now he slid his spectacles over his
nose and peered at Janine and Mark with keen blue
eyes that Janine well knew could see straight through
anyone.

"Papa!" cried Janine, hurling herself into her
father's arms.

He hugged her, kissed her tenderly on the forehead,
then held her at arm's length, staring at her as though
he couldn't believe the evidence of his own eyes.

"What on earth are you doing here, *ma petite*? How
did you get here?"

Janine motioned to Mark. "This—this gentleman
brought me home. He's Lieutenant Furneaux of the
Pennsylvania militia."

Dr. Mercer stepped forward and pumped Mark's
hand energetically. "Well, we needn't stand here all
night. Come in, come in, and tell me what you're doing
with my daughter!"

Mark's brows lifted and the corner of his mouth
turned down in a wry grin. "It's more a question of
what she's doing with me, sir."

Janine shot him an angry, indignant glance, but
Dr. Mercer laughed and his voice held a trace of
irony. "That I can well believe! Truth to tell, you
look as though you could use a tot of brandy."

The lieutenant raised his hand in a gesture of refusal. "Thank you, no. I can't stay . . . and I think your
daughter requires your attention."

Zoë, hovering over Janine, shook her turbaned head
worriedly. "Miss Janine look like she give up living,
Doctor."

Taking the candle from Zoë, Dr. Mercer turned to
Janine and brought the light close to her face, studying
it clinically, noting her flushed skin and too bright
eyes.

"Don't fuss over me, Papa. I've had a nasty chill,
that's all."

"Begging your pardon, Doctor Mercer," said Mark
authoritatively, "your daughter's been quite ill. I

wanted her to remain at the inn, but she insisted upon pushing on. . . ."

Dr. Mercer smiled ruefully, shaking his head. "I see my headstrong daughter hasn't changed an iota. I'm sorry for any trouble or inconvenience she's caused—"

"Not at all," Mark interrupted smoothly. "It was my pleasure. And now I must be on my way."

Stunned by his airy dismissal of their harrowing journey, Janine stood silent beside her father, supported by his arm around her shoulders.

"Surely we can put you up for the night," said Dr. Mercer.

"Thank you, sir, but duty calls." Mark gazed directly into Janine's eyes, his lips curved in the familiar mocking, challenging smile that never failed to antagonize her. He touched his hand to his forehead in a mock salute.

"Au revoir, little darling."

Good riddance to this rude and insolent man, thought Janine venomously. She forced herself to step forward, extending her hand, but before she could bid him good-bye, he turned and was gone. All of a sudden she felt a stab of sadness, a sense of loss, as though something were going out of her life forever. The emotion was puzzling but she decided she was simply feverish and bone-tired, that was all.

She followed Papa into the parlor and sank down gratefully on the rose brocade sofa. He poured them each a glass of brandy and eased into the green Windsor chair across from her.

She took one sip of brandy, and then the thought struck her with the force of a blow.

"Papa," asked Janine with her heart in her throat, "isn't Jonathan here?"

"Jonathan! Jonathan Burke?" Dr. Mercer gazed at her, a baffled expression on his kindly face. "Why on earth would he be here?"

Overwhelmed with fatigue, disappointment, and

despair, she put her head in her hands to stem the sudden flow of tears.

Dr. Mercer rose from his chair and went to her. He fished a handkerchief from the pocket of his night robe and wiped her eyes. "Blow your nose, child, and tell Papa all about it."

She blew her nose obediently, and Papa patted her arm. "Now, now," he said soothingly, "everything's going to be all right."

Janine fought back her tears and took another sip of brandy. The liquid burning her raw throat revived her. With lips that trembled, she told him of her ill-starred love for Jonathan, Aunt Ellen's violent opposition to their marriage, and their flight from Heritage Hall. She paused, shuddering at the horror of the memory of Jake and Lige pawing her, tearing her clothes from her body.

Dr. Mercer returned to his seat. He placed his glass on a side table, and leaned forward, his elbows resting on the arms of the green Windsor chair, his hands clasped before him, listening attentively. "Go on, go on, *ma petite*."

In a low, tremulous voice she went on to tell of the brigands' attack in the clearing, her wild flight on Beauty and subsequent capture, her ill treatment suffered at the hands of the renegades, and her rescue by Lieutenant Furneaux. She skipped the details of their arduous journey, though why she had done this, she could not have said.

She bit her lips to still their trembling; her hands were white with anxiety.

"Papa, even though those savages told me that Jonathan was dead, I can't believe it. Won't believe it! All the while I kept hoping he'd escaped and had come here to wait for me."

Dr. Mercer's eyes were full of sympathy, his expression grave. He sighed deeply. "I can understand your not believing Jonathan is dead unless you know it for a fact. And the fact that he isn't here doesn't signify

the renegades have done away with him. If Jonathan
had been killed, someone would have found his body
and let the Burke family know. Ellen would have sent
word by post rider, or one of the servants. After all,
it was the horses and money your abductors wanted.
From what you tell me, the clearing where you were
waylaid is much nearer to Alexandria than Philadelphia. Jonathan may well have headed home. I'll
write to Ellen. Surely she'll have heard from him."

He stood up and went to her and ran his hand
gently over her long black hair, his face filled with
compassion.

"Come, Janine. What you need now is rest."

She felt somewhat comforted by Papa's cheerful
optimism, although she couldn't understand why
Jonathan wouldn't have sent her word if he was safe.

The next morning Dr. Mercer sat at Janine's bedside, a worried frown on his kind countenance. He
had diagnosed her illness as pleurisy, and now she saw
Zoë enter the room bearing a bleeding basin and a
fleam.

"No, Papa, no!" cried Janine, shrinking down under
the covers and pulling them over her head. Too often
she had watched while Papa ordered a patient to
breathe deeply and cough while he drained twelve
ounces of blood from his jugular vein.

Papa gazed at her thoughtfully, as though debating
the question in his own mind. Finally he said, "On
several occasions when I've put off bleeding a patient,
I seemed to have had good results. For now we'll
settle for emetics and laxatives." He drew the covers
away from her head. "But if those chest pains don't
diminish within twelve hours, you can expect to be
bled!" His voice was stern, but he smiled as he
smoothed back damp tendrils of hair from her flushed
face.

Looking up into his eyes, Janine could see that he
was more worried than he cared to admit of the dread

disease of the lungs and chest that took a high toll of those who contracted it.

"If anything happens to you, Janine, life will not be worth living," he said huskily.

"Nothing will happen to me, Papa!" she said lightly in an effort to reassure him. She knew that his world revolved around her, and this often worried her. Long ago Zoë had told her that after her mother's death, he couldn't bear the thought of marrying again; that Janine, so like her mother, was all his joy and delight; and Zoë herself had taken good care of them and the house as well. His life had been full, teaching at the Philadelphia College of Medicine, working day and night to establish a practice. Later, when his practice flourished, he had little time for courting. Janine smiled to herself, recalling an attractive young widow with slanting green eyes and golden hair who'd set her cap for Papa. She'd had a passel of children and Papa had said he'd no desire to take on a brood, nor was their home large enough, nor did he have enough money—physicians were not well paid—if at all. Anyway, Papa had escaped matrimony, claiming he was accustomed to peace and quiet and he intended to keep it that way.

Now he sat down at Janine's writing desk and drew paper and quill pen before him, dipping the quill into the silver inkpot. "I'm trying to think how best to approach my austere, God-fearing sister in the light of your hapless elopement, Janine. It's difficult at best, and to make matters worse, from what you've told me, the old wounds haven't healed as I'd thought."

Janine's eyes widened in surprise. "What old wounds, Papa?"

Dr. Mercer set down the quill and rocked back in his chair, regarding Janine solemnly. "It may be my fault that she hasn't accepted you, *ma petite*. Ellen had always expected me to return to Virginia after I finished my medical studies in Edinburgh. She was angry and disappointed when I went on to the *Hotel Dieu* in Paris, but I had to go, for it was a prestigious hospital and I knew I'd gain invaluable experience. I also knew the breadth and depth of Ellen's devotion. She's the kind of woman who insists upon sharing the lives of those about her, and much as I loved and appreciated her, I'd no wish to be smothered. So when Nicole—your mother—and I returned to America, I thought it best to keep a friendly distance between them and settled down here. It disturbs me greatly that Ellen's love and affection for me has not extended to you. I'd hoped she'd take you to her heart and 'mother' you as she once mothered me." A resigned sigh escaped him. "I suppose the old adage that two women in the same household are one too many must have some basis in fact." He went on, smiling ruefully. "It is true, you are impulsive, fearless, and perhaps a bit stubborn, but you come by it honestly. In any event I'm happy to have you home, Janine," he said firmly. He dipped the quill in the inkpot and bent to his task.

During the days that followed, Janine battled fever and chills and spasms of coughing that left her weak and exhausted. Gradually, under Papa's watchful eye and Zoë's unremitting care, she regained some of her strength. Even so, Papa insisted she stay in bed until she was stronger. As the days drifted by with no word from Jonathan and no reply to Papa's letter from Aunt Ellen, her spirits flagged. Tortured day and night with worry about Jonathan, she began to grieve for him. She grew pale and listless, and life seemed to lose its zest.

One evening after supper she lay in bed trying to read the *Pennsylvania Gazette*. She felt restless and out-of-sorts, and her mind refused to fasten on the words. It was unseasonably warm for May, and Zoë had not yet closed the window against the night air. Outside she heard a cricket's shrill song and a whippoorwill calling in the hush of twilight. Suddenly there came the clear, sweet sound of bells chiming.

She sprang from her bed and ran to the window, leaning far out on the sill. The sound came from the direction of Christ Church. How curious, thought Janine. The chime of eight bells rang out on all public occasions as well as for funerals of prominent people. Who could have died? She listened for the strains of "Roslyn Castle," the tune usually rung at such times, but the pealing bells rang the tune "Nancy Dawson."

Of course. She'd forgotten the "butter bells." The bells of Christ Church were always rung on Tuesday and Thursday evenings, heralding the market the next day. And tonight they seemed to summon her. No matter what Papa thought, she'd had enough of languishing in bed, she told herself firmly. Tomorrow she'd be out and about.

She rose at dawn and, moving quietly so as not to wake Papa, dressed in a soft blue muslin gown edged in wide lace at the neck and sleeves. As she stole downstairs, she heard a familiar *swish, swish* coming from the parlor, and peeked inside. She saw Zoë's tall, oblong figure vigorously wielding a broom, sweeping up old sand to which clung dust and dirt from the floor. After telling Zoë where she was going, Janine took up a wicker basket for purchases and left the house.

A rosy hue streaked a pale gray sky like watered silk and gave promise of a fine day. She walked slowly down Second Street past Captain John Cadwalader's red brick mansion, recalling that Papa had told her the captain drilled his "silk stocking" company of the Pennsylvania militia here in this very street. Ever since the skirmish at Lexington the streets of Philadelphia reverberated to the sound of fife and drum. In fact the militia was constantly out, morning and evening, and sometimes Janine caught a glimpse of the men from her window. Papa had said there were already thirty companies in the city in uniform, well armed and making most surprising progress; the thought of soldiers and fighting sent a shiver down her spine.

She glanced across the way at Loxley House on the corner of Taylor's Alley, hoping to see Lydia Darragh. She was fond of this quiet little Quaker woman who made burial clothes and laid out the dead. It was Friend Darragh who years ago had taught her how to dry herbs and roots to make remedies.

Ahead she saw other women with baskets, some followed by little serving maids, hurrying toward the long open sheds that stretched from Front to Third, down the center of High Street.

She hastened her steps, passing the milliner's and the shoe shop without stopping to gaze in the windows. By now the roads to Philadelphia would be crowded with farmers in Conestoga wagons bringing produce from as far away as Lancaster. Barking dogs and squealing pigs scampered among sedan chairs, horse-drawn carts and wagons, all of which were made to stand outside the marketplace.

An air of excitement pervaded the crowd, and her pulse quickened at the smells and sights and sounds flowing about her. Soon she was threading her way through the throng milling about the stalls where meats and produce were laid out neatly.

She paused at a display of fish to buy a gleaming silver fillet of sole, whose bright eyes guaranteed freshness. At the meat stalls she cast a critical eye over beef, pork, lamb, raccoon, possum, and bear meat, finally deciding upon a small leg of lamb. She strolled past stands heaped with colorful fruits and vegetables, admiring big healthy cabbages, bright carrots, lettuce, beets, and potatoes.

Oh, it was fun being out again, mingling with people, hearing the buzz of conversation and bursts of laughter. Eagerly she searched the faces of the crowd for one she knew, to no avail. She sighed inwardly, supposing it was not strange that having been gone for two years, she saw no one she recognized.

Pausing at a stall laden with butter and cheeses, she took a coin from her purse and scooped a bit of butter from a sample mound, savoring the cool, sweet taste.

"Janine!" cried a voice at her elbow. "Is it truly you?"

Janine whirled to face a dainty, petite girl, wearing a pale green, lace-trimmed gown, who looked as delicate as a Dresden figurine. Her golden hair was swept high on her head, with two shining curls falling coquettishly over her left shoulder. Blue-gray eyes danced with pleasure in her pert, oval face, and her smile radiated warmth and charm. Behind her stood a grinning serving maid carrying a wicker basket.

"Peggy!" cried Janine. "How wonderful to see you!" They embraced in an affectionate hug.

Peggy Shippen, though somewhat younger than Janine, was a childhood friend who belonged to an aristocratic and wealthy family that had helped rule Pennsylvania along with the Penns. Peggy, too, lived on Second Street in a splendid red and black brick mansion with her parents, her brother, and three older sisters. Fortified by a large number of servants, the family lived in great style, and many a day Janine and Peggy had romped through the formal garden and orchard behind the house. They had attended Miss Cavendish's school together and had suffered under the same tutors of reading and the arts so necessary for young ladies of culture and refinement. Peggy was quick-witted and intelligent when a subject interested her and had quite a head for figures. But she was unabashedly scornful of those classes that were intended solely to prepare a young lady for society.

"Your Papa's well?" asked Peggy solicitously.

Janine nodded. "And your family?"

Peggy rolled her gray-blue eyes ecstatically. "My sisters and I are besieged with suitors—a mad, gay whirl! Brother Edward threatens to go out and shoot rebels, and Papa's in fine fettle, nervous as a scalded cat, as usual."

"And your mother?"

Peggy gave a helpless shrug and raised her eyes heavenward. "She survives."

It was no secret that Peggy was her father's favorite and that she adored him, while regarding her mother, whom she considered weak, with impatient disdain.

"You've returned from Virginia to stay, I hope."

"I daresay," Janine agreed, thinking this was neither the time nor place to tell her about Jonathan.

"Oh, I'm so glad you're home," bubbled Peggy. "You must come for tea, and a game of whist. Philadelphia is so exciting—marvelous balls and concerts. . . ." A frown of annoyance puckered her smooth brow. "The Southwark's closed down since Congress has declared there will be no more plays, and Mr. Douglass and his American Company have sailed for the Indies."

Janine recalled that Papa had told her Congress had banned plays because of the growing unruliness of the audiences who interrupted the action, insulted the performers, and injured people in the pit. But he confided to Janine that he suspected the real reason was that any sizable gathering could be dangerous when partisan conflict grew by the week, and the play or the opera was no longer the thing.

Peggy babbled on, her expression bright and eager. "We'll see to it you meet some nice young men. The king has sent some handsome specimens to put down what he calls 'the tyrannical and arbitrary rabble of America,' " she said, laughing.

They finished chatting, and Peggy waved a hand as she moved away into the crowd.

Meeting Peggy lifted Janine's spirits considerably. She had always been fond of the gay, light-hearted girl whose extravagance and passion for parties was the despair of her doting father, Judge Edward Shippen. Janine smiled to herself. Peggy's family thought

her a gentle and timorous child. And with strangers,
she was shy. But Janine recalled with startling clarity
scenes from their childhood when she and Peggy Chew
had gathered in Shippen's playroom. More than once
they'd squabbled over dolls or games, and when Peggy
was not given her way, she'd erupted into a wild fit of
hysteria that ended the afternoon.

Now, on her way home, something Peggy had said
tugged disturbingly at her mind. With an effort she
called to mind their conversation. The king has sent
men to put down the rabble—that was it. Surely it
wasn't necessary for the king to take up arms. Everyone
had agreed that Lexington was only a skirmish. Aunt
Ellen was right in one thing, thought Janine bitterly.
It was foolish for the colonists to oppose the king's
regiments. And Mr. Franklin was right too when he'd
said the colonies' radicalism was a threat to the peaceful and prosperous society; there were peaceful means
of settling things. A thoughtful frown creased her
brow. She herself had gone along with the colonists
in protesting the hated importation taxes by boycot-
ting English tea and fabrics, but if she could believe
Adam Burke, these radicals—"rabble," as Peggy called
them—would bring chaos to the economy. She certainly had no sympathy for the revolutionaries. At
the thought the image of a bold, handsome, dark-eyed
lieutenant rose unbidden to her mind. "Particularly
Mark Furneaux," she muttered vehemently under her
breath.

She hastened her steps, grateful for the strong cedar
posts that were sunk every few yards along the edge
of the pavement to protect pedestrians against the
overcrowded street traffic. The brick pavement, level
with the street, now swarmed with people. Carpenters,
bricklayers, and painters hurried along, carrying the
tools of their trade. Apprentice boys pushed wheel-
barrows piled high with paper for a printshop, or
colorful cloth for a tailor shop, or beaver skins for a
hat shop.

She circled round a young apprentice who had stopped to flirt with a doe-eyed girl drawing water at the public pump. At least the long, dreary April rains had kept down the dust, thought Janine, breathing in deeply the warm, sunny May air.

When she reached home, she found Zoë on her hands and knees, diligently scrubbing the marble doorstep.

"Mercy, Zoë! The steps are already gleaming. Couldn't you skip today?"

Zoë sat back on her heels and grinned, shaking her head. "I scrubs them twice a week, Miss Janine. That's why they's gleamin'."

Janine ran lightly up the steps, and Zoë bent back to her task.

Exhilarated by her jaunt to the market and her meeting with Peggy, Janine was filled with optimism. *Maybe today when Papa stops at the coffee house*, she thought, *he'll find the post rider has brought a letter from Jonathan.*

But when Papa came home that night, he had no letter for Janine.

"Oh, why doesn't he write?" mourned Janine in disappointment and despair.

"Have patience, *ma petite*," said Dr. Mercer gently. "A letter will come."

"Then why is the post so slow?"

Dr. Mercer smiled encouragingly. "It's far better since Mister Franklin took over its management. Just think, fifteen years ago there were only eight deliveries a year!"

Janine sighed, taking no comfort from the thought, and led Papa into the dining room to supper.

"I do have some news, however," said Dr. Mercer, easing into a chair across from her at the table. "It seems that a frontiersman from Vermont named Ethan Allen and his Green Mountain Boys along with a militia commander from Connecticut—a druggist, of all things—named Arnold, stormed Fort Ticonderoga in upper New York."

Janine's fork halted midair and her blue eyes widened in alarm. "Were they all killed, Papa?"

Dr. Mercer chuckled, shaking his head. "Far from it! They invaded the garrison before dawn, demanded the British surrender, and they did! In ten minutes the Americans took over their artillery and ammunition, and not a drop of blood was shed!"

"I don't believe it," said Janine flatly.

Papa fell back on one of the aphorisms he was so fond of quoting. "Fact is more strange than fiction."

Chapter 10

Two evenings later Papa came home rubbing his hands together in exultation, his blue eyes sparkling with the news that he had been elected to serve on the staff of Penn's Hospital, which cared for the sick-poor.

"But, Papa," protested Janine, "you've more patients than you can care for now, without taking on charity patients."

"Someone has to look after the sick-poor, Janine. Besides, it's not only a matter of charity. It's also an opportunity that offers both honor and experience— experience I'd never get anywhere else. I'll be better able to diagnose and treat my own patients."

Janine knew that most physicians didn't treat the sick-poor particularly well, because, like everyone else, physicians greatly respected a person's social position, and unlike Papa, regarded their calling as a trade and did business with those who could pay best. She sighed, gazing fondly at her father.

"If you have time to see them," she said, smiling wryly.

"It's only two days a week, Monday and Thursday, for four months of the year. I'll work in tandem with Adam Kuhn, a fine man. I've known him since our student days in Edinburgh." Enthusiastically he went on. "When I'm not on duty, I'll be called in as a consultant in extraordinary cases."

Shuddering, Janine recalled the poor creatures raving, crying, yelling, clinging to the grates on the windows, to the delight of the spectators who made great sport of tormenting them.

"But, Papa, the place is filled with lunatics!"

Dr. Mercer shook his head. "The poor devils need care, Janine, and there are only twenty-five or thirty among almost a hundred residents. Penn's Hospital is, in the main, for the care of the sick-poor. After the managers admit as many sick-poor as they can support, they accommodate paying patients: servants, slaves whose masters pay, the insane and sick from wealthy families. And, of course, we have out-patients as well."

"Will you give up teaching at the medical college, then?"

Dr. Mercer shook his head. "On the contrary. My apprentices will have the advantage of making rounds with me."

Janine's face brightened, and a thoughtful expression lighted her eyes. "That should be interesting, Papa. Perhaps one day I may make your rounds with you."

Dr. Mercer smiled and waved a hand in dismissal. "It's no place for you, *ma petite*. You can help me most by carrying on here. I'm counting on you to keep my apothecary well stocked."

"That will hardly fill my days, Papa."

"Nevertheless it is better to light one candle than to curse the darkness, *my petite*."

It was two weeks later, on a brilliant May afternoon, that Janine, astride Brandy, rode west on Pine Street beside Papa, mounted on his black mare. Soon the cobbles gave way to a dry, rutted road, through the rolling countryside, past fenced farmland surrounding Penn's Hospital. A row of buttonwood trees planted along Eighth Street provided welcome shade. And beyond them rose a cupola crowning the huge, T-shaped Georgian building whose heavily glazed, reddish-brown bricks gleamed in the sun. If you counted the dormer windows under the hipped roof and the "English" basement with windows just above the ground, Janine thought, it was four stories high.

"Why is it called Penn's Hospital, Papa, when Thomas Bond and Benjamin Franklin founded it?"

"Certainly a misnomer," said Dr. Mercer. "Franklin, of course, was the author of the act passed by the Pennsylvania Assembly establishing the hospital in seventeen fifty-one. But ten years later Thomas Penn and his brother Richard, both grandsons of William, granted them the remainder of the square not already owned and occupied by the hospital, and they also provided an annual grant of forty pounds, which they still pay. But I suspect the citizens simply shortened Pennsylvania to Penn's for convenience."

At the arched gate they dismounted and looped their reins through a ring on an iron horse's-head mount. Walking toward the hospital they passed a washhouse, stable, and garden, and farther on, a long narrow red brick building three stories high.

"What's that, Papa?"

"That's the Elaboratory, built in seventeen sixty-eight, where they prepare drugs for the hospital apothecary."

As they mounted the stone steps of the hospital, Dr. Mercer said, "You understand that you are making rounds with me today only. I've not agreed to let you accompany me every day."

Janine smiled. "Of course, Papa." She glanced at the keystone over the doorway in which was carved 1755 and stepped inside.

Dr. Mercer nodded toward the corridor on his right. "The consultation room, apothecary shop, and apartments for the steward, matron, and other staff are down there, and the men's ward is to our left."

Just then a slightly-built young man wearing a neat but threadbare mustard-colored suit approached them and greeted Dr. Mercer with a broad smile. His dark red hair, clubbed with a black ribbon, accentuated the thinness of his face. But the most striking thing about him was his eyes: sparkling, vibrant in a pale, angular face, they reminded Janine of Madeira. Now, as she looked at him, his eyes met hers with a level, questioning gaze.

Dr. Mercer introduced him as Dr. Richard Ransom, one of the hospital apprentices. "My daughter takes great interest in my work, Doctor Ransom. She's making rounds with me today."

Richard Ransom's straight sandy brows lifted in surprise, his wide mouth stiff and unsmiling.

"It's quite unusual for a young lady to wish to be here. . . ." He paused as though waiting for her to speak, his bright eyes speculative, appraising.

Janine lowered her gaze and said nothing. Her interest was difficult to explain, and besides, she was trying to place his accent. Was there a trace of a burr in his speech?

"Well, come along, Ransom, we'll work from the bottom up." Dr. Mercer led the way down the stairs to the ground floor where the lunatics were housed in cells. Each had a bed, a table, and a window fitted with grates. While Dr. Mercer checked a patient, Janine and Dr. Ransom waited in the corridor. She could see his eyes on her in the dim light, studying her curiously. She lifted her chin and looked him square in the eye. Hastily he glanced away, redness creeping into his pale face, and an awkward silence stretched between them.

He's struck dumb now that he's alone with me, perceived Janine, stifling a grin. At last he blurted: "The patients are permitted to exercise here in the corridor."

Janine shivered and, turning to glance through the barred doors, bit her lip to keep from crying out at the sight of iron manacles that circled the patients' wrists and ankles. From these, chains were attached to staples embedded in the walls.

Noticing her expression, Dr. Ransom said kindly,

"It's not as cruel as it seems, for otherwise many of them would injure themselves."

"I know they're often fractious," said Janine, "but they seem very quiet now."

"They've just finished eating."

She said nothing, but her heart went out to the poor creatures who were no better off than the prisoners in the Walnut Street jail. Several napped and others sat listlessly gazing into space. One haggard-looking woman stood on her bed and stared out the window.

"At present we have only female patients," Dr. Ransom went on. "Most are victims of religious melancholy or disappointed love."

She noted that none were naked or indecent. Even in their folly, thought Janine, they preserved a primitive characteristic of decency. Turning to Dr. Ransom, she said, "It's pleasantly cool down here now, but isn't it terribly damp and cold in the winter?"

Dr. Ransom gave her a solemn smile. "It's common knowledge, Mistress Mercer, that the insane are not affected by extremes of temperature."

Again she made no reply, and after an uncomfortable silence Dr. Ransom went on.

"We lay claim to being the first public hospital in the colonies. The Almshouse for the care of the aged and infirm poor of the city was established in seventeen thirty-one, but they didn't appoint physicians to look after them until seventeen sixty-nine, and even at that they only looked after such paupers as might be ill."

"It's a fine building," said Janine lamely.

"This is really only the east wing," said Dr. Ransom, his russet eyes sparkling with pride. "The structure is modeled on the Royal Edinburgh Infirmary. The west wing and central wing are yet to be built."

Just then Dr. Mercer returned, and they followed him to the floor above and into the men's ward. Windows without curtains on both sides of the room let in light and air, and Janine noted a large open wood fireplace that would provide some warmth in winter. As they made their way slowly down the wide aisle, she counted twenty-five beds on each side, all filled. Halfway down the room she saw a huge beefy man with an assistant who limped along behind him setting down hand trays, water cans, and slop buckets at each bed.

An emaciated-looking youth waved a feeble hand in greeting to Dr. Ransom. The doctor smiled and tousled his rough straw-colored hair. Janine heard him speak softly to Papa. "John Pierce, here, suffering from Hydrops Ascities Siccus. . . ."

Dr. Mercer nodded and suggested treatment.

"The next man," Dr. Ransom went on, "Thomas Hall, fell from a ship's mast and broke his thigh—and his companion in the next bed had his feet mashed on board his frigate. Doctor Kuhn has seen to him."

They stopped before the bed of a gaunt, hollow-eyed man with a white scar running from temple to chin, whose frizzled gray hair lay damp upon his forehead.

"He's suffering with ulcers in his toes caused by chiggers in his feet," her father explained to Janine. "I suspect he acquired the disease in the tropics."

Gently Dr. Mercer removed the dressings, and Janine and Dr. Ransom drew close, watching as he examined the ulcerated area. Janine's stomach turned over at the sight of the red, swollen feet, the diseased tissue yellow-crusted and seeping. Suddenly she felt Dr. Ransom's steady gaze upon her, as if he expected her to faint or flee from the sight.

Calmly she turned to Papa. "Is he improved today?"

"I believe so, yes."

Dr. Ransom had water brought, and with great care and gentleness he swabbed the infected area. When it dried, he dusted the man's feet with a powder and wrapped them in fresh linen cloths.

The expression in the man's eyes as he thanked Dr. Ransom was one of doglike devotion, and it came to

Janine that all the patients viewed the slim, straight-backed, capable resident with admiration and respect.

The third floor, laid out as the second, with beds lining the walls, housed female patients. Janine followed Papa and Dr. Ransom down the ward as they examined patients and discussed their ailments. She noticed that several patients had visitors; others stared vacantly into space; a few read Bibles or religious tracts. Beside one bed a Negro woman, bent over a spinning wheel, looked up expectantly as they passed. Dr. Ransom paused to look at the woman's work, watching a red thread spinning from the shuttle under her expert hand.

"You do well." He smiled, fingering the flaxen thread. "Soon you'll have enough to make me a pair of britches!"

The woman's dark face split in a grin, revealing a gap where her two front teeth should have been, and Janine could see that Dr. Ransom's words were heaven to her.

To Janine the man was an enigma. With his patients he was relaxed and confident. And with Papa he was respectful and diffident, she thought. But he seems to regard me with a curious, puzzled air, as he would a patient with an unknown disease. She hadn't missed the way his eyes followed her when he thought she wasn't looking. But she had no time to ponder over that now.

After visiting the garret that housed hospital employees and cases requiring isolation, they returned to the first floor to take their leave. Dr. Mercer's hand was on the door when Dr. Ransom asked, "Have you heard the latest news?"

"I was here Tuesday last. Is it something since then?"

The young resident's expression was grave. "The managers have agreed that the present state of public affairs will not permit further importation of drugs from London."

Dr. Mercer's blue eyes flashed with anger and indignation. "But we've purchased drugs from Thomas Corbyn and the firm of Sulvanus and Timothy Bevan from the start. They're Quaker firms—nothing to do with politics—and both make generous contributions to the hospital!"

"Nevertheless," said Dr. Ransom, "the managers have already notified Thomas Corbyn. I hope they haven't acted in too great haste."

Dr. Mercer's voice rose and his face flushed in agitation. "It will never do to alienate our friends in England. Contributions in pounds sterling from David Barclay, John Hyam, and John Fothergill *and* English Parliament are not to be sneezed at! As Candide would have pointed out," he added testily, *"Cela est bien dit, mais il faut cultiver notre jardin!"*

Dr. Ransom appeared baffled, and an embarrassed flush suffused his face.

"Papa means to say it's all very well for the managers to talk, but it's necessary to cultivate their garden," said Janine gently. "Anyway, you can purchase drugs here, can you not?"

Dr. Ransom's sandy brows lifted in surprise. "We have done, in the past, but they are quite dear, and our funds are limited," he said stiffly. His attitude plainly showed that the affairs of the hospital were none of her concern.

As Janine and Dr. Mercer trotted homeward in the soft May sunset, her mind seethed with all she had seen and heard at Penn's Hospital. Her eyes had been opened to a world she had known existed, but now the stark reality of it struck her like a thunderbolt. In the face of such misery her frivolous pastimes seemed dull and stupid, even boring. Thinking of the managers cutting off their supply of drugs from England was an unpleasant reminder that once again this silly rebellion was proving the undoing of the colonists. And then her mind turned to Dr. Ransom.

"Tell me about Doctor Ransom, Papa."

Mercer shot Janine a sidelong glance from the back of his black filly. "Two years ago the managers decided to receive medical apprentices into the hospital, and Doctor Ransom, who had recently finished his studies at the medical college, was appointed to serve a five-year term of indenture. He's a brilliant young man, dedicated to his work."

"He has rather a strange, rolling accent," she said casually.

Dr. Mercer laughed. "That's right enough. He's a Scot—the son of a farmer who came over with a wave of Scots from the Highlands in forty-five."

"He seems terribly solemn."

"Oh, he is that. But he's had little time for pleasure. He worked on his father's farm and later became a tutor to earn money to attend Philadelphia College. He's always wanted to become a doctor, you see, and is driven by this singleness of purpose."

"Is he married? asked Janine curiously.

"No." Dr. Mercer suppressed a smile. "He once told me that he'd had little time to court a wife and the girls he's met since coming to Philadelphia were flighty and empty-headed as filly-lou birds . . . he's a terribly serious young man."

"He appears to be dreadfully shy and unsophisticated," said Janine airily and, clucking to Brandy, dismissed Dr. Ransom from her mind.

Chapter 11

As the summer of 1775 wore on, Janine's days fell into a routine. There was the marketing to do on Wednesdays and Fridays and, on occasion, she would mount Brandy and ride five miles to the mill in Frankford for flour.

After she brought the food in the house, she spent much of her time preparing it. One day she would lose herself in a frenzy of baking; another day she and Zoë made ten large cheeses from the milk of their one-and-only cow, tethered in the yard. Though Zoë did most of the cleaning and the monthly washing of clothes, Janine pressed all her own clothes and Papa's shirts, a task she found most tiresome. It gave her time to think—to give in to hopeless despair of ever seeing Jonathan again. And yet, even in these darkest moments, she would never allow herself to believe that Jonathan was dead.

Zoë would shake her head sadly, lamenting, "The blue devils has got you, Miss Janine."

And on such occasions, when anxiety and fear threatened to overwhelm her, Janine would escape outdoors to the gardens. Her greatest delight was the herb garden near the kitchen door. Here mint, sage, fennel, summer savory, and rosemary, along with the other herbs she used to prepare the medicines to stock Papa's apothecary chest, grew in profusion. Those she could not cultivate herself, she purchased from the country women at the market. Just the feel of the soft dark earth under her fingers and the sharp, pun-

gent scent of mint and thyme helped to drive out the
terrible worry and loneliness that had often oppressed
her since she'd come home.

Beyond the herb garden she had put in a good store
of vegetables: lettuce, squash, cucumbers, beans, carrots, and turnips, which she watered and weeded with
a vengeance. When she was not beset by Zoë's blue
devils, she liked to tend the garden early in the morning before the town awakened, with only the twittering of sparrows, robins, and the raucous blue jays for
company.

At the back of the yard near the stable stood a small
orchard of peach, pear, and apple trees. And as spring
lengthened into summer she'd taken pleasure in
watching the clusters of pink and white blossoms give
way to small green fruit, which promised a good crop.

Janine also took pleasure in the small circular rose
garden on the far side of the house, ablaze with pale
yellow, parchment-white, and deep red velvet blooms.
A dusty pink climber covered the arbor where she
loved to sit in the gathering twilight, surrounded by
the soft sweet fragrance of the roses and lilacs, watching the fireflies come out. The mosquitoes would eventually find her and drive her inside.

From dawn till dusk she drove herself with the fury
of one possessed, until her bones ached with weariness
and her mind was numb.

During the long, sultry summer evenings she forced
herself to spin and weave cloth, from which she
fashioned clothes for Papa and Zoë and augmented
her own meager wardrobe for the coming winter as
well. As much as she detested needlework, it was more
satisfying when someone could wear the fruits of her
labors. And sewing didn't seem nearly so tedious on
the evenings when Papa kept her company in the
parlor.

One evening around the middle of June she sat in
the parlor mending Papa's stock while Papa read the
Pennsylvania Gazette. That night, though the windows

were open, they were still suffering from a warm muggy heat wave that had hit a week ago, soon after the delegations arrived for the Continental Congress.

Janine sighed and let her mending fall to her lap. She noticed that the soft rose brocade on the arms of the Chippendale sofa on which she sat were worn thin —and the ivory brocade draperies frayed. Her gaze wandered absently over the room to the polished walnut tea table flanked by carved side chairs, the fireplace faced with delft tiles, and the landscape painting over the mantel—shepherdesses by an artist named Watteau that Papa had picked up in Paris. Her eyes rested on Papa, reading in the Windsor chair under the warm glow of the lamp. The paper rustled as he turned a page. "I see Congress has agreed to the appeal from the Massachusetts Committee of Safety. . . ."

"What appeal, Papa?"

"They've asked Congress to adopt the New England army as an American army. They wanted Congress to create an army of men from every colony, not separate armies. John Adams has been pushing a Grand American army, and now they're going to have at it!" He smiled at Janine over his spectacles. "And a friend of yours is going to be General and Commander-in-Chief."

"Oh? Who might that be?"

"Colonel Washington of Mount Vernon. John Adams proposed his name and after some talking around, Washington was unanimously chosen."

"Colonel Washington!" cried Janine in startled surprise. The image of the modest, six-foot-two, two-hundred-pound planter-soldier sprang to her mind. He was quiet, unassuming, and confident. And he *had* commanded a regiment on the frontier for five years. He knew how to move through forests, and how to fight. And he knew land—had surveyed it, explored and mapped it, planted it. Now he would defend it! A cold tremor of fear ran down her spine. With an effort she kept her voice low and even.

"Papa, this means the patriots are going to take action against the king, does it not?"

Dr. Mercer peered at her over the top of the paper. "I think we can assume that, yes."

Janine drew in her breath sharply. "Must we choose sides, then?"

Papa thought for a moment, picking his words carefully. "Not tonight, little one. Let's hope it never comes to that. Much noise and little wool, as the devil said when he sheared his pig."

Janine took up her mending, and her fingers trembled. Jonathan and Adam would surely side with the rebels, she thought morosely. Her mind went back to the days she had ridden up to Alexandria to watch them drill with the train bands on the square, fifes and drums striking up merry tunes. One danced through her head now: "The Girl I Left Behind Me." Every able-bodied male between sixteen and sixty had come to these mustering outs that took place one day a month. Oh, it had all been so gay and exciting—especially the games that began around two o'clock with prizes for cudgels, wrestling, and best marksmanship. It had all been like a holiday then.

Dr. Mercer, struck with a thought that might reassure Janine, lowered his paper and gazed at her directly. "It's all very well for the colonial militia to drill, to fight to the death to protect their homes and families, but leaving their homes unprotected and marching off to a long drawn-out campaign on some distant battlefield is something else again!"

"Surely it won't come to that, Papa!"

She thought of the ragtag militia, the men in leather breeches and homespun jackets, the officers and gentlemen in waistcoats and ruffles, and they conjured up a ludicrous picture against the well-trained British regiments, drilled with machinelike precision.

Voicing the fear clutching at her heart, Janine said, "The militiamen aren't professional soldiers, Papa. The men I saw in Virginia were farmers, merchants, clerks, doctors, lawyers, tradesmen, mechanics . . . even under Colonel Washington they can't hope to win against the king's men."

Dr. Mercer removed his spectacles and began polishing them on his sleeve. "Nevertheless Congress is raising ten companies of riflemen from Pennsylvania, Maryland, and Virginia to serve for a year, and Washington leaves from the State House tomorrow to take command."

An idea struck her then, and her blue eyes kindled with excitement. "Oh, Papa, let's go to see him off. I'd so like to see him again, and he may have news from Mount Vernon—he may even have news of Jonathan!"

Dr. Mercer put his spectacles on and regarded Janine tenderly. Her face was bright with anticipation, her eyes shining with hope, and his heart ached for her. Privately he thought it highly unlikely that Colonel Washington would have news of Jonathan— unless the boy were dead. Bad news traveled quickly.

"Of course we'll go, *ma petite*. But don't raise your hopes too high. The mails are no better from Mount Vernon than from Heritage Hall."

Sunday, June eighteenth, was warm and sunny. Puffy white clouds driven by a light breeze scudded across a brilliant blue sky. Janine had gone to great pains to look her best. Her hair, brushed to a glossy sheen, was caught up in back by a pale blue ribbon and she wore a newly sewn white muslin gown embroidered with forget-me-nots that matched her eyes. Janine and Dr. Mercer hurried up Chestnut Street to the State House and threaded their way through the people thronging the yard.

An air of excitement and anticipation rippled through the crowd waiting before the handsome Georgian building. Built of brick, two stories high, it was flanked on each side by wings joined to the main structure by means of a brick arcade. It was easy to see why it was said to be the grandest building in the colonies, thought Janine. Her admiring gaze traveled up the brick tower past the open arches of the wooden cupola topped by a lofty spire. Then turning to Dr. Mercer she asked, "Do you think they'll ring the bell in honor of General Washington, Papa?"

Dr. Mercer looked skeptical. "I doubt it. 'Tis said the steeple is in such ruinous condition, they're afraid to ring it lest it should fall down."

The State House clock struck ten. A momentary hush fell over the crowd, and an instant later it erupted into cheers as Colonel Washington strode from the building and mounted his great mahogany steed.

"Papa, he's in uniform!" exclaimed Janine, gazing at the blue jacket faced in red, the buff breeches, and tricorn hat.

"A colonel's garb from the French and Indian War," said Dr. Mercer. " 'Tis rumored he donned military blue to indicate his mood, to let everyone know that though the delegates talk of peace, they are prepared for war."

Shrilling fifes and thudding drums beat a steady tattoo and the flags of the color bearers whipped smartly in the breeze as the procession paraded slowly through the yard. Janine stood on tiptoe, waving frantically.

"Colonel Washington, Colonel Washington!" cried Janine with all the breath she could muster, completely forgetting that he was now a general.

With noble and solemn mien, the general doffed his tricorn in a sweeping bow as he passed the waving, shouting spectators. The band struck up a martial air. Janine's breath caught in her throat, her knees went limp, and she clutched Papa's arm for support as General Washington swept through the gateposts at the head of the cavalry parading down the cobbled street in a sea of shouting admirers, oblivious to her presence.

Whether he hadn't recognized her or hadn't seen her in the press of the crowd, she would never know. Tears welled in the corners of her eyes as she stood on tiptoe watching the procession march out of sight. Suddenly her view was blocked by a tall figure whose head and shoulders rose above the crowd. Her breath left her body in a rush at the sight of the thick, clubbed black hair, the set of the brown-coated shoulders and broad back that she would never forget.

"Papa, I do believe that's Lieutenant Furneaux ahead!"

Dr. Mercer tucked her hand in the crook of his arm. "Then let's hurry, so we can speak with him."

All her distress and disappointment that she'd had no chance for a word with General Washington turned to irritation with this bold, insulting man who'd treated her like a trollop, refused to believe the truth, then mocked her for refusing him.

"But, Papa," cried Janine, "I've nothing to say to him."

Ignoring her protest, Dr. Mercer hurried her through the thinning crowd to the lieutenant's side and clapped him on the shoulder. "Lieutenant Furneaux?"

The lieutenant spun around and Janine stifled a gasp. He wore a brown coat whose lapels and cuffs were faced in red, and buff-colored breeches—the uniform of the Pennsylvania militia. *He is more handsome than I remembered him*, she thought, becoming annoyed. Clutching his arm was a woman dressed in a pink brocade gown and a silk bonnet bristling with pink feathers. Blond curls framed a startlingly white face with rosy cheeks and a beauty patch on her right temple. A pink and white confection, thought Janine, nonplussed.

Swiftly the woman's light blue eyes swept Janine from head to toe in shrewd appraisal, and just as swiftly dismissed her as of no consequence. Turning to Mark, the woman glanced imploringly into his eyes, as though to ask if they must endure the unwelcome presence of these people who had accosted them.

With easy grace the lieutenant doffed his hat, made them an exaggerated bow, and, smiling cordially, said, "Mistress Mercer, Doctor Mercer, may I present Mistress Anne Delaney?"

The woman acknowledged the introduction with a slight incline of her head and clung to Mark Furneaux's arm with a possessiveness that made Janine want to strike her. What was Anne Delaney to Mark, and she to him, that she assumed such a proprietary manner, fumed Janine—though she herself wanted nothing whatever to do with the arrogant, insolent wretch, she thought perversely.

As Mark met Janine's astonished gaze one brow rose and his lips turned down in the mocking smile that never failed to antagonize her. His dark brown eyes glinted in amusement.

"I'm happy to see you restored to good health, Mistress Mercer."

Reminded of their journey, Janine blushed furiously as scenes of Mark bedding her, bathing her, feeding her . . . flashed through her mind. And now he was laughing at her! thought Janine wrathfully. Oh, if only they were alone, she would tell this cad what she thought of him!

Dr. Mercer extended his hand and grasped the lieutenant's in a firm clasp. "I've never thanked you properly for your kindness to my daughter."

Janine's gaze shifted to Anne Delaney and she noticed that frosty light had come into her pale blue eyes and the line of her cupid's bow mouth had hardened.

"Had you not come to her rescue and taken such care of her," Dr. Mercer went on, "I'm sure she would have lost her life."

And my virginity too, if Mark Furneaux had his way, thought Janine venomously.

Mark accepted Dr. Mercer's thanks with what appeared to Janine to be excessive gallantry, considering all that had transpired between them. Oh, the effrontery of the man! thought Janine, biting her lip in vexation.

"Won't you join us in some refreshment at the London Coffee House?" asked Dr. Mercer.

Lieutenant Furneaux glanced at Anne Delaney, his thick crescent brows raised in question.

The woman's lips curved in an arch smile. "Darling, we have an appointment . . . remember?"

For an instant he appeared perplexed, and with swift feminine intuition Janine surmised that their "appointment" was with one another.

"Another time perhaps," said Mark smoothly.

Anne Delaney turned her cold gaze on Janine and in the patronizing tone of one speaking to a child said, "It was so lovely that your Papa could bring you to see the ceremony today, wasn't it Mark?" Again she smiled fatuously into his face.

A rush of anger and indignation brought hot blood to Janine's cheeks. How could this woman make her feel as though she were five years old? Though her own slender height gave her the advantage of looking down on Anne Delaney, the woman somehow succeeded in making her feel gauche. *She's smaller than I, but much more curvaceous, fuller in the bosom— and in the bottom too,* thought Janine enviously. The woman displayed such presence, such self-assurance and sophistication that Janine was struck dumb. Desperately she racked her brain for something to say. Now, gazing at Mark, she saw a glimmer of laughter cross his face, as though he knew her predicament and found it amusing.

With all the dignity she could muster, she turned to her father and said in a cool, controlled voice, "Papa, we must be on our way. I'm sure Lieutenant Furneaux and his—his friend have better things to do than stand here in the hot sun melting like tallow."

Dr. Mercer smiled and tipped his hat. "Please do call upon us whenever it's convenient."

Oh, why did Papa encourage this rogue, thought Janine furiously. But she forced a semblance of a smile and said nothing.

"Attractive woman, that Anne Delaney," remarked Dr. Mercer as they strolled down Chestnut Street under the shade of leafy poplars.

"I've never cared for women with that starchy white-powdered skin and painted cheeks," said Janine more sharply than she'd intended. "They always have the appearance of being so hard and callous."

"Well, that's understandable in Anne Delaney's case," Papa said easily, "considering who she is."

Janine's head swiveled toward Papa in startled surprise. "Oh? Who is she?"

"Why, Anne Delaney is an actress, well-known for her performances with David Douglass's American Company at the Southwark. I once took you to see a play there—*She Stoops to Conquer*, I believe it was. Anyway, when Douglass and his troupe left for the Indies last February, she stayed behind."

And why had she stayed behind? wondered Janine. Was it because of Mark Furneaux? She marched beside Papa in tight-lipped silence, staring straight ahead.

At last, noticing her dour mood, Papa asked, "Why so pensive, little one?"

Janine shook her head and managed a smile. "No reason, Papa. I'm fine."

But deep in her heart she knew that she was in an exceedingly ill humor for absolutely no reason at all.

Chapter 12

It was several days later that news was brought of what had happened in Massachusetts only the day before Washington had headed north to take command of the Continental army. Rumor, later confirmed by dispatches, was now fact, reported in the *Pennsylvania Gazette*.

Papa rushed in from the London Coffee House waving the paper excitedly, shouting, "Incredible! Incredible news, *ma petite*!"

Alarmed, Janine sank down on the sofa, trying to make sense of what Papa was telling her.

"You know that Artemus Ward and his New England army have General Gage hemmed in in Boston. Poor devil is cut off from the countryside and his nearest supplies come from England, three thousand miles away."

Janine nodded.

"Well, it seems that Ward decided to tighten his grip by fortifying the Charlestown Peninsula."

Noticing the vague expression on Janine's face, he went on impatiently. "This was of strategic importance, you see, because from the hills of Charlestown, the American artillery could rake Boston and drive the British out. Ward ordered his men to fortify Bunker Hill, and on the night of June sixteenth some twelve hundred Americans moved out with picks and shovels and guns to build and hold a redoubt. Unfortunately someone made a mistake and they fortified Breed's Hill instead. Be that as it may, you can imagine how shocked the British were when they woke up the next morning and saw the fortifications going up."

Again Janine nodded. She could certainly imagine that!

"General Gage immediately ordered His Majesty's ships to bombard the redoubt, but the rebels stuck with it. That afternoon Sir William Howe, commanding twenty-eight barges and long boats filled with British regulars, set out to take Breed's Hill."

Papa held up the paper and ran his index finger down a column. "It says: 'Waiting till the enemy was less than fifteen paces distant, the Americans met their advance with deadly fire from their Brown Bess muskets.' " Papa looked up from the paper. "What's beyond belief is that no one was in charge! No one issuing orders until Col. Prescott took command of the fighting urging them on!"

Again his eyes fastened on the paper: " 'The British retreated, reformed and attacked again. Again the Yankees beat them back.' " Papa glanced up, his blue eyes bulging in astonishment. "Twice their soldiers broke and fled, *ma petite*! British soldiers! Then Howe sent orders to General Burgoyne to burn Charlestown to clear it of snipers."

He read aloud: " 'The fleet set the town on fire with red-hot cannon balls, and while the town went up in one great blaze, the church steeples rose like great pyramids of fire above the rest. Howe immediately attacked the Americans a third time. On the third assault the Yankees, having almost no ammunition left, and spent, having had no food or drink except for rum, retreated, keeping up a hot fire. The British carried the earthwork and drove the defenders from the hill.' "

Dr. Mercer looked up, his brow puckered in a thoughtful frown. "Though the Redcoats won the battle, I'd say they lost the day. All Gage won was a useless peninsula!" He adjusted his spectacles on his nose and consulted the paper again. "Howe lost one thousand and fifty-four of his twenty-five hundred men —two hundred and twenty-six killed and eight hundred and twenty-eight wounded. The rebels lost one hundred killed and two hundred and seventy-one wounded. Howe admits the success is too dearly bought—and General Clinton is quoted as saying, 'A dear bought victory, and another such would have ruined us.' "

"God's death!" exclaimed Dr. Mercer, flinging the paper down in outrage and indignation. "Can you imagine what a slaughter that must have been? The hillside running red, littered with wounded, maimed, dead and dying—dreadful, dreadful! It's not to be borne!"

A cold, sick fear lodged in the pit of Janine's stomach as she envisioned the horror of the battle that had been fought so uselessly. The British claimed to have won, yet Papa said the Americans had won. She didn't care who won as long as the rebellion was over. Surely this must have taught them something. But exactly who had been taught what, she wasn't certain.

On several occasions that June, Janine had taken tea with Peggy Shippen and her three sisters at the elegant mansion on Second Street. Once, in desperation for the companionship of girls her own age, she'd gone to a sewing bee. And one Sunday afternoon she'd attended a lawn party where, good as her word, Peggy had introduced her to several young men. They were handsome and charming and squired her to balls, parties, and concerts. She had enjoyed herself, but those swains were not Jonathan. Being in their company only made her more acutely aware that he was lost to her and she often returned home feeling lonely and depressed, missing him all the more. It was only to please Papa that she continued to go out. More and more often on these occasions, however, the conversation turned to the king and the rebellious colonies.

The talk oppressed her and the threat of war seemed to hover over them like a pall. Janine resolved to decline all such invitations in the future.

Despite her resolve, on a hot, muggy Saturday early in July when she was feeling particularly bored and restless, Peggy persuaded her to accompany her and Debbie Morris on a picnic in the Governor's Woods.

They rode their horses at a slow trot out Pine Street past Penn's Hospital and entered a huge tract of primeval forest. In a sun-dappled glade they dismounted, spread a quilt on the ground, and sat down to enjoy the food in Peggy's hamper. Afterward they took up their baskets and began to gather plump ripe strawberries growing wild in a field at the edge of the woodland. When their baskets were filled, they sank down, hot and perspiring, under the cool shade of an elm tree to rest, fanning themselves with their bonnets.

How quiet and peaceful it was, thought Janine, grateful to escape the noise and bustle, the sultry heat of the town.

Peggy's bright, eager voice cut sharply through the stillness. "Have you read in the *Gazette* of the Declaration by Congress of the Causes and Necessity of Taking up Arms?"

Janine sighed and said nothing. Peggy's busy mind was always working over politics. She supposed it was because her papa was in government and he confided his worries to her.

"Imagine the temerity of Congress to do such a thing," Peggy went on, her blue-gray eyes flashing with outrage. "The rebels are asking to be put down! Papa says the remedy for evil statutes is to have them repealed—and that when 'natural law' supersedes the enactments of proper authorities, the way is open to anarchy."

Janine, leaning her back against the tree trunk, her arms wrapped about her knees, turned toward Peggy, smiling. "Don't worry, Peggy. I'm confident that

Mister Franklin will avert further hostilities. He believes in compromise."

"Avert hostilities!" cried Peggy, incensed. "If anything, he's over there in London furthering, nay *encouraging* rebellion." Warming to her argument, she went on. "Taxes on goods and stamps are no longer the issue. Mister Samuel Adams sees to that! And Mister Franklin too is promoting this ridiculous pipe dream of independence. What fools they are to resist the power of Great Britain!"

Janine said nothing, but one of Papa's favorite Shakespearian sayings came to mind: "Methinks the lady doth protest too much!" Nevertheless she found herself resenting Peggy's attack on Mr. Franklin. And she did not like to think of Jonathan and Adam in the militia and her friend General Washington commanding the Continental army as being fools for resisting the tyranny of the king, even though she didn't believe in taking up arms. No, thought Janine, she couldn't agree with Peggy's views, as she seemed to wish her to do.

Debbie, a staunch follower of the Quaker persuasion, said quietly, "Perhaps Janine has no wish to choose sides, Peggy. Nor have I." Her gentle voice held a note of reproach. "We cannot countenance this conflict."

Peggy bent an indignant gaze on Debbie. "Oh, I'm against conflict. And so is Papa," she said vehemently. "He insists that all our family stay neutral. But the colonists are stirring up a hornet's nest."

Janine well knew Judge Edward Shippen's reputation for steering a middle course. Now she wondered if his professed neutrality was due to his hatred of conflict or, as some townspeople said, because he could not decide whether he had more to lose by British intervention or American resistance. She began to suspect that under Peggy's show of bravado, she was ridden with fear. For the fact was years ago the governor had appointed Edward Shippen to the Provincial

Council. As a member of Pennsylvania's highest governing body, it was more than ever his duty to enforce British laws.

Gazing at Debbie through narrowed lids, Peggy rushed on. "Janine, of all people, should understand how ridiculous this idea of independence is. She was born in Europe. Her *real* parents were French. The French know you can't revolt against a king!"

Stung, Janine's chin rose in defiance. She had always thought of Dr. Mercer as her 'real' father, despite Aunt Ellen's constant jibes reminding her that her parents were French. And no one had ever questioned her loyalty to King George! Peggy was putting her on the defensive, and her cheeks were growing hot with irritation. With an effort she bit back a sharp retort and said calmly, "I'm every bit as loyal to the king as you are, Peggy, but I can't see men killing each other when matters could be settled amicably. If only the king would stop sending troops and listen to Mister Franklin. . . ."

Peggy laughed derisively. "Rather the colonists would listen to the king! Who is Mister Franklin that the king should listen to *him*! La, Janine, you're daft over Mister Franklin. The old roué has charmed you out of your senses, along with hundreds of other rebels. Why, he himself has been heard to say that he has great difficulty following the advice he dispenses in *Poor Richard's Almanac*!"

Janine's face burned with anger and annoyance. Impatiently she brushed a twig from her skirt. "I'm defending Mister Franklin only because I admire him as a statesman—and for his accomplishments," she said heatedly. "That doesn't make me a rebel, does it?"

Without waiting to hear Peggy's reply, Janine jumped up and ran toward a clump of Queen Anne's lace growing nearby and began to pluck a bouquet. She had no desire to continue an argument that would end with Peggy flying into one of her wild fits of hysteria—and even worse—to part on ill terms. To

Janine's relief, Peggy let the matter drop, but the afternoon ended on a tense, unpleasant note.

During the days that followed, Janine read one after another of Samuel Adams's fiery exhortations, and their discussion of that afternoon came back to her. Her mind grew increasingly uneasy—disturbed over where her allegiance lay and what the future would bring.

The August days grew intolerably hot. Flies and mosquitoes bred in the swampy land on the outskirts of the town, and dysentery, fevers, and other sicknesses ran rampant through the sweltering city. Dr. Mercer was away much of the time. Whenever he wasn't teaching at the medical college or on duty at Penn's Hospital, he would rush from one patient to the next. Often he would not come home till well after dark, his face lined with exhaustion.

Though she deplored the diseases gripping the citizens, Janine was grateful to be kept too busy to let gloomy thoughts occupy her mind. It seemed to her that she answered the door fifty times a day for those who came to summon Papa to the bedside of the sick. Frequently an ailing citizen himself would appear on the doorstep, and if Janine recognized the complaint, she would treat the patient with medicines from Papa's apothecary chest. She administered countless doses of chamomile tea to settle children's stomachs and the juice of hot ash for earaches.

With a neat, precise hand she began to add to her red leather-bound recipe book all the remedies she knew for the common ailments, and in the evenings added others that Papa told her. Mixed in with recipes for doughnuts, for candied orange peel, and for preserving eggs were recipes to cure rheumatism and ringworm and dysentery and the itch, followed by remedies for the whooping cough, for the bleeding piles, for the jaundice, as well as potions to kill rats, to destroy bedbugs, to cleanse the skin and prevent

pimples. One day she was delighted to find a new cure
in the newspaper: A roasted fig beat up with white
sugar finely powdered is used as a suppuration to
plague boils at Constantinople.

Though they stifled under the oppressive heat, they
had to keep the windows closed at night, lest they be
eaten alive by mosquitoes, which made the heat more
oppressive and sleep difficult. The fashionable feather
ticks laid over the cornhusk mattresses further induced
bedbugs to multiply.

One hot and humid morning Janine came downstairs to find Zoë in the kitchen diligently sprinkling
elder-flower powder over the rice, wheat, and fruit.

"I do the bed sheets next, Miss Janine. Ain't no way
them ants, moths, and weevils is going to live here!"

Janine smiled, thinking that Zoë's zeal and determination alone would discourage any varmints.

From early morning till late at night, Janine threw
all her energies into running the house and keeping
the apothecary well stocked. But when she dropped
wearily into bed her mind strayed to Jonathan. Oh,
where was he, and why didn't he find some way to
get word to her? Her heart ached with longing for him
and lately a new thought had crept insidiously into
her mind to plague her: He no longer cared what had
become of her. Resolutely she pushed down the treacherous thought, reliving all their days together at Heritage Hall, feeding on the thin store of memories,
keeping Jonathan's memory fresh in her mind.

Chapter 13

Autumn crept over the town slowly, frosty nights followed by the sunny warmth of long Indian summer days. Leaves lingering on elms, poplars, and oaks deepened to shades of old gold, rust, and wine. For Janine the days drifted by like smoke.

One stormy evening she sat in the parlor, mending the frayed hem of her blue muslin gown, waiting for Papa to come home for supper. It was not like him to be so late. Anxiously she set her gown aside and went to the window to peer out into the darkness. The faint glow of the streetlamp shone feebly through a driving rain, and wind blustered about the house, whirling leaves from the trees, plastering them to the street, and scattering fluffy balls from the buttonwood trees onto the glistening pavement.

Shivering against the chill in the parlor, she drew her chair nearer to the fireside and sat down again. She had no more taken her gown in hand when she heard the front door burst open and Papa's voice shouting her name.

Alarmed, she jumped up and ran to the hall to greet him.

Dr. Mercer draped his dripping cloak on the hall tree and, putting an arm around her shoulders, led her into the parlor.

"Sorry to be so late, *ma petite*, but the post rider was due at the coffee house and I waited for him to come. And," he grinned broadly, "patience is rewarded."

He reached inside his jacket, pulled out a soiled white envelope, and waved it before Janine's startled eyes. "I've a letter from Ellen!"

For a moment she stood paralyzed, heart thumping, mouth dry. Then she sank into a chair, stiff and tense, bracing herself for whatever was to come, clutching her mending in her lap.

Papa crossed the room and stood warming his back at the fire burning in the grate while he broke the seal and began to read the letter aloud.

Impatiently she listened to Ellen's acknowledgment of Papa's letter, her excuses for not writing, and at last Papa came to the heart of the letter.

" 'You will be greatly relieved to hear that Jonathan has come home. . . .' "

Janine's hand jerked, and a bright drop of blood oozed from her pricked finger. Papa shot her a jubilant smile. "Good news, indeed!"

"Go on, Papa!" cried Janine.

" 'Having been set upon by renegades in the forest, Jonathan was robbed, suffered a brutal beating and a gunshot wound through his right side. The renegades, leaving him for dead in a thicket by the roadside, stole Brandy and fled. There he lost consciousness. He has no recollection how long he lay thus, a day, or two, or three. He was found by the post rider who carried him upon his horse to City Tavern in Alexandria. Having suffered a severe concussion, Jonathan could not recall so much as his own name. Fortunately one of the customers in the tavern recognized him. The tavern keeper laid him up in a room and summoned Mr. Burke and myself as well as Dr. Craik. Dr. Craik removed the bullet from his side, but found the flesh had mortified and his body was burning up with fever. For a time we feared for his life, but after profuse bleedings he rallied and we brought him to Heritage Hall. After a time his health and his memory were restored.' "

Janine's heart swelled with joy, and tears glistened

in the corners of her eyes. Jonathan was alive and
safe! Alive and safe at Heritage Hall!

Ellen's letter was full of news as to how Governor
Dunmore had threatened to free and arm the slaves,
and had made off with the gunpowder stored in the
magazine at Williamsburg. Mr. Jefferson had protested to the king, and a conciliatory overture was
made by Lord North, which Mr. Jefferson had rejected. She went on to say that all Virginians were
arming themselves and that independent companies,
from one hundred to one hundred and fifty men in
every county of Virginia, were training in the art of
war in preparation for their defense. Papa frowned
and his voice slowed as he came to the end of the
letter.

" 'When fully recovered, Jonathan left home to join
the Virginia militia under General Washington at
Cambridge. We have had no word from him since, and
fear for his safety.' "

Janine's heart went leaden, and for a moment she
was too stunned to hear what Papa was saying. Jonathan, fighting with the Continental army? thought
Janine. Why, he might be killed! No! She wouldn't
think that. The thought was too much to be borne!

Dr. Mercer crossed the room and, heaving a long
relieved sigh, handed Janine the letter. "Well, *ma
petite,* you must be happy indeed to know that Jonathan is at least safe and sound."

"Happy?" repeated Janine distractedly. "Oh, yes,
Papa. Of course."

Dr. Mercer picked up the *Gazette* and stood reading
before the fire. Janine read through Ellen's letter once
more. What Ellen hadn't said, thought Janine abashed,
was of as much interest as her news. That Ellen had
made no reference to her elopement with Jonathan
and had asked no questions as to her welfare made her
feel like an outcast. It was as though Ellen had wiped
her from memory, as if she no longer existed. The

letter dropped to Janine's lap, and she rested her head on the back of the chair and closed her eyes.

Thoughts darted through her mind like frightened hummingbirds. Had Jonathan joined General Washington's troops with the hope of seeing her in Philadelphia? If so, surely he could have found her. Why hadn't he come to see her, or sent word? Had Jonathan, like Ellen, put the past behind him? But surely a love as strong as theirs could survive separation. She tried to conjure up an image of Jonathan with the Virginia militia. Washington was deadlocked in Boston. She recalled that in September Lord William Howe had taken over from General Gage as commander of the British forces in Boston. She opened her eyes and gazed at Papa reading the *Gazette*.

"General Howe will soon put an end to this rebellion, won't he, Papa?" Her blue eyes, wide with anxiety, begged for reassurance.

Dr. Mercer removed his spectacles and polished them on his sleeve, considering his reply. "I can't promise you that . . . I fear our noble British general fails to understand the determination and resolution of the colonists." He set his spectacles astride his nose and returned to his paper.

Sighing, Janine folded Ellen's letter and put it away in her sewing box along with her needle and thread. There must be some good reason why Jonathan hadn't written. She must keep up her courage, her faith in him. He was alive and well and that was all that mattered, she told herself firmly. General Howe would soon put down the rebellion. Meanwhile she must let Jonathan know that she loved him, missed him, and waited only for the day when he would come home to her.

Folding her blue muslin gown over her arm she rose from her chair. "I'm going to my room, Papa, to write a letter to Jonathan."

Dr. Mercer looked up from his paper, a doubtful expression clouding his blue eyes. "I doubt it will ever reach him, *ma petite*. The post is so unreliable—not to mention that you've no address for *one* soldier among thousands."

Janine's lips set in a determined line. "I must try, Papa. I'll address it care of the Virginia militia under General Washington. Surely he'll get it eventually." She blinked back tears of joy and relief stinging her eyelids. "And meanwhile maybe a letter will come from Boston."

The weeks dragged past, gray and cold, and the word Janine was longing to hear did not come. Her hope of hearing from Jonathan ebbed away, leaving her desolate, hollow as a shell.

One evening at supper, Papa said casually, in the voice he always used when trying to slip a sugar-coated tablet down a patient's throat, "I had a pleasant chat with Doctor Ransom today at the hospital."

Janine's forkful of meat pie paused halfway to her mouth. "Oh? And what did Doctor Ransom have to say?"

"As a matter of fact he asked to borrow a few medical books. Seems he's exhausted those in the hospital library." He looked down at his plate, avoiding Janine's gaze and cleared his throat. "I invited him to call and browse through our library in the study."

Janine eyed him speculatively, her head cocked to one side. "Papa," she said, her voice holding a note of suspicion, "you're not matchmaking, are you?"

Dr. Mercer had the grace to blush. He thought he'd been rather subtle about the matter, and, truth to tell, he'd had no thought of matchmaking, but now that she mentioned it. . . . He put the thought aside for further consideration. He had merely hoped to bring a bit of cheer into the house. It worried him that Janine had grown so thin and pale, so gloomy and quiet. He missed her bright laughter, her cheerful singing about the house. He'd hoped that young Ransom could bring the child to life.

"Of course I'm not matchmaking!" He managed to look indignant and surprised at the same time. "I simply offered to lend him a few volumes—" Papa broke off, realizing too late he'd betrayed his hand in initiating the offer of his library, and flustered and red-faced, he compounded his faux pas. "I thought he could do with a change from hospital fare, a home-cooked meal—"

"When is he coming, Papa?" asked Janine, grinning at her father's obvious discomfiture over his gaff.

"Friday. For dinner," said Papa, smiling like a cat who'd devoured a canary.

Friday was cold and sunny, with a blustering wind that swept through the streets, bending the poplars. Richard arrived shortly before noon, looking rather as though he'd been blown here by the wind, thought Janine. When she stepped forward to greet him, she noticed that he was not quite a head taller than she. There was a smattering of freckles across his cheeks, pink from the cold, and his rumpled hair was redder than she remembered. Now, standing here before her in his well-brushed homespun suit, he appeared stiff and shy, ill at ease away from his familiar surroundings in the hospital.

Richard stared at her mutely, wishing he'd had more time to learn a few social graces—like chatting amiably about small, everyday things. All he could think of was how beautiful the girl was in her gown the color of sunshine. He saw the blood rising in her cheeks as he gazed at her appreciatively, taking in her raven black hair piled high on her head, the two glossy curls curving over her left shoulder, the lace flounce above her bodice, her trim waist, her yellow silk gown, down to the tips of her slippers.

Janine, wanting Papa to be proud of her, had taken great pains to look her best, and to plan a sumptuous dinner as well. Now she was rewarded by the look of approval in Richard's sparkling, amber-colored eyes.

He was no less approving of the meal laid before him on the candlelit table set with gleaming pewter and fine white linen. He devoured the snapper soup, roast beef, ham, sweet potatoes, peas, and crisp golden brown wheat bread baked by Janine herself, as though he hadn't eaten in weeks.

All during dinner Janine studied Dr. Ransom covertly, noticing the pleasant sound of his soft, rolling speech, the eager expression on his lean, freckled face, his enthusiasm when he spoke of his work at Penn's Hospital. And more often than not when she looked up, she found his intense gaze upon her and quickly lowered her lids.

Lingering over their dessert of raisins, almonds, spiced peaches and pears, Papa asked, "Did you attend Doctor Bond's lecture today?"

"Indeed!" said Dr. Ransom. "Wouldn't miss one for the world."

Janine had often heard Papa speak of the controversial Dr. Thomas Bond, for he'd been instrumental in founding the hospital and now he'd become famous for his clinical lectures for medical students. "But Doctor Ransom," Janine broke in, "you've finished your requirements. Surely you no longer need attend—"

Solemnly Richard shook his head. "I learn something new every time I hear the man." He turned to Dr. Mercer. "It's said he was strongly influenced by Morgagni. . . ."

"That well may be. Morgagni's a great pathologist. But whether or not, Bond's first lecture was an extraordinary statement at the time," said Dr. Mercer, warming to his subject.

"I was there, you see. It was in November of sixty-six at his home. The gathering included the managers of the hospital, professors, some thirty students at the new medical school, and leading citizens." Papa grinned and shook his head. "He shocked them all out of their boots when he remarked quite casually that hospitals are justly reputed the grand theaters of medical knowledge—and here on our doorstep we had over a hundred live patients for study. He insisted that much more study was needed of actual cases by the clinical method, especially in the fevers that raged every summer in the South. He cited some of the treatments used for yellow fever and made a strong case for study of its causes and methods of prevention."

Janine shifted restlessly in her chair. How Papa did go on. But Richard was soaking up his words like a sponge.

"Of even more significance for medical education," Papa continued, "Doctor Bond insisted that equally important was the examination of the dead; for how else could our errors in judgment be rectified for the benefit of survivors? In fact it wasn't till then that the managers permitted the bodies of patients who died to be taken by the matron and laid out in a suitable apartment there—" Papa broke off, as though suddenly deciding that cadavers were not appropriate table conversation.

Dr. Ransom leaned forward, his intense gaze fastened on Dr. Mercer's face, clearly fascinated by Papa's shop talk.

"Why was it that Doctor Morgan, and Rush and William Shippen Junior tried to do away with Doctor Bond's lectures last year?" asked Richard curiously. "After all, they are a degree requirement of the medical school."

Dr. Mercer chuckled. "Just between the two of us, I think they wanted to give the clinical lectures themselves. Doctor Kuhn and I stood up for Bond, however."

"Wasn't it Doctor Morgan who advocated separating the practice of physic from surgery and pharmacy and kept insisting that anatomy cannot be learned by listening to a lecture and reading about it in a book?"

"Heavens, yes," said Papa, popping an almond into his mouth. "John Morgan said that in his discourse at the first commencement—a revolutionary idea then, although he'd already said it several years earlier, in sixty-five I believe it was—at the same time he proposed a plan for establishing a medical school in the College of Philadelphia."

Dr. Ransom leaned back in his chair, looking thoroughly confused. "But Doctor William Shippen, Junior also takes credit for first proposing the medical school."

"And well he may have." Dr. Mercer's blue eyes twinkled. "Another vendetta! Doctor Shippen studied in London, then got his M.D. from the University of Edinburgh. While in London, he'd talked with his good friend Doctor Fothergill about his plans to give courses in medicine after his return to America in seventeen sixty-two. That same year Doctor Fothergill shipped a gift of seven cases of marvelous anatomical drawings and casts to the hospital with a letter recommending that Doctor William Shippen Junior give a course of anatomical lectures—said he was well qualified for the subject and would soon be followed by an able assistant, Doctor Morgan. He hoped they'd be able to erect a School of Physic here that would draw students from all over America and the West Indies. The following May, seventeen sixty-three, Doctor Shippen began his lectures, once a fortnight, a dollar a head, for the benefit of the hospital."

"And by seventeen sixty-six the medical school curriculum was established, and you joined the staff in seventeen sixty-nine," finished Dr. Ransom, smiling.

Janine was surprised and gratified to see the respect and adulation for her father reflected in Dr. Ransom's warm brown eyes. How Papa was enjoying this, she thought, with a surge of affection for him.

"Another new idea Doctor Morgan brought back from Europe in seventeen sixty-five, in addition to the umbrella," said Papa, chuckling, "was that of employing an apothecary to put up his prescriptions and perform other related duties instead of doing such work himself, as had been customary. It caused a great sensation in medical circles at the time." He glanced at Janine, pride glowing in his eyes. "And, of course, I now have my own apothecary."

Dr. Ransom, following his gaze, flushed and smiled embarrassedly and in general looked like a shy and sheepish boy. It was obvious to Janine that he'd been so engrossed in their conversation, he'd forgotten her presence.

"I'm sorry," he said. "We must be boring you with our talk."

"Not at all," said Janine, smiling, thinking she'd never met a man who was so terribly earnest and sincere.

"Perhaps you'll show me your apothecary," he said politely, trying to make amends.

"Gladly." She rose and led the way down the hall to the warm, cozy kitchen, fragrant with sweet-scented hickory burning low on the grate in the fireplace. She crossed the room to a great walnut hutch whose shelves were crowded with bottles and jars containing ointments, salves, powders, and tablets.

"We keep our medical supplies in here," said Janine, pulling open a drawer containing surgical dressings, lint bandages, fracture pillows, splints, sponges, twine, and flannel. "And in here, our equipment for making remedies." She bent over and opened the doors below to reveal balance scales and weights for measuring ingredients; two sets of ceramic mortars and pestles, one large and one small; spatulas for making boluses, pill-rolling tiles, and various knives.

Dr. Ransom's lips pursed in a low whistle of approval, but when Janine glanced up, his eyes were resting on the neck of her bodice. Flushing, she straightened up and added hastily, "I grow a number of herbs—I've boneset, summer savory, and fennel drying—hanging on the rafters in the garret. I gather others in the country or purchase them at the market."

Richard's bright gaze startled her. There was a quirk
tugging at the corners of his lips, and she felt a flash
of annoyance that he didn't appear to be taking her
seriously.

"And how do you know how to brew all these remedies?"

She motioned to a row of books on the shelf of the
hutch. "I've E. Smith's *Compleat Housewife* and *The
Art of Cooking Made Plain and Easy*, and my own
book containing recipes passed down, many that Papa
has given me." She lifted a red leatherbound book
from the shelf and flipped it open.

"Here's snakebite, treated by doses of olive oil and
applications of mercury ointment; kidney ailments
dosed with a glass of horseradish roots and mustard
seed in gin; earache cured by the hot juice of ash . . .
rickets. . . ."

Richard, reading over her shoulder, pointed to a
recipe at the top of the page. "And what does this
cure?" he asked, grinning.

Janine blushed, gazing at a recipe for apple tarts.

"And that!" Richard's finger slid down the page to
a recipe for lemon pie. He was standing so close to her
that she could smell the fresh, well-scrubbed scent of
him, and his warm breath on her neck sent prickles
running down her spine.

Nettled by his attitude and disturbed by the feelings
his nearness aroused in her, she snapped the book
shut. "I've all sorts of recipes—for everything!"

To hide her confusion she stepped forward and
lifted a glass bottle from the shelf. "Mary Bannister's
Drops of Spirit of Venice Treacle, handed down by
Mother Bannister herself, in Boston," she said lightly.
"And Catherine Deimer's Tar Water, for curing the
scald head, and Deimer's Pills for the Gravel and Pain
in the back."

She held up another jar. "An extraordinary ointment for clearing the skin, taking off freckles—"
Janine halted abruptly, suddenly horribly aware of

the freckles scattered across Richard Ransom's cheeks. Scarlet with embarrassment, she stood as if frozen.

Dr. Ransom's face grew solemn. "I'll strike a bargain with you. I'll use your magic ointment if you will apply it personally, at least twice weekly."

Looking up into his face, she saw his russet eyes sparkling with merriment and at the same time they both burst into laughter.

"What other magic potions have you?" asked Richard good-humoredly.

"We've calomel, ipecac, Peruvian bark, tartar, all the usual remedies." She picked up a small jar, opened it, and waved it under his nose. "Here is a smelling nectar that will cure the itch, or any other breaking out, only by the smell!"

Richard's clear, skeptical laughter filled the room. "I do believe you're better equipped than our apothecary at the hospital. If we're not careful, you'll be taking over our patients!"

A voice from the doorway said, "It's not beyond belief!" Dr. Mercer entered the room and put an arm around Janine's shoulders. "Last week a neighbor was suddenly seized with a great pain in his right hip. His wife summoned doctors Cadwalader, Bond, and Kearsley to his bedside, but they could give little relief. Then she called upon Janine, and with her help he got some relief by clyster."

"I'll remember that," said Richard, trying without success to conceal his disbelief. "Perhaps I may call upon you in the future?" His tone was facetious, his eyes challenging.

"Please do," Janine replied stiffly, more than a little miffed with this self-assured physician who refused to take her seriously.

It wasn't until after Richard Ransom had gone that Janine paused to wonder whether his calling on her in the future was to be professional or social. He was rather intriguing, she thought, despite his lack of respect for her work and his painful self-consciousness, except of course, when the talk turned to medicine. However, if by any chance he should call again, she would make it quite plain that she was spoken for; that her heart belonged to Jonathan, and that calling on her would avail him nothing.

Chapter 14

Several weeks later on a bitter cold November night Janine was curled up in Papa's big leather armchair before the fire in the study reading a book when there came a sharp rapping on the front door. Clutching her pink flannel wrapper about her, she ran to answer. Her blue eyes widened in astonishment and she started back in surprise. On the threshold stood Dr. Ransom, red-faced and shivering, clutching Dr. Mercer's two volume *De Sedibus* under his arm. She had thought the shy, serious, red-haired doctor had forgotten her entirely, much less that he would call on her, and had dismissed him from her mind.

"Forgive me for calling unannounced," he said with an appealing, apologetic grin, "but I wish to return your father's books."

Taken aback, Janine felt her face turn scarlet. He'd not come to call upon her after all! "I'm sorry, Papa is not at home this evening," she said stiffly, holding out her hands for the books. "I'll be glad to give these to him when he returns."

Dr. Ransom continued to smile and clutch the books under his arm. "You're most kind, Mistress Mercer. However, Doctor Mercer said I might borrow additional books from his library. . . ." He let his words trail away and stood shivering in the doorway.

Janine tried to maintain her composure in the face of this eager, smiling young man. After all, she told herself, he had come to see Papa and Papa was out.

There was no reason to invite him inside. "Yes," she said uncertainly, "what books do you wish?"

He frowned, pursing his lips, staring thoughtfully at the star-studded sky overhead. "I'd have to browse through his collection." Abruptly his bright, innocent gaze swung to meet hers. "Depending on what is available."

Janine eyed him speculatively, hesitating. She started to say *I* am not available, Doctor Ransom, and thought better of it, for of course he was speaking of books. The man was completely devoid of guile.

"I don't often have the opportunity to come into town, but I can call again, when Doctor Mercer is at home—if you're afraid to allow me inside. . . ."

Challenged, Janine lifted her chin and she stepped back into the hallway, holding the door wide. "I'm afraid of nothing, Doctor Ransom. Come in."

Richard followed her down the hall to the study and gazed appreciatively around the warm, cozy room. Lamplight cast a soft glow over the mahogany kneehole desk, the bookshelves that stretched to the ceiling, and the red turkey carpet. A fire burned cheerily in the grate. He set the books on a table and strode to the fireplace, warming his hands over the fire.

Studying his trim, straight-backed figure, it struck Janine that he was wearing the same threadbare mustard-colored suit he'd worn the day they met, and the day he'd come to dinner, and that he wore no cloak against the bitter cold night. And awkward silence fell between them. He'd appeared eager to come inside and visit her, thought Janine, but now that he was here, his tongue seemed to be stuck in his throat.

Silent as a shadow, Zoë appeared in the doorway. She wore her red turban, and her coffee-toned skin gleamed in the lamplight. She gave them a gap-toothed smile. "Will you be wanting some refreshment, Miss Janine?"

Dr. Ransom turned from the hearth, a pleased, hopeful expression on his lean face.

Janine hesitated. Some deep instinct told her that she could send him on his way, but she couldn't bring herself to turn him out—poor, hungry, shivering from the cold. She should be hospitable. After all, he was Papa's apprentice.

"Bring us some hot rum, and the meat pastries left from dinner, please, Zoë."

Dr. Ransom eased into Papa's brown leather chair and stretched out his legs toward the fire. Janine sat primly across from him in a rush-bottomed rocker. The firelight lit her eyes and her black hair tumbled about her shoulders. She saw Richard's gaze wandering from her face, downward, pausing at the gentle swell of her breasts, lingering on the long, slender curve of her thigh. She clutched her pink night robe around her and her eyes frosted a bit.

Color crept up Richard's face to the tips of his ears and he turned his head and stared intently at the gilded bronze clock on the mantel. Nodding at the two figures mounted on one side, he said, "A Greek god subduing a goddess?"

Following his gaze, Janine said conversationally, "They are Roman warriors. I suppose they are lording over their captives. Papa brought the clock from France. . . ."

"It's quite handsome," said Richard, a shade too eagerly, then fell silent again.

The cat's got his tongue, thought Janine, sighing inwardly. She made polite chatter about this and that until Zoë returned with a tray bearing two steaming mugs of rum and a plate of golden brown pastries. Janine took one and nibbled at the edges, trying to make it last.

Dr. Ransom munched one, then another and another of the light, flaky pastries. Clearly his hysop of tea and bread at the hospital had far from satisfied the gnawing hunger in his stomach, thought Janine.

Soon the pastries were gone. But Richard remained.

They sat in silence, broken only by the hissing of the fire and the ticking of the clock that seemed to echo in the room. Richard sipped the hot buttered rum and licked his lips nervously.

"What's new at Penn's Hospital?" asked Janine finally.

His face lighted with enthusiasm, and he began to describe in great detail an operation he had witnessed—the removal of a kidney stone, performed by Dr. Bond.

Janine listened, as though fascinated by every detail.

"Doctor Bond is the best surgeon in the colonies," Richard said flatly, draining his mug of rum.

Janine smiled. "You'll be as good someday."

He shook his head. "I'm sticking with medicine, like your father. Right now I've all I can handle with ulcers and carriers, dropsy, scorbutick ulcers, and consumption."

As though realizing he'd lingered too long on his work at the hospital, he broke off and asked, "How do you occupy your days when you're not keeping house for your father and stocking his apothecary?"

"My duties take all my time, Doctor Ransom," she said emphatically. "In the evening if I have no mending to do, I read—*The Vicar of Wakefield, Tristram Shandy, Robinson Crusoe.* . . ."

"Hum . . . you're quite well-read," said Richard. "I wish I could discuss books with you, but I've had no time to read novels.

"I also read the *Pennsylvania Journal* and the *Gazette.*"

"And well informed, also," he said lamely.

With an effort Janine smothered a giggle and said nothing. He was so solemn and serious, speaking to her as though she were one of the pupils he'd tutored in the past.

He cleared his throat and rushed on, "Too few young ladies take an interest in what's going on around them. Of course I can understand why. They are excluded from honors and from offices, deprived of a voice in legislation, obliged to submit to those laws which are imposed on us. No wonder they're indifferent to the public interest."

Janine could feel her temper rising. "Doctor Ransom, I am quite aware of what's going on around me and most concerned with the public interest. For instance I do think that the colonies are justified in protesting new taxes and other restrictive regulations passed by Parliament and that we should be represented . . . but this can be achieved by peaceful means."

Dr. Ransom gave a rueful laugh. "You sound like our Quaker managers at the hospital."

"I'm not of the Friendly persuasion," said Janine coldly, "but we *are* British subjects. It's pure folly to cut off the hand that feeds you."

A red flush spread over his thin face and he bent a penetrating gaze upon her. Quietly he asked, "What of the hand that strangles you?"

Her breasts rose sharply as she drew in her breath. "I'm certain that right at this moment Mister Franklin is effecting a reconciliation."

"Don't count on it! Even Lord North has tried to tell King George that we must be given certain rights—"

Janine interrupted him. "Doctor Ransom, I'm afraid we must agree to disagree. We cannot discuss politics further, for I see you have a closed mind. You've already thrown in with the rebels!"

Richard retorted sharply, "And have you not chosen sides?"

"Of course not!" said Janine heatedly. "I'm remaining neutral. This rebellion will soon end, you'll see."

His expression was somber, and a cynical half-smile touched one side of his mouth. "I fear you're hiding your head in the sand, Mistress Mercer. There will come a day when you'll be forced to choose, mark my words."

Abuptly he stood up and went to the shelves lined with books, quickly scanning the titles. "I must be going. It's a cold night and the gatekeeper will be drowsy with rum to warm his innards—it will be a task to wake him to let me into the hospital."

He drew *An Experimental History of the Materia Medica* from a shelf above his head and turned to her. "This will do nicely for the time being. Please thank Doctor Mercer for me."

Janine showed him to the door, and just before he stepped out into the dark, cold night, he turned to face her. His straight sandy eyebrows rose, and there was a gleam in his russet eyes. "Keep reading, Mistress Mercer. You may be further enlightened." He left, closing the door firmly behind him.

Further enlightened, indeed, fumed Janine, nettled. His lofty, positive air annoyed her. Did he think because he was so much better educated than she that she had no mind for thinking? That her opinions were of no value? With a slight shiver of dread she recalled Dr. Ransom's prophecy that the day would come when she would have to choose sides. This was the second time she'd crossed swords over the rebel cause: first Peggy Shippen, now this hardheaded Scottish doctor. She recalled the look in his eyes before he went out the door—one of censure, disapproval. Clearly he thought the less of her for "hiding her head in the sand." Even though she wasn't interested in him as a suitor, it disturbed her to have him think ill of her. It was not until then that she remembered she'd not told him of her betrothal to Jonathan. She shrugged. It was of no matter. He'd not asked to call upon her again. And if she had anything to say about it, he never would!

As events turned out, she had nothing to say about it, for it was Papa who accepted Dr. Ransom's invitation to attend Francis Hopkinson's concert at Christ

Church on Christmas Eve, and Papa who invited him to sup with them beforehand.

Janine welcomed Richard with the same warmth and cordiality she would have shown any other guest of Papa's, and to her relief, Richard seemed to have forgotten that they hadn't parted on the best of terms. During the meal his face was lighted with pleasure and his eyes betrayed a subdued air of excitement. Soon she, too, was swept up in anticipation of the evening's entertainment ahead.

A short time later they settled themselves in the carriage Richard had hired to take them to Christ Church.

"I'm eager to hear Hopkinson conduct *The Messiah*," said Papa enthusiastically as they rattled down Second Street.

"I'm afraid I'm not acquainted with his work," said Richard.

"His soirees at his home are famous," said Dr. Mercer. "He's quite a composer, you see. Plays his own compositions on the harpsichord—saloon music—songs to be sung. In fact he's a pupil of Bremmer's."

Richard grinned appreciatively. "I do know of James Bremmer!"

Dr. Mercer turned to Janine. "Bremmer's a Scot—the first Philadelphia composer of any consequence."

Nodding abstractedly, Janine gazed out the window. They crossed High Street and she saw the lofty spire of Christ Church silhouetted against the bright, moonlit sky. The clear sound of bells chiming "O Come All Ye Faithful" floated on the brisk, cold air. The carriage pulled up before the church gate. When Janine alighted, Richard held her arm in a firm clasp that gave her a pleasant sensation of being looked after. He did not release his grasp as she walked between him and Papa down the brick path to the entrance below the tower.

In the narthex she paused while Papa and Richard dropped coins in the poor box. Standing in the doorway of the sanctuary, she gazed enchanted at the gleaming brass chandelier brought from England years ago. Tonight it blazed with candles that shed a golden radiance over the rows of people crowded into white wooden pews. Chancel, altar, and balcony were swathed in evergreens and loops of holly and ivy.

Slowly they made their way down the wide aisle and took their places in a straight-backed pew on the left. Janine's gaze traveled over the chancel whose blue-green walls were softened by candles flickering on the altar, their light reflected in the dark squares of glass in the great Palladian window, the graceful wineglass pulpit, and the English font in which William Penn had been baptized. She glanced covertly around the congregation. There were the Cadwaladers; Mayor Samuel Powell and his family; Philip Syng, the silver-smith; and almost hidden behind a fluted pillar, the little seamstress Betsy Ross.

She heard a rustling and shuffling in the balcony as the choir rose to its feet. A violin note sounded, and a hush settled over the crowd. Janine, seated between Papa and Dr. Ransom, soon became caught up in the majesty of the soaring music and voices. Sometime near the end of the program, shifting uncomfortably in the crowded pew, she became aware of Richard sitting close beside her. His arm brushed against her arm, his thigh touching her own. She looked up into his face. Their glances met, and for the first time she saw reflected in his clear brown eyes more than casual friendliness or the camaraderie that had sometimes sprung up with the pitting of wits between them. For a moment she saw adoration shining from his eyes. She smiled uncertainly, not knowing how to defend herself against such bald admiration. *I'm imagining things*, thought Janine. *It's a trick of the candlelight.* Hastily she looked down at her hands in her lap and began folding and unfolding her white kid gloves.

Richard reached over and gently placed his large warm hand over hers. She stole a glance at him. No, there was no mistaking the fondness of his expression. Oh, how pleasant it was, to be loved and desired again! Her heart began thumping with the old familiar quickening. But she did not want to feel this way about Richard Ransom. She must not! And worse, if he grew truly fond of her, he'd be dreadfully vulnerable, and she had no wish to hurt him. Why, oh, why, hadn't she told him about Jonathan, she thought, vexed with herself.

All the way home in the carriage Janine cast sidelong glances at Richard to reassure herself that she had misread the expression in his eyes. But in the pale gleam from the moon and stars Janine found his warm, affectionate gaze upon her, and she could hardly wait to escape to the safety of her room.

But when they drew up before the house, Papa invited Dr. Ransom in for hot mulled cider. They sat in the parlor where Zoë had lighted a fire that blazed merrily on the hearth, sipping the hot, spicy brew.

"Play something for us on the spinet, *ma petite*," said Papa.

Reluctantly Janine sat down before the spinet. She had no wish to play, for she felt ill at ease under Richard's intense, affectionate gaze. But to please Papa she ran through several popular tunes, hoping to dispel the sentimental mood that seemed to have enveloped them.

"Play a few carols, Janine," urged Papa, smiling warmly.

Obediently she struck up one of his favorites, "God Rest Ye Merry Gentlemen." Papa and Richard came and stood behind her and began to sing. In spite of herself Janine joined in, singing "Hark! The Herald Angels Sing," "Joy to the World," "While Shepherds Watched Their Flocks," and others. Papa and Richard sang in loud, clear, enthusiastic voices. They were having a jolly time, thought Janine, smiling to herself.

Gradually a feeling she could not put down crept over her—a helpless feeling of being caught up by a current and swept into an intimacy against her will. Finally she could stand it no longer and rose abruptly from the spinet.

"It's late, Papa, and Doctor Ransom has a long way to travel. . . ."

"Quite so, *ma petite*," said Dr. Mercer with a jovial smile. "Illness is no respecter of holy days, I'm afraid, and I've a busy day ahead tomorrow." His right eye dropped in a sly wink behind Richard's back. He bade them goodnight and left her alone with Dr. Ransom.

Janine's heart sank to her slippers. Papa had mistaken her suggestion that they end the evening as a hint for him to retire! She stood motionless before the fireplace, her hands clasped at her waist in an attitude intended to convey that she expected Richard to take his leave. Though she was outwardly calm, her heart was fluttering against her breast.

Smiling shyly, Richard drew from his pocket a small package wrapped in white paper and tied with a red bow, and crossed the room to stand before her.

"A small remembrance, Janine," he said, pressing the package into her hands.

"Richard!" exclaimed Janine, embarrassed. "You shouldn't, really. I can't accept—"

"Please. It's nothing."

His face shone with such pleasure and anticipation that she couldn't bear to disappoint him by refusing his gift. Slowly she tore the paper from the box and lifted the lid. Inside lay a gold heart-shaped locket on a thin chain. Opening the trinket, she found a lock of Richard's dark red hair. A common gesture of friendship between friends, thought Janine.

"Richard, it's lovely!" Impulsively she reached up and kissed him on the cheek. Before she could step away, his arms came round her waist; he bent his head to her face and his lips met hers, tender and warm. Her heart beat rapidly and she felt a quickening of her emotions. Her arms crept up around his neck. She could feel his strong, slender body pressing against her own. Then suddenly aware of her own response, she drew back, whirling away from the circle of his arms. Ignoring the surprised look in his eyes, she took the locket from the box. Sliding the chain around her neck, she fastened the clasp under her hair.

"Richard, you're so kind," said Janine, smiling with delight. "It's beautiful!"

He moved toward her, arms outstretched. "Janine, I. . . ."

She backed away, holding her hands out before her as if to fend him off, her heart racing, afraid of the ardor she saw in his eyes, afraid of the passion rising within her.

He stepped forward, seized both her hands in his and drew them close against his chest. She stiffened against him, but she could feel his heart pounding, his breath coming in short, quick gasps.

"Richard, it's late, and you *must* go," she said firmly.

"I have all the time in the world—and patience— the waiting kind," he said, smiling ruefully. But his eyes held a look of pain and disappointment that stabbed at her heart. They stood for a moment in a sort of frozen silence. Wordlessly she shook her head.

"May I see you again?"

She wanted only for him to leave. Hastily, and without thinking, she said, "Yes, of course. But now go. You'll never find a carriage."

"It's a fine night. I'd welcome a brisk walk to the hospital . . . if I could stay. . . ." His eyes were pleading, imploring.

She stood smiling at him regretfully, shaking her head from side to side.

"The pond near the hospital is freezing over. Will you go skating with me?"

"Yes, yes!" she blurted. If he didn't go, she would scream.

"When?"

"When the pond is frozen. Now go, please!"

When the door shut behind him, she leaned her back against it and closed her eyes. She felt shaken and confused, out of tune with the world. Who would have thought that under Richard's shy, homespun exterior smoldered the heart of a cavalier. She wished with all her heart that Richard Ransom had never come into her life. . . .

Chapter 15

January of 1776 came, and with it the exhilarating news of the Continental Army's conquest in Montreal under General Richard Montgomery and Colonel Benedict Arnold. The joy and hope the victory raised in the hearts of the rebels was quickly dashed by the debacle at Quebec in which Montgomery was killed and Benedict Arnold wounded. Washington, still deadlocked at Boston, was plagued by desertions and the unwillingness of "sunshine patriots" to reenlist. Jonathan would never desert, Janine thought morosely. She resigned herself to not hearing from him until the British drove the rebels back home or his enlistment expired.

The freezing cold had apparently cooled the fevers and distempers of the citizens, and Janine, no longer besieged by the ailing who had flocked to her door for remedies, was bored to distraction. Early in January Peggy Shippen invited her to attend a quilting bee at the mansion on Second Street. Despite her resolve not to attend such gatherings, and thinking rather to mend the coolness that had sprung up between them at the picnic last summer, Janine accepted the invitation.

As though by common consent everyone avoided speaking of politics and kept up an endless chatter of new fashions, new hairstyles, and new beaux. Peggy, her pert face glowing with excitement, could talk of nothing but a handsome young British officer named John André, taken prisoner at St. Johns, whom she had met passing through Philadelphia on his way to internment at Lancaster. Janine, restless and weary of their babble, finally made her excuses to leave early.

Peggy showed her to the door and told her, with a peculiar light in her slate-blue eyes, that she must read *Pamela*, a popular novel published in England, whose purpose was to instruct young ladies in how not to behave. It would benefit her greatly.

"Promise me you'll read it!" Peggy teased.

Whether or not Peggy was trying to tell her something, she didn't know, but she nodded a smiling agreement and left.

The following week the weather turned mean. Swirling clouds of snow came down thickly, blanketing the streets. When at last it stopped, a pale sun shone only long enough to melt a little of the snow, then disappeared behind the clouds. During the night the slushy snow froze, glazing the streets with ice.

On a dark, gloomy afternoon in that same week in January, Janine stood gazing moodily out the parlor window. The heavy sky threatened more snow. If she were to be snowed in, she thought, she needed something to occupy her mind, something to take her mind off Jonathan. She smiled to herself, recalling Peggy's admonition. "Why not?" she whispered aloud. Hastily she donned her blue velvet cloak and bonnet and set out for the bookseller's on High Street.

The shop was dark and shadowy despite the oil lamps casting cheerful halos of light. A dry, musty odor, not unpleasant, assailed her nostrils. She nodded to the bookseller who was talking with an elderly silver-haired gentleman at the counter and edged past two buxom, well-dressed ladies lingering over a stall that held Bibles and prayer books. Farther along she paused at a stall to glance through a book of music, put it down and picked up a new cookbook. She had been browsing for some minutes when a deep voice at her elbow said,

"I doubt you have need of that, Mistress Mercer—or is it Mistress Burke?"

Janine whirled around and her blue eyes widened in astonishment. Mark Furneaux made a slight bow and stood gazing down at her, grinning like a court jester. Thunderstruck, she stood as if paralyzed. He looked devastatingly handsome in his dashing uniform of the Pennsylvania militia. In the crook of his arm, he carried a tricorn hat and a thick pamphlet. His broad shoulders glistened with melting snowflakes. His hair was thicker and blacker than she remembered; and his crescent brows, lifted questioningly over sparkling black eyes, gave him the look of a demon. He had an air of utter assurance, of annoying insolence about him that set her nerves on edge.

Mark seized her hand and gazed pointedly at her ring finger, noting the absence of a ring. "Am I addressing Mistress *Mercer*, then?"

A tremor shook her from the top of her head to her toes, and she could feel her face turning scarlet. Speechless, she nodded. He was watching her intently.

"Still awaiting the phantom lover, I presume."

Again she nodded.

A skeptical glint appeared in his dark eyes, and his mouth twisted in a mocking grin. Surely he didn't think she had fabricated Jonathan for the purpose of putting him off! He released her hand and went on. "I've bought Thomas Paine's *Common Sense*." He took the thick pamphlet from under his arm and held it out to her, grinning. "Just published and it's a bestseller. Three bookstores were sold out. Perhaps I could purchase *Common Sense* for you also?"

Janine's chin rose in disdain. "I've no need of *Common Sense*, thank you!" she said haughtily.

His eyebrows rose in mock surprise. Suddenly realizing what she'd said, she could have bitten her tongue. "I'm here to purchase a book recommended by a *friend*," she said hastily, stressing the word *friend*. "Good day, Lieutenant Furneaux."

She turned away toward the shelves lining the wall from floor to ceiling and stared hard at the rows of books.

Mark's deep, genial voice boomed over her shoulder. "Perhaps I can help you, if you tell me what you're looking for."

Her head jerked around. "Shh!" she hissed. "Everyone in the shop can hear you!"

"So?" he said loudly, his black eyes dancing in merriment.

Abruptly she turned and marched briskly to another table stacked high with the newest plays and poems of Francis Hopkinson, Philip Freneau, and John Trumbull. Mark followed and stood close beside her. She could feel his warm breath like a caress on the side of her neck, and she smelled the scent of tobacco and leather. His very presence was somehow disconcerting. Of all the people to turn up here, thought Janine. This odious wretch who had shamed and humiliated her beyond belief, this despicable man who would not believe she was a lady! Memories of their days and nights together flashed unbidden through her mind: the wild passion of his embrace, his gentle bathing of her fevered body, his strong arms holding her close against him as they rode Brandy through the forest, the comforting warmth of his body next to hers in their bed on the pine needles. . . . Her face grew hot and her heart was beating so hard, she thought he could surely hear it. Now, he was embarrassing her, that's all it was. She took a deep breath.

"I'm looking for *Pamela* by Mr. Samuel Richardson, and I'm certain I can find it, thank you," she said in a tone plainly intended to dismiss him.

"*Pamela!*" Mark snorted. "You certainly won't find her there! Anyway, I think *A Father's Legacy to His Daughters* would be more appropriate reading for you," he said with a mocking smile on his face.

Oh! He was so impertinent and ill-bred, she'd have

liked to slap his face. She pressed her lips firmly together and said nothing.

He turned to a stall of popular English novels and began to peruse the titles. "I understand that *Pamela* has a hearty appetite for seduction," he said nonchalantly.

Janine's face flamed with embarrassment, and she felt that she would strangle at the expression on Mark's tanned, piratical face. "You've read it, then?"

Mark shook his head. "No, but an acquaintance of mine has. . . ."

Anne Delaney, no doubt, thought Janine, unaccountably annoyed.

"*Pamela*! Here she is!" He picked up the book and turned toward her. "Please allow me to give it to you," he said, grinning. "A memento of our journey. . . ."

"No thank you, Lieutenant Furneaux," said Janine coldly.

"Then at least let me see you home. I wouldn't want you to be set upon by renegades," he said with elaborate concern.

With great effort Janine controlled her temper. He seemed to be taking great delight in forcing his attentions upon her. She disliked him heartily, lounging there against the book stall. But there was something stimulating about him, something warm and vital and electric. . . .

"You're making a nuisance of yourself," she said vehemently. "And it won't be necessary for you to see me home, thank you!"

The two plump matrons turned to stare at them. A tall horsefaced woman in a corner frowned over her spectacles, and the silver-haired gentleman and the shopkeeper stopped talking to watch the drama unfolding before them. Janine snatched *Pamela* from Mark's hand and started toward the shopkeeper. Mark followed at her elbow.

"You didn't mind traveling with me on your flight

from Virginia!" he said in a loud and indignant voice that carried to the corners of the bookstore.

Janine heard a gasp and a titter from the ladies who continued to stare, wide-eyed and disapproving. Oh, Lord, thought Janine, suppose they recognized her as Dr. Mercer's daughter? Her reputation would be ruined! She bit her lip in vexation. All she wanted to do was to flee from the shop, away from this impossible scoundrel! She flung her money down on the counter and bolted out the door.

Mark, following hard on her heels through the doorway, caught himself just in time, gripping the doorjamb to keep from tripping over her as he ran down the steps. Janine sat sprawled on the snowy pavement in a muddle of blue velvet, her bonnet askew. Glaring up at him like an enraged kitten, her blue eyes blazed with anger and humiliation.

One glance at her face told Mark that her pride was more injured than her body, well-padded by voluminous petticoats, gown and cloak. He noted the skid marks her heels had left in the newly fallen snow and rightly surmised what had caused her downfall. His lips twitched with suppressed laughter.

"A step in time saves nine," said Mark good-naturedly. "Permit me." He bent down and scooped her up in his powerful arms.

"It's a *stitch* in time, you dunderhead!" snapped Janine. "And put me down!"

His dark eyes gleamed in merciless merriment. "My, aren't we prickly today! I suppose it's my fault that you slipped and fell!"

"Of course it is!" The moment she spoke, the folly of her words and the ridiculousness of her plight struck her, and tears of anger and frustration glistened on her eyelids.

"You're not hurt, are you?" His voice held a note of alarm, and there was no mockery in his eyes now.

"No! So put me down this instant!"

He swung her down and set her on her feet on the

icy pavement, letting his arms fall to his sides. An agonizing pain shot through her right ankle and she toppled toward him, thrusting a hand against his chest
to keep from falling. Swiftly he swept her off her feet
into his arms.

"Once again it seems you can't get along without
me, little darling." He bent his head to hers, looking
deep into her eyes, his mouth an inch from her own.

"I'm quite all right," she sputtered. "You've no
need to carry me. I can walk perfectly well if you
place one hand under my elbow."

"But *I* can't walk with one hand under your elbow."
He spoke with the exaggerated patience of one speaking to a small child. "You see, little darling, the slush
of the morning has now frozen into ruts that have been
covered by newly fallen snow, on which you, or both
of us, can break our necks—as you have just so clearly
shown."

"Pecksniff!" said Janine wrathfully.

Ignoring her remark, Mark hailed the driver of a
passing carriage for hire. Flinging open the door, he
lifted Janine to the seat inside and jumped in beside
her.

The carriage, whose wheels had been replaced by
runners, glided smoothly up High Street on thick-
packed snow, and Janine was pressed snugly beside
Mark in the narrow seat. He put an arm around her
shoulders as though it were the most natural thing in
the world for him to do. Janine started to protest and
immediately thought better of it. He would only laugh
at her, and an arm around her shoulders was nothing
to make a scene over, considering the past intimacies
they'd shared.

The snow was falling thickly now, and the whirling
white flakes like a curtain outside the window created
the illusion that they were in a private world all their
own, an illusion of time suspended in an oasis of
silence. Mark, sitting beside her in the stillness, seemed
unnaturally quiet. Janine turned her head to look at

him, and at the same moment he turned toward her. Their gaze locked and held, their eyes reflecting a startled wonder, an overpowering awareness of each other.

Janine's eyes closed. Mark's mouth came down on hers and suddenly she was in his arms. The softly falling snow, the muffled creak of the carriage ceased to exist, and in the whole world there seemed only the two of them.

The carriage lurched over an icy rut, slid around the corner into Second Street, and abruptly they were thrust apart. Janine's face felt flushed and her heart was thudding like a drummer's tattoo. She caught her breath and folded her trembling hands primly in her lap, not daring to look at Mark. She knew she should take umbrage with him but she could not find the strength. She felt as though she were spinning, whirling like the snowflakes falling past the window of the carriage.

She ventured a sidelong glance at Mark. *He* apparently did not feel as though he were spinning, whirling like a snowflake, thought Janine ruefully. He was peering out the window through the drifting snow at the dim shapes of houses on their left, whistling softly under his breath, "The World Turned Upside Down."

He signaled the driver to stop. "This is it, isn't it?" he asked her. "The house next to the alley, with the Hand-in-Hand fire mark . . ."

"Yes." The word was a hoarse whisper.

She made no protest when he carried her up the marble steps and rapped on the door. They waited in silence there in the gathering dusk for Zoë to let them in. Snowflakes fell on their heads and shoulders, glistening like diamonds. They watched the bent figure of the lamplighter trudging down the street. He braced his ladder against the lamppost outside Cadwalader's mansion, mounted the steps, and touched his wand to the wick. A flame sprang to life, bathing him in an aureole of golden light.

Janine shivered, wondering what could be keeping Zoë. Impatiently, Mark rapped sharply on the door. There was no answer. Flustered, Janine finally remembered she had a key, fished it from her purse, and handed it to Mark. He unlocked the door, carried her into the parlor, and lowered her onto the rose brocade sofa.

She let out a long sigh of relief. Home, safe and sound. Casually Mark dropped his hat and their books on a table. Surely he didn't mean to stay, thought Janine, alarmed.

Janine tried to make her voice sound calm over the fluttering in her breast. "Zoë has probably gone on an errand and will return shortly. Thank you for your help, Lieutenant Furneaux. I can manage now."

"You're welcome." He grinned, making no move to go. Instead he eased Janine's blue velvet cloak from her shoulders and draped it over the Windsor chair near the fireplace. Then, hunkering down before the hearth, he struck a spark from flint and steel from the tinderbox and lighted a fire under the pine knots on the grate.

Janine pulled off her galoshes and kicked off her slipper, and, while his back was turned, slid her stocking down over her knee. Abruptly Mark stood up and turned to face her. His glance traveled appreciatively down her calf to her ankle.

"I'd best take a look at that," he said, striding toward her.

His tall, powerful body seemed to fill the small parlor and there was a look of animal strength about him that excited her.

"Never mind," she said quickly. "Papa will see to it when he comes home."

Ignoring her protest, Mark knelt down before her and grasped her slender foot between his large warm hands, cautiously running his fingers over the smooth

ivory skin of her ankle. He gazed into her eyes with
genuine concern. "Does that hurt?"

She shook her head. The touch of his fingers seemed
to burn her skin and set her senses reeling so, she
wanted to scream. It took all her self-control not to
jerk her foot away. His dark head was bent over her
ankle, and she pushed down a wild impulse to run her
fingers through his hair. To cover her confusion she
blurted out the question that had been nagging at her
mind since they'd first met. "What are you doing here
in Philadelphia, Lieutenant Furneaux?"

He sat back on his heels, his dark eyes level with her
own, and gave her a long, direct stare.

Embarrassed, she said, "Your shipping—your
import-export business must have been cut off by the
war." She wanted to stop, but the words tumbled out.
"You're really a privateer, aren't you? A common pi-
rate, preying on—"

Coldly he interrupted her.

"It appears to me, Mistress Mercer, that you're
overly concerned with the history of a man who has
only your welfare at heart." His tone was frigid and
impassive, and his eyes glinted dangerously. "Either
you're uncommonly curious—for a lady—or living in
Virginia has bred this unfortunate trait."

Janine felt a hot flush of anger suffuse her face. Why
should he be so secretive?

Before she could speak, Mark went on. "Since you
insist, my grandfather migrated with the Calvinist
Huguenots when they fled from France in sixteen
eighty-five and settled in Nova Scotia. My parents were
born there, as was I. In seventeen fifty-five, during the
French and Indian War, my father refused to sign an
oath of allegiance to the British king. I was six-years-
old when our colony was driven from Arcadia, scattered throughout the colonies. My family settled here
—in the City of Brotherly Love. They are now de-
ceased." He smiled grimly and stood up.

Nonplussed, she started to tell him she had only

wondered what had brought him to Philadelphia at this time. But fearing he'd take offense, she said nothing.

Glancing down at her foot, he said, "Impossible to tell if any bones are broken, but we should soak it—take the fever out."

"Never mind," said Janine more sharply than she'd intended. "Zoë will be here any minute."

A look of quick impatience crossed his face, and the corners of his mouth turned down in a grimace. "Maybe." He turned and strode from the room, closing the door behind him.

Janine heaved a sigh of relief and stretched out on the sofa, leaning back against one arm, resting her foot on the edge of the seat. Her ankle felt much better already, she decided. No more than a minor sprain. The fire hadn't yet driven the chill from the room, and she shivered, wishing Mark hadn't removed her cloak. Why did that impossible man always put her on the defensive, she thought, frowning in annoyance. Every time they met she was at a disadvantage. Now, true to form, he'd gone without even bidding her good-bye!

Moments later she heard footsteps echoing down the hall. Startled, she realized she'd not locked the front door after the redoubtable lieutenant had left. Suddenly the parlor door was flung open and Mark appeared, holding a copper kettle.

"Mark!" gasped Janine, jerking upright on the sofa.

"Who else?" he asked, smiling sardonically. He crossed the room to the hearth and hung the kettle on a hook over the fire. "I'll wait for this to heat."

"There's no need for that," she said tartly.

Mark came and sat down beside her on the sofa, his arms spread across the back, his legs stretched out before him. He gazed at her quizzically, as though she were a strange animal whose likes he'd never seen. Turning his amused, condescending smile upon her, he said, "Now tell me how a lovely child like you has escaped matrimony."

Nettled, she said abruptly, "That's none of your affair, Lieutenant Furneaux. You made it quite plain when we were—" Flustered, she broke off, searching for the right words.

He raised one eyebrow and laughed softly. "Traveling together?"

Janine blushed and stumbled on. ". . . plain that you wished to be rid of me, and you are. I don't know why you're here now!" She intended to sound stern, but her voice held an unaccountable mixture of curiosity and surprise.

His fingers plucked the lace ruffle edging the neck of her gown and his expression turned suddenly grave.

"Come now, you wouldn't have me abandon a damsel in distress, would you?"

She shivered and jerked her shoulder away from his hand. Again he was jeering at her, throwing her very words up to her.

"You've performed admirably, Lieutenant Furneaux," said Janine stiffly, "beyond the call of duty."

"Aren't you going to award me a medal?" His dark eyes mocked her. "Have you forgotten I've saved your very life at the Boar's Head Tavern, and most certainly your virtue!"

She drew in her breath sharply, her blue eyes blazing with indignation. "Not for want of trying to take it for yourself! And, as I've told you before, saving my life doesn't warrant you own me!" She turned away from him and sat stiff and straight, staring hard at the flickering fire.

"I haven't asked to own you, little darling." His right hand clasped her shoulder and he drew her gently into the curve of his arm in a comforting hug. "Come here, I'll keep you warm."

She turned her head to protest, but the expression in his dark eyes, the same wonder and recognition she had glimpsed in the carriage, held her motionless for a fraction of a second. In an instant his full sensuous lips were on hers, warm, gentle, seeking. Swiftly her hands came up hard against his chest, pushing him away.

With his free hand he grasped her wrist and drew her arm around his neck. He thrust her other hand away, and she collapsed against his chest. He sank back against the arm of the sofa, pulling her with him. Entwining his fingers in her hair, he loosened the pins, smoothing the soft silken strands and breathing in the sweet fragrance.

Janine pounded his shoulders with her fists, but her passion only seemed to inflame him further. His fingers held her chin firmly and he tilted her head back. With a sharp intake of breath she strained against him, his strong and muscular body challenging hers. He parted her lips with his own.

She felt giddy and light, as though she were falling, falling as in a dream—lost. She must save herself, must stop him, thought Janine frantically. Into her mind flashed the memory of the way she'd repulsed him that first night in bed at the tavern. All at once she went limp against him, lying detached and unresponsive, a dead weight in the curve of his body, hardly daring to breathe. His fingers under her chin trailed lightly down her neck, paused at the pulse throbbing in the small hollow of her throat, and moved downward, holding her breast in a firm caress. Shadows cast by the firelight danced like demons in the corner of the room. She closed her eyes and held her breath, steeling herself against his embrace.

Gently his hand moved to her other breast, stroking, savoring its fullness. She must stop him, she thought fervently, trying to summon the strength to move. In a second now she would leap up from the sofa and run from the room. The fire hissed softly on the hearth, and the shadows in the room deepened. Bracing her hands against the sofa, she struggled to sit up.

"I must go now," she murmured. Confusion muddled her thinking. Her mind was playing her false.

What she had meant to say was *"You* must go now." Somehow she spoke the words.

Mark pulled her down on his chest, his strong arms pressing her against him. "You don't want me to go now," he whispered in a soft, husky voice that sent a shiver rippling down her spine.

To her own horror and astonishment she realized he spoke the truth. Her heart was hammering so wildly, she feared she could not stand, and her breath was coming in gasps as if she had been running hard.

"Yes," she murmured, not knowing what she meant.

Her gown slipped from her shoulders and yet she was no longer cold. Warmth crept through her body and a delicious languor stole over her. She felt as though she were floating, carefree as a kite far above the earth.

From far away came a small, alien sound as of metal clicking upon metal, slicing into her consciousness. Then she heard the familiar creaking of a hinge, the slamming of a door. She sat bolt upright and quickly tugged her dress into place. Mark, his face flushed with passion, rose up on his elbows, muttering an oath. At the sound of boots stamping in the hallway, he leaped to his feet, shook his head as if to clear it, then strode to the fireplace and, taking up the poker, jabbed savagely at the blazing fire.

With fingers that shook, Janine had barely finished pinning her hair into a semblance of a chignon when the parlor door burst open and Papa stamped into the room, his cheeks pink from the wind and cold. His bright eyes were surprised and questioning as he gazed from Janine's glowing face to Lieutenant Furneaux, who seemed to be studying the fire intently.

"Papa!" said Janine in a voice that trembled with an emotion too quickly suppressed, "I've had an accident."

Dr. Mercer's penetrating gaze swept her from head to toe. "Nothing serious, I trust."

She poked her foot out from under the hem of her skirt.

"I slipped on the step outside the bookseller's and turned an ankle, that's all," said Janine breathlessly. "Fortunately Lieutenant Furneaux happened to be there and brought me home," she added, her face flaming.

Oh, dear God, thought Janine. Did Papa suspect what had taken place before he'd walked in? It seemed to her that the air was heavy with passion. What would he think of his daughter allowing herself to be compromised, all the more disgraceful for her being betrothed! Overwhelming feelings of guilt mingled with shame and remorse swept through her. But worst of all, she'd enjoyed herself beyond belief!

Dr. Mercer's gaze shifted to Mark, who stood lounging against the mantelpiece, bold as brass, impertinence and bland mockery shining from his dark eyes, as though he knew she'd been helpless to resist him and was savoring his triumph.

"I'm grateful to you, sir," said Dr. Mercer heartily. "It seems you're constantly rescuing my daughter from misadventures." Gazing with fond concern at his daughter, he bent to examine her ankle. When he felt the bones and twisted her foot this way and that, she barely winced.

"Seems a bit swollen. You might soak it in warm water with a few salts."

"Yes, Papa," said Janine a shade too eagerly. "That's what we intended. Lieutenant Furneaux filled the kettle and we're waiting for the water to heat."

"Hum, just so." He rubbed his chin and stood looking at her, a silent, thoughtful expression in his eyes.

"Zoë's gone, Papa," said Janine hastily, hoping to divert his mind from what he might be thinking. "She's usually home by dark. I'm fearful for her safety. . . ."

Dr. Mercer patted Janine's shoulder reassuringly. "Zoë's in the kitchen starting supper, *ma petite.*

"We've been to tend her sister—down with childbed fever." He turned to Lieutenant Furneaux. "Care to join us in a glass of brandy?"

Mark nodded. A lazy smile crossed his face as he met Janine's eyes across the room. "I believe we could all do with a tot of brandy."

It wasn't until they were sipping the fiery amber liquid and Mark was peering out the window at the falling snow that Dr. Mercer lifted the kettle from the hook in the fireplace. He pursed his lips, but said nothing. The water in the kettle had boiled dry.

Chapter 16

Janine fervently wished that Mark Furneaux had never entered her life. She was more than a little disturbed by the feelings he stirred in her. Whenever she was in his presence, some undercurrent flowed between them that she could not deny. There was something exciting about him that she could not define. Maybe it was the bold way his eyes looked out of his olive-tinted face with an annoying air of insolence, as if all women were his property to be enjoyed in his own good time. She'd certainly made it clear to him that she wasn't one of the throng of worshipers waiting to fall at his feet and yet, with utter disregard, he made love to her and she was helpless as a child to stop him. Anger and humiliation burned inside her at the thought. To make matters worse, she never had discovered what business had brought him to Virginia, or Philadelphia, and the little he'd told her of his past only served to make him more mysterious and exciting. Sternly she told herself she'd been caught off-guard, caught up by the romantic aura of a dashing officer of the militia. He was impossible, ill-bred, and no gentleman, and she vowed she would have nothing to do with him. She clenched her fists in an agony of impatience and frustration. If only she would hear from Jonathan, she thought for the thousandth time. Surely he could have written! Surely he *had* written and his letter had gone astray. Maybe tomorrow. . . .

* * *

As January of 1776 wore on, winter took over in earnest, holding the city in a grip of bitter cold. Harsh winds swept down from the north over frozen streets and patches of grime-covered snow in a succession of gloomy, cloud-covered days that seemed unending. And as the days dragged past with no word from Jonathan, Janine's heart grew heavy and her spirits flagged. She felt irritable and listless by turns and had no energy for anything. Even Papa's tonic of sulfur, molasses, and herbs had failed to revive her spirits.

Papa always came home early now, for during the winter, days at the hospital were governed by the sun, causing breakfast to be served early, lunch at noon, and after an early evening meal, lights out.

One evening late in January Papa returned from the hospital and found Janine curled up in his leather chair in the study, reading by the fire.

"Doctor Ransom tells me the pond near the hospital is frozen over," he said casually, warming his hands at the fire.

"Oh," said Janine, not looking up from her book.

Dr. Mercer picked up the pipe tongs and bent over the grate to light his pipe. "He mentioned he might ride home with me on Thursday and take you skating in the afternoon."

Janine sighed, letting her book drop in her lap. "Please tell Doctor Ransom I've no desire to go skating on Thursday, or any other day," she said wearily.

Dr. Mercer stood before his daughter, feet astride, drawing on his pipe, regarding her with a worried frown.

"You look pale and drawn, *ma petite*. You're too thin. You're not eating well. . . ."

"I'm not hungry, Papa."

He pushed out his lower lip, scowling. "Yes, and your refusal of food worries me more than anything else. Frankly I'm fearful you'll go into a decline and into an early grave."

Janine laughed. "Oh, Papa. What foolishness."

He lowered his head and peered sharply at her over the rims of his spectacles. "A little sunshine and exercise would be the best thing in the world for you. An afternoon skating on the pond is what your physician orders. Doctor Ransom is a fine young man. He's pleasant company, well-mannered, intelligent. . . ."

"But, Papa, he's so solemn and so serious and—"

"You could do worse than to keep him company," Papa plunged on. "At least he would take your mind off Jonathan. Slavery under one's own passions is worse than under tyrants! Dr. Ransom is a most attractive young man, you must admit. And if you'd give him half a chance, well, you might even marry someday!" Dr. Mercer waved his pipe agitatedly in the air. Clearly he was saying more than he'd intended, but he couldn't seem to stop. "It would be an excellent match!"

"Papa! You can't mean what you're saying!"

Dr. Mercer sank into a chair across from her. "Oh, I know, I know! There's Jonathan. But to tell the truth and shame the devil, I'm not at all certain Jonathan's the right husband for you, *ma petite*."

Janine gazed at him, her eyes wide and incredulous. "Surely you jest!"

He leaned toward her, looking her straight in the eyes. "Ellen will never give up the reins at Heritage Hall, Janine. And it's quite obvious that you will submit to Ellen's domination no better than I, myself, have done."

Janine saw a flicker of sadness in his eyes, then his expression turned grim.

"Your life at Heritage Hall is more apt to be a bed of thistles than roses," said Papa drawing deeply on his pipe.

Janine stared at him, stunned speechless. Papa was being so ridiculous, there was no point in discussing the matter. Then it came to her with startling clarity

that Papa was trying to prepare her in the event that
Jonathan never returned. Did Papa believe he
wouldn't? Her heart twisted painfully. It wouldn't
bear thinking about. As for her life at Heritage Hall,
Ellen would have to accept her as Jonathan's wife.
Jonathan would see to that!

Dr. Mercer smiled and his tone changed to one of
indulgent concern. "You understand, I'm not trying
to tell you whom to marry, but you can at least go
skating. . . ."

Vehemently Janine shook her head. "I've no need
for skating, nor for Richard Ransom. I'm not going,
Papa." She took up her book and gazed determinedly
at the page she had read before.

Dr. Mercer shrugged and blew a cloud of smoke
toward the ceiling. "Do what you think is best, *ma
petite.*"

On Thursday afternoon Papa came home early from
the hospital. Janine ran to the hallway to greet him
and stopped short in surprise. With him was Richard
Ransom, his lean freckled face tinged with red, his
amber eyes sparkling with pleasure and anticipation.
Janine greeted them pleasantly, but as Richard turned
to hang his cloak on the hall tree, she bent a sharp eye
on her father, her face crimson with annoyance, her
look speaking plainer than words: You old scoundrel,
you brought him home anyway!

Papa, standing behind Richard, gazed at the ceiling
and threw up his hands in a helpless gesture. With an
effort Janine controlled her irritation and led the way
into the parlor. Summoning a polite smile, she turned
to face Richard.

"Richard, I'm sorry. I asked Papa to tell you—I'm
not going skating with you today."

A perplexed, hurt expression flashed across his face
and was immediately gone. He was in an ebullient
mood that would not be put down and he spoke with

a cheerful air of optimism that Janine imagined he used when talking to a balky patient.

"Of course you're going. What nonsense. Hurry now, get your cloak and skates."

Janine's chin rose in stubborn defiance. "No, Richard."

He gave her a long, level stare, his voice was hard and unyielding. "Janine, you gave me your word . . . Christmas . . . remember?"

She faltered before his intense gaze and her cheeks grew hot. "I'm not good company, Richard. I'd only spoil your pleasure."

He said nothing, but his eyes held a reproach and the stubborn set of his jaw matched her own.

"Go along, Janine," said Papa smiling encouragingly. "You'll enjoy yourself once you're skimming over the ice."

She stood silent for a moment, biting her lip in vexation, thinking that, short of facing the two of them and making a tiresome scene, she had no choice. There was nothing but to give in gracefully. She would go now and get it over with, once and for all.

Janine rode beside Richard as they trotted up Spruce Street, out of town, past snow-covered farmland. In the distance ahead rose Penn's Hospital, the sun glistening on the ice-coated branches of the surrounding buttonwood trees. In an effort to make conversation Janine remarked, " 'Tis said the buttonwoods are used as a landmark by mariners sailing up the Delaware River."

Richard smiled, nodded, and said nothing until they drew rein between Sixth and Seventh Streets. Here the land sloped downward like a giant platter where the pond froze in winter. A throng of skaters were whirling over the ice, their long, colorful scarves flying out behind them. Richard laughed and nodded at a dashing figure clad in red coat and buckskin tights.

"Look, there's Doctor Foulke, skating High Dutch and cutting the letters of his name at one flourish!" For a moment she watched him gliding over the frosty white surface crisscrossed with slashes and curves. Distracted by a fragrant aroma, her gaze traveled across the pond. Smoke curled from a roaring bonfire where skaters were roasting chestnuts over hot coals. At the sight of everyone having such a merry time, her annoyance at being inveigled into coming out today faded. Skating with Richard may be fun after all, thought Janine, feeling considerably more cheerful.

They tethered their horses among the others under the bare branches of the elm trees and walked to the edge of the pond. Richard knelt before her and, taking up her skates, steel runners on wooden soles, bound them to her boots with leather straps. She placed one hand on his shoulder to keep her balance, shivering as the wind stung her cheeks and the cold crept through her skirts and jacket. It wasn't until they were skating side by side, circling the pond, that she began to feel warmth seeping through her body.

She leaned forward into the wind, breathing deeply, and the crisp, cold air filling her lungs was invigorating. Gliding swiftly over the ice in long, easy strides gave her a heady sense of freedom, as though she had wings. Despite herself, she was swept up in the happy mood of the laughing, shouting skaters. A feeling of exhilaration came over her, as though she'd wakened from a long sleep.

After a while Richard slid his left arm around her waist, clasped her right hand in his, and they struck out together. The soft hiss of the blades, their matching strides set up a pleasant rhythm that brought a sparkle into her blue eyes and a smile to her lips. She glanced up into Richard's face and in his eyes was an expression of warmth and utter devotion that sent a prickle of alarm down her spine. Abruptly she stiffened and her easy, swinging stride faltered.

"Tired?" asked Richard solicitously. "Come, we'll rest awhile."

They hunkered down by the fire and pulled off their gloves, warming their hands at the heat of the crackling flames. Then, donning his gloves, Richard scooped some chestnuts from the fire. They went to sit away from the other skaters under the stark branches of an elm, savoring the taste of the hot sweetmeats. When they finished, Richard sat beside her, silent and preoccupied. For once Janine was glad he was not good at idle chatter. She was enjoying the scene before her, watching the late afternoon sun moving slowly down the sky, bathing the white frosted pond in a golden light, casting cobalt shadows on the glistening snow. Her gaze traveled to Richard, staring at the pond, a faraway look in his eyes.

Finally he said, "We had a pond much like this one on the farm where I grew up. The day it froze over was a big event for my brothers and sisters and me. Skating was our main entertainment all winter long." He looked at Janine and grinned. "When we played crack the whip, I was always at the end of the tail—I was the youngest and smallest, you see. I skated across the ice on my bottom more often than my feet! And all summer long, we swam in the pond, in the evenings mostly. The rest of the time it seemed as though we all worked like Trojans to keep food on the table."

"Sounds like a terribly bleak existence," said Janine sympathetically.

Richard's sandy brows rose. "Oh, we were a happy family. At least we children were. We had each other—there were nine of us."

"Nine children!" exclaimed Janine. "Your mother must have been quite a woman."

"That she was." He nodded and a tender expression crossed his face and quickly vanished. "There were other children born after I was, who died in infancy. My mother died when I was twelve—of childbed fever—bearing yet another child—" He paused, his voice grew husky, his burr more pronounced.

"That's when I decided to become a doctor—a proper one with a degree, not a self-styled sawbones. . . ."

"An ambitious goal indeed for the son of a poor farmer!"

Richard nodded, smiling. "I was too young to realize it was impossible. And in reality, though we were poor as church mice, it was a blessing in disguise. It was because there were so many of us that I could get away. My older brothers and sisters stayed on—helped my father run the farm, so I was free to go. In fact they were glad to be rid of me—one less mouth to feed."

To Janine it sounded as though they'd all but booted him out the door. A surge of indignation mixed with sympathy flowed through her and her heart went out to him.

"Go on," she said. "What did you do after you left home?"

"Became a tutor to a wealthy family in New Jersey. My mother had taught me to read and write, you see. I hoarded every farthing I could lay my hands on to go to medical college. I'd dreamed of going to Edinburgh, but that was impossible." His words were a calm statement of fact, holding no self-pity. "Eventually I gained admission to the medical school of the College of Philadelphia. It was a great stroke of fortune to become an apprentice to your father."

He turned his head to look deeply into her eyes and Janine had the uncomfortable sensation that he felt fortunate in more ways than one. Nevertheless she felt a new respect and admiration for Richard Ransom.

"Your father must be very proud of you," said Janine.

"I suppose so, though he doesn't say much." Richard laughed. "A dour Scot, and a prime example of

the Presbyterian work ethic. Poor man never had any
time for the pleasures in life. But work must agree
with him. He's lived to a ripe old age—well over
fifty!"

"Incredible!"

"He's from tough stock. He was a Highland Scot, a
stern, fearless, hot-tempered rebel. When he was
twenty-two, he joined Bonnie Prince Charlie in the up-
rising of seventeen forty-five. Became a public enemy,"
said Richard with a wry laugh. "It's strange to think
of my sober father as a public enemy. He had to leave
Scotland or be taken as a political prisoner, so he fled
to the colonies. He'd planned to settle in North Carolina with the others, but his ship put in at Annapolis.
He was a redemptioner."

Janine frowned, puzzled. "A redemptioner?"

"It's like being an indentured servant. He couldn't
leave the ship till he was 'redeemed.' Had to agree to
a term of servitude to whoever would pay the captain
for his passage. Fortunately a wealthy tobacco farmer
named Johnson, also a Scot, from Southern Maryland,
redeemed him. My mother was an orphaned cousin
who lived with the Johnson family—a woman of gentle birth. She liked to write poetry, and I've often
thought this sustained her during the lean years with
my father. Anyway, they were married and when
father's contract expired, he received a land grant
along with a sum of money, tools, clothing, and food.
He was again one of the fortunate redemptioners.
Many of the men never collected their due. He farmed
his own land then, and reared our family. . . ." His
words trailed off and he stared reflectively across the
pond.

If Richard had inherited any of the qualities of the
stern, fearless, and hot-tempered rebel who had been
his father, Janine thought dryly, they had been
obliterated in his childhood either by the necessity of
scrounging for a living or of keeping out of harm's

way in the crowd of children swarming about the small farmhouse. Now it was easy to understand why he was so shy, so unsophisticated, so idealistic, and at the same time so dauntless and so determined to wrest what he wanted from life. She felt an overwhelming compassion for this earnest red-haired young doctor. Caught up in a closeness, an intimacy they had never before experienced, it occurred to her that it would not be unpleasant to share in Richard's life. The silence lengthened between them as they sat in the orange glow of the sunset, thinking their own thoughts. Richard sighed and turned to face her.

"Well, enough of my past." As if to lighten their mood, he asked, grinning, "Have you heard the story of Doctor Chapman and his friend?"

Janine shook her head.

"They were strolling up Spruce Street the other night past Mikveh-Israel Cemetery when the friend said, 'I think there's a light in the graveyard.' And Doctor Chapman said, 'Do not bother. It's only an Israelite!' "

Janine burst into laughter. "What a tease you are! I'd no idea you'd such humor lurking beneath that solemn exterior."

"I've never seen *you* so cheerful and lighthearted, my lass. Are you truly enjoying the day so much?"

To her own astonishment Janine found herself saying, "I haven't enjoyed myself so much since . . . I can't remember when!"

Suddenly his face was lighted with a happiness that became a palpable thing, enveloping them like a cloak; and in his eyes she read a look of love and longing so intense, it frightened her. Oh, dear lord, thought Janine, she would have to tell him now, before it was too late.

Gently she put her hand on his arm. "Richard"— she paused, searching for the right words—"I must tell you about Jonathan."

When she finished, the ardent light in his eyes had died and he gazed at her with the look of a wounded animal.

"Janine, that was an age ago." His voice was low and urgent. "You were a child then. You couldn't have known your own mind. You simply wanted to escape an unfortunate situation at Heritage Hall."

"No, Richard," said Janine quietly. "Jonathan and I truly love each other."

"Surely a man who truly loves you would have let you know he's alive! If he hasn't, it's because he knows that your love, or whatever you felt, was an infatuation. He has no wish to embarrass you by holding you to a pledge you've no wish to keep."

"He may have tried to let me know he's alive, Richard." Now that she voiced it, the hope sounded feeble to her own ears, and she felt close to despair. Silently she thanked Richard for not suggesting that it was Jonathan who no longer wished to honor their pledge. She looked down at her gloved hands, lacing her fingers tightly together. "And I do wish to keep my pledge."

Impulsively he took both her hands in his own, as though to give her strength to face what must be done. "Janine, sometimes we must put the past behind us. Cast out old memories to make room for the new. You can't go on living in the past."

"I'm not living in the past," said Janine in a choked voice, "but for the future. I'm waiting. Jonathan will come back to me. As soon as this rebellion is over, he'll come back. I know he will," she insisted with such vehemence that she couldn't have said whether she was trying harder to convince Richard or herself of the truth of her conviction. She withdrew her hands from his, and though it distressed her to say it, she said, "Richard, you must find someone else."

He drew back as though she'd struck him a blow, abject misery written on his thin, sensitive face. Her heart contracted with pain at having hurt him.

"All right, Janine." He bit off the words, his voice husky with emotion. He was trying to smile, but his eyes were somber. "I'll look for someone else. But while I'm looking, there's no harm in our continuing to see each other, is there?"

With an effort she suppressed a sigh. Thinking of his drab existence at Penn's Hospital and of Papa's fondness for his apprentice, she couldn't find the courage to cast him out entirely.

"As you wish, Richard." She shivered and stood up, brushing snow from her skirt. "We'd best be going now."

"Once more around the pond. All right?"

At her nod he sprang up and clasped her elbow lightly, leading her back to the pond. The sun had slipped down toward the horizon, and flaming orange and yellow ribbons streaked across the pewter sky beyond the skeletal army of trees in the distance. Only a few solitary skaters remained, blurred figures skimming over the ice. Janine was well aware that Richard was trying to recapture the carefree, jubilant mood they'd shared earlier, but it had gone, evanescent as their steamy puffs of breath on the cold air.

They rode home in silence in the gathering dusk. The only sound was the uneven beat of the horses' hooves on the frozen, rutted road and the raucous cry of crows circling the fields. Janine felt as though a pall of gloom had settled upon them.

That night, snug and warm behind the close-pulled curtains of her tester bed, sleep eluded Janine. Conscience-stricken, she tossed and turned. Oh, why had she told Richard she'd continue to see him? She berated herself for giving him false hope. And yet, she reasoned, she'd been honest with him, had told him there was no future for them together. Deep in her heart she knew she would never stop loving Jonathan and turn to Richard Ransom. Her emotions toward Jonathan had not changed since the day she first knew she was in love with him.

She rolled onto her stomach, burrowing under the quilt, her face pressed into her pillow, yearning, aching for Jonathan, her body taut with her need for him. At last she drifted off to sleep, thinking longingly of Jonathan riding Brandy at her side, smiling, his hair shining gold in the sunshine.

Chapter 17

During the weeks that followed, Richard continued to call on her. At first she was on her guard, alert for any sign of affection or romantic intent. But never once had he betrayed to Janine by one look, one word, anything but the casual interest one would show the daughter of a friend and colleague. An easy camaraderie sprang up between them that she thoroughly enjoyed and she came to look forward to his visits.

They skated on the pond on sunny afternoons; went on sleigh rides on clear, cold, starlit nights; attended concerts and balls; and once weekly or more Richard would take supper with Janine and Dr. Mercer. Afterward Janine would play the spinet—tunes of Mozart and Haydn, or lively arias. More often than not Papa and Richard, charged with fervor and enthusiasm, would boom out the words to "Chester" and other popular tunes of the day. Frequently they would gather round the card table for a game of cards, or they would discuss puzzling ailments of patients or the news of the Second Continental Congress and the rebellion.

When the talk turned to war, Janine sat quietly, her heart fluttering with anticipation and dread, listening to the bits and pieces of news that Papa and Richard had heard in the coffee houses and taverns. At the London Coffee House on post days the latest English and American newspapers and magazines were to be found, and the latest news brought by special corre-

spondents elsewhere. Members of the Congress who
frequented City Tavern, Frye's, The Indian Queen,
and other taverns, kept the town informed of all that
transpired in the State House.

Although Janine was desperate for news of General
Washington's army, she lived in constant dread of
hearing that fighting had broken out. With great effort
she pushed her anxiety down in a dark corner of her
mind. Boston was a long way off and a battle seemed
remote. She told herself over and over that battles
were not fought in the winter and when spring came,
the rebels would have to go home to plow their land
and plant their crops.

She was jolted back to reality by news that caused
a cold knot of fear to settle in the pit of her stomach.
Early in March the Yankees, under General Washington, had, overnight, erected two powerful forts on
Dorchester Heights overlooking Boston. Supported by
more than fifty cannons, mortars, and howitzers hauled
from Ticonderoga by Henry Knox on a forty-two sled
ox-train, they bombarded Boston unmercifully. Sir
William Howe had ordered his fleet and shore batteries to fire upon the Americans, but the cannonballs
fell short. Finally the British drew back, and on
March 17 General Howe evacuated Boston. More than
one hundred black-hulled ships carrying 9000 soldiers,
1200 women and children dependents, and 1100 unhappy Loyalists lingered in the harbor for ten days,
then departed for Halifax, Nova Scotia.

Richard Ransom summed up the Yankee point of
view one rainy evening, pacing to and fro in the
warm, cozy parlor.

"Not only is it a great victory for the colonists, but
Washington has won his first victory without fighting
a battle!"

Janine's heart sang with joy. If there had been no
battle, then Jonathan must be safe! Naturally she was
happy over General Washington's incredible victory,

and said so. That Howe's failure to put down the rebellion was a British defeat did not occur to her.

"The most incredible thing of all," Richard went on, his russet eyes gleaming with satisfaction," is that there's not a single Redcoat on the Atlantic coast from Falmouth to Savannah. Our thirteen colonies are unoccupied, united and, for all practical purposes, independent."

Janine stared at Richard in stunned disbelief. Saying they were independent did not make it so.

"The problem," said Dr. Mercer, rubbing his chin thoughtfully, "is where will Howe strike next? I wouldn't be surprised if he sailed to New York. It would be a rich prize, for from it runs the strategic waterway to Canada, the control of which could decide the war."

Janine's mind fastened on the word *war*. Papa thought there would be a war! She hadn't thought of the rebellion as war. War meant long drawn-out fighting and killing and devastating the land, and the thought struck terror into her heart.

It did nothing to relieve Janine's mind to learn that General Washington apparently concurred with Papa. Around the middle of April news was brought that Washington had rushed his troops overland to New York City. At the same time they heard that the British had ordered General Clinton to set sail along the coast.

"It's rumored he's to meet Sir Peter Parker's fleet out of Cork," Papa told her one night at supper. "Parker's bringing two thousand troops under Cornwallis, who's expected to attack somewhere in the South."

Janine frowned. "Putting down rebels who have taken up arms is one thing, Papa. But initiating an attack. . . ."

"Congress is trying to counter him. They've sent General Charles Lee to dodge about the seaboard."

Papa's blue eyes danced in amusement. "Lee says he's confused as a dog in a dancing school—that the British can fly in an instant to any spot where they choose with their canvas wings, whereas he can act only from surmise."

Janine drew a deep breath and said nothing. She wished Papa would stop talking about the war.

"In point of fact," Dr. Mercer went on, "that could be an advantage to the colonists. True, the British move at will upon the sea while the Americans move on land, but they've the whole country at their disposal. If their armies retire a few miles back from the navigable rivers, ours cannot follow them."

Thoroughly confused, Janine sighed and set down her fork. "If the British can't send enough troops to subdue all the colonies at one time, Papa," she said unhappily. "How can they expect to win a war?"

"With the help of colonials loyal to the king," said Dr. Mercer confidently. "There are hundreds of citizens in every province well disposed to government from whom they'll no doubt have assistance. New York is a hotbed of Loyalists. There's South Carolina, and our own town is seething with them."

The memory of Peggy Shippen's fiery tirade flashed into her mind. And wasn't she herself loyal to the king? Oh, if only things could be the way they were before this dreadful business began!

Late in May Papa came home with the news that Mistress Washington was in town visiting the John Hancocks and that one of his colleagues had inoculated her against smallpox.

Janine's heart leaped to her throat. "Is General Washington here in Philadelphia?" Maybe he'd come to tell the Congress the cause was hopeless. . . . Maybe he—

Dr. Mercer shook his head. "Still in New York, waiting for Howe's missing fleet to appear."

Disappointed, Janine turned and stared out the

window. "Was the inoculation painful?" she asked absently.

"Nothing to it. You just scratch the skin with a needle that has been tipped with scrapings from a victim of the disease. Dr. Kuhn gave me some of the scrapings and I thought we'd inoculate ourselves as well. Seems a good idea, don't you think?"

Janine shrugged dispiritedly. "If you think so, Papa."

One hot, sultry evening early in June Dr. Mercer and Janine were scanning the *Pennsylvania Gazette* in the parlor when a familiar name leaped up at her from the page she was reading.

"Papa!" she cried, clutching the paper. Have you read this. . . . ? Richard Henry Lee's resolution introduced in Congress on Friday last?"

Without waiting for his reply, she read in a voice that shook with indignation and outrage:

Resolved that these United Colonies are, and of right ought to be, free and independent States, that they are absolved from all allegiance to the British Crown, and that all political connection between them and the state of Great Britain is, and ought to be, totally dissolved.

"Thomas Paine and his *Common Sense* caused this," fumed Janine. "Attacking the British government, the king himself, the very institution of royalty. He ridicules the king, depicting him as a harsh and savage brute. Doesn't he realize that we have friends in England worth keeping on good terms? Nobody wants a war, Papa!" she cried in despair. "How can we hope for a reconciliation in the face of such ravings from Paine and Lee?"

Dr. Mercer looked up with startled eyes, as though astonished at his daughter's outburst. "Dear God,

Janine. Where have you been? The time for reconciliation is long past! Why, on the very day the *Common Sense* went on sale in Philadelphia, the king concluded a contract with Duke Karl of Brunswick to hire thirty thousand Hessians to put down 'the rebellious Americans.'

"As for Paine, he's answered the colonists' doubts and fears with simple, clear arguments. When I read his pamphlet I realized that unconsciously I'd been thinking the same thoughts."

"Papa!" she burst out aghast. "How could you!" She felt betrayed, as though her own father had deserted her and gone over to the enemy.

Dr. Mercer leaned forward in his chair, looking her directly in the eyes. "*Ma petite, Common Sense* is working a powerful change in the minds of everyone. Paine writes with sound doctrine and unanswerable reasoning. Conviction is replacing the sentimental attachment we've had for the past." He sighed and pushed out his lower lip. "I'm afraid the desire for independence has become, in John Adam's words, a torrent."

"That well may be, Papa," Janine said, "but we can't exist without England! What can they be thinking of?"

"Independence!" said Dr. Mercer shaking his head emphatically. "I heard today that Congress has appointed a committee of five to prepare a draft—they call it a declaration of independence—and John Adams, Roger Sherman, Robert Livingston and Doctor Franklin will serve, as well as your friend Thomas Jefferson, who's been entrusted with the task of writing it."

"A declaration," repeated Janine uncertainly. "I'm surprised that Doctor Franklin isn't writing it."

Dr. Mercer leaned back in his chair, grinning. "It's said at the tavern that Dr. Franklin told Jefferson: 'I have made it a rule, whenever in my power, to avoid becoming a draftsman of papers reviewed by a public body.' Says he took his lesson from an apprentice hatter."

Janine smiled wryly, considering Papa's news. "Mister Jefferson has a reputation for literature and a happy talent of composition, but nothing will come of it, will it, Papa?"

Dr. Mercer threw his head back and laughed heartily. "It's hardly likely that the king will recognize our status as self-governing dominions almost on a par with Great Britain."

"*Our* status, Papa?" asked Janine with a lift of her brows.

Dr. Mercer smiled ruefully. *"Touché, ma petite!"*

June passed into July of 1776, hot, humid, enervating, with no cooling breeze at night to bring relief. As the city sweltered under the intense heat spell, Janine put out of her mind all disturbing thoughts of Richard Henry Lee's Resolution, Thomas Paine's *Common Sense*, and Thomas Jefferson's Declaration. She had enough problems on her own doorstep, for dysentery, fevers, and smallpox ran rampant through the town.

The vast swamp areas bordering the town were thick with mosquitoes, and exposed piles of garbage in the city stenched with rot. The ships, lying at anchor on Water Street, brought disease along with their cargoes. And the mosquitoes fed upon diseased passengers or crewmen who lay in squalid hotel rooms near the wharves. They swarmed over the city spreading disease among the hapless citizens. The wealthy packed up their families and drove out of town to spend the summer at their country estates in Germantown. People walking on the street or in carriages held to their nostrils sponges soaked with boiled wine, vinegar, and herbs to ward off smallpox, and Janine kept a pot of the brew boiling inside the house.

Despite the annoying invasion of mosquitoes, she threw open the windows hoping to catch a breath of air, only to be assaulted by the racket of coaches, wagons, and drays thundering over the cobblestones, and the reek of slop that seeped from the necessaries in the yards into the brick gutters.

One evening she sat by the window in the parlor, listlessly waving a bamboo fan, feeling as though she would expire of the heat pressing down on them. In the distance she saw heavy black clouds riding down the valley of the Schuylkill and the Delaware. The curtains billowed, filled by a gust of wind. A crash of thunder and streaks of lightning slashed the sky while huge drops of rain spattered on the sill. Janine jumped up and ran to close the windows against the sudden storm that now pelted on the roof and rattled the shutters.

"Thank God," said Janine, sighing with relief. "At last the heat spell is broken."

Dr. Mercer shook his head. "It's no good, *ma petite*. These abrupt changes in weather only weaken people's resistance. I fear the diseases will only grow worse."

Papa's prediction proved correct. For those who remained in the city, the environment was becoming increasingly more dangerous. Many people were dying of smallpox, dysentery, and fevers. The victims were largely the poor who could not afford the cost of medical treatment. Dr. Mercer was gone from early morning till late at night, treating the sick. And when he came in, his shoulders sagged and his face was etched with weariness. Janine dosed all those who came to her door, gaunt, hollow-eyed, ridden with fever, whether they paid or not. By the end of the day she fell into bed exhausted, grateful that she was too tired to think. She hated to go out, for she could scarce walk a square without quailing at the shocking sight of a death cart rumbling down the street bearing five or six coffins.

"The poor creatures die without number," she told Papa despairingly. "Where are they taking them?"

"They dig large pits in the Negroes' burying ground and put forty or fifty coffins in the same hole." Dr. Mercer sighed tiredly. "Disease is the truly hopeless battle, I'm afraid."

At the same time came news of another battle that had raged several days earlier on the coast of South Carolina where General Clinton had joined Admiral Sir Peter Parker and his nine-warship fleet. The patriots were not caught unprepared, for they had learned from an intercepted letter of the projected capture of the important port of Charleston. General Charles Lee with two thousand troops had hurried south to defend the town. In order to take Charleston the British had to silence the guns on Sullivan's Island which commanded the channel into the harbor. On the morning of June 28 the British men-of-war launched the attack, letting loose incessant broadsides upon the island. Colonel William Moultrie, manning his palmetto fort, returned a furious cannonade in an almost continual blaze and roar until he ran out of powder at eleven o'clock that night. Clinton's army, attempting an amphibious landing, discovered that the channel was deeper than they thought and abandoned the effort. Three of Sir Peter Parker's frigates ran aground. In fact the British ships suffered so incredibly under Moultrie's relentless bombardment that in the dead of night the men-of-war cut their cables and stole away.

Janine listened skeptically to Papa's account, thinking the report was impossible to believe even though he assured her that the news was quoted directly from a letter written by General Lee to Congress.

"Lee claims it was one of the most furious and incessant fires he ever saw and heard," said Dr. Mercer, "and Moultrie said never did men fight more bravely!"

Janine closed her ears and mind against Papa's

words, shrinking inside herself, wishing he'd stop talking about fighting and killing.

To make matters worse, on the third of July came the rumor, later confirmed by dispatches, that on June 29 Sir William Howe's missing British fleet had appeared in New York harbor. He had sailed from Nova Scotia and was threatening New York. All Janine's worry and anxiety came back tenfold. She tried to listen to Papa babbling excitedly over the debate raging in the State House over Thomas Jefferson's declaration, but her mind, grappling with the thought that Jonathan was in danger, refused to take in what he was saying.

The next morning Janine awoke to the sound of the cowherd blowing his horn in Dock Street. Drowsily she rolled over and parted the bed curtains. Thank goodness Zoë would let out their cow so the cowherd could drive it off to a neighboring pastureland for the day. She went to the window and stared out at the burning sun climbing the sky. In the predawn darkness she'd heard rain pattering on the roof and now a steamy heat lay like a blanket smothering the town. Her gaze dropped to the street below. A farmer's cart rumbled past. Women hurried toward the new factory, flax spinners, thought Janine from the looks of them. A man with a barrow hawking oysters trundled by. Zoë was scrubbing the front stoop. Janine sighed heavily. The day promised to be like any other. And then she remembered. It was not like any other. Howe was threatening New York! Where was Jonathan now? Was he fighting the British this very minute? The clock on the State House struck seven, startling her from her gloomy thoughts. She mustn't spend the day torturing herself with what might be happening to Jonathan.

After breakfast she threw herself into a frenzy of distilling bitters, boiling syrups and making ointments and salves to replenish her ravaged apothecary. By the end of the day her feet were leaden, her back was stiff, and her head ached from bending over the steaming kettles, mixing, stirring, filling bottles and jars. Perspiration beaded her forehead and her dress clung to her skin. She had all but finished stacking the bottles and jars on the shelves of the hutch when she heard the front door burst open and footsteps stamp down the hall, into the kitchen. Papa stopped short before her red-faced, eyes bright, breathless with excitement.

Janine pushed a damp strand of hair back from her face with her hand. "Papa! Slow down. You'll have apoplexy rushing around in this heat."

"Janine," he said puffing, "I've just come from Mister Smith's tavern. The deed has been done! The declaration. It's said the declaration was reported by the committee, agreed to by the house, and signed by every member present except Mister John Dickinson who put forth a fervent protest, but I expect he'll come round."

Janine felt her knees go weak and prickles rise at the nape of her neck. "That can't be!" she cried. "Surely it's only another rumor."

"Twelve colonies voted for it!" said Papa in a loud, triumphant tone. "Only New York abstained."

She sank down in a chair by the fireplace, feeling as though the earth had dropped from under her feet. The day she'd thought would never come was upon them. It was beyond belief. Papa went on, recounting who'd said what, but she wasn't listening. She bit her lip, thinking, trying to grasp the significance of this declaration. Would this mean she'd have to choose sides? If so, was she a Tory like Peggy Shippen or a rebel like Jonathan? She stiffened her back, and her chin rose in determination.

"I wouldn't vote for it either," she burst out, her blue eyes sparkling with outrage. "I'd refuse to be coerced into a decision I'd no heart to make!"

Papa stood before her, regarding her with a grave expression. "It's said at the tavern that Doctor Franklin told the Congress, 'We must hang together, or assuredly we will all hang separately.' "

Janine's eyes met Papa's, their gaze locked and held. She could feel the blood rushing to her face, pounding in her ears. "I shall remain neutral," she said in a low, quiet voice.

Chapter 18

Four days later Janine and Dr. Mercer stood among the crowd in the heat of the morning sun in the State House yard. The leaves on the elm trees drooped. Even the birds were still. It seemed the world was holding its breath waiting for what was to come. Janine gazed hastily about the yard. The only person here she knew was the august personage of Charles Biddle, whose thick brows seemed to be drawn in disapproval. The most respectable citizens were conspicuous by their absence, she noted. Strange, considering it was they who had spoken out most strongly for independence.

A murmur rose from the crowd, and standing on tiptoe, Janine could see members of Congress striding through the doorway and down the steps of the State House: tall, red-haired Mr. Jefferson; Dr. Franklin's long thin gray hair and spectacles; Sam Adams, wig askew. All were solemn and unsmiling, as though weighed down by the seriousness of what they'd done, thought Janine. A shiver of excitement ran down her back as Colonel John Nixon, carrying a scroll, mounted a platform and in a powerful voice began to read: "When in the course of human events. . . ."

Janine listened intently to the clear, precise words of Jefferson's document justifying the steps taken on July second when Congress had voted for independence. Plainly it was intended to persuade the world that the colonists were in the right in this family quarrel. There was a statement of purpose, Jefferson's theory of inalienable rights, specific grievances, followed by an account of tyrannous acts of George III, concluding with the colonies declaring themselves independent. As John Nixon finished reading, a hum of conversation rippled through the crowd, mixed with shouts of approval. A thunderous roll of drums reverberated around the yard and suddenly the bell in the flimsy wooden steeple began to toll, ringing out deep-throated and clear across the town.

To Janine it held a triumphant tone, as though heralding a victory that had already been won, that struck the very fiber of her being.

"No one's afraid to ring the bell today, Papa," said Janine smiling.

Shading his eyes against the sun, Dr. Mercer gazed up at the tower. "That old bell's been hanging there for twenty-five years. I suppose it will hang a few more. The Pennsylvania Assembly ordered it in fifty-one to commemorate the fiftieth anniversary of the signing of the charter of Philadelphia by William Penn." He turned to look at Janine, a peculiar smile on his face. "Come to think of it, the inscription is prophetic—a Biblical verse from Leviticus that begins, 'Proclaim Liberty throughout all the land, unto all the inhabitants thereof. . . .' I don't recall the rest."

How ironic, thought Janine, smiling to herself, that the great bell should once again proclaim liberty! Her attention was distracted by a small knot of men clamoring about the doorway of the State House. She watched while in a frenzy of patriotic ardor a man climbed a ladder and hauled down the king's Royal Arms of gold, red, and blue from over the doorway, carried it to the street and set it ablaze. Her gaze was riveted to the scene in horrible fascination while the lion and the unicorn stood proudly in flames to the end.

A sense of foreboding swept through her so strong that it left her weak-kneed and trembling. For the first time she faced squarely the turmoil going on

about her, the events she had chosen to disregard. The
time had come to put aside her fantasy of returning
to the peaceful, ordered existence she'd known as a
child. At last she perceived the truth of John Adams's
ominous warning: "We shall have a long, obstinate,
and bloody war to go through." Unconsciously she
squared her shoulders and stiffened her spine. Her
expression changed to one of grim determination.
Whatever happens, thought Janine, *I'll put a good
face on it.*

Several days later, as though bearing out John
Adams's prediction, Dr. Mercer told Janine that a few
wounded soldiers had been admitted to the hospital.

"But, Papa," cried Janine, dismayed, "Penn's Hospital is for the sick-poor!"

Dr. Mercer shrugged and smiled. "It's no hardship,
Janine. We've only fifty-six patients now, half our
capacity."

The following day it was reported that more than
one hundred British ships, commanded by Sir Peter
Parker, had anchored off Sandy Hook. To Janine it
seemed the war was closing in around them as relentlessly as a noose tightening about their necks. Janine's
fears for Jonathan's safety returned to plague her in
full measure when news came that on August 22
Howe's troops had landed unopposed on Staten Island.
General Clinton had returned with his 3,000 men.
And to command his squadron, in sailed Admiral
Viscount Howe himself. Washington had mustered
less than 10,000 men to oppose the 25,000 British and
German soldiers who had not yet disembarked from
the fleet, dividing his army between Manhattan and
Brooklyn Heights. The battle for Long Island was
about to begin.

Though she tried to conceal it, a deep melancholy
possessed Janine. If Richard noticed her somber mood,
he made no comment. His visits to the narrow brick
house on Second Street occurred with increasing fre-

quency, but Janine attributed it to the easing up of admissions to the hospital. She was grateful for their outings, for being with Richard took her mind off her anxiety over Jonathan's safety. Richard took her to the Rittenhouse orrery to watch the stars plough their relentless course across the heavens. They visited the waxworks to view Biblical characters and such notables as George Whitfield, the evangelist, and to see the seventeen-foot model of the City of Jerusalem carved by two Germantown men. They attended the horse races held at Center Square. Once they stayed home to listen to Papa and his friends perform chamber music in the parlor, entranced by the soft intimacy of music by Handel and Bach.

The last week in August Richard surprised her by buying tickets to the assembly. The assemblies held at Alexander Hamilton's on Front Street were always gala occasions. This particular evening was to begin with a concert, after which there would be dancing followed by a candlelight supper. Janine was delighted. Then, on second thought, she decided she would have to tell Richard she couldn't go. What could she be thinking of, wondered Janine guiltily, dashing off to a party, kicking up her heels when poor Jonathan was probably lying in some mudhole being shot at by the British.

In a sharp, indignant voice Papa took her to task, pointing out that she could do Jonathan no earthly good by staying home; that he could hardly expect her to hibernate during his absence; and furthermore, that since she had accepted Dr. Ransom's previous invitations, it would be rude and unkind to deprive him of her company on this special occasion.

Janine listened to Papa's heated remonstrance in wide-eyed astonishment. Suddenly everything he said seemed perfectly logical. Her heart beat excitedly at the prospect of going. It seemed like ages since she'd had a chance to dress up and go to a dance. Finally she allowed him to persuade her to accept Richard's invitation.

Three days before the assembly Janine sat before the mirror over the lowboy in her room, struggling with her hair in an effort to arrange it in the new style, swept up in a tower atop her head.

"We'll practice now," said Janine, smiling into the mirror at Zoë's tall slender figure standing behind her, "so we can dress it right for the assembly."

Zoë nodded, frowning in concentration, her deft fingers sweeping up the mass of shining black hair, putting in a bodkin here, taking one out there, and at last it was done.

Janine took up a hand mirror and turned to see the effect from the back. Then, facing the mirror, she surveyed her reflection critically and burst out laughing.

"Oh, Zoë," wailed Janine. "I look as though I've taken a fright! It will never do. I don't know why I ever told Richard I'd go!" She threw up her hands in a helpless gesture. "I haven't even a decent gown to wear."

"'Course you do, Miss Janine!" Zoë strode to the wardrobe, rummaged through the gowns hanging inside, and brought out a rich apricot silk trimmed in lace. "You look grand in this one. . . ."

Janine shook her head. "I tried it on, Zoë. It hangs on me like a shroud."

Zoë hung the gown back in the wardrobe and turned to face Janine, an implacable expression on her dark face.

"They's a trunk in the garret where your mama stored yard goods, long time ago. You can just sew you a gown right quick."

Janine crossed the room and flung herself on the bed in despair. "Zoë, you know how I hate to sew. I could never make a gown!"

Zoë's soft black eyes grew hard, her voice stern and commanding. "Miss Janine, you got to git up and git.

You git up in that garret and find you some goods and
I help you make you a gown."

Janine lay on the bed unmoving, staring disconso-
lately up at the ceiling.

Zoë marched across the room and stood over her,
hands on her hips, glowering. "You go 'long with you
now," she said fiercely, "else I take a switch to you!"

Her tone reminded Janine of days long ago when
she was a child and Zoë had used the same words and
the same threat to make her behave. She laughed in
spite of herself and reluctantly rose up from the bed.

"Hold your fire, Zoë. I'm going!"

The garret was dim and shadowy and dust motes
danced in the pale light that filtered in from the
dormer window overlooking the river. She made her
way through a welter of cast-off furniture, hatboxes,
and traveling cases, past a discarded birdcage and a
dress form to a battered leather-bound trunk shoved
back in a dark corner. Inside, as Zoë had thought, were
lengths of yard goods. She lifted out a bolt of embroidered white linen, yellowed with age. There were
gray bombazine, too somber, decided Janine; a rich
brown velvet, stifling in the August heat; several
lengths of rich silks, an emerald green, pale pink, and
teal blue, none of which were enough to fashion a
gown. Sighing, she reached for the last length of fabric
wrapped in tissue paper at the bottom of the trunk.
Impatiently she ripped off the layers of paper and beneath its rustling folds glimpsed a delicate blue brocade. She shook out the fabric and a pang of nostalgia
swept through her. It was not a length of fabric as she'd
thought at first, but a gown—the gown her mother had
worn to sit for the portrait on the medallion Papa had
given her.

Clutching the dress to her bosom she ran downstairs
to her room and held it up to her shoulders before the
mirror. Trimmed with garlands of rosebuds, the voluminous skirt was caught up on each side to display a

flower-embroidered petticoat. *Oh, how lovely it is!* she thought.

Quickly she undressed and slipped the gown on over her head. With shaking fingers she fastened the hooks. If only it weren't too tight! She sucked in her breath. Worry and anxiety had melted away enough weight so that if she stood up straight and breathed carefully, it would do. Smoothing out the wrinkles, she gazed at her reflection in the mirror, pleased with what she saw. The blue brocade turned her eyes the color of hyacinths and accentuated the whiteness of her skin. It was a bit long, but surely she could manage to sew a hem!

On the evening of the assembly Janine dressed her hair with a cluster of curls caught up at the back of her head and a soft wave combed from a center part falling softly over her brow. Among her jewelry she found her medallion, and smiling fondly at her mother's portrait, she fastened it around her neck. "Mercy," she murmured, surveying herself in the mirror, "I'd almost forgotten what I look like!"

She picked up her ivory fan and went downstairs to the study where Papa was reading a new medical book sent from England. She tiptoed into the room and stood before him.

"Papa?" she said softly.

Dr. Mercer glanced up from his book and gazed at her as though thunderstruck.

"Will I do, Papa?"

Dr. Mercer removed his spectacles and brushed away a sudden mist that rose before his eyes. *"Ma petite,* you are so beautiful, you take my breath away!"

"Thank you, Papa!" Smiling, her eyes shining with happiness, she pirouetted before him.

Dr. Mercer cleared his throat. "Do you know, the dress you're wearing is Nicole's—your mother's wedding dress—the dress she wore the day we married. You are the image of her. . . ."

At that moment Zoë appeared in the doorway to announce Dr. Ransom.

The admiration that lighted Richard's eyes at the sight of Janine was no less than Papa's, Janine noted with satisfaction. Blushing, he blurted, "How lovely you look!"

Janine smiled to herself. Though Richard was sparing with words, it was enough. Enough to reassure her that her gown would do nicely and that she looked her best.

By the time they arrived at Alexander Hamilton's, the long room was crowded with elegantly dressed ladies and gentlemen. Evidently her gown was not the only one to have been brought out from storage, thought Janine amused. She and Richard mingled with the other guests, admiring banks of yellow, rust, and white chrysanthemums and thick stands of potted palms that graced the candlelit room. They sat quietly on stiff-backed chairs listening to the musicians playing selections for the violin, trumpet, and woodwind choirs. A cool breeze from the river wafted in through the open windows, bringing relief from the late August heat, but Janine fanned herself restlessly, her toes tapping under her skirts, eager for the dancing to begin.

When at last the concert ended, someone pushed forward a waist-high walnut box on legs that reminded Janine of the lowboy in her room at home. Everyone rose and crowded around the strange-looking object, questioning, murmuring excitedly.

"What on earth is that contraption?" Janine whispered in Richard's ear.

"It's a glass armonica—one of Doctor Franklin's miscellaneous inventions," said Richard, grinning. "I saw one on exhibit at Annapolis two years ago."

A potbellied man in a plum-colored suit came forward and raised the lid. Janine edged nearer, gazing down at the instrument in fascination. Inside, a row of colorful glass hemispheres, at least three dozen, she

thought, were fastened on their sides to an axis. A
hush fell over the audience. With a bow and a flourish
the man in the plum-colored suit began to turn a
handle that projected from one end.

"He's turning the glasses to keep them wet," Richard whispered. "They revolve through a trough of
water."

Intrigued, Janine leaned forward to see, and as the
man rubbed the glass discs with his finger, they yielded
a strangely sweet tune. A chorus of delighted ooh's and
ah's rose from the guests.

When the man finished, a spontaneous murmur of
approval and applause went up, then the cluster of
people around the armonica began to mill about,
chatting of this and that while servants pushed the
chairs back against the walls so the dancing could
begin. With Richard following behind her, Janine
threaded her way through the crowded room and was
brought up short by a uniformed militiaman blocking
her way. Glancing up, she met the dark-eyed gaze of
Mark Furneaux.

Startled, she gave a little gasp of surprise and one
hand went to her throat. What in the world was *he*
doing here? His lips curved in a sardonic smile and he
nodded his head slightly in greeting. Janine's gaze
darted to his companion. She could see only the
woman's back and Mark's hand clasping her elbow.
At that moment the woman turned around as if to see
what was occupying the attention of her escort.

Janine froze. On Mark's arm was Anne Delaney,
dressed in a scarlet satin gown revealing a most daring display above the low-cut décolletage. Her silver-
blond hair, piled high in the newest fashion, was
adorned with red feathers and jewels that sparkled
like diamonds. A beauty patch graced one rosy cheek.
Overdone and ostentatious, thought Janine waspishly.
She looks like a bird of paradise. By sheer determination of will she resisted a mad impulse to reach out

and snatch the feathers from the woman's towering coiffure.

Anne Delaney swayed against Mark's side, curling her hand around his arm with a possessive air, and stared at Janine with lofty condescension, her light blue eyes cold under stiff, pale lashes.

Janine managed to return Mark's smile, but she wanted desperately to bolt and run. Under Anne Delaney's cool, scornful appraisal, she felt like a naïve child in her dainty, blue brocade gown and flowered underskirt. Rigid and tense, she introduced Dr. Ransom, and as the men shook hands she saw Mark Furneaux taking Richard's measure with that lazy, insolent grin on his face. Richard shifted his feet and looked ill-at-ease. The four of them stood staring at each other for a long, awkward moment, a small island among the guests eddying about them.

Finally Janine said in a high, choked voice, "Do tell us of your recent travels, Lieutenant Furneaux. I'm sure we'd be very interested. . . ."

Before he could reply, Anne Delaney broke in imperiously, "We've no time to chat." Then, gazing up into Mark's face with wide, adoring eyes, she said, "Mark, darling, the music is starting." Abruptly she turned her frosty gaze on Janine.

"Mark and I are dancing," said the woman in a haughty voice that plainly indicated that the conversation was at an end. She turned her back and, tucking her hand in the crook of Mark's arm, started to move away, pulling him with her.

Mark cocked one eyebrow at Janine and shrugged as though he were powerless to resist being summarily dragged away by this painted witch. Fuming, Janine watched them move across the room, Anne Delaney clinging to Mark's arm with a familiarity that to her mind bespoke a closeness she had observed to exist only between lovers. Her heart twisted painfully in her breast and she was astonished to realize that she could quite cheerfully have wrung Anne Delaney's long, beautiful neck. Sternly she told herself that a man who was content to let himself be led around by the nose wasn't worth his salt and that it mattered not a farthing to her what Mark Furneaux did.

She bent her mind to being pleasant to Richard, dancing quadrilles and minuets with sparkling eyes and merry laughter on her lips that swiftly changed to a disdainful glance and a stiff smile whenever they passed Mark and his scarlet woman.

When the musicians struck up a tune heralding the start of the country dances and jigs, Richard begged off and disappeared into the card room to engage in a game of brag. Janine excused him good-humoredly and, having no lack for partners, whirled dizzily from one to the next. Toward the end of the evening she found herself grasped firmly about the waist by a pair of powerful arms and, looking up, met the dark, laughing eyes of Mark Furneaux.

She drew in her breath sharply, so conscious of his nearness, the warmth of his body, the touch of his hand on hers, that her knees trembled under her.

He drew back from her, holding her at arm's length, as his bold eyes roamed her body appreciatively. She could feel her cheeks burning in embarrassment. Unaccountably she wanted him to see her at her best and yet she was apprehensive too. Would he remember their last meeting as she did, as though seared in her mind with a branding iron? Flustered, she asked, "How do I look?"

She was watching him, her eyes big and uncertain, and she broke into a delighted smile as Mark gave a long, low whistle. "How do you look? Like an angel!"

She gazed up into his face, laughing. "Oh, do I, Mark?" There was no mockery in his eyes now, and for an instant it seemed that his smile had more in it than friendship. Suddenly realizing how her response must sound to him, her face sobered and she looked down at her fan, murmuring in confusion, "I'm most surprised to see you here. I'd have thought by now your enlistment would have ended and you'd be aboard your ship, searching the seas for easy prey."

"That I have done," said Mark agreeably. "I'm sure you've heard that Congress has authorized privateering."

"No," said Janine, taken aback, "I hadn't heard. . . ."

"Last spring," Mark went on. "So you no longer need concern yourself over my illegal piratical pursuits, as you seemed to on the day we met at the booksellers."

"I suppose there's nothing left for you to do since Congress put an embargo on exports to Britain and the British West Indies," she said coldly.

"It's much more rewarding to rescue ladies in distress," said Mark, his eyes dancing in merriment.

"I'm sure," remarked Janine tartly.

Was he jeering at her, she wondered. Though she searched his face carefully, she couldn't be sure what he was thinking. Was he, too, remembering their frantic embraces, their passionate kisses on the sofa in the parlor? It was on the tip of her tongue to ask if he'd also rescued Anne Delaney, but she caught herself in time.

When the musicians paused to rest, Mark drew Janine's arm through his and led her toward a bench in a corner of the room partially concealed by the thick potted palms. At his touch a warm tide of tingling excitement flooded through her and she sank down on the bench, hot and breathless. Suddenly her gown felt much too tight, squeezing her about the waist and bosom so that she thought the seams would burst. She sat quietly fanning herself, not daring to look up, wishing Lieutenant Furneaux back on the deck of his ship where he belonged.

He eased down beside her and his eyes dipped briefly to the curve of her breasts. Quickly she raised her fan, glancing over the lacy edge. "And where have your travels taken you?"

Mark's eyes slid away from her face, and in his expression was the old evasiveness of former days when the talk had turned to his past.

"That's of little importance, and I'm sure it wouldn't interest you. And what of you?" he went on, his voice heavy with sarcasm. "Have you forsaken your erstwhile fiancé for a new suitor who fulfills all your requirements? Someone who fits your notion of a proper gentleman, as tallow fills a mold? One whom you can admire as well as love?"

Oh, the odious wretch! thought Janine furiously. He knew her mind better than she knew it herself, and his patronizing, cavalier attitude only made matters worse. She felt like slapping his arrogant face.

"My heart is not so lightly taken as yours, Lieutenant Furneaux," said Janine stiffly. "I'm afraid you forget that I'm not like the passel of adoring females swooning at your feet. I'm still betrothed to Jonathan Burke. Doctor Ransom is simply a good friend who recognizes and accepts my loyalty and devotion to my fiancé." She started to add, Which you so flagrantly disregard and take advantage of, but remembering just in time her feeble protests on the last occasion he'd compromised her, she lacked the courage to speak the words.

Mark's eyes glinted in amusement and his lips curved in that infuriating, insolent grin. "I quite understand," he said with elaborate gravity. His smile faded and his face assumed a bland expression. "And what of your loyalty to your country? Has that, too, remained steadfast?"

Something in his voice challenged her spirit and brought back her strength in a surge of dislike. What was it to him where her loyalty lay? She inclined her head, her chin at a stubborn tilt, but made no comment.

He was watching her intently, as though her answer were of the utmost importance.

"Have you no loyalty to the colonies?"

"Naturally! But I, like so many others, am torn by

doubts and misgivings. Therefore, I have chosen to remain neutral," said Janine with a proud lift of her head.

"Neutral!" Mark threw back his head and laughed derisively. "Impossible! Haven't you read Tom Paine's pamphlet that I left in your parlor?"

The mention of the bittersweet memory of that cold and snowy afternoon when he'd made love to her before the fire threw her into confusion. Was that *all* he remembered, Tom Paine's pamphlet? Her heart raced and a flush rose to her cheeks. "I'm not so easily swayed by the writing of a hot-headed demagogue who wishes to incite people to rebellion merely to make a name for himself! Opposing the claims of the British is one thing. Proclaiming independence is quite another!"

"Do you then doubt the wisdom of Washington, Jefferson, Adams, and your hero Doctor Franklin?"

Damn him! thought Janine, nettled at his gibe. He was deliberately baiting her. Truth to tell, the stand taken by these men whom she respected had given her cause to doubt her own convictions, but she'd die before she'd confess it to Mark Furneaux. He always managed to put her on the defensive and she would not be gainsaid by him now.

"Mister Franklin shares my views," said Janine heatedly. "He's always spoken out for reconciliation."

"I grant you that," said Mark soberly, "but when he perceived the futility of that course, he had the wisdom to change his views. . . ." His words trailed off and his gaze darted somewhere over her shoulder. The next instant Richard appeared and stood looking down at Janine, a quizzical light in his eyes, a peculiar half-smile on his lips.

"Are you ready to go into the buffet supper?"

At her nod, Mark rose, made an elaborate bow, and left.

* * *

Janine's argument with Mark had upset her more than she cared to admit. Though it was true that the rebels had committed treasonable acts, she had to agree that the Crown had brought down an iron fist upon the colonies, holding them by the throat. In a moment of reflection she examined her conscience. She would not, could not, profess conversion to their cause out of simple expediency. Yet she was beginning to perceive with terrible clarity that remaining neutral was like walking the edge of a blade, for in the eyes of these hotheaded rebels, anyone not *for* rebellion had to be *against* it. Already the townspeople were looking upon the Quakers next door, the Darraghs across the street, even the managers of the hospital, with suspicion and hostility. Nevertheless, thought Janine, she would hold firm to her resolve to remain neutral.

Chapter 19

Several days later Janine read in the *Pennsylvania Journal* that in the dead of night, under cover of rain and blessed fog, the Americans had evacuated Brooklyn Heights on Long Island and taken a stand on Harlem Heights in Manhattan.

To her chagrin she came upon an item that bore out Mark's statement as to Dr. Franklin's wisdom in changing his views. Franklin, along with John Adams and Edward Rutledge had met with Lord Howe on Staten Island. It was said that Lord Howe tried to negotiate peace, but Franklin was reported to have written Lord Howe:

> Were it possible for us to forget and forgive . . . it is not possible for you . . . to forgive the people you have so heavily injured. Britain must first recognize American independence. But I know too well her abounding pride and deficient wisdom, to believe she will ever take such salutary measures.

Lord Howe's secretary, Ambrose Serle, summed up the situation when he said, "They met, they talked, they parted. And now, nothing remains but to fight it out. . . ."

Until this very day two hopes had been left to sustain her. She had hoped that with the show of British power and the reluctance of the sunshine patriots to fight, the rebellion would fizzle out and life would

gradually resume its old face. She had hoped that
Jonathan's return would bring back some meaning
into life. Now both hopes were gone. It seemed
the war would never end. The bitterest fighting, the
most brutal retaliations were just beginning. And she
might never see Jonathan again.

Janine threw herself into household tasks with a
zeal that surprised even Zoë. They aired all the linens
and bedding, polished all the pewter, dusted, swept,
and scrubbed; and when the house was spotless, Janine
insisted upon making candles to supplement the light
from the lamps during the long, dark winter ahead.
It was a back-breaking task. They gathered wood to
build a fire under a huge kettle out in the yard, then
carried bucket after bucket of water from the pump
half a square away to fill it. When at last the water
boiled, they added to it tallow from beef and deer
that Zoë had collected and hoarded for months. As
they bent over the steaming kettle the rancid brew
assailed their nostrils, but Zoë and Janine boiled and
skimmed, boiled and skimmed, till at last they ob-
tained a clear tallow. This they poured into long tin
cylinders, each containing six candle molds, then set
them by to harden. But no matter how hard Janine
labored, how exhausted she was at the end of each
day, always at the back of her mind niggled her desperate fear for Jonathan's safety.

Then on a sunny day around the middle of September came news that struck terror into her heart. British warships in the Long Island Sound moved into the
East River and pounded Kip's Bay, scattering the
militia. The defenders fled in panic, and the British
occupied New York. In a torment of mixed emotions
Janine read that the 'triumphal entry' was a melancholy spectacle, the town having been deserted by its
twenty-two thousand inhabitants, of which only five
hundred remained.

While Howe dawdled at the beachhead, some three
thousand Americans slipped out of the city to the

Harlem lines. The next day crack British and German troops were lured into a trap at the Hollow Way below Harlem Heights. The Yankees attacked.

Janine started to cast the paper aside. Reading the news only confused her and cast her into despair. Then the word *Virginia* leaped at her from the page, and she read on in spite of herself. With Reasin Beall's Maryland militia pressing on with them, George "Joe Gourd" Weedon raced into action with the rest of Andrew Leitch's 3rd Virginia. Suddenly the British began to retreat, with New Englanders, Marylanders, and Virginians in pursuit.

Janine's eyes widened in astonishment as she kept on reading. As if the victory were not enough, the paper went on to say that the important thing was that this startling achievement was a national one, not sectional. Although troops from many states had been committed to the battle, for the first time Washington's force had been transformed by him, and by its own efforts, from a rabble into an army and every man at Harlem Heights knew it. Their stunning victory gave them a confidence which they had previously lost. However, the report went on to say, the victory was not without a price, for Colonel Thomas Knowlton of Connecticut and Major Andrew Leitch of Virginia were lost. Janine's mouth went dry and the blood pounded in her ears. And what of Jonathan, she thought, torn with fear and anxiety. Was he with Andrew Leitch's 3rd Virginia? Was he, too, lost? She could only hope and wait and pray.

On September 20, less than a week later, Howe's prize, the city of New York, was swept by a fire that gutted the town, which the British declared had been started by some rebels. One fourth of the city burned that night and all the next day in an unimaginable scene of destruction and horror.

The news reached Philadelphia almost simultaneously with the news that the same day the British seized a young man named Nathan Hale, a Connecti-

cut captain wearing civilian clothes within British
lines. The man, in the guise of a Dutch schoolmaster,
having been betrayed by his Tory cousin, admitted
that he was a secret agent. Howe, distraught over the
fires and suspecting trickery from the Americans, gave
orders for Hale's execution the next morning. Without benefit of trial, clergyman, or Bible, Nathan Hale
was hanged at eleven o'clock on Sunday morning,
September 22, furthering the colonists' sense of outrage.

Cousin against cousin, thought Janine dispiritedly.
It was bad enough to have to fight the British, but
monstrous to have to fight one's own cousin. Then it
came to her with a small shock of recognition. She
and Jonathan were cousins, if only by an accident of
marriage.

It was mid-October before General Howe resumed
his attack, landing a force in Westchester. In a game
of cat-and-mouse Howe delayed and Washington withdrew. On October 28 Howe advanced on White
Plains, then delayed, waiting for reinforcements, letting victory over Washington's army slip from his
grasp. Again Washington withdrew, ferrying the bulk
of his army into New Jersey.

As the gray November days dragged by, Janine
waited in an agony of suspense for word from Heritage
Hall. Surely Aunt Ellen and Uncle John would have
news of Jonathan. Papa kept telling her that no news
was good news until she thought she would scream if
he said it once more. She kept up her courage by telling herself that if Jonathan were dead, she would know
it in her heart. Her fervent hope that the fighting
would soon end soared when General Howe captured
Fort Washington on the Hudson. Everyone said that
the fort's loss was the greatest disaster the Americans
had so far suffered and that the outlook for the future
was dismal indeed. Lord Rawdon was quoted as saying,
". . . the Continental Army is broken all to pieces and
the spirit of their leaders and abettors is also broken.

However, I think one may venture to pronounce that it is well nigh over with them."

Two days later, on November 18, the British crossed the Hudson to surprise General Nathanael Greene at Fort Lee. Greene barely escaped with his life, leaving behind precious cannon and supplies, and a thousand barrels of flour. Washington's troops, now reduced to less than 3,000, retreated south through New Jersey, and Cornwallis boasted that he would catch Washington in New Jersey as a hunter bags a fox.

Meanwhile a small, ominous cloud appeared on the horizon over Philadelphia in the form of a letter written by General Mifflin to Robert Morris that was handed about City Tavern. Philadelphia and the control of the Delaware were thought to be the new objective of Sir William Howe, even though he had settled down in winter quarters in New York, letting the Hessians guard the outpost at Trenton.

On a snowy evening the first week in December Dr. Mercer came home with news that brought the stark reality of the war to the doorstep.

"The Council of Safety has ordered that our hospital is to be used by the Continental Army!" said Papa in a loud and indignant voice that Janine knew masked worry and anxiety. "Fifty soldiers were admitted late this afternoon," he added, sinking wearily into a chair. "Doctor Bond asked me to be there early tomorrow. He's going to need all the help he can get."

"I'll go with you, Papa," said Janine. "Surely I can put my time to better use there than here."

"Dear God, Janine. It's no sight for you to see," said Dr. Mercer, running his hands through his hair in a hopeless gesture. "These men aren't our ordinary run of raving lunatics, or suffering from the usual diseases. The best of them suffer from blood poisoning, scurvy, gangrene, putrid fever, and pleurisy—the worst are mangled, wounded—gruesome sights. It's no place for a lady."

The next morning, ignoring Papa's protests, Janine mounted Brandy and cantered along the frozen road beside him to Penn's Hospital at Eighth and Pine. They tied their horses at the hitching post near the gateway and mounted the steps to the entrance of the red brick building. The moment Dr. Mercer opened the door, Janine almost choked on the stench of unwashed bodies, the foul smell of putrid flesh, the odor of death floating out on the cold December air. She turned her head away, took a deep breath of fresh air, and plunged inside the entryway. Moans and cries that raised gooseflesh on her neck warned her of the sight she would see as she followed Papa into the long room lined with narrow iron beds.

In the pale winter sunlight that filtered through the windows, she could easily distinguish the soldiers from the resident patients. The soldiers, emaciated, lice-ridden, clad in tattered, blood-caked clothes, lay like discarded rag dolls on the beds. Some writhed in pain, moaning, crying out. Others lay with clenched jaws and tense white faces waiting for the doctor to get to them. Several appeared to be sleeping—or dead —thought Janine shuddering. At the end of the ward Janine saw a lone male attendant washing a patient, followed closely by a maid holding a basin.

Janine started as a sharp voice at her elbow asked, "What are you doing here?"

She whirled around. Dr. Ransom, his mustard-colored suit spattered with blood, stood staring at her, his arms folded across his chest, frowning in disapproval. His eyes were red-rimmed, his face pale and drawn with weariness.

"She insisted upon coming along," Dr. Mercer explained with a resigned shrug. "She wants to help."

The corners of Dr. Ransom's mouth turned down in a skeptical grimace. "We can certainly use her." He eyed her doubtfully. "If she can stomach the carnage."

At his words she determined to stay and help no matter what she was asked to do. She draped her cloak over a chair, and rolling up the sleeves of her green muslin gown, she said flatly, "I'm ready to work, Doctor Ransom."

For a long moment he studied her appraisingly, then apparently reserving judgment, he turned to Dr. Mercer.

"Doctor Bond is in surgery, taking care of the most crucial cases. I've seen to the first three." He nodded toward the beds on his left.

Janine blinked and tried not to stare at a man whose underjaw was shot off, calling to mind the dark red butchered beef she'd seen hanging on a hook at the market. Hastily she turned to the man in the next bed who lay staring with glazed eyes at the blackened stump of his left leg. Dr. Ransom followed her gaze.

"He suffered a rottenness in the large bone of his leg—the tibia being carious from one end to the other and the head of the thighbone being likewise injured. Doctor Bond amputated through the thigh."

Dr. Mercer nodded without speaking and they moved on to the next bed. "A farrier let blood from this poor fellow and accidentally punctured the radial artery, and an aneurysm of the artery has developed. He's awaiting surgery." Dr. Ransom frowned. "I wish you'd take a look at him, Doctor Mercer."

Dr. Mercer nodded, strode to the man's side, and bent to examine him.

Janine followed silently at Dr. Ransom's elbow. Her legs were shaking and her throat closed with horror at the sight of the ravages wrought by men fighting. They paused at the bedside of a soldier who couldn't have been more than seventeen. His white pasty face bore a pinched look and there were dark hollows under his eyes, his body long and painfully thin under the linen sheet.

"We've requisitioned some blankets," murmured Richard in Janine's ear, "but God knows when we'll get them."

Though the room was chilly this far from the feeble heat given off from the large open wood fireplace, Janine noticed that the boy's forehead was beaded with sweat.

Dr. Ransom smiled and touched the boy lightly on the shoulder as if in reassurance. He introduced Janine, then asked, "Well, Tim, ready to go after that bit of lead now, lad?"

Tim blinked his pale, pain-filled eyes in agreement. Dr. Ransom turned to Janine and explained in a low voice, "We remove bullets only if they're not beyond the reach of a finger. This one is especially tricky, for the tear in the flesh indicates it was made by a mutilated musket ball."

Again Janine nodded, though she had no idea what he was talking about.

"Give him a tot of rum from the flask there."

Janine held the flask to the boy's parched lips, dribbling rum down his throat. Dr. Ransom turned to a cart standing beside the bed, and from a leather case holding his surgical instruments he removed a lead bullet pitted with teethmarks of former patients. He placed it between Tim's teeth.

"Bite down, hard."

Dr. Ransom pulled back the sheet and Janine stifled a gasp at the sight of the gaping gangrenous wound in the right side of the boy's thin chest. He gasped in pain and Janine could see his ribs rising and falling rapidly as Dr. Ransom continued to probe.

"I think I've found it. Give me the forceps."

Janine handed Dr. Ransom the long iron tongs cupped at the ends and held a damp cloth to the boy's glistening forehead. With cool deliberation and exercising great care and gentleness, Dr. Ransom eased the forceps into the jagged wound. Tim grabbed Janine's arm with both hands, holding fast with a viselike grip, arching his back, his jaw clenched with the force of biting the bullet, trying not to cry out.

It seemed to Janine that Dr. Ransom took forever to find the devilish bit of lead. At last he withdrew the small round ball.

"God's death!" he exclaimed, holding it up for her to see. Through the center, out the side, protruded the sharp end of a nail that had been sunk in the bullet. Appalled, Janine shook her head, swallowing hard. So this was the "mutilated" musket ball! Swiftly she bent to mop the blood that gushed forth from Tim's wound, then helped Dr. Ransom bring the wound together with plaster and clean linen bandages.

"Later we'll apply a dressing of soft flannel dipped in oil, followed by a poultice of bread and milk."

They moved on to the next bed where a husky, black-bearded man lay, eyes closed. Janine held her breath against the terrible stench that rose from his lice-ridden body.

"Putrid fever," said Dr. Ransom quietly. "The man needs bloodletting to rid the body of disease poisons." He handed her a curved brass basin from the cart. "Hold the basin and watch carefully. You can learn to do this."

He picked up a fleam, slipped out one of the blades that folded into the handle, and cut a vein in the patient's arm. Janine flinched as though it were her own, but if Dr. Ransom noticed, he gave no sign. A bright stream of blood spurted out into the bleeding basin that Janine held snugly against the man's arm. When he'd drawn about twelve ounces of blood, they moved on to the next patient.

Janine helped Dr. Ransom strip off the man's tattered breeches and filthy shirt, exposing his body which was covered with a mass of crusty, pus-filled boils. Janine clenched her teeth, watching while Dr. Ransom dipped a blistering iron in a caustic solution in a cup and applied it to the man's arm. He jerked in pain, his eyes rolling back in his head.

"The irritation draws out the inflammation," explained Dr. Ransom.

To Janine it appeared that it succeeded only in changing the character of the soldier's pain, but she said nothing. She followed Dr. Ransom through the ward, carrying out his orders, noting his gentle manner, his soothing voice, his hands bringing some measure of relief to the wounded soldiers. Here was a different Dr. Ransom than she'd seen before. Competent, sure of himself, inspiring confidence in his patients.

By the time the deep tones of the dinner bell in the basement rang out six o'clock, Janine had dispensed jalap, niter, and calomel for purging out sickness; mixed up emetics of tartar, warm water, and honey; administered cinchona to those suffering from the ague; bathed and dressed more wounds than she could count. Her shoulders ached, her feet were killing her, a sharp pain knifed between her shoulder blades down her back, and the moans and cries of the soldiers flowed together like one long wail echoing in her ears.

Dr. Ransom came up to her and put an arm around her shoulders. "You're ready to drop. Go home and rest."

Janine shook her head. "What next?"

"We've done all we can do for them today. Tomorrow we start over—bloodletting, purging, dressing wounds. . . ."

"I'll be here early in the morning."

Dr. Ransom's eyes rested on her with something like admiration, and he reached out and smoothed back a damp tendril of hair that had fallen over her forehead.

"I won't say there's no need, Janine, for you've helped more than I ever believed you could."

She gave him a grateful smile. "I'm quite strong. Stronger than I appear to be, Richard."

"Well I know that," he said ruefully, looking deep into her eyes. "For once your strength is being put to proper use—rather than resisting my advances."

Janine blushed, her indigo eyes lighting with
amusement. "I've nothing to fear from your patients,
Doctor."

"Nor have you anything to fear from me," he whispered in her ear as he led her down the aisle between
the rows of beds out to the entrance hall. He left her
sitting on a bench under the portrait of a staunch
Quaker manager of the hospital and returned to the
ward.

Waiting for Papa to come down from surgery,
Janine considered Richard's parting words. *Had* she
nothing to fear from him? He was remarkably kind,
gentle, compassionate, and she perceived that beneath
his unsophisticated, shy exterior lay a solid core of
strength. Maybe he was, under the skin, a stern, fearless, hot-tempered rebel like his father, thought
Janine, intrigued. As Papa would say, blood is thicker
than water! Her heart warmed toward this red-haired
Scot. She admired him more than she cared to admit.
She could no longer deny that she was drawn to him—
and it came to her with startling clarity: That's what
she had to fear. She was exhausted with war, with
waiting, and her defenses were down. She was astonished to find that she yearned for the love and security
he held out to her. She tried to bring reason to bear.
It was only because Jonathan had been gone so long
that she felt so warmly toward Richard. That's all it
was. If Jonathan should return to her tomorrow, there
would be no doubt in her mind at all where her heart
lay.

The next day passed much as the day before, assist-
ing Dr. Ransom, dispensing medicines, bathing and
feeding patients, dressing wounds. Under Richard's
supervision Janine performed two bloodlettings, drawing half a pint of blood from each side of her patient's neck. She loathed this treatment, and it was
with great difficulty that she forced herself to keep

silent, for it seemed to her that rather than draw out the poisons, bloodletting only weakened the patients further.

Watching her closely, Richard nodded his approval. "You're quite skillful, Janine." He glanced down the room at the boy from whose chest he'd removed the bullet. "Tim Abernethy isn't responding the way he should. Let a pint of blood from his left arm. See if that doesn't bring him around."

He strode away and Janine started down the aisle at Tim's bed. The boy was sleeping soundly. His face was deathly pale, his breathing shallow. Deciding he needed his rest, she turned away. She would see to it later. She wanted to get to the soldier who suffered so with boils and change the dressings. No sooner had she finished with him than Dr. Ransom summoned her to attend a patient who had just been admitted— a courier who'd taken a shot in the leg.

She hurried to his bedside. Papa, Dr. Bond, the attendants, and all the patients who could walk had gathered round him like bees to a honeypot. Weakly he gasped out the news that drove all other thoughts from Janine's mind. General Cornwallis and his troops were marching south, threatening New Jersey. The English fleet had been sighted on the Delaware River below Philadelphia, blocking American passage. The inhabitants expected the fleet to sail up to the city at any hour and were fleeing to the country. And a handful of citizens, determined that the British would not take Philadelphia, had hatched a plan to set fire to the city.

For a moment they all stood there in stunned silence, looking at the wounded courier as though he'd gone soft in the head. Then they looked at each other in shocked disbelief.

"Thank God we're well out of the city," someone murmured. There was a buzz and hum of conversation until Dr. Bond ordered everyone back to work. They dispersed then, intent on the tasks at hand that de-manded immediate attention. The cold, gray Decem-ber afternoon wore on without further news, but Janine noticed that she wasn't the only one who cast furtive glances out the window in the direction of town, half-afraid, half-expecting to see an ominous red glow staining the horizon.

Darkness had fallen by the time Janine and her father finished their duties at the hospital. As they urged their mounts into a trot down Pine Street to-ward town, the countryside seemed unnaturally quiet, as though waiting for something, dreading what was to come. Janine's stomach churned with nervousness, her hands were wet and her mouth dry. She sniffed the cold, crisp night air.

"Papa, I smell smoke!" exclaimed Janine. "Do you think the rebels have waited till dark to set fire to the city?"

Dr. Mercer's strong, reassuring voice reached across the darkness. "It's only woodsmoke from the fire-places, *ma petite*. Don't let your fancies run away with you."

She sat stiff and tense on Brandy's back as they rode into town, but the only flames she saw burning were from the streetlamps, casting pools of light on the de-serted streets. Shops and houses were dark and closed up tight. When at last they reached the row of homes on Second Street, she sighed in relief at the sight of their shuttered brick house intact.

Once inside, Zoë relieved their fears. Word had got-ten about that Congress had summoned the instigators and strictly enjoined them to drop their horrid pur-pose. There had been no further reports on the whereabouts of the wily Cornwallis.

It wasn't until after Janine had gone to bed and heard the night watch under her window calling "Ten o'clock and all is well" that she remembered she'd forgotten to bleed Tim Abernethy. Feelings of guilt and remorse swept through her and she prayed that the boy would survive the night.

The next morning when she arrived at the hospital, she hurried to Tim's bedside, and stopped short in amazement. He was sitting up, propped against the pillow, spooning up the last bit of porridge from a bowl. Color had returned to his cheeks, and the faded, pained expression had gone from his eyes. Janine placed a hand on his forehead. It felt cool under her touch.

"Feeling better today, Tim?"

He grinned up at her, his eyes crinkling at the corners. "Yessum. I'm rarin' to go back and chase the lobsterbacks!"

"Best wait a day or two," said Janine, smiling.

Suddenly Dr. Ransom appeared at her side. "He's looking much more lively today, don't you think, Janine? Shows what proper treatment will do."

Janine held her breath while Richard removed the dressing and examined Tim's wound, fearful of what he would find after she'd forgotten the bloodletting.

"It's coming along nicely." He turned to Janine. "Put on a fresh dressing and let another pint of blood. He'll soon be good as new." He moved on to the next bed.

"You ain't be bleedin' me, are ye?" Tim asked.

Janine gave him a long, level look. "You heard the doctor. I'm giving you the same treatment I gave you yesterday," she said firmly.

Dr. Ransom glanced up from the next bed, a question in his eyes. Janine averted his gaze and bent over Tim's chest, busy with the dressing.

"Yessum," said Tim. His eyes locked with Janine's in silent understanding.

She finished changing the dressing on Tim's wound and straightened up. "I'll be back soon with the bleeding basin." She turned away and started toward the apothecary to pick up her medicines for the day.

* * *

Two days later the town was in a turmoil, thrown into a frenzy of fear and excitement over the rumors creeping in from New Jersey. It was rumored that 5,000 of Washington's men had been taken prisoner; that General Charles Lee had been captured at Basking Ridge; that Cornwallis was only waiting for the Delaware to freeze to march his men across and push on to Philadelphia. The question on everyone's lips was: Where was Cornwallis and his troops?

After supper that evening Dr. Mercer leafed through the paper, poked the fire, cleaned his pipe, and moved restlessly back and forth from the parlor window. At last he said, "I think I'll stroll down the street to the Golden Fleece. Maybe another courier has brought news. . . ."

Janine smiled in spite of herself. Papa was as eager for news as she was—and as fidgety until he found out what he wanted to know. She curled up in the wing chair by the fire and tried to read. The words blurred on the page and her head nodded. She heard the clock strike ten before she dozed off.

It was shortly after midnight when she felt Papa's hand on her shoulder, shaking her awake. Startled, she jerked upright, fear clutching at her throat.

"Papa, what is it?"

"Cornwallis has chased Washington's army all the way to the Delaware!"

Papa was smiling, as though elated, and this news didn't sound like cause for celebration. She felt as though a giant hand were squeezing her heart.

"And General Washington?" she asked fearfully.

Papa continued to smile expansively. "Somewhere around New Brunswick Washington commandeered all the boats he could lay his hands on and ferried his men across the river." Papa chuckled in satisfaction. "Old Cornwallis showed up just as the last of Washington's troops were crossing over the Delaware into Pennsylvania, safe as a fox in a hole. They left Cornwallis stranded on the banks, madder than a hornet!"

Janine's hopes soared. Washington in Pennsylvania! If Jonathan were still with the army, surely he'd find a way to see her. Surely they'd stop this senseless fighting for the winter—maybe even for good and all!

Chapter 20

As 1776 drew to a close virtually all the news was bad.
On Lake Champlain, Guy Carleton had swept past
General Benedict Arnold's makeshift fleet and could
now move on to Fort Ticonderoga at his leisure. Eight
thousand British troops had landed and taken possession of Rhode Island. On the last day of November,
two thousand enlistments had expired and the men
went home. Others were waiting only until their service would end on New Year's Eve. But many had
refused to wait. Desertions increased sharply.

The delivery of Boston and victory at Charleston
were far outweighed by defeats at Long Island, Fort
Washington, and Fort Lee, and the loss of New York
and New Jersey. Although General Charles Lee's 2,700
soldiers had joined Washington across the Delaware,
raising the strength of his force to 7,500, many of them
were entirely naked and most so thinly clad as to be
unfit for service. It was estimated that only 4,707 were
fit for duty. Faith in General Washington's army was
flagging. The future looked dismal indeed.

Winter had seized the town in a cruel grip. Snow
lay thickly on the frozen ground, and before the sun
could do its work, another layer of fine wet snow
covered the frozen earth. Determined to keep her mind
and hands occupied, Janine labored from morning till
night at Penn's Hospital. She had never become hardened to the sight of the mutilated bodies, the mangled
limbs, the bleeding, and the incurable wounds, and
could never face them without quailing inside. "I'm

of no real use to the badly wounded and dying soldiers," she told Papa one day in a fit of discourage-
ment. "It's like trying to fill a sieve with water!"

"You have been a great help, nonetheless," said
Papa, patting her arm.

Sighing deeply, she wished this horrible war would
hurry and end. But there was no end in sight. One
bright spot cheered her. Tim Abernethy continued to
improve, and by Christmas Day, he, along with many
of the other soldiers, had been discharged.

Christmas day dawned bright and clear. The sun
shone warmly upon the town, melting the snow on the
bare branches of the poplar and elms lining the streets,
dripping down the icicles hanging from the eaves. All
morning Janine and Zoë worked in a fever of preparation for the guests they had invited for dinner.

Shortly before four o'clock Janine donned the pale
blue brocade gown she'd worn the night of the assembly. Recalling that night made her think of that arrogant Mark Furneaux. Where was he now, she
wondered. Her fingers fumbled on the hooks of her
gown and she quickly put him from her mind. To her
dismay she found that the gown hung loosely on her
slender body. She hoped Papa wouldn't notice how
thin she was, for he'd surely insist that she stop working at the hospital. She brushed her hair till it gleamed
blue-black in the lamplight, swept it up in back, and
arranged it in a cluster of curls pinned high on the
back of her head.

By the time she'd finished dressing, Dr. Williams, a
colleague of Papa's, and Dr. Rush and his wife, Julia,
fourteen years his junior, had arrived. Dr. Rush,
though much younger than Papa, was a professor of
chemistry at the college. He also had a private practice and was deeply involved in politics. In fact, she
recalled, he'd signed the Declaration. Idly she wondered why Papa had invited him tonight. The man
was a firebrand, she knew, advocating separation from

England; and he'd promoted that troublemonger Tom Paine and his *Common Sense* that Mark Furneaux had left in the parlor. But she didn't want to think about Mark Furneaux, she told herself sternly.

She descended the stairs just as Richard Ransom and Mr. and Mistress McAlister came in the door, stamping the snow from their feet.

"Goodness!" cried Mistress McAlister, brushing wet flakes from her cloak. "It started out to be such a fine day and now it's fearfully cold and raw—looks to be a real storm setting in."

"A good night to be inside," said Papa cheerfully, ushering them into the parlor.

Richard looked particularly distinguished this evening, thought Janine. He was wearing a new suit, a dark green woolen coat and breeches, his stock was freshly laundered, his burnished coppery hair neatly tied in a queue instead of escaping its ribbon as it usually did when he was making his harried rounds in the hospital. Yet in the light of the parlor lamp she noted that his face showed the strain of the past few months. His high cheekbones seemed more prominent in his thin, bony face; his eyes sunken and shadowed.

Everyone was in a festive mood, made more so by the repast Janine had hoarded and brought out for the occasion. Steaming snapper soup, huge platters of ham and beef done to a turn on the spit, sweet potatoes and peas, and for dessert, floating island, raisins, and almonds. After dinner Papa brought out the Madeira and poured glasses of the sparkling amber liquid.

Richard, sitting next to Janine, raised his glass to his lips, his eyes saluting her over the rim in a wordless toast. He seemed in a particularly jubilant mood tonight, she decided. His eyes burned with a strange light and there was an air of excitement about him, as though he were suppressing a secret. Men can never keep secrets, thought Janine amused. If she kept silent, he would tell her all in good time.

They adjourned to the parlor, and while Janine played the spinet, everyone gathered round and in lusty voices sang the carols that Papa loved so well. When the carols were done, they ran through the most popular tunes of the day: John Dickinson's liberty song and a raucous drinking song written by Benjamin Franklin. Every time Janine looked up from the keys, she met Richard's gaze upon her. Yes, he was hiding something, she was sure.

The party broke up earlier than Janine had expected, for a northeast wind had begun to howl around the corner of the house, blowing before it a fine, pelting snow, and the guests said they must be going before they were snowed in. Richard lingered before the fire talking with Dr. Mercer while Janine showed the other guests to the door.

Retracing her steps down the hall to the parlor, Janine heard Papa's voice, hearty, jovial, "I hope the matter we spoke of today will come to a happy conclusion. . . ."

As Janine entered the room he broke off abruptly, and she had the strong suspicion that they'd been discussing a private matter between them, one which they had no wish for her to hear.

She stood behind Papa, her hand on the back of his chair. "I hope you'll excuse me. It's been a long day," said Janine smiling. "Good night, Richard, Papa." She bent down and kissed Papa on the forehead and turned to leave the room.

Dr. Mercer rose to his feet and grasped Janine's elbow lightly. "Stay, Janine. Richard here wants a word with you." He grinned, a conspiratorial gleam in his eyes and gave her a benevolent look, as people do when they know a secret. "I'm about to retire." He bid them goodnight and strode from the room.

Janine perched stiffly on the edge of the rose brocade sofa. A feeling of apprehension swept over her. What could Richard and Papa have spoken of this morning? Had something gone wrong at the hospital?

She knew that the Quaker managers weren't sympathetic to the rebel cause. Had Richard locked horns with them? Dr. Morgan had left last October to become Director-General and Chief Physician of the Continental Army Hospitals. It wouldn't surprise her in the least if he'd persuaded Richard to serve with Washington's army. God knows, they were desperate for doctors. She braced herself for the words she was certain would come.

Richard sat down beside her, resting his arm on the back of the sofa, and gazed directly into her eyes. Meeting his gaze, she saw gold flecks dancing in their depths, reflecting the light in the warm, candlelit room.

When he spoke, his voice was low and halting, as though it was hard for him to find the words he sought.

"Janine, I've an admission to make, an apology. . . ."

"Go on, Richard."

"When you first came to work at the hospital, I thought you were playing at being Lady Bountiful, spreading charm and largess among the sick and wounded . . . that working there was no more than a novel way of passing the time. . . ." He took her slim hands in his, clasping them gently. "But after working with you these past few weeks, I confess I was surprised and, well, impressed with how capable you've proved to be, how well you've handled the patients. I no longer doubt your sincerity. You've done marvelously well. . . ." He paused and swallowed, gazing at her as though she were a rare porcelain.

An apology, thought Janine, astonished. Why was he groping for words, talking all around Robin Hood's barn over this! He was so grave, so serious, she bit her lip to keep from smiling. He'd misjudged her and he was sorry. She could imagine what it had cost this proud Scot to make such an admission.

"Thank you, Richard," she said softly.

"I—I'm proud of you." He paused again, looking

down at her long, slender fingers, stroking them with
his thumb. "And you know how fond I am of
you. . . ." His words trailed off and color suffused his
face to the tips of his ears.

Janine stared at him, bewildered. As though time
had reversed itself, the Richard she had first known,
awkward, ill-at-ease away from his medical milieu, sat
tongue-tied before her. She nodded without speaking.

"You'd be a fine wife for a physician. . . ."

Small prickles of apprehension ran down her back.
Again she said nothing.

Abruptly he blurted out the words. "Will you marry
me, Janine?"

She opened her mouth to speak, but before she
could answer, he rushed on.

"In another year I'll finish my residency," he said,
his face bright with eager enthusiasm. "Then we can
be married. I'll set up a private practice right here in
town. We'll have a fine life together. . . ." His voice
died away and he gazed at her with eyes filled with
love and longing.

His proposal struck her with the force of a blow.
Unable to bear the intensity of his gaze, the naked
adoration in his eyes, she looked away without speaking.

"Janine, I love you. I need you!" He put an arm
around her shoulders, turning her to face him. With
his free hand he entwined his fingers in the cluster of
thick curls at the back of her head. He leaned toward
her, his lips meeting hers in a firm, hard kiss.

Her pulses raced, her heart quickened, not with
passion, but alarm. After a moment she drew back and
looked up into his face. Myriad thoughts darted
swiftly through her mind like swallows. Marriage to
Richard would be like living on a broad, vast plain.
There would be no peaks and valleys with this steadfast, reliable man, but long, steady years, the days
blending one into the other, much as her life had been
with Papa. Still, it would be a good life, one to which

she was accustomed, a role she could well fill. *I do admire and respect him*, she thought. *He adores me, and I'm truly fond of him. Many good and happy marriages are built on much weaker foundations. At least that's what Papa is always saying.* Immediately a louder voice deep inside chided her. How could she even think of marrying Richard when her heart belonged to someone else? Her voice was gentle, imploring.

"Surely you've not forgotten that I'm betrothed to Jonathan?"

Quick anger leaped to his eyes. "Jonathan be damned!" he exploded. "You're not being fair to me, Janine, or to yourself either for that matter, putting me off because of a girlish infatuation with some Virginia dandy!"

A lump rose in her throat, and misery flowed through her body. The last thing in the world she wanted to do was to hurt Richard, and now he sat before her, hurt, angry, bewildered.

She held out her hands in a helpless gesture. "I thought you understood that I was waiting for him," she said softly. "If I were betrothed to you, you'd expect me to wait."

Richard jumped up from the sofa and began pacing the floor with angry, impatient strides, his hands clenched behind his back.

"I don't deny it, Janine. I know you said you were waiting for him. And I'd expect you to wait for me, but I wouldn't leave you languishing for a year and a half with no word!" He halted midstride in the center of the room, his chin jutting forward indignantly. "Are you going to wait forever for this man, wasting your life away, withering on the vine?"

In the silence that followed, the candles burning low in the brass wall sconces sputtered and crackled. To give herself time to think, Janine rose, crossed the room, and picked up the snuffer from the mantel. She turned her back to him and with hands that trembled, touched the snuffer to the wicks. There was no sound but that of the north wind blowing up a gale, rattling the shutters against the house.

"These are unsettled times," she murmured. Reluctantly she faced the unpleasant truth that Richard was right. She *could* wait forever, withering on the vine, as he said, and Jonathan might never come back to her. She stood at the window, her back to him, staring out at the white flakes whirling through the darkness, so he couldn't see her face, see how near she was to giving in to an impulse she knew would be wrong . . . to marry without love. She tried to compose herself, to appear calm, though her mind was in a turmoil. She crossed the room and replaced the snuffer on the mantel. When she turned around, Richard stood looking at her, a long desperate look. His eyes clung to hers.

"Janine"—his voice was earnest, pleading—"you must marry me!"

Her throat went dry and the words came out in a harsh whisper. "Richard, I'm sorry. . . ."

His eyes turned bleak and flat, calling to her mind the eyes of the wounded, dying soldiers in the hospital who had lost all hope. His lips pressed together in a thin line and there was a sadness, a resignation in his face that made her shrink inside.

"Good-bye," he said hoarsely. Without another word he turned and strode from the parlor, closing the door firmly behind him.

Janine longed to run after him, to beg him to understand, but she stood fast, as though rooted to the spot before the hearth, knowing that nothing she could say would ease his disappointment. She heard the outer door slam as he let himself out into the whirling snow. She sighed deeply and lifted a candle from the table. As she lighted her way up the stairs to bed, she felt weighed down with sorrow and regret. She wished with all her heart that she could love Richard Ransom. Most of all she wondered at her own folly, throwing away a chance for happiness in favor of gambling on the unknown future.

Dr. Mercer and Janine did not learn until two days later that about the time they and their guests were finishing their Christmas dinner, General Washington's regiments, in the frozen hills of Pennsylvania, were finishing their evening parade. And before Janine slept that night, the soldiers were on the march. Starving, shivering, coatless, some in threadbare shirts, some whose feet were wrapped in rags, some barefoot, they plodded doggedly through a snowstorm toward McKonkey's ferry on the Delaware. Here they clambered aboard forty-foot-long Durham ore boats manned by John Glover's Marblehead sailors who set about ferrying a cargo of twenty-four hundred soldiers, eighteen field pieces, and some horses across the ice-choked river. By three A.M. the troops were all landed, and the Americans marched at breakneck speed over the sleet-glazed roads, nine miles to Trenton.

Colonel Johann Gottlieb Rall, commanding the Hessian post, had been celebrating Christmas with his men and was now, in the early light of dawn, sleeping it off. Washington's twin columns charged both ends of town simultaneously, cutting off escape from the village, sweeping down on the sleep-dazed Germans with bayonets and murderous musket fire. Rall flung on his clothes, mounted his horse, and frantically called his men to arms. The American artillery cut up the Hessians before they could form and according to Colonel Knox, "the ensuing hurry, fright, and confusion was not unlike that which will be when the last trumpet shall sound."

Soon after Rall toppled from his horse, mortally wounded, his men surrendered. Now, with one thousand prisoners and stores to tend, Washington again crossed the Delaware in a raging storm to the safety of Pennsylvania. His forces had suffered two killed and three wounded. It was a glorious victory that raised the drooping spirits of the starved and ragged army.

Several days later Washington made the most daring gamble of all. Leading fifty-two hundred men, he again crossed the Delaware and occupied Trenton, thinking to strike another blow at his disorganized enemy. Instead, he found himself in grave danger of being cornered by General Charles Cornwallis and eight thousand crack regulars behind Assonpink Creek, with further retreat cut off by the Delaware.

An exultant Cornwallis exclaimed, "At last we have run down the old fox, and we will bag him in the morning."

During the bitter cold night British sentries watched the light of the colonials' campfires, heard the clink of their shovels working through the night. It wasn't until the next morning that Cornwallis learned of the ruse. Leaving their campfires burning, Washington's entire army had slipped away on the frozen ground, not to retreat, but to move around Cornwallis's flank in the direction of Princeton.

A little before daybreak the Americans hit the British rear guard at Princeton and swiftly routed the enemy. With their commander-in-chief shouting "It's a fine fox chase, my boys!" they proceeded to take the town. Washington had planned to march seventeen miles on the British base at Brunswick, but seeing his men were fought out, he retreated to Morristown.

Word came that the British were hurrying from Trenton, according to Henry Knox, "in a most infernal sweat-running, puffing, blowing and swearing at being so outwitted." An hour after Washington's army left, the British arrived in Princeton, and believing that the Americans were heading for New Brunswick, marched there. Once again the fox had outwitted his enemies. Howe withdrew his army to the safety and comfort of New York.

"It appears that Washington has out-generaled the

generals," Papa told Janine enthusiastically. "And it appears to me this victory at Princeton is just what we need to turn the red tide from our shores, so to speak."

To Janine the entire account seemed beyond belief, as unreal as battles she'd read about in history books that happened long ago in another land. She wanted it to seem unreal, because then she could go on believing that Jonathan was safe—except that the victims lying in Penn's Hospital were *real*.

Chapter 21

January 1777 came full of cold rains and wild winds, and Washington's ragged scarecrows took up winter quarters at Morristown on the south slope of Thimble Mountain.

Because a number of patients had been released from Penn's Hospital before Christmas, Janine was not needed until mid-January. She fidgeted at home, restless and out-of-sorts until the gray, gloomy Monday morning when she returned to her duties at the hospital.

Richard Ransom, aloof and unsmiling, greeted her perfunctorily and walked with her down the aisle between the beds, assigning her patients to bleed and blister, wounds to dress, and dosages of medication to administer.

Taken aback, she bided her time waiting for him to recover his good humor. But as the days passed and his attitude toward her remained cool and aloof, she perceived with a slight sense of shock that this was the way things were going to be. Damn his stiff-necked Scots pride, thought Janine irritably. He was so wounded by her refusal to marry him that he'd retreated behind a wall of reserve that she could not penetrate. The distance between them may as well have been miles rather than the length and breadth of the men's ward.

Chaffing under his treatment, she longed for the easy camaraderie of their former days together. Frequently she sought his advice or called his attention to some improvement in a patient, or told him of a humorous incident that had happened on the ward to try to draw out a smile. But try as she would, he remained stiff and remote, speaking to her only when driven by necessity. His cold, impersonal manner grieved her sorely, but as time wore on, she saw there was nothing she could do to change him, and at last she ceased trying to mend the breach between them.

Near the end of January more soldiers were admitted to the hospital, including nineteen Hessians captured at Trenton. Again and again Janine put off the detestable bleeding of patients suffering with fevers and, as with Tim Abernethy, within a day or two, she noticed that the color returned to their cheeks and new vigor seemed to take hold of their emaciated bodies.

One of these soldiers was Willie Zunt, a barrel-chested, florid-faced fellow with shaggy yellow hair and big ears, who had taken a musket ball in the forehead. At first the doctor thought that the ball had fallen out, but after several days they had discovered that the ball lay flat on the bone and spread under the skin. The ball was removed, with the comment that it was fortunate that his skull proved too thick for the ball to penetrate.

Whenever Janine fed him, bathed him, or dressed his wound, Willie made a feeble effort to utter a few words in his guttural German. But seeing that Janine didn't understand, he gave over to staring gratefully at her with smiling, parched lips and bright, burning eyes.

This morning as she bathed him, it seemed to her that Willie's fever-ridden body shed more heat than the open fireplace at the end of the room. Despite his bath, his fever raged on unabated and that afternoon when she checked him again, he looked at her with a bright-eyed expressionless stare and a slack-jawed smile. Quickly she summoned Richard to his bedside. Richard felt for the man's pulse, looked into his eyes, and closed the lids with his thumb. Janine felt her legs go weak and clutched the footrail of the bed for support.

Richard sighed heavily. His voice was rough. "He's dead. And he shouldn't have died. When did you last bleed him?"

Janine shook her head wordlessly.

"This morning, yesterday afternoon?" demanded Richard impatiently. He stood waiting for her answer, regarding her with a cold, implacable stare. "Speak up!"

"I never bled him," said Janine dully, meeting his gaze.

"What!" exclaimed Richard aghast. "You deliberately ignored my orders!" Dr. Ransom's brows lifted over russet eyes burning with outrage.

Janine rushed on, unable to stem the torrent of her words. "Nor did I bleed Tim Abernethy. That first day he was sleeping and I thought he needed rest. And the next day I saw he was the better for it, so I never bled him, nor some of the others either!" She raised her chin in defiance. "And clearly they were all the better for it!"

He looked her directly in the eye. His voice was hard and filled with reproach. "Tell that to Willie Zunt!"

Her heart pounded and her mouth was dry. Her tongue flicked over her lips, but she couldn't speak. She wanted to say, "He would have died sooner if I'd bled him, I know he would!" Tears of guilt and sorrow for Willie stung her eyelids.

Dr. Ransom's eyes raked her unmercifully and his voice was like steel. "In the future, Mistress Mercer, please follow my instructions to the letter."

She nodded mutely. She would have felt better if Richard had shouted at her, upbraided her. His frigid, disdainful air, conveying greater indifference than that he would have shown a stranger, wounded her like the stab of a knife. From that day on, in tight-lipped silence, she went about doing exactly as she was told. Nevertheless twenty-two men died. By the end of February there were fifty-five soldiers and only thirty-seven civilian patients residing in the hospital.

As a shield against Richard's steadfast indifference Janine retreated into a shell, and as the days passed she discovered that he could no longer hurt her. The shell of hardness was slowly thickening. She had changed to meet this new world for which she was not prepared, and the vulnerable child she once had been was gone.

Though she was still deeply affected by the wounded —their hoarse, cracked, frightened voices, singing, whistling, cursing, swearing, calling Doctor, Doctor, Doctor, from morning till night and the foul stench of sickness, putrid flesh, vomit, feces, their lice-ridden bodies—she summoned the courage to accept their illness and death with quiet resignation. She no longer gagged at the foul odors or quailed at the sight of maimed bodies and mangled limbs. She kept up the pretense of a calm, unruffled exterior as she went about her duties, and gradually the change became part of her.

Now, standing in the sun between the rows of beds, her back breaking from the eternal bending, her hands roughened by the constant washing of bodies, she felt in some obscure way she couldn't define that by caring for these soldiers, no matter which side they fought on, she was helping Jonathan, for she was now convinced that he must be lying ill or wounded some-where in New Jersey. She would never allow herself to think he may be dead. She nurtured a desperate hope that someone was caring for him as she was caring for these poor helpless creatures in Penn's Hospital.

By late spring of 1777, however, most of the soldiers had been discharged from the hospital. One brisk, sunny afternoon when Janine had finished for the day, she heard Richard's footsteps following after her through the entrance hall. Without looking around, she donned her cloak, and as she opened the door Richard stepped past her and pushed it closed.

She turned to look at him, her eyes raised to his impassive face.

"I want you to know how much we all appreciate your help here at the hospital. . . ." His tone was polite and distant.

Nevertheless her heart gave a little skip of anticipation and hope. Words had never come easy to him, she thought. And now that the terrible pressure of treating so many soldiers was relieved, he'd had time to think, to reconsider shutting her out of his life. He was trying to make amends. She smiled encouragingly. "Thank you, Richard."

"However," he went on in the same distant tone, "since most of the soldiers have been discharged, your services here are no longer needed." He summoned a stiff smile that did not reach his eyes. "Good day, Mistress Mercer."

Thunderstruck, Janine stood speechless, watching his slim erect figure stride briskly down the wide entrance hall into the ward. Tears brimmed on her eyelids as she fled out the door, down the steps, and across the grounds. Oh, she thought, choking in distress, to be so summarily dismissed! He knew full well there would soon be other patients—that help was impossible to find. To think he could be so relentless! She leaped on Brandy's back, jerked the reins, and rode pell-mell back to town, the cool April wind whipping the tears of hurt and anger that rolled unbidden down her cheeks.

During the days that followed she turned the house inside out in such a frenzy of cleaning that even Zoë was exhausted. When they finished housecleaning, they made butter and cheeses. May and June dragged past and Janine attacked the gardens, digging, planting all manner of vegetables and herbs. They gathered apples and peaches and pears from the trees in the yard and made cider and jellies and preserves. And always she kept Papa's apothecary chest well stocked.

But no matter how she filled her days, Janine felt a terrible sense of loss. Her spirits drooped and she felt a strange restlessness that would not be stilled. When Papa asked in a gentle, roundabout way what the matter was, she told him she missed working at the hospital, which was true as far as it went. She did not tell him she missed Richard Ransom more than she thought possible. Even though he had been cool and distant, sharing tasks, a common interest, his very presence had been more comfort to her than she had realized.

Then the last week in July came the startling news that two hundred fifty warships, transports, and miscellaneous vessels under Sir William Howe had hoisted their sails in New York harbor and headed out into the Atlantic hazes. A flood of rumors spread up and down the coast. Where was Howe's fleet? Where would he strike?

"General Washington evidently has some notion," said Papa one evening at the supper table. "Talk at the tavern has it that he's moved his army down from Morristown Heights near Neshaminy Bridge."

"Neshaminy!" cried Janine. For a moment hope fluttered in her breast, then died. Though it was much nearer to Philadelphia than Morristown, it could be a world away for all the chance she had of seeing Jonathan. "What good will that be?"

"I'm not certain," said Papa thoughtfully, "but I think he's keeping one eye on the coast in case Howe's fleet should appear and one eye over his shoulder on General Burgoyne in the Champlain Valley."

Janine sighed heavily. The whole thing was incomprehensible to her. "How can Washington fight a battle when he doesn't know where the enemy is, let alone with a ragged army and no weapons or ammunition?"

"It's said that Washington commandeered supplies and has whipped his army into shape," said Papa, "and that a French ship, the brig *Mercury* out of Nantes, has docked in Portsmouth with arms, clothes, gunflints, and Lavoisier's gunpowder—that there are no less than thirty-four similar ships clearing French ports for America, from a firm called Hortalez et Cie." His brow wrinkled in a puzzled frown. "I can't say I've ever heard of it."

On the hot, humid morning of August twenty-second, ships were sighted at the mouth of the Delaware. Their sails were big and square, not the sails of small merchant vessels, but of frigates and sloops of war. The town was in a panic. Howe's two-hundred-fifty-ship fleet was about to invade Philadelphia. But the invasion was not to come from the Delaware. At the mouth of the river the fleet was blocked by an elaborate *cheveux de frise*, strong iron-clad spikes placed menacingly below the water's surface.

Howe, persuaded that the navigation of the river was too hazardous and its defenses too impressive, sailed on to the head of Chesapeake Bay. Philadelphia breathed a sigh of relief. He would have a sixty-mile march overland to reach the town and then General Washington and his colonials would soon put him to rout.

Washington promptly marched his sixteen-thousand-man army to Philadelphia. News spread through the town that he would review the troops on their way to meet Howe, Cornwallis, and von Knyphausen.

Janine's heart soared, and all fear of an invasion of Philadelphia was driven from her mind by the knowledge that Washington and his entire army would march through the town.

"Papa!" she cried, "This means he'll be here, marching right before my eyes!" She felt she could hardly contain the wild happiness that flooded through her.

Papa blinked, uncomprehending. "Well, you've seen the general before, *ma petite*. And surely you understand that you won't have a chance to speak with him."

"No, no, Papa. Not Washington. Jonathan! He's bound to be here, marching with the army!"

Dr. Mercer pushed out his lower lip and cocked his head to one side. "Possibly—but don't place your hopes too high. I've no wish to put a damper on your spirits, but it's highly unlikely that you can find Jonathan among sixteen thousand men."

"They can't march faster than the eyes, Papa!" Her heart swelled with hope. "I'll watch every second. And even if I shouldn't see him, maybe he'll see me!"

A shadow of disbelief crossed Dr. Mercer's face, but he smiled gently. "It's possible, it's possible. Even so, he can hardly break ranks to step aside and chat."

"Oh, I know, Papa," said Janine airily. "I wouldn't expect him to. All I want is to see him, to know he's alive!"

Janine slept little that night, her dreams invaded by an endless parade of marching men in all manner of uniform, but their faces were those of the soldiers she had tended at Penn's Hospital, none of whom faintly resembled Jonathan.

Early on the morning of August 24, the fine misting rain of the night before was driven away by the sun and there was an air of great excitement in the town. By seven o'clock Janine could hear the artillery rumbling through the streets, and a faint sound of music and cheering. It sounded as though the whole town had turned out to see the American Army parade through the city.

She dressed quickly in her blue muslin gown and fastened her medallion around her neck. Snatching up her straw bonnet from a chair, she tied it under her chin, then raced down the stairs to see if Papa was ready.

He was finishing the last of his breakfast at the table in the kitchen. "Oh, Papa," cried Janine in a frenzy to be off, "the soldiers are coming! Do hurry!"

Dr. Mercer shook his head regretfully. "I'm on duty at the hospital. You go, and tell me all about it when I come home. And don't forget to watch for our French general."

"Yes, Papa, I'll remember!"

She gathered up her skirts and flew out the door, down Taylor's Alley to Front Street, elbowing her way through the crowd toward Chestnut Street where Washington was to review the troops. Papa's general was a young French nobleman named Marie Joseph Paul Yves Roch Gilbert du Motier, Marquis de Lafayette, who had joined Washington's army, demanded the rank of major general, and offered to serve without pay, and she herself was curious to see this audacious soldier.

Shopkeepers stood in the doorways. Men, ladies with parasols, children, dogs, and sailors jammed the pavements. People were cheering, shouting, waving, while vendors were hawking oysters. In her haste she stumbled and almost fell over a carriage block. She quickly righted herself and, gathering up her skirts, mounted the carriage block. She stood on tiptoe, balancing precariously, craning her neck to see between the heads and bonnets and parasols blocking her view. Her heart beat wildly and her hands grew moist. Here came the advance guard! A shiver went down her spine as the fifers and drummers struck up "Yankee Doodle."

There came General Washington! How handsome he was in blue and buff, riding his mahogany steed, escorted by Henry Knox and Tench Tilghman. And beside him must be the young marquis. The red-haired, blue-eyed, youth sitting straight and tall on his mount appeared older than his nineteen years.

Four regiments of light horse pranced past the calm, dignified general and his officers and aides, who were all mounted on horseback. Next marched divisions of the army and the artillery and infantrymen, twelve deep, accompanied by the colonels and other field officers on horseback. Oh, it was magnificent! She saw John Adams standing on the corner across the street, smiling confidently, as though the entire army were there to protect him.

"I trust you're impressed with the army about to defend your city and protect your virtue, Mistress Mercer," drawled a deep, insolent voice in her ear.

Startled, she whirled around, lost her footing, and would have fallen from her perch on the carriage block had not someone standing behind her caught her in his strong, powerful arms and set her on her feet. She caught a glimpse of his fringed hunting shirt and breeches. Now, crushed in his close embrace, her heart hammered against his chest, her pulses raced. Quickly she disengaged herself from his grasp.

"Mark Furneaux! What in the world are you doing here?"

He laughed softly. "Viewing the general's troops, even as you are, little darling. Do you mind?"

Recalling the way she'd lashed out at him at the assembly, her face turned crimson. How haughtily she'd assured him she was remaining neutral—and here she was, singing and shouting like a mad woman, cheering the colonial army on to victory.

"Of course I don't mind," said Janine coldly. "It's a public demonstration."

His lips curved in a broad smile and his white teeth glistened in the brilliant sunlight. "And you don't censure the rebellious Continentals marching off to protect your neutral hide?"

"Oh!" said Janine furiously. "You're rude and arrogant and . . ." she tried to think of some other words to tell him what she thought of him, ". . . and impossible!"

"And I'm right," said Mark, arching one eyebrow and grinning like a tom cat.

"You're in the militia," said Janine wrathfully. "Why aren't you out there marching with the troops?

Or did you desert the cause when your enlistment
was up?"

His eyes ran up and down her figure with that cool
look of appraisal that always made her feel un-
clothed. "I find I'm needed more to rescue ladies in
distress."

"Oh! Oh!," said Janine angrily. And unable to
think of anything more cutting to say to him, she
whirled around, bent on flight. But there was nowhere to go, no inch of space in the solid wall of
people jam-packed like sardines on the pavement. She
hopped back up on the carriage block and stood with
her back like a ramrod, staring hard at the militia
marching past, stepping smartly, if not in time, in
their patched, ill-fitting uniforms the colors of dry
leaves.

Again Mark's deep voice spoke close to her ear,
sending a tremor down her spine.

"Though they're dressed in ragtag clothes, their
arms are certainly well burnished," he remarked in a
casual, conversational tone. "They even carry them
like soldiers and they look as if they might face an
equal number with a reasonable prospect of success."

Janine bit her lip in vexation and said nothing.
He was trying to bait her with his talk of Washington's army. She wouldn't let him goad her into losing
her temper as he had the night of the assembly. Why
did he insist upon annoying her? Why didn't he go
away?

She stood stiffly on the carriage block, and once
when the crowd surged back to make way for a skit-
tish horse, she teetered sideways and immediately felt
Mark's hands spanning her waist, holding her firmly
and securely. His touch went through her like fire.

They had been watching Washington's men tramp
over the cobbled streets for more than an hour before Janine saw the colors of the Virginia regiment
flowing past. She leaned forward, straining her eyes,
searching for a shining blond head, examining every

face, every gaunt figure from the tallest to the impossibly short. There was one! Her heart leaped to her throat, and at that moment he turned his head away and she saw his dark hair tied in a queue dangling over his collar. The bright sunlight suddenly clouded and the faces blurred through tears. She blinked rapidly and struggled not to cry. She thought she would strangle, trying to hide her disappointment. Maybe he'd joined another regiment. Maybe there was still a chance, she told herself, dabbing at her nose with her handkerchief. She lifted her chin and stared at the rows of marching men.

The sun, like molten brass, soared upward, and the August heat beat relentlessly upon them. Janine wiped the perspiration from her brow with the back of her hand. Her face was burning and her knees felt weak. Suddenly the lines of soldiers before her began to swim, waver, shimmer in the scorching sunlight. The throng of people had pressed farther back from the street, and smelly, sweating bodies pressed close against her. Her clothes, damp with perspiration, clung to her body. The air was hot and heavy, and she gasped for breath. Her vision blurred and a cloud seemed to pass over the sun. She felt herself swaying, sinking down and down, as though she were drowning and could not save herself.

Chapter 22

Gradually she became aware of the strong smell of tar, the stench of rotting fish, the sound of water lapping against a dock, the creaking of a ship's mast and a gentle, rolling motion. She lay flat on her back, rocking slowly, gently, as though in a cradle. Something cool was pressing on her forehead. She reached up and felt a damp cloth, wondering how it came to be there. Raising her head, she stared about a sunlit wood-paneled room. Her breath left her body in a gasp. Though she had never before been in such a place, she recognized the wide sweep of windows, the round table fastened to the floor, and the sea chest. A ship's cabin!

Over the back of a chair lay her blue gown and her petticoats. Lord in heaven, what could have happened to her? Her legs felt weak, her stomach felt queasy. She closed her eyes and sank back on the pillow.

She heard the door open and footsteps crossing the cabin floor. She turned her head and saw Mark Furneaux carrying a tray on which were a teapot and cups. He set the tray on the table, came to the bunk, picked up the damp cloth, and wiped her brow.

"Feeling better?" His voice was low and gentle and bore none of the insolence and mockery she had come to expect.

"I think so," said Janine uncertainly. "I don't know what came over me. . . ."

"A touch of the sun, little darling. You dropped into my arms like a ripe peach from a tree."

Just then the ship gave a slight lurch. God in heaven, thought Janine frantically, this—this villain has abducted me and now we're on the high seas bound for who knows where!

"Where have you brought me?" she demanded wildly.

His smile reminded her of a lion about to devour a mouse. "You're in the captain's cabin, my cabin, of the *Adventure*. It seemed the handiest place to take you away from the press of the crowd."

"Your ship!" cried Janine, sitting bolt upright in the bunk. Her voice rose in agitation. "How dare you spirit me away like this? Where are you taking me? Tell your men to head back to port this instant!" Fury and indignation sparkled in her eyes, but to her ears her tirade sounded like the feeble mewing of a kitten.

Mark threw back his head and laughed, his eyes mocking the rage in her face.

"My dear, I wouldn't dream of taking you as far as Hog Island in my ship. With your penchant for misadventure it would undoubtedly sink halfway across the Delaware. I assure you, we're securely moored at the dock."

"Nevertheless I wish to be put ashore immediately!"

"As you are?"

Janine looked down at her thin linen shift barely concealing her nakedness and felt the color flooding her neck, creeping up to her face. She lay back on the pillow and pulled a sheet up to her neck.

"If you'll be kind enough to leave, I'll get dressed," she snapped.

He smiled that maddening, superior smile and crossed to the table, poured a cup of tea, and brought it over to the bunk.

"Stop ruffling like a hen and drink this—if you can stomach liberty tea," said Mark grinning. He put an arm around her shoulders, easing her upright, shoving the pillow behind her back. He held the cup to her lips while she sipped the hot brew. The warmth began spreading through her body, and strength flowed slowly back into her legs. When she had finished, he refilled her cup and, handing it to her, sat down on the edge of the bunk.

She sipped the tea in silence, watching him, the way his thick black hair shone in the sunlight, the crescent curve of his brows over black eyes that at this moment were soft as velvet, the set of his broad shoulders. Though his mouth was set in a line that he doubtless considered firm and unyielding, there was a pleasant softness about the corners of his lips. She looked up into his eyes and found him staring at the medallion hanging from the ribbon around her neck. His eyes continued downward to the fullness above the lace edge of her shift.

Her heart beat rapidly, her face flushing with embarrassment. She handed him her cup. "I'm feeling much stronger now. I must be on my way."

He made no move to rise from the bunk, but sat there looking at her, a dark, inscrutable expression on his face. As always there was something hot and vital and exciting about him. Something in the depths of his eyes warned her to go—and quickly. She knew there was no use asking him again to leave while she dressed. Being what he was, he would only laugh at her and she could not bear to hear it.

She gritted her teeth and, casting modesty to the winds, drew up her knees and swung past him. The minute her feet touched the floor she ran across the cabin and, turning her back, hastily began to pull on her clothes. He didn't stir from the bunk, but she could feel his eyes watching her and her face flamed. She had the feeling that he knew she was afraid of what he might do and was amused.

She had donned her petticoat and gown and was reaching around the back to fasten it when she felt his fingers on the hooks. For a moment she froze, and then she realized he was fastening them for her. She was breathing easier now. In a moment she would be away, free from this man who had the power to turn her knees to pudding with a glance. Apparently he'd meant what he'd said on that terrible night at the tavern—that he'd never take a woman against her will and for that she was thankful. Whether it was because it would be ungallant, or because of his inordinate pride, she didn't know, or care.

When he finished hooking her gown, she raked her fingers through her hair and from the corner of her eye saw him sitting on the edge of the table watching her intently. With trembling fingers, she pinned it up as best she could, then turned to Lieutenant Furneaux.

"You've been very kind. Thank you again for rescuing me."

His smile was lazy and indolent. "Any time."

He'd not made any unwelcome advances toward her, and she relaxed, her confidence restored. She picked up her bonnet and set it on her head.

His black eyes turned challenging and mocking. "Tell me," he pursued blandly, as though she had not signified that their conversation was at an end, "what have you been doing since we last met—languishing after your fiancé, or stepping out with your doctor, or sewing a fine seam waiting for the king and the colonies to reconcile their differences?"

"Indeed not!" said Janine bristling. She told him of her work at Penn's Hospital. "Tending the soldiers of *both* armies!" she finished vehemently.

"Ah, neutral to the bitter end," he jeered.

She knew he was baiting her, but as always his baiting maddened her.

"You're a fine one to make sport of me!" she flared. "If you're so all-fired devoted to the rebel cause, why don't you give up your privateering and join them? But oh, no! You couldn't wait till your enlistment expired so you could join your fellow privateers, plundering the king's ships! General Arnold told Congress that if those damned mercenaries on the seaboard hadn't put all their sailors and all their money into privateers so that there was nothing left for the defense of the country, they could fight off twice their strength in ships and guns."

Something in his face stopped her and the minute the accusing words left her lips she could have bitten her tongue.

Mark glared down at her, his black eyes shining like coals, his mouth set in a grim line.

"May I remind you, Mistress Mercer, I'm not accountable to you for my actions. As a matter of record I'm not a privateer, but engaged in trade with a reputable firm—Hortalez et Cie."

The name rang a bell in her mind, but she was so upset, she could not think where she'd heard it, and Mark's voice was pounding in her ears like a hammer.

". . . and furthermore, I don't denigrate you for being a Tory—and that's what you are, a Tory!"

He spat the word like an epithet, and it was like an arrow piercing her heart. Hurt and anger coursed through her.

"How many times do I have to tell you, I'm neither rebel nor Tory?" she cried, furious that her voice shook. "I'm for peace and an established government, Lieutenant Furneaux, which is more than I can say for you!"

Mark leaped to his feet, towering over her, clenching his fists as if to keep from striking her. She refused to back down, but stood her ground, her chin raised in defiance, her blazing eyes a deep blue, her cheeks suffused with crimson.

His voice was hard and tight with barely controlled rage. "Your behavior is hardly that becoming a lady, Mistress Mercer. Perhaps I can teach you some manners."

"Manners!" shrieked Janine. "You! I'm ashamed to be seen in your company, you—you blackguard!" She turned and fled across the cabin. She was halfway to the door when he gripped her arm, his fingers biting into her flesh.

"Let me go!" she cried wildly.

His strong arms went around her, crushing her to him, and the breath ran out of her lungs in a rush. He placed a finger under her chin, raising her face to meet his, his eyes devouring her. In an effort to catch her breath she opened her mouth, and his mouth covered hers, warm and eager, seeking. Her head fell back. She arched her body, leaning away from him, and his arms slid up her back, pressing her close to him, his solid, muscular body bending to mold with her own.

She reached up and clasped his shoulders, trying to push him away, and felt his brute strength and knew it was no use. A long, tremulous sigh escaped her. In a moment he would release her and she would fly out the door. She felt desire stirring deep within her and knew she must escape before it was too late, before her treacherous body betrayed her.

His violence subsided and tenderly he kissed the lobe of her ear, her neck, her throat, the delicate rounded flesh rising and falling rapidly above her bodice.

Oh, Lord, thought Janine, the tea had done no good at all. Weakness flowed through her and she felt like thistledown blowing in the wind. From somewhere deep in the recesses of her mind echoed the thought that he would not take a woman who was unwilling. . . . A violent trembling shook her and her knees gave way.

Mark gathered her up in his arms and carried her across the cabin, kissing her forehead, her eyelids, her lips, and bore her down on the bunk, covering her body with his.

"No, Mark, no!" she murmured faintly.

His passionate kisses silenced her protests. Kisses that stirred her to depths she'd never dreamed of. Her arms slid around his neck, her body on fire with longing for his. She knew that she was helpless to stem the desperate fury of their desire for each other, knew she would yield to his ultimate embrace.

His hands caressed her body with a knowledge that set her senses reeling, her skin tingling. The restraint he had shown thus far now vanished swiftly, giving way to a passion that was savage, violent, ruthlessly selfish, a passion that she was challenged to match.

From a great distance she heard the receding sounds of fife and drum. Suddenly the drumming grew loud and insistent. *The parade is marching through the cabin,* thought Janine dimly, and she didn't care. . . .

Mark raised his head and bellowed, "Go away!"

The pounding on the cabin door stopped and a voice from the other side shouted, "All I need is your signature on the manifest, Cap'n—cargo going on board."

"Lie still, little darling," Mark whispered huskily.

He rose from the bunk, clutching his breeches around his middle, and strode to his desk. He dipped a quill in the ink pot then went to the door and opened it a crack.

Dazed, disheveled, she sat up. Dear God, she whispered, almost sobbing as the enormity of the folly she was about to commit struck her. Her emotions confused and overwhelmed her. She was furious with Mark for trying to seduce her and even more furious with herself for wanting him to. She thrust down her skirts and flung herself over the edge of the bunk. Snatching up her bonnet, she raced toward the door.

Mark had finished scratching his signature on the manifest and closed the door. Now he leaned against it, his arms folded across his chest, his dark eyes smoldering with pain and disbelief.

"Janine, you're not leaving?" he asked in a hoarse voice.

"The sun has addled my brain!" cried Janine, close to hysteria. "Let me go!"

His gaze was hard and level and his mouth twisted

with rage. "No woman has ever before so filled me with desire—or so angered me! I'm courting disaster even to be seen in the company of a Tory sympathizer, but you've driven my caution to the winds and now you're leaving! You can't go now!"

With a swift lunge she tried to dart past him, her hand reaching toward the door. He grabbed her wrist and held it in a cruel, viselike grip. She had never felt so trapped in her entire life.

"Let me go!" shrieked Janine. "You womanizer! You've shamed me so that I dare not look at my own reflection in the glass! You who never take a woman against her will!"

"Against her will!" thundered Mark. The anger and rage which had threatened to boil over into violence erupted in a shout of laughter.

"What's so funny?" demanded Janine wrathfully.

"Never have I encountered a lady more willing—and able!" He whooped with delight and slapped his knee.

"Beast!" spat Janine, stamping her foot.

He leaned against the door, shaking with laughter, while Janine stood, hands clenched, consumed with fury. At last he composed himself enough to say in his calm, superior tone, heavy with sarcasm, "Don't fret yourself, little darling. I'll shame you no further. Tomorrow I sail with the tide."

"I'm leaving this minute!" cried Janine.

He stepped aside, flung open the door, and made a deep, exaggerated bow. She plunged headlong through the doorway and fled down the narrow passageway toward the ladder leading to the deck above.

Swiftly Mark adjusted his clothes and raced after her. When he gained the deck, she had disappeared. Leaning over the rail, he saw her stepping from the end of the gangway onto the wharf and merging with the crowd that watched the last of Washington's army parade along Front Street.

"Good riddance," he muttered savagely. "Best to

forget you!" He stamped back to his cabin and, staring down at the bunk, he saw a small object shining on the rumpled bedclothes. He reached out and picked it up. On his palm lay the medallion that Janine had worn on a ribbon around her neck. The face that smiled up at him was the image of Janine. For a long moment he stood staring at the soft, full lips, the haunting eyes the color of bluebells, the silken black hair, then he went to his desk, unlocked a drawer, and drew out a small box inlaid with rare woods. Opening the box, he dropped the medallion inside and locked it away in the desk.

Chapter 23

September 1777 came, warm without the humid heat of August. Washington waited on the banks of the Brandywine to repel the British army and protect Philadelphia, capital city of the colonies.

About eight o'clock on the morning of September 11 Janine went out to her garden to gather herbs. She was kneeling down, cutting sprigs of sage, the sun warm on her back when there came to her ears a far-off sound like thunder of an approaching storm. Rain, she thought. We certainly need it. Shading her eyes with her hand, she looked up into the brassy sun. Rain? No! Not rain! Cannon! She gripped the shears tightly and strained her ears, and the faraway booming sound seemed closer. With a fear that threatened to overwhelm her, it occurred to her that what she was hearing was artillery fire from the guns at Brandywine twenty-five miles away. The armies were engaged!

Her heart racing, she ran around the side of the house to the front and stopped short in astonishment. Carriages, carts, horses loaded with all manner of possessions were laboring up the street. The inhabitants were fleeing the town! A bearded old man with a wizened face who was pushing a barrow shouted, "Better be packin'—men-o'-war coming up the river!" and hurried on.

Janine dashed inside the front door and collided with Zoë in the entryway, her eyes rolling with fear.

"Zoë," said Janine breathlessly, "the fighting has

begun!" Pushing past Zoë, she dashed upstairs to the garret and leaned out the dormer window at the front of the house. The roofs and chimneys of the houses across the street blocked her view to the south. She turned and raced to the rear window overlooking the river.

Zoë, who had followed close on her heels, panted, "What you see, Miss Janine?"

With an effort she presented a calm face, though her heart thumped in her breast. "I don't see any warships, Zoë, but the townspeople are leaving. Papa will never leave. He'll be needed here to tend the sick and wounded. But you must go. Pack up as much as you can take with you and fly."

Zoë turned a stoic face toward Janine and said with dignity, "Thank you, but this here is my home too, Miss Janine."

Janine's mouth fell open in surprise. It had never occurred to her that Zoë had nowhere to go. Now she nodded her head in assent and put a hand on Zoë's brown arm.

"Don't worry, Zoë. General Washington will never let the British occupy Philadelphia."

Papa didn't come home for dinner at midday as was his habit. Janine sat down at the table alone and tried to force down the chicken and potatoes Zoë had prepared for her. But the food was like paste in her mouth and she could swallow nothing over the fear clutching at her throat. She paced to and fro in the parlor, leaning out the window time and again, watching the street, frantic with worry. Papa wasn't on duty at the hospital today, but maybe he'd gone there anyway—maybe they were bringing the wounded soldiers in from Brandywine. . . .

It was well after dark before Dr. Mercer stamped in the house, slamming the door behind him. Lines of weariness were etched in his face, and he dropped into the chair by the fireside, his shoulders sagging.

"I've been at the hospital," he said tiredly. "The managers, they're taking them away. It's unthinkable! unthinkable!"

Janine's heart leaped to her throat. Papa had tried to explain to her earlier on what was happening, but she had failed to take it in. She knew there were questions in the minds of many Pennsylvanians concerning their Quaker neighbors. Because Friends generally were either neutral or passive loyalists, the revolutionary government of Pennsylvania and many of the rebels as well looked upon Quakers as spies and informers. They had vented their hostility in double taxation, imprisonment, and even exile. Early in September, frantic with the threat of their enemy at their back door and well aware of the loyalists in their midst, the Executive Council of Pennsylvania had looked about for enemies in their own camp. Then, shocking the town to the core, Colonel William Bradford of the militia had arrested a number of prominent and wealthy Quaker citizens. Among them was Henry Drinker, a prosperous merchant and co-owner with Abel James of one of Philadelphia's leading export-import firms, and, beyond belief, four prominent members of the Board of Managers of Penn's Hospital: Israel Pemberton, James Pemberton, Thomas Wharton, and Edward Pennington.

"Taking them where, Papa?"

"Virginia!" His blue eyes sparkled with anger and indignation. "They are to be taken away tomorrow— and without even benefit of trial—even though the Pennsylvania Chief Justice has granted them that right!" He leaned back in his chair, sighing heavily. "Not only that. A part of Washington's army has been routed at Brandywine and they're tramping into town in droves. On my way home I saw hundreds of their muskets lying in the road, thrown down by those who made off. I hadn't the heart to ask them the particulars of the battle, but rumor has it the slain are

said to be very numerous, upwards of a thousand."
His voice trailed off into silence.

A cold, sinking fear gripped her so, that she could
hardly speak. At last she forced herself to say, "Go
on, Papa."

"Our French general, Lafayette, took a bullet in the
leg. . . ."

She could hardly listen to Papa for the blood
pounding in her ears. Jonathan! What of Jonathan?
She forced herself to pay attention to what Papa was
saying.

". . . reported that Washington's forces fell back
toward Philadelphia under a shattering attack from
Howe's army and Howe has moved on to occupy
Chester."

Chester! Only fifteen miles from Philadelphia! Oh,
where was Jonathan tonight while she sat here helpless to do anything at all. Was he alive, and did he
think of her as he lay on some godforsaken field? Or
was he dead months ago, rotting in some ditch with
hundreds of other rebels?

Papa slumped in his chair, and in his face, which
she could see only dimly in the lamplight, there was
none of the vitality, the indomitable courage she had
come to depend on. The eyes that looked into hers
had the same fear-ridden look she'd seen in the eyes
of others who'd refused to leave the city. And now
fear of unknown things seized her and she could only
sit and stare at him, all the flood of questioning
dammed up at her lips.

In a low voice Dr. Mercer went on. "Last night
several of our friends lost their horses—stolen from
the stables by the rebels. I locked our horses and cow
in the wash house for safekeeping."

"Oh, Papa," cried Janine, "when will they give up?
Surely such a defeat will convince General Washington
that he can't hope to win!"

He eyed Janine thoughtfully, pushing his underlip
out and up a little. "Defeat it may be, but his army

is still intact. There's still a chance that he can keep
Howe out of Philadelphia."

But after Brandywine all the news was bad. Howe
swung west of Philadelphia and charged the cavalry
and Washington withdrew his troops to Reading
Furnace. On the twentieth of September Philadelphia
held its breath. Howe had crossed the Schuylkill at
Swede's Ford, driving a wedge between Washington's
troops and the town. A battle was expected hourly.
Boats, carriages, and footpads had taken flight all the
night before, and now all the boats were put away
and the shipping all ordered up the river on the next
tide, on pain of being burnt should Howe's vessels
approach.

To Janine's astonishment some of the citizens who
had fled the city were returning. In the early afternoon she had gone outside to see what was going on,
and glancing down Second Street, she saw a sight
that brought her up short. A carriage was drawn up
before the Shippen's house and Peggy and her three
older sisters and her parents tumbled out and hurried
inside their brick mansion. That evening Zoë reported
that one of the servants had told her that they had
returned in order to prevent their home from being
appropriated for quartering British officers.

Quartering British officers, here in their own homes?
thought Janine aghast. How would she feel if she and
Papa were forced to harbor the king's soldiers? A
sudden chill went through her. Even the Shippens
balked at that. But the city was teeming with friendly
Loyalists, and now many of the Quakers, incensed
that some of their leaders had been arrested and
banished, would look on the Redcoats as their de-
liverers. But the very thought was incredible. Washington would never let them take the city.

The next day continued quiet and Janine's nerves
were so on edge, she paced from one room to the
other, taking up her mending, putting it down, trying

to read, tossing the book aside. She felt she would fly into a million pieces if something didn't happen soon.

It was not until the following morning that they learned of the bloody attack on Anthony Wayne commanding a small detachment at Paoli. Major Samuel Hay who had escaped, staggered into town wild-eyed with horror, gasping the news. Shortly after midnight a British force swept down on the camp and, holding their fire so as not to reveal their presence, the light dragoons had charged with bayonets and swords, killing and capturing at least three hundred men. "A dreadful scene of havoc and slaughter," babbled Major Hay, white with shock, "a scene of butchery unsurpassed in the annals of the age." A massacre, they called it, and Janine felt an impotent rage and a suffocating sense of dread descend upon her.

On September 24 reports continued to come in of the English approaching, but no one knew what to believe. The Continental Army continued pressing horses, and Joshua Fisher's goods were taken from him for the army. Cannon were placed in some of the streets and there was talk of the city being set on fire. Janine and Dr. Mercer sat up until two in the morning, along with many of the citizens, guarding their homes against whatever calamity might leap out at them from the darkness. At last Papa fell asleep in his chair. Janine, numb with waiting and watching, stumbled upstairs to her room and dropped exhausted across her bed.

September 25 dawned cool and damp with thunderheads banked to the north. Tension mounted unbearably while they waited, ears straining for the sound of artillery and marching feet. Dr. Mercer set out on his black mare to make his rounds, but returned soon after to tell Janine he'd met up with Enoch Story who'd told him that the British were within four or five miles from them—that they were by John Dickinson's place and were expected in the city that evening. Then he was gone again.

She leaned against the door, her mind in a ferment. Was this another rumor soon to be refuted by another more terrifying one? Four or five miles? Soon now, any minute, General Washington and his army would swoop down on the British. He was holding his fire, waiting for the enemy to come to him, she told herself.

The town seemed ominously quiet. The shops and warehouses were locked and boarded. Even her own house seemed sinister, it was so quiet and still. She thought she wouldn't be able to stand it another minute. She ran outside and gathered apples into a basket with the idea of making cider. She began to peel one of the apples, but her hands were shaking so badly, she dropped it. She made herself finish peeling it, then ran out to the front stoop to listen. Nothing! She ran back again to the kitchen and took up the knife and another apple. She cut her finger and was not even aware of the pain. Doggedly she kept on. The waiting was worst of all, she decided. She longed for the British to come and get it over with.

Late in the afternoon rain came down in a steady torrent and was still pelting down when Dr. Mercer came home for supper that evening. Janine flew to meet him, desperate for news, yet frightened for what she might hear. He hung his dripping cloak on the hall tree and turned to face her, his eyes weary with fatigue.

"Thank the good Lord it's still raining," he said, taking out a handkerchief, then mopping his face. "It's said that tarred faggots are laid in several outhouses in different parts of the town. If anyone should make an attempt to fire the town, providence may prevent it."

Sitting across from him at the supper table, Janine listened while he told her of the great confusion in the

city, but there was no word of General Washington.
Papa paused and speared a piece of beef with his
fork.

Janine felt the color draining from her cheeks.
"Papa, where is Washington's army?"

Dr. Mercer gave a hopeless shrug. "Lord knows.
Somewhere beyond Germantown, I think."

Her fork clattered to her plate and she stared at
him incredulously. "Dear God, Papa! Way out there
in the country? Why isn't he here, defending the
town?"

Dr. Mercer shook his head and looked down at his
plate. "There's nothing to defend. Congress has fled
to York, most of the citizens have gone. Why should
he risk his army? Howe has wasted weeks of fighting
and now he's going to find he's gained an empty
victory."

Janine's heart went leaden as the last hope left
her. Fool that she was, why hadn't she thought that
Washington wouldn't defend an empty town? For a
moment she was too stunned to listen to what Papa
was saying, but she pulled herself together to hear
the rest of his news.

"The magistrate has warned us that the citizens
must take care of the town tonight. . . ." He paused
again, as if undecided whether to tell her the rest
and then went on. "Because of the rain, the British
have set up their camp within two miles of the city
for the night, but they will be in in the morning."

So they were coming at last, thought Janine dully.
And General Washington wouldn't lift a finger to stop
them. There would be no fighting in the streets,
no killing or burning or pillaging, and for that she
was thankful.

As though eager to end the conversation, Dr. Mercer
jumped up from his chair, wiping his mouth hastily
on his napkin.

"I must be off, Janine. The men of the town are
gathering at the State House at eight o'clock. We're

going to form companies to watch the town. Don't
expect me till you see me!" He kissed her quickly
on the brow and left.

Janine rose from the table and wandered into the
parlor. Parting the curtains, she looked out the
window at the rain-darkened street. The town was
quiet, as though holding itself in readiness for what
was to come. She was astonished to find that she herself no longer felt any fear, but rather a mounting anger that the British should take the town unopposed.
She turned from the window, and thinking to occupy
her mind and her hands, she dragged the spinning
wheel from its corner in the kitchen over to the fire
burning in the hearth and sat down to spin. The
thread was rough and uneven under her nervous fingers, but the hum of the wheel soothed her. The
evening passed without any disturbance, and at midnight she went to bed. Under her window she heard
the singsong bawl of the watchman crying the hour.

The next morning shortly before eleven o'clock
Janine heard shouts and excited cries coming from
outside, and the faint rhythmic sound of marching
feet on cobblestones. She rushed to the parlor, flung
open the window, and leaned out. Citizens poured
from their homes, lining the pavement. Far down
Second Street she saw a slow moving line of men advancing toward her, an endless tide of red coats and
white breeches flowing relentlessly up the street. Bands
played, colors flew in the stiff September breeze. Even
though many inhabitants had fled the town, it seemed
as though thousands were yelling and cheering as
Howe led British and Hessian soldiers into Philadelphia. Scanning the throng below, Janine noticed
that they were mostly women and children. Tory
sympathizers, she thought, surprised at the bitterness
in her heart.

Now Cornwallis rode by on horseback and she
stared intently at him, taking in the thick brows over

heavy-lidded dark eyes, his long nose and full-lipped mouth, the sloping forehead, the heavy jaws. A formidable enemy, she thought, shrinking inside. Now marching along with the British was Joseph Galloway and a man she recognized as Tench Coxe, who had earned the undying hatred of his countrymen by resigning from the militia and turning Loyalist. Uneasily she remembered that John Adams had called Philadelphia "that mass of cowardice and Toryism."

Awestruck, Janine stood watching as the red tide advanced. Now came the Hessians of Knyphausen's regiment in dark blue coats and white breeches, followed by the jaegers in green coats faced with red. There was no plundering on either side of the street, and it was hard to think of these stalwart red-coated men as the enemy. What the victors would do with the town remained to be seen. Everyone knew of the looting, raping, shooting, stabbing, and other atrocities committed by Cornwallis's army in New York and New Jersey!

Eagerly she watched for General Howe, but when the red tide ended, he had not appeared. Later it was reported that three thousand troops had entered the town and had taken up their post at Germantown and that Howe had made his headquarters not at the home of a devoted Tory, but had commandeered John Cadwalader's elegant mansion on Second Street.

As though that were not enough, late the following afternoon Dr. Mercer stormed into the house, red-faced and fuming. "Without a by-your-leave or previous notice, the British have brought their sick and wounded soldiers into the hospital!" he raged. "They're crowding the wards, incommoding our patients!" He flung up his arms in a hopeless gesture. "It's impossible to keep order in the place!"

"Oh, Papa, how dreadful!" She could well imagine the commotion that would cause. "Tomorrow I'll go with you—"

"No, no!" interrupted Dr. Mercer testily. "I asked Doctor Ransom if he needed you and he said he could manage without your help."

Janine pressed her lips together in a tight line and said nothing, but a bright, burning anger flared up inside her. There was a time when she would have ignored Richard's stubborn refusal and, knowing he needed her, rushed to his aid. But now she determined he would crawl on his knees before she would come!

Chapter 24

The fall of Philadelphia was a staggering blow to the rebel cause. The talk in the taverns and coffee houses was of little else, and the newspapers made much of it. Gloom hung heavily over the Continental Army, they said, and many civilians, as well as Washington's own officers—Pickering, Green, and Lee among them —started doubting Washington's capabilities. Forgetting his daring strokes at Princeton and Trenton, mutterings against him and demands for his removal bombarded Congress from disgruntled officers and civilians. But the majority of his men had not lost faith, and Washington, it was said, appeared calm and unshaken throughout the rumblings.

During the crisp autumn days that followed, the citizens were constantly in a state of nerves and excitement, expecting the worst to happen yet not knowing what the worst could be.

Early on the morning of September 27 Zoë rushed home from the market gasping out the news that the American frigates *Province* and *Delaware*, with several gondolas, had sailed up the river with the intention of firing on the town to destroy it along with the hated Tories. Now they were being fired upon by a battery which the English had erected at the lower end of town.

Janine and Zoë rushed to the garret window and by craning their necks could see the ships spouting puffs of smoke and some figures running around on deck. Her heart pounding with fright, Janine watched spellbound until at the end of half an hour the *Delaware* ran aground, took fire, and struck her colors.

Pale and shaken, Janine turned to Zoë. "Do you realize that the British have saved our town from destruction by the patriots! It's beyond belief!"

Later Janine learned that the British boarded the ship and took Admiral Alexander and his men prisoners. A number of citizens were taken up and imprisoned. Someone sent fire rafts down the river to annoy the British fleet. But life went on.

Several mornings later an autumn mist rose with the sun, shrouding the town in a glowing pall. Janine awoke to a sound she now recognized as cannon fire. Hastily she threw on her clothes and ran downstairs looking for Papa, but he had already left the house.

"He say for you to stay put," said Zoë vehemently. "He don't want you be mixed up in all that shooting."

Janine ran to the door and, flinging it open, cocked her head, listening. She could hear the rumbling of the batteries and see the smoke, which rolled like low-hanging clouds over the town. The firing seemed to be coming from the northwest, from the direction of Germantown, but it sounded loud enough to be in the next block. She spent the morning in a swivet of anxiety and worry, unable to set herself to complete the smallest task, wishing Papa were safe at home. What could be happening to Jonathan wouldn't bear thinking about.

It was shortly after noon when Dr. Mercer returned with astonishing news. Washington's army had marched toward Germantown and made a surprise attack upon Howe's nine thousand men at Mount Airy!

"The rebels had them on the run!" exclaimed Papa with a triumphant smile. "They were retreating!"

"Go on, Papa, go on!"

"Then Howe rallied his men and a party of Loyalists and took refuge in Chew's place."

Janine nodded, envisioning the square stone mansion where Peggy Chew lived.

"Scotch Willie Maxwell's Jerseymen tried to clean them out, but"—Papa shook his head hopelessly—"the Continentals were blinded by musket smoke and a terrible fog. In the melee the men were firing on each other. When their ammunition began to run low, Washington and his men withdrew."

"Withdrew!" cried Janine despairingly. "He withdrew all the way through New York and New Jersey!"

"Now hold on a minute!" Papa bent a sharp gaze on his daughter. "It was a bold stroke. Though they lost the day, they came so close to victory that they now believe it's within their grasp. It will stand them in good stead in the days to come."

Following the battle at Germantown, two Presbyterian meeting houses, the playhouse, and the State House, were turned into hospitals for the wounded American soldiers. Janine went to the State House and once again moved quietly and efficiently among the wounded and dying, serving coffee and whey, binding wounds, offering words of encouragement till her back ached and her knees buckled from weariness. Her green muslin dress was streaked with blood, dirt, and sweat. When she could do no more, she went home, enraged and sick at heart at the sight of these men brought down by a cause they could not hope to win.

On a brisk evening in mid-October when the poplars had turned yellow and the smell of woodsmoke was in the air, Janine went next door to take tea with Rachel Lindley, a gentle, rosy-cheeked Quaker with two small children. She returned home to find Papa pacing the parlor in a state of high excitement.

"Colonel Boudinot is here, in Philadelphia! I've invited him for supper."

"Colonel Boudinot?" Janine's brows drew together

in a perplexed frown. "I've not heard you mention him. . . ."

"Elias Boudinot is a former patient—a delegate to Congress from New Jersey. Now he's involved in the New Jersey Committee of Correspondence—an ardent patriot. He sent powder to the beleaguered Bostonians, and . . ." Dr. Mercer hesitated ". . . similar missions."

Janine's eyebrows rose. "Similar missions?"

"Well, he's involved with the care of British prisoners and . . . this is in strictest confidence, *ma petite,* he also manages the intelligence of the army."

"And why is he coming here, Papa?"

Dr. Mercer thrust out his lower lip, considering. "I suspect he's scrounging about for physicians for Washington's army—for all intents and purposes."

Colonel Boudinot was a tall, angular man with a narrow head and a large nose that was set between eyes that gleamed like those of a hawk. Tonight he wore no uniform. Janine thought that in his snuff-colored coat and breeches he would easily pass unnoticed among the citizenry walking the streets. His mood was jubilant, for news had just been received of General Burgoyne's surrender to Gates at Saratoga.

After supper they adjourned to the parlor and Colonel Boudinot eased into the Windsor chair and stretched out his long legs before the fire. Papa poured glasses of Madeira.

"This time Gentleman Johnny Burgoyne started a conquest he couldn't finish!" said Colonel Boudinot, elated. "You know what his intentions were, of course. He wanted to knock the northern colonies out of the war. He was moving his army south to Albany to meet St. Leger's force driving east through the Mohawk Valley. But Arnold smashed him at Fort Stanwix, sent his Mohawk Indians packing. Howe was to march north to join him and instead he's sitting on his haunches here in Philadelphia!" Colonel

Boudinot chuckled in delight. "Gates was waiting for Burgoyne at Bemis Heights with upwards of six thousand men. . . ."

Janine shuddered and stopped listening as Colonel Boudinot went on to describe the battle in all its horrifying detail. At last he finished and the talk turned to camp hospitals and physicians. Janine pricked up her ears.

"Washington's moved on to Whitemarsh, you know, and we're in desperate straits. We've only one surgeon and five surgeon's mates for every thousand men of the army. And many of our surgeons have had no training except that of apprenticeships. . . ."

Dr. Mercer shook his head. "I'm no surgeon, Elias."

Colonel Boudinot waved a hand in dismissal. "No matter. We suffer not only from wounded and maimed. We're plagued with all manner of diseases—putrid fever, dysentery, white plague, pleurisy, ague, scurvy, smallpox—though we've managed to hold down the smallpox—made inoculations routine last summer." He bent his sharp gaze on Dr. Mercer. "I don't think you realize, Robert, that disease in camp has proved far more formidable than the Redcoats on the battle-field. Last year alone we lost ten thousand men to illness! In God's truth, lucky is the soldier who can leave those infested rabbit warrens we call hospitals alive and free of some new malady."

Janine's mind fastened on the news that Washington had moved to Whitemarsh and her heart thudded with excitement. If only she could go to General Washington's camp, she could find Jonathan! She knew she could. Eagerly she blurted out, "I could help, Colonel Boudinot. I've cared for the sick and wounded at Penn's Hospital." Flushing, she added, "I'm no longer needed there."

An amused smile lighted Colonel Boudinot's long, narrow face. "Conditions are far beyond your help, my dear. Besides, to General Washington's extreme annoyance, we've a hoard of camp followers. Wives, sweethearts, all the women in camp act as nurses to look after the men. What we're desperate for are medicines"—he glanced hopefully at Dr. Mercer—"and physicians."

Dr. Mercer shook his head. "I've too many responsibilities here, Elias. I'm needed not only at the hospital, but right here in the city to treat the citizens—and the poor souls who can't afford a doctor." He smiled ruefully.

At that moment there came a violent pounding on the front door, and seconds later Zoë appeared in the parlor doorway, motioning frantically to Dr. Mercer.

"You come quick. Mistress Galloway took bad. . . ."

Dr. Mercer jumped up from his chair, excused himself, and went out, leaving Janine to entertain Colonel Boudinot.

With an effort she concealed her disappointment at his refusal to accept her help. But why not tell the truth and shame the devil? she thought. Color rose from her neck, creeping over her face.

"I must confess, Colonel Boudinot, I've an ulterior motive for going to Whitemarsh. My fiancé, Jonathan Burke, is with General Washington's troops and we've had no news of him for more than a year." She swallowed over the lump that rose in her throat and hurried on. "I thought if I were there, in the encampment, I might find him."

Colonel Boudinot's piercing hawk eyes registered astonishment. "I doubt you'd have much success in a camp of eleven thousand men." He sipped his Madeira and gazed thoughtfully at her over the rim of his glass. "However, there is a possibility I could be of some help in finding him for you." He leaned back in his chair and looked at her appraisingly. "And perhaps you could do something for me as well."

"I'd be happy to!"

Colonel Boudinot cleared his throat and set down his glass. "You're well aware, of course, that General Howe was headquartered at the home of Captain

John Cadwalader. I believe he's turned the house over to a German general now, but there are staff meetings held from time to time. . . ."

Janine nodded. "The Cadwaladers live only three doors down the street from us."

"Just so. I'd like you to keep an eye on Cadwalader's house. Note who enters and leaves, how often. In fact, every move the British make is important, no matter how trivial it may seem. You see, I gather information on the arrival of reinforcements, changes of bivouacs, assemblage of wagons and other heavy equipment—even the movement of a gun emplacement is of interest to me and General Washington."

Janine's eyes widened in astonishment. "Surely you enlist much more skillful and efficient observers than I who keep you abreast of what goes on in the town."

"Quite true," said the colonel dryly. "Unfortunately, there are those among them in the employ of the British who feed us false information. So we prefer to hear reports from several sources to verify their authenticity. Then, too, my men cannot be everywhere at once. An extra pair of eyes and ears often comes in handy, especially if a man is unable to meet his contact to pass on intelligence." A regretful sigh escaped him. "And, of course, we occasionally lose a man. It's well to have a replacement on the scene."

Janine listened intently as he explained what she should be on the lookout for, straining to remember every word.

"We'll meet at the Rising Sun Tavern. It's kept by the Widow Nice, and my presence there goes unnoticed, for I've made it my habit to dine there every afternoon. It lies six miles north of the town and two miles west of Frankford. Do you think you can find it?"

Janine nodded, her heart pounding with excitement and anticipation.

Colonel Boudinot's brows drew together in a

thoughtful frown. "We need some pretext for your being there. . . ."

With the thought of action, her head went up and her shoulders went back. "That's of no concern, Colonel Boudinot," said Janine smiling. "I'm in the habit of riding out to Frankford mill to buy flour."

Colonel Boudinot's sharp black eyes gleamed with approval. "You'll say nothing of this to anyone, not even your father. Both for your own protection and his, I must swear you to secrecy. Agreed?"

Again Janine nodded, and they made plans to meet the following Saturday.

If Janine's sudden interest in knitting woolen stockings for Papa and Zoë aroused their curiosity, they made no comment. By the hour she sat at the parlor window behind the sheer glass curtains keeping a sharp watch on the comings and goings at British Headquarters in Cadwalader's brick mansion, peering frequently into the double-paned busybody outside the window.

Saturday dawned, cold and sunny, and a bitter wind whipped about the corners of the house, rattling the windowpanes. Shortly after three in the afternoon Janine donned her warm green linsey-woolsey gown, wrapped an old brown cloak around her, and set off for the home of Abraham Carlisle to get a pass to ride out to Frankford Mill. Impatiently she waited her turn in line. For once she was thankful that provisions were scarce. After Howe's troops had occupied the town, the country people driving the great Conestoga wagons filled with produce dared not come in to market lest their produce be commandeered by the British. The citizens had to rely on their own meager gardens, dried fruits and vegetables, and stores they'd put by last summer. They were given passes to go to the mills for flour, and some had little else.

When Janine's turn came, her pulses raced and she

lowered her eyes as she took the pass, certain her guilt was written on her face for all to see.

Sternly she told herself that today was no different from the many other trips she'd made to Frankford. With an effort she forced herself to walk, not run, to Brandy. She set off at a brisk mount trot for Frankford.

She had timed her ride carefully so as to arrive at the tavern a little before four, when Colonel Boudinot should have finished his dinner. Her progress was slowed by deep ruts and sharp, frozen ridges. It was with difficulty that she held on to her patience while Brandy carefully picked his way along the slippery road. By the time she reached the inn, the lowering sun told her it was late afternoon. With shaking fingers she tethered Brandy to a post outside and entered the crowded tavern. Gazing anxiously about the dimly lighted room, she saw several men lounging at tables, eating, or playing cards. Surely Colonel Boudinot would be alone. Suppose he wasn't here? thought Janine with a sinking heart. Then in a corner near a window she saw an angular figure sitting at a table, hunched over a tankard of ale. As she started toward him, the Widow Nice, polishing glasses behind the bar, looked up questioningly. Colonel Boudinot gave her a nod and she looked away. Quickly Janine threaded her way through the tables and slid into a chair across from Colonel Boudinot, her back to the room.

He smiled and raised his tankard of ale in greeting. "Will you join me?"

Though the room was warm, Janine felt chilled to the marrow and her teeth were chattering. "Hot cider, please."

Colonel Boudinot gave her order to a serving maid, and when the steaming mug of cider was set before her, Colonel Boudinot leaned toward her, folding his arms on the table.

"You'll be pleased to hear I've found your fiancé."

Janine's hand flew to her lips, stifling an exclamation of joy. "Jonathan!" she whispered eagerly. "Where is he? How is he? When can I see him?"

Colonel Boudinot grinned and raised his hand as if to stem her flood of questions. "As you thought, he's serving with Washington's troops at Whitemarsh. . . ." He paused.

Tears of joy and relief brimmed on Janine's eyelids. "Yes, go on. . . ."

"I wasn't able to see him. I had only a few moments to spare. . . ." Again he hesitated, his expression suddenly grave. "One of the subalterns scanned the rolls. . . ." His words trailed off and suddenly an uneasy foreboding seized her. He was holding something back!

"Colonel Boudinot, you can't imagine how grateful I am, just to know Jonathan's alive and well!" She let out a vast sigh of relief and cupped her cold hands around the pewter mug, sipping the hot brew, savoring its warmth.

Colonel Boudinot hunched his shoulders and cleared his throat. "I'm afraid he's not as well as could be," he said gently.

Her eyes widened in alarm as she stared at him across the table. She saw him looking at her appraisingly, as if he were trying to decide how much to tell her. Dimly she recalled the night he'd discussed the camp hospitals with Papa. Into her mind floated the image of men stuffed into tents, lying head to toe in damp and filthy clothing on rotten straw, no medicine, no blankets to fend off the cold seeping in, the putrid air. . . .

"What do you mean, he's not as well as could be?" demanded Janine in a strangled voice.

Colonel Boudinot took a sip of ale. "He's suffering from putrid fever—camp fever, we call it."

Janine felt the color drain from her face. She'd

seen men suffering from putrid fever in Penn's Hospital. She had a horrible vision of Jonathan lying helpless, his chest and abdomen covered with rose-colored spots, suffering the indescribable agonies of alternating bouts of delirium and coma. Her knees turned weak at the thought of Jonathan, handsome, robust, laughing, brought down by this dread malady.

She leaned forward, her eyes pleading. "Colonel Boudinot, please, couldn't you request that Jonathan be transferred to Penn's Hospital?"

The colonel sighed. Sympathy and regret were written on his face as he shook his head slowly, relentlessly. "I'm sorry, Janine."

Her thin shoulders sagged in despair, but she managed a wan smile and looked up into his kind face. "At least if he's in the camp hospital, he's not out in the woods and fields being shot at like a turkey. . . ." Her voice trailed off.

Colonel Boudinot stared hard out the window at the bare-limbed trees. "Yes, there's that to be said, of course." He turned to face her and hesitantly, as though against his better judgment, he said, "There is a slight possibility that I could get you a pass to see him—though General Washington has a particular dislike for camp followers."

Janine's face brightened. "General Washington and I are acquaintances," she said eagerly. "When you give him my name, he'll know I'm no camp follower. Oh, please, you will try to get me a pass. . . ."

"I'll do my best, Janine. But don't count on it."

Her hope would not be dimmed. Gazing at Colonel Boudinot, her cheeks grew pink and her eyes sparkled with anticipation. "You *will* see him for me, won't you? Tell him that I love him, that I'm waiting. . . ."

Colonel Boudinot's dark eyes glistened in the lamplight. "I'll try." He cleared his throat and assumed a brisk, businesslike tone. "Now, what news have you brought me?"

In a low voice Janine poured out all the seemingly
unrelated and unimportant bits of information she'd
gleaned during the past few days while watching the
comings and goings at the Cadwalader house and
while shopping, marketing, and strolling on Water
Street along the wharf. Colonel Boudinot listened
intently, nodding from time to time.

"Friday last, from our garret window, Zoë and I
saw a number of Hessians crossing to Jersey in flat-
bottomed boats."

"How many, would you say?"

"I heard it said upward of two thousand. The *rumor*
was that their intentions were against Fort Mercer
at Red Bank."

Colonel Boudinot's dark eyes burned with an intense light. "It was Washington's intention to block-
ade the British in Philadelphia to force Howe to call
on the Royal Navy for help in opening up the Delaware to his supply ships. Go on."

"The night following, the Hessians who'd crossed
the river were driven back two or three times endeavoring to storm the fort. We heard that two
hundred were slain and great numbers wounded. Now
it's said they've attacked Fort Mifflin on Mud Island.

"Yesterday it seemed the firing was incessant from
the battery, the gondolas and a British man-of-war,
the *Augusta*. Near noon we were all panicked by a
blast that shook the town to its foundations. Those
pouring from Quaker meeting said they thought it to
be an earthquake. The windows of the prison and
many homes were shattered—it sounded like a hundred cannon. Later we heard it was the *Augusta*—
that it had taken fire and, after burning nearly two
hours, blew up. Some say she took fire by accident;
others that it was caused by red hot fire from Mud
Island battery. Another smaller English vessel also
took fire and burned. Last night we saw the fires of
the British and Hessians camped across the river
in Jersey."

Colonel Boudinot pursed his lips, his intense gaze never leaving Janine's face. "What else?"

"General Howe's men have been felling trees in the Governor's forest beyond the hospital like rushlights," said Janine angrily. "Hauling away great wagonloads and building huts south of town. . . ."

"Interesting," said the colonel. "The information ties in with other intelligence we've gathered. Building a camp in the city could mean that Howe plans to remain in Philadelphia."

". . . and his men are using the weather vane atop Carpenter's Hall for target practice!" added Janine, her blue eyes blazing in indignation.

Colonel Boudinot allowed himself an amused smile. "Anything more?"

"Tom Prior was arrested by the British on suspicion of sending intelligence to General Washington."

Colonel Boudinot took another sip of ale, and an expression of pain and sorrow crossed his usually bland countenance. "Yes, we heard that. A good man. Most unfortunate."

"That's all I have to tell you, Colonel. Very little of consequence that you haven't already heard, I'm afraid."

Colonel Boudinot smiled and patted her hand. "It doesn't seem much by itself, perhaps. But like a puzzle, when all the bits and pieces of information we gather are fitted together, they make an interesting picture for General Washington to see and consider."

He gave her a long, penetrating look. "Do you wish to continue serving your country?"

She drew a deep breath, and her voice was low and tense with determination. "I'll help in any way I can."

A gleam of approval shone from Colonel Boudinot's dark eyes. "You're a courageous young woman, Janine. A credit to your countrymen."

Before she left the tavern she agreed to meet him

the following week if she had further intelligence to pass on. And if not, the week after.

Urging Brandy homeward in the soft gray dusk, past oaks and pines that cast long shadows across the stubble of snowy fields, her heart sang with joy. The words *Jonathan is safe, Jonathan is safe* pounded in her ears in time with Brandy's steady hoofbeats. General Washington would surely grant her a pass to see him. Somehow she would find nourishing food and medicine, and even if she couldn't stay in camp, she could ride out every day to care for him.

Now, thinking of her impulsive promise to Colonel Boudinot to help in any way she could, the significance of what she had agreed to do came to her with startling clarity. She had thought only to return his favor of finding Jonathan by relating what was going on in the town. She had simply told him what anyone with eyes and ears could observe. She had not actually looked upon it in the light of serving her country. Now his words rang in her ears.

She was astonished at her own actions, for when the moment was suddenly thrust upon her that she was forced to choose sides, no doubts clouded her mind. Papa was right when he'd said that revolutions had a way of upending ordinary values. And though she'd die before she'd admit it, that odious Mark Furneaux was right. She could no longer ignore the evidence of her own eyes and ears.

She thought of General Washington and Thomas Jefferson and Dr. Franklin. And of Jonathan and Tim Abernethy and the other soldiers in Penn's Hospital, all willing to fight to the death for the colonies, for their beloved independence, for their homes and families. Then, thinking again of Jonathan, she muttered in Brandy's ear, "King George be damned," and spurred the horse to a canter through the small village of Nicetown. She wanted to be home before dark.

When she finally arrived, she slowed Brandy to a

walk and turned him toward the stable behind the
house. Then, thinking better of it, she locked him
in the washhouse for safekeeping against the maraud-
ing Hessians. She noted with relief that Papa's mare
wasn't there. Thank goodness Papa was gone. She
wouldn't have to explain her whereabouts this afternoon.

Once inside the house she hung her cloak on the
halltree and to her surprise she saw a strange surtout
hanging on one of the hooks. Who could be calling
at this hour? She heard Zoë's footsteps in the bedroom
above. Zoë must have told the caller that Papa was
out. Someone wanting medicine, most likely.

Swiftly she crossed the hall and opened the parlor
door. She started in surprise at the sight of the visitor
who stood with his back to her, warming his hands
at the fire blazing on the hearth.

"Richard!"

He spun to face her, and his lean face colored to
the roots of his auburn hair; whether from the heat
of the fire or embarrassment at seeing her appear in
the doorway instead of Papa, she could not tell.

"Papa is making calls, Richard. He should be home
shortly if you wish to wait." Her tone was sharper
than she'd intended, but she was still nettled over
his cold, aloof treatment at the hospital, smarting
from the memory of his curt dismissal last spring.

"I came to see you, as well as your father, Janine."
His tone was formal, but his eyes clung to her like
those of a starving man at the sight of food.

Her heart quickened in spite of herself, and she was
surprised at how happy she was to see him again.
She inclined her head. "Oh?"

"Last night at the hospital after the explosion we
heard all sorts of dreadful rumors about an earthquake and fire in the town. . . ." He seemed at a loss
for words and shifted uneasily before the fire. "I came
as soon as I could . . . I couldn't get away till now. . . ."

When she said nothing, he went on. "I was concerned for your safety. . . ." His words trailed off as though it were painful for him to continue.

"I appreciate your concern," said Janine awkwardly, "and I'm sure Papa will too."

She turned to leave the room. Richard's face seemed to crumple and he started toward her, his hands outstretched imploringly. "Janine, wait! Listen to me, please! I know you're angry with me. I treated you like a leper and I'm sorry. I was distraught. I thought it best to forget you. But when it seemed your life was in danger, well, I realized that forgetting you was futile. I can't forget you, Janine. Just now when you came in, I was so relieved to see you safe and sound, I—" His hands dropped to his sides in a helpless gesture.

Janine's heart went out to him and she put her hand on his arm. "Don't take on so, Richard, please! Do sit down and calm yourself. Papa will be home soon."

They settled themselves by the fire, catching up on each other's news, and when they finished, a silence fell between them. Richard's eyes held hers and he gazed at her longingly. At last he said in a low, passionate voice, "My life is barren without you, Janine. I've searched for someone else, but all other women suffer by comparison. Couldn't we see each other occasionally?"

Janine dropped her gaze to her fingers pleating a fold in her gown. Richard was pleasant company. She had missed him. And she was tired of war and waiting alone.

"If you wish," she said softly. "As long as you understand—"

"I understand." He smiled ruefully. "We're friends again, then?"

She nodded and looked up into his eyes, wondering how long they would remain friends.

The next morning when Janine told Papa of Richard's embarrassed apology, he grinned and patted her shoulder benevolently. "A bird in the hand is worth two in the bush!"

"Oh, Papa," said Janine in mock indignation, "you old reprobate!"

Chapter 25

During the golden, frost-nipped days of October 1777, Janine continued to meet Colonel Boudinot at Rising Sun Tavern. He sat facing her across the scarred oak table, his dark eyes gleaming, hanging on her every word, no matter how insignificant the news seemed to be.

Early in November she reported that a soldier had been hanged on the common for striking an officer. Provisions had become more scarce among the citizens. To make matters worse, the Hessians were plundering at a great rate such things as wood, smoked meats and fish, potatoes, turnips, apples—whatever they could find among the small stores the citizens were trying to hoard to see them through the cold winter months.

"One of Howe's soldiers came to demand blankets, and when I refused him, he barged inside and tramped upstairs and took one!" said Janine fuming. "Then he had the insolence to beg me to excuse his borrowing it!"

A small smile creased Colonel Boudinot's leathery face. "As we surmised. The British are languishing on empty stomachs and feeling a chill in the air! Their supplies are not getting through as long as we hold forts Mifflin and Mercer."

"Butter cannot be bought for love or money," Janine went on. "All we have is from our cow, and many citizens have none at all."

Two weeks later on a cloudy Thursday in Novem-

ber Janine mounted Brandy and galloped all the way
to the tavern in high excitement. In a low, strangled
voice she told Colonel Boudinot of the terrible bombardment that thundered all the day long the previous
Tuesday from the *Vigilant* and *Somerset*, British men-
of-war, upon the formidable Mud Island battery pro-
tecting Fort Mifflin.

"The colonel nodded gravely. "Yes, we heard. We
were certain the English were about to storm the
fort, that our troops would be wiped out, but then
it was reported that our men had withdrawn and
slipped across to Fort Mercer."

"And none too soon," added Janine, her face flushed
with excitement. "Last night at two in the morning,
Cornwallis left the city with three thousand men. I
heard them clattering along the street under my
window, dragging their artillery, cursing the cold
and darkness."

The colonel's eyes gleamed with admiration.
"You've done well, Janine." Once again she had cor-
roborated the sometimes questionable reports of other
informants. "To misquote your father. 'Once again
the enemy has locked the barn door after the horses
have stolen away.'"

Just before dawn on November 21 Janine awoke
to the heart-stopping thunder of cannon fire. She
jumped out of bed and flung her night rail around
her. Snatching up a candle, she dashed upstairs to
the garret. The window across the room blazed red
with a glow that lighted the dark sky outside. *Oh,
God,* she thought, *they've set the town afire!* She ran
to the window and peered out. Her hand flew to her
throat and her mouth fell open in horror. In the middle of the river, enveloped in an inferno of flames and
billows of red-tinged smoke, stood the American fleet
blazing like the fires of hell, the orange and yellow
flames licking up the masts like pennants in the
breeze.

Breathlessly she counted the masts etched against the blackness. Eight vessels were engulfed in red haze and smoke. Suddenly a shattering explosion erupted from the blazing flotilla, then another, quickly followed by two more. The windows rattled and the floor under her feet shook with the impact. Clapping her hands over her ears, she raced downstairs to rouse Papa.

But Dr. Mercer had already flung on his clothes and rushed outside to see what was going on. Standing in the doorway, shivering with cold and fright, Janine saw lights flickering on in houses along the street, and soon frightened knots of citizens were gathered on the pavement. It was Chalkley James who hurried up from the riverfront with the news. The firing was from the *Delaware* that lay at Cooper's Point. The Americans had set their entire fleet afire, seventeen ships in all gasped Chalkley, except one small vessel and several of the galleys that passed by the city in the night.

The next morning an American schooner was burned in the river by the British nearly opposite Drinker's house, and the day was shattered by the firing of cannon and small arms.

Toward the end of November Janine reported to Colonel Boudinot several skirmishes between the Americans and the picket guards in which seven or eight were killed. On the morning of the twenty-second a thousand men attacked the picket guards and were quickly driven off. They fled for their lives, some taking refuge in John Dickinson's house and in the homes of neighbors who offered shelter. The British immediately set fire to Dickinson's house and a number of others whose owners were suspected of sheltering the rebels, burning them to the ground.

"It's rumored that the British planned to burn the houses anyway because they served as hiding places for our soldiers," said Janine in a low-pitched, angry voice. "In fact the British threatened to burn all the houses within four miles of the town outside the lines.

Everyone is in a panic, locked and barricaded inside their homes, not daring to leave, not knowing who will be suspect next.

"The day after, a British vessel came up the Delaware to Philadelphia, and now the wharves are lined with ships bringing supplies to the English."

Colonel Boudinot shook his head and sighed, lines of weariness etched more deeply in his weathered face. "The British control the waterway from the Cape to Philadelphia now. They can bring in all they want." He allowed himself a rueful smile. "Since the Congress in York has declared today a day of Thanksgiving, we're giving each and every man half a gill of rice and a tablespoon of vinegar." He sighed again and an expression of resignation replaced the ironical twist of his lips. "I suppose we can be grateful that we're still alive."

Janine returned home and went dutifully to the Thanksgiving service at Christ Church to give thanks, but for the life of her, she could not see what for. It seemed to her that God would be most displeased with the behavior of his divine humans.

Early one bitter, snowy morning in the first week of December, Janine heard a loud pounding on the front door. Running to answer, she found a young red-nosed, mustached British officer standing on the threshold. He looked at her with eyes as cold as gray marbles, his manner pompous and overbearing. He told her that he was Sergeant McMickle and that he was commandeering horses.

"We have no horse to spare," said Janine flatly and started to close the door.

He placed a big rough reddened hand against the door, holding it open. "You don't mind if I take a look in your stable, ma'am?" His face split in a leering grin and his eyes raked her from head to toe.

"No—no," she stammered, "of course not." Papa had left early, riding out to the hospital on his mare.

If she agreed to let this cur search the stable, perhaps he'd not think to look in the washhouse where Brandy was hidden. She slammed the door and raced to the back of the house, her heart pounding wildly. Parting the curtains at the window, she saw the scarlet-clad figure in a whirl of snowflakes tramp through the kitchen garden and enter the stable.

An instant later he reappeared, head down, trudging back toward the house. Whether he heard a sound that caught his attention, or whether he was simply curious, she didn't know. But as he passed the washhouse, his head jerked up and he strode to the door, kicked it open, and glanced inside.

Janine's breath caught in her throat and she thought surely her heart would stop beating. The man stepped through the doorway and moments later emerged, leading Brandy through the yard by a rope attached to his halter.

Stricken with rage, she flung up the window and leaned out, shrieking, "You can't take that horse! Let go of him this instant!"

In reply the officer leaped on Brandy's back, grinned, raised his hand in salute, and, clucking to the horse, rode around the corner of the house toward the street.

Janine sped through the house, down the hall and yanked open the front door. Lifting her skirts, she flew outside into the pelting snow just as the man rounded the front of the house.

Screaming "Stop, thief!" at the top of her lungs, she flung herself at horse and rider, clutching the man's scarred leather boot, tugging on his leg with every ounce of strength she could muster in an effort to pull him from Brandy's back.

Halfway down the street two men paused to stare, then strode inside the Golden Fleece Tavern. The officer's leering grin changed to snarling fury. He kicked out violently with a force that sent Janine reeling, knocking her off-balance, and she tumbled to the ground. Rage numbed the pain of her fall and she raised up on her hands and knees in time to see the British sergeant urge Brandy to a trot and ride swiftly away down the street. Janine buried her face in her hands and burst into tears.

Shortly before three that afternoon Dr. Mercer returned home to find Janine in despair over the theft of Brandy. They sat down to dinner, but she could eat nothing.

"I'm going down to British Headquarters and demand they return my horse!" she raged. "I'll steal him back if I have to!"

Dr. Mercer gazed at his daughter with sad, hopeless eyes. "You would go on a fool's errand, *ma petite*. They would only laugh at you. As for stealing him back, well, even if you should find Brandy, you'd be shot on sight if you tried to make off with him. If it's any consolation, you're not alone. Coming home I saw Redcoats everywhere taking horses and wagons from farmers, commandeering carriages, everything on wheels. They're crossing the Schuylkill. Must have been upward of five hundred of them. You can feel the excitement crackling in the air. Something is surely afoot."

Janine's red-rimmed eyes narrowed and her lips pressed together in a hard line. Colonel Boudinot would certainly be interested in this. She'd have to take Papa's horse and ride to Frankford. And she must think of a good reason to borrow his mare.

"Go on, Papa," said Janine, tense with excitement. "What else?"

When he finished telling her of all the commotion going on in the town, he pushed his chair back from the table and stood up. "Well, I must be off, Janine."

Her heart sank to her toes. "Surely not in all this snow, Papa!"

Dr. Mercer smiled. "It's nearly stopped. Mrs. Reed requires a clyster. I promised Mistress Galloway I'd look in on her, and I want to see how Cyril Harvey's coming along. I'm afraid he's taken pleurisy." He patted Janine on the shoulder. "Be glad you don't have to venture out. I'll stop at the tavern on the way home—see if I can find out what's going on."

After Dr. Mercer left, Janine paced the floor in an agony of indecision. Should she go out and see what news she could gather along the wharf, or keep watch on British Headquarters at the Cadwaladers' house? She was dying to go out, but Papa could probably learn more than she from the men at the tavern.

With a sigh she took up her knitting and sat in her chair at the window in the front parlor, glancing up frequently to scan the snowy street opposite and to peer into the busybody tilted to mirror her own side of the street. She wound the black wool through her fingers, thinking wryly that surely Papa will have the warmest feet in the town.

Her needles had been clicking busily for almost an hour when her eyes caught a flash of scarlet marching purposefully down the street. With a start of surprise she saw two British captains enter Loxley House, directly across the street from the Cadwaladers'. Janine's brow wrinkled in a puzzled frown. This was strange indeed, for Loxley House was the home of schoolmaster William Darragh and his wife, Lydia—Quakers who steadfastly refused to take part in the war. Had the British learned that Darragh's son Charles was serving as a lieutenant in Washington's camp at Whitemarsh? Would they too be arrested and sent away to exile in Virginia with James Pemberton and other Friends? Her hands shook, and several stitches slipped from her needle. She sat tense and alert, her gaze riveted upon Darragh's white front door.

After about ten minutes the officers emerged from the house and crossed the street to headquarters. Almost immediately Darragh's door flew open and the short, slight figure of Lydia Darragh in her Quaker gray ankle-length dress emerged. She marched across the street and mounted the steps of Cadwalader's red brick mansion. A scowl darkened her fair complexion, her blue eyes were stormy, and her mouth turned down at the corners. It was obvious even from this distance that Friend Darragh, usually so calm and composed, was madder than a wet hen.

Burning with curiosity, Janine hitched her chair closer to the window, parted the curtains, and pressed her cheek against the cold glass, the better to view the street in the busybody fastened outside the window.

Ten minutes later Lydia Darragh emerged from British Headquarters. Her face was composed, her brow serene as she walked sedately to her house and went inside.

As the afternoon wore on, scarlet-clad officers who carried themselves with an urgent, purposeful air continued to pass in and out of Loxley House. As darkness came on, the lamplighter, bundled against the cold, bent against the sharp wind, trudged down the street. Mounting his ladder against the streetlamp that stood before Darragh's house, he touched a flame to the wick. The light sprang to life, casting a golden aureole on the snowy pavement.

Shortly before seven o'clock Zoë stuck her white-turbaned head around the parlor doorway.

"Miss Janine, what for you sitting here all 'lone in de dark, like a cat on a fence?" scolded Zoë.

"I'm waiting for Papa," said Janine without turning her head.

Zoë crossed the room and lighted the lamp on a table before the fireplace. "Well, I've done laid out your supper. You just come eat your oyster stew. No telling when your Papa come home."

Janine wouldn't leave her post now for all the oysters in Chesapeake Bay. "Just bring it here on a tray, please, Zoë."

Zoë shrugged and went out; she returned moments later with the tray. She set it on the table before the fireplace.

"Bring it over here, please, Zoë," said Janine, motioning to a table by her side. "I'm watching for Papa."

"You ain't never had to watch for him before."

When Janine said nothing, Zoë frowned and flounced out of the room, closing the door with a slam of disapproval.

Quickly Janine rose and blew out the lamp. In the light of the streetlamp sifting through the window, she sipped the hot stew abstractedly, never taking her eyes from the door of Loxley House.

Shortly after dark Janine saw two red-coated officers mount the steps and go inside, followed moments later by three more British officers. Her heart leaped to her throat. In the pale yellow glow of the streetlight, she could not be certain, but she thought she recognized two of the figures—General Cornwallis and General Howe!

She sat tense and unmoving, straining all her senses, waiting, watching for them to come out. Her mind was seething with questions. What business could the British have with Friend Darragh? She kept coming back to the fact that Lieutenant Charles Darragh was serving in Washington's camp at Whitemarsh. Surely his quiet mousy little mother could not be aiding the British! What could she tell them that would warrant a meeting of high-ranking officers?

Shortly before nine Dr. Mercer walked in and found her sitting in the darkened parlor. "Heavens, child, why don't you light the lamp?"

"I—I must have fallen asleep, Papa. I suppose the wick has burned down. . . ."

Dr. Mercer lighted a taper from the glowing coals in the fireplace. "Looks all right to me!" He turned up the wick and touched the taper to the lamp.

Janine regarded him in the soft glow of the lamplight. His face looked gaunt and gray, and his shoulders slumped with weariness.

"You look exhausted, Papa. Why don't you have

your supper and go on to bed? I'm going to knit a while longer."

"Physician, heal thyself, eh?" said Dr. Mercer, grinning. "Well, I believe I'll follow your advice."

She let out a slow sigh of relief, and as soon as the door closed behind him, she doused the lamp and sat down once more by the window.

Shortly after the State House clock struck ten Darragh's white wooden door swung open and several officers strode from the house, crossed the street, and disappeared inside Cadwalader's. Moments later two more officers stepped out the door. The light of the streetlamp shone on a stocky blond-haired youth and his rangy, dark-haired companion. They donned their hats and continued down the street, the sound of their steps crunching on the icy pavement, and turned into the Golden Fleece Tavern at the corner of Taylor's Alley.

Impulsively Janine leaped to her feet, ran to the entry hall, and snatched her old brown cloak from the halltree. Flinging it around her shoulders, she slipped out the front door, closing it softly behind her. Heedlessly she ran down the street and followed the soldiers inside the tavern.

Her gaze swept the low-ceilinged room, scanning the faces of the men—old men in ragged homespun, British soldiers sprawled at tables cluttered with trenchers and tankards, who had clearly been there for some time. Keeping a sharp eye out for her quarry, she threaded her way past the crowded tables toward the gray-haired bewhiskered tavern keeper behind the bar.

In a breathless voice, frantic with urgency, she asked, "Have you seen Doctor Mercer about? There's an emergency—one of his patients has broken a hip!"

The innkeeper shook his grizzled head. "Haven't laid eyes on him all day."

Janine gazed at him imploringly. "Oh, dear, I must find him!" She turned and looked anxiously about the room. There they were! Sitting at a table in the corner near the stairs. A serving maid was taking their order. Quickly she turned back to the tavern keeper, her eyes wide and appealing.

"Papa told me he'd be here . . . I don't know where else to look. . . ." She let her words trail off and bit her lip, waiting. . . .

"He's bound to turn up. Why don't ye wait a bit? The boys'll make room here." He grinned and nodded at a table nearby. "Or ye can sit at the back table—there's only two lobsterbacks." He jerked his head toward the table where the two officers were sitting.

She thanked him and turned toward the soldiers, approaching the table boldly, swinging her hips as she'd seen Anne Delaney do. She managed a wide, glittering smile. "May I sit here to wait for my papa?"

The tall, dark-haired officer grinned at her, disbelief mirrored in his heavy-lidded eyes.

"Our pleasure, miss." He pulled out a chair next to his. "Sit right here, miss. We'll see no harm comes to you while you're waiting for your papa."

His expression reminded Janine of a fox about to pounce on a chicken. She summoned a grateful smile and slid into the chair beside him. She had a quick impression of a man of about twenty-eight or thirty with close-set eyes, a long sharp nose, pointed chin, and a small, thin-lipped mouth.

"Lieutenant Cooper here, and"—he gestured toward his companion—"Lieutenant Widgery, at your service, miss."

She bobbed her head at Lieutenant Widgery, a rotund, red-faced man whose bushy blond eyebrows matched the mustache gracing his full upper lip. They ordered her a hot rum punch and she sipped it slowly, chatting of this and that, leading the conversation around to General Howe, of whom she spoke in glowing terms. She called up all the phrases Peggy Shippen had voiced, praising the Loyalists and King George, and before long she knew she'd convinced them that she was one of the many Tory sympathizers who'd flocked to the tinsel-gay town with the arrival of Howe's army.

Calling to mind Anne Delaney's brazen mannerisms and flirtatious gestures, she tried to mimic them, raising her eyes boldly to meet those of the dark-haired lieutenant, then quickly lowering her lids demurely. She edged closer to Lieutenant Cooper and felt his hand cover her own in a cozy squeeze. Though she was gratified to see that her effrontery was having the effect she wished, her knees began to tremble with fear and apprehension.

She saw Lieutenant Cooper's calculating gaze taking in her trembling body and knew he was mistaking her tremors for passion roused by the spell of his charm. She smiled, fluttered her lids, did everything she could think of to encourage him to think she found him irresistible, until she could see there was desire in every line of him.

"Listen, sweetheart," whispered the Lieutenant in her ear, "why don't we go upstairs where we can have more privacy?"

Coyly Janine demured, saying she had to wait for her papa. Basking in the pleasure of her flattery and admiration, her provocative glances, augmented by several tankards of rum, the soldiers grew mellow. Lieutenant Cooper eyed her hungrily and ordered her another tot of rum. His fingers stroked the back of her neck, loosened the pins in her hair, and it tumbled about her shoulders, covering his hand. In an effort to distract him, from time to time Janine would call their attention to the customers taking aim at the dart board, or a soldier clowning at the far end of the room. And when they turned to look, she would upend her mug of rum into their tankards.

"Don't think Papa's coming," said the lieutenant in a slurred voice. He smiled wolfishly, gazing at her through heavy-lidded eyes, and his arm crept around her waist. He half-rose from his chair, drawing her up with him.

"C'mon upstairs, swee'heart. My friend here will keep an eye out for Papa." He waved a hand in the direction of his friend.

Janine said nothing. Lieutenant Widgery sat slumped over the table, his head on his arms, snoring loudly. They're both drunk as lords, thought Janine happily. Twisting gently from Lieutenant Cooper's grasp, she sat down and looked up into his flushed, bleary-eyed countenance with teasing eyes filled with promise.

"I'd best wait a bit longer."

Held at bay for the moment by the promise he read in her eyes, he sat down again and ordered another tankard of rum. When he'd drained it, he ran his fingers through her hair, caressing the long silken strands. "Le's go upstairs *now*."

She cocked her head like a kitten. "If I stay with you tonight, tomorrow you'll forget all about me," said Janine with a mournful sigh. "You'll love me and leave me. I'll never see you again. I wager you have a girl in every city from Boston to Savannah."

Ardently he denied her accusations. "Never, m'love. Can't see you t'morrow or the nex' day, but the day after I'll be campin' on your doorstep."

Janine suppressed a smile. Thank God the man was tiddly enough not to ask where her doorstep might be. Raising her face close to his, she pouted prettily. "But I want to see you tomorrow. Why can't I see you tomorrow?"

He leered at her through rum-glazed eyes. "I'm busy t'morrow and the nex' day."

She gave him a withering stare. "Shooting at the weather vane atop Carpenters' Hall?" she asked scornfully.

He hiccuped and laughed at the same time. " 'Tis much more impor'ant than firing at weather vanes, swee'heart."

She drew back from him, feigning an injured air. "Well, if whatever you're doing is more important than I am. . . ."

"Nothing's more impor'ant than you are, swee'-heart. And if I had my way, I'd hold up the whole shootin' match for you. But 'las, I'm not in command. . . ." He hiccuped again.

Janine assumed a disappointed air and tossed her head as if to dismiss him. "You are of no importance in your regiment, then. . . ."

He gave an indignant snort and tried to raise his lolling head. "Impor'ant! Well, swee'heart, let me tell you, I'm the mos' impor'ant man in my regiment."

Janine listened, her heart in her throat, while Lieutenant Cooper told her how important he was. By the time he finished, she had all the information she sought. She knew as much as the lieutenant did about what would take place tomorrow, and the knowledge struck terror in her heart, and her palms were damp with fear. With an effort she pushed down the sick, sinking feeling in the pit of her stomach and pretended to be overwhelmed by awe and admiration for the redoubtable lieutenant.

He slumped back in his chair, his legs sprawled out before him, grinning with obvious pleasure at her astonishment and warm approval.

She continued to tell him how wonderful he was while her mind worked frantically trying to think of a ploy to escape him. The plan she hit upon was chancy, but it would have to do. She kept a weather eye on the door of the tavern and the next time it opened an ancient derelict with a scraggly black beard lurched through the doorway.

"Oh, there's Papa, now!" cried Janine. "I must fly!"

Lieutenant Cooper gazed at her stupidly and before he could gather his wits about him, she stood up quickly, gathered her cloak about her. As comprehension slowly came to him his chin jutted out and an angry flush spread across his face. He clutched the edge of the table, pushed back his chair, and stood up. He lunged toward her and his arm shot out, grabbing her elbow. Janine whirled away from him and he fell back onto the seat with a grunt of rage.

Seizing the table with both hands, he hoisted himself to his feet and stumbled after her. Swiftly she wove her way between the crowded tables, dodging the hands reaching out for her, past the bearded old derelict, out the door.

She fled down the icy pavement, slipping and sliding toward her house halfway down the block. Her heart was pumping wildly. *Dear God,* she prayed, *let me get inside before he reaches the door and sees me running, sees where I live!*

Once inside the dark entryway she locked and bolted the door and leaned her back against it, gasping for breath. With shaking hands she lighted a candle and hurried upstairs to her room. She had not dared look back, and now at any moment she expected to hear the enraged lieutenant thumping on the front door. Thank God Zoë had pulled the draperies. From outside the house would appear dark.

She peeked through the curtains and for a moment she thought her heart would stop beating. A scarlet-clad figure stood on the steps of the Lindleys next door, shouting, demanding to see her, hammering on the door. Holding her breath, she listened, heard the door open and Friend Lindley's low voice. Soon all was quiet. Peering out the window, she saw him trudging up the street, mumbling to himself.

She crossed the room and sat down at her writing desk. She must set down all the details before they escaped her mind. Taking up her quill, she scratched the information on a piece of tissue paper, then searched among the linens stored in the walnut chest until she found what she was looking for. She drew out the faded blue needlebook she'd used as a child and had hidden away in despair, hoping never to use it again. Carefully she folded the paper in the form of a pipe shank and inserted it in one of the various small pockets inside the needlebook.

She hid the book under her pillow and got undressed. Safe in bed at last, she racked her brain as to how she could pass the information on to Colonel Boudinot. If it were true, the intelligence she'd coaxed from the tipsy Lieutenant Cooper was vital to Washington's defense. She must reach Colonel Boudinot as soon as possible. Damn that miserable McMickle, stealing Brandy! thought Janine, her anger rising to choke her. It was no use asking to borrow Papa's mare. He would need the animal tomorrow and she couldn't tell him why she was in such desperate need of a horse. She could trust no one to carry her message. There was only one thing to do. . . .

Chapter 26

The morning of December 3 dawned gray and cold. No ray of sun ventured forth to melt the crust icing the deserted streets, and a promise of snow was in the air. Janine dressed quickly and rushed upstairs to the garret to peer out the dormer window. Though she had known what to expect, she gasped at the sight. In the gray light of dawn flatboats were ploughing dauntlessly across the choppy waters of the Delaware. Boats, particularly, were a clue to the enemy's intentions. She raced to the dormer overlooking the street. Crawling along Second Street in a seemingly endless line were a number of carriage and scantlings—timber —presumably for road surfacing or bridge building, thought Janine. It appeared that the lieutenant was telling the truth.

Janine hurried downstairs, donned her brown cloak, and snatched up a flour sack. She found Papa eating breakfast at the table, engrossed in the *Pennsylvania Gazette*.

"I must go to Frankford Mill today, Papa, and I'm leaving now, before it begins to snow." She kissed him lightly on the top of the head, and before he could answer, or question how she was going to get there, she was down the hall and out the door.

At Abraham Carlisle's she waited on the doorstep in a fury of impatience for her pass. When at last she got it, she began walking at a brisk, steady clip through the frozen streets and lanes toward Frankford. Thinking now of Brandy's capture brought on a fresh surge

of anger and despair that made her spine stiffen and
gave her strength. Sternly she told herself that other
women, poor women who had no horses, always
walked to Frankford Mill; that five or six miles was
not too much of a walk for a sturdy young woman of
eighteen. She could make it easily. She must make it!

Janine arrived at Frankford in the early afternoon,
ploughing through mud churned up by horsemen
and carriages that splashed her cloak, past wretched
houses and barking, snarling dogs that made the hair
prickle on the back of her neck. Still, it was a relief
to be outside British-held terrain. She had no wish
to be caught with the information she carried, even
though it was well hidden in her needlebook.

Upon reaching the mill, she asked the miller to fill
her sack and promised to be back shortly. Then,
turning westward, she trudged along Nice Town Lane
toward Rising Sun Tavern. Her fingers and toes were
numb, her body ached with cold, and her boots were
caked with mud. She glanced worriedly at the pale
sun filtering through bare-limbed oaks and pines. It
must be well after three o'clock, and well past the
Colonel's dinnertime. *Dear God,* she prayed, *don't let
me miss him!* She tried to walk faster, but her legs
were weak with weariness, and several times she
stumbled and almost fell. Surely it couldn't be much
farther now!

She heard hoofbeats cantering down the rutted
road behind her and quickly moved out of harm's
way to the side of the road. She didn't turn around
until a voice commanded, "Hold up, there, ma'am."

The horseman, wearing a snuff-brown uniform faced
in red, reined in beside Janine, staring down at her,
his eyes wide with surprise. His astonishment was no
less than her own as she gazed at the stocky rider,
recognizing his big-toothed grin, his snub nose and
ears that stood away from his head. She'd known him
for a coon's age. A good-natured boy who lived only
a square away from her on Third Street. They'd

shared the same dancing master, attended Christ Church, skated on Dock Creek in winter.

"Tom Craig! What are you doing here?"

Lieutenant Colonel Thomas Craig of the Third Pennsylvania Mounted laughed and swung down from his chestnut gelding to walk along beside her.

"I was about to ask the same question of you, Janine. I've orders to challenge anyone traveling along Nice Town Lane."

A tremor of apprehension coursed through her and with great effort she kept her voice calm and even. "I'm going to see my fiancé, Jonathan Burke."

Tom Craig smiled and his teeth gleamed white in the sunlight. "Oh, yes. I heard you were promised. A lucky fellow."

"He's ill, in the camp hospital at Whitemarsh—"

Tom shook his head. "You're headed in the wrong direction. The camp is east of here, and you can't go that way. My orders are—"

Janine's pulse quickened. She'd have to brazen it out. "My pass is from General Washington himself, Tom. It's all right, truly it is."

Tom regarded her with a troubled expression in his eyes. "Sorry, Janine. Much as I'd like to, I can't let you go on."

Janine bit her lip in vexation. She was sorely tempted to confide in him, but recalling Colonel Boudinot's warning, his swearing her to secrecy, she thought better of it. She looked up into his face, her lip quivering. "At least let me pick up my pass. Colonel Boudinot told me he'd have it for me today at Rising Sun Tavern."

Tom hesitated, indecision plainly written on his honest, open face, torn between desire to please his appealing young friend and dedication to duty.

"Please, Tom," pleaded Janine. "You can come with me, if you like."

His gaze wavered. "Even if you have a pass, you're

still miles from the camp hospital, and I can't let
you go there!"

Janine smiled. "I've no wish to cause trouble by
disregarding your orders. Only let me obtain my pass
from Colonel Boudinot."

The young officer frowned and licked his lips nervously. "It's well past the dinner hour. He's most
likely gone from the tavern by now."

She clenched her teeth to keep from crying out, Oh,
Lord, stop prattling and let me go!

"Colonel Boudinot will have left the pass with the
tavern keeper," she countered smoothly. "He knows
how desperate I am to have it."

"All right," said Tom reluctantly. "But I must have
your promise to go straight home, immediately upon
leaving the tavern."

Gazing directly into his trusting eyes, Janine
nodded.

"You have my word, Tom."

He bade her good day, leaped astride his horse,
turned, and clattered down the lane in the direction he had come.

Janine hurried on, trying to push down a terrible
sinking feeling that Colonel Boudinot would have left
the tavern long since.

Once inside, her gaze traveled quickly over the
room. The table in the corner by the window was
deserted. Janine sank wearily on a chair and let out a
long sigh. She must think of some other way. She
looked around her and saw a ragged, pimple-faced
subaltern seated by the fire, carving a piece of wood.

She went over to him and asked if he'd seen Colonel
Boudinot. The youth scratched his head as though
to get his thinking processes going. "I think the
colonel has gone, ma'am."

Just then the door at the rear of the tavern leading
to the necessary burst open and Colonel Boudinot
entered, stamping snow from his boots. Janine could

have flung herself upon him and kissed him in sheer relief.

Once again she faced him across the scarred oak table in the corner of the room. In a low, urgent voice she related the events of the preceding days. Then from her bodice she withdrew the tattered needlebook and passed it across the table to him.

"I've no further use for this," said Janine, smiling, "but I think you'll find it of great value."

A flicker of surprise crossed his face and quickly vanished as he slid the needlebook inside his coat pocket. His hawk eyes met hers and a look of understanding passed between them. He drained his tankard of ale and left.

On her way home in the dull twilight of the winter afternoon, Janine smiled to herself, trying to imagine Colonel Boudinot's surprise when he read the piece of paper on which her neatly written figures would tell him that Howe was coming out of the city with 5,999 men, 13 pieces of cannon, baggage wagons, 11 boats on wheels. . . .

At eleven o'clock on the night of December 4 Janine blew out the candle on her bedside table and was drawing the curtains round her bed when she heard the rumble of wagons and field artillery rolling through the cobbled streets below. She jumped from her bed and ran to the window, parting the curtains to peer out. British troops were heading toward the Schuylkill—not the Delaware! She watched them intently, a small smile tugging at the corners of her mouth, until her feet grew cold on the bare floor. She crawled back into bed, snuggling under the warm covers. It seemed to her that men, thousands of them, rolled through the city all night long.

Shortly before midday the next morning Janine was sitting by the window, knitting, when Papa rushed into the parlor and blurted out the news.

"Howe's army made a surprise attack on Washington's camp at Whitemarsh at three o'clock this morning!"

Janine sprang up from her chair, spilling her knitting to the floor. "Oh, Papa, no!"

Dr. Mercer beamed, rubbing his hands together gleefully. "The surprise was on Howe, because the Old Fox was ready and waiting for him, his men entrenched, the cannon mounted. It's said the Redcoats pretended to be crossing the Delaware, as though to cross at Bristol and hit the Americans from the rear. But Washington was wise to the deception. Just before midnight a cavalry captain spied their lanterns bobbing along the Skipjack Road near the Schuylkill.

"Howe and his men are digging in like gophers along a ridge beyond Chestnut Hill and the two armies are sitting there glaring at each other like strange dogs." Dr. Mercer's blue eyes gleamed with excitement, his expression exultant. "Howe's surprise was a complete failure, and if he knows what's good for him, he won't try a frontal assault or he'll wind up with another Bunker Hill!"

Janine picked up her knitting and sat down in her chair by the window, a half-smile curving her lips. That afternoon it was reported that British General "No-Flint" Grey had a brush with Morgan's and Gist's riflemen that cost a hundred British lives. Otherwise the two forces merely looked at each other all day long.

Early the following morning Dr. Mercer was in the study working over his ledgers and Janine was in the kitchen boiling up a kettle of foxglove when she was startled by a vigorous pounding on the front door. She stopped stirring the iron kettle and cocked her head, listening. She heard Zoë open the door. A harsh voice demanded to see Mistress Mercer.

Moments later Zoë appeared in the kitchen doorway, her dark eyes rimmed with white. Her chin quivered, her voice shook. "Two British soldiers, Miss Janine, asking for you. I tell them and tell them you busy, but they say for me to fetch you right now!"

Janine drew a deep breath to compose herself and with as much dignity as she could muster, she entered the parlor. Two scarlet-clad officers, one a lieutenant and the other a sergeant, stood before the fireplace, feet astride, staring at her with hard, cold eyes. The sergeant had ice-blue eyes and a vivid white scar that stood out against his flushed, angry face. She shifted her gaze to the lieutenant's gray glare. They both looked eight feet tall, formidable, and threatening, and a foreboding swept through her that raised goose-flesh on her skin. Her chin rose in haughty disdain.

"What can I do for you gentlemen?" she asked coldly.

The flint-eyed lieutenant spoke in a harsh, clipped voice. "We understand that you were in the Golden Fleece Tavern night before last."

Janine tried to still the panic rising in her breast. Should she admit she was there, or deny everything? She had been careful not to tell Lieutenant Cooper her name, but if they'd questioned the tavern keeper, he may have identified her. She swallowed hard, but when she spoke her voice was husky with fear.

"I was there for a short time waiting for my father, Doctor Mercer. However, when he didn't come, I returned directly home."

"You were seen consorting with two British officers far into the night," said the lieutenant sharply. "Officers who had just come from a council meeting with General Howe at Loxley House," he continued in a cold, implacable tone.

Janine shrugged and ran her fingers lightly over the carved wooden back of a side chair. "The tavern was crowded. I waited at a table that may have been occupied by your soldiers." Above the rush of blood pounding in her ears, she could hear Papa's footsteps hurrying down the hall.

"Waited at a table!" shouted the scar-faced officer with a contemptuous sneer. "The customers at the tavern report that a wench was drinking, carousing, even propositioning our officers. You were heard telling Lieutenant Cooper you'd accompany him to his room! So don't waste time trying to play the virtuous innocent with us!"

Papa burst into the room, cutting short the man's furious tirade. "I'm Doctor Robert Mercer. What's the meaning of this intrusion?"

The flint-eyed officer's condescending gaze swept Dr. Mercer from head to foot, taking in his shabby black suit, his tired, lined face.

"Someone informed General Washington of our intended attack upon his camp at Whitemarsh." His harsh voice cut through the room like the slash of a sword. "We've reason to believe the informant was your daughter."

Dr. Mercer's eyes blazed; his face turned scarlet with indignation. "Preposterous! I arrived home at nine o'clock and found my daughter awaiting me in this very room, after which we both retired. What you suggest is impossible. Impossible!"

Thank God she hadn't told Papa of her dealings with Colonel Boudinot, thought Janine, for his outraged indignation and innocence could not be doubted.

The man regarded Dr. Mercer with a disbelieving stare. "That may well be, Doctor," he replied, "but three persons present in the taproom at the Golden Fleece have identified the wench talking with our officers as your daughter."

Janine felt as though the blood were draining from her body. Her knees went weak and she gripped the back of the chair for support. Dr. Mercer's head swiveled around to Janine, his penetrating blue eyes questioning.

"She need not trouble to deny it," said the angry, red-faced sergeant.

"Of course she needn't," bristled Dr. Mercer. "Your drunken, addlepated witnesses are mistaken."

"She has already admitted being there," said the lieutenant with a superior smile.

"I—I was there a short time looking for you, Papa," stammered Janine, wishing the floor would open up and swallow her. "When I couldn't find you, I returned directly home."

Dr. Mercer threw up his hands as though that ended the matter. "There, you see?" he blustered. "There's no possible way she could have passed on information to General Washington, even if she *had* overheard some chance remark made by your loose-tongued officers."

"That remains to be seen," said the lieutenant sharply. "Perhaps a more thorough questioning will refresh her memory." Turning to Janine, he said roughly, "Come along. We're taking you to headquarters."

Chapter 27

Drawing himself up to his full height, Dr. Mercer glared defiantly at the British officers. "I cannot permit you to take my daughter from this house!"

The sergeant stepped forward, his mouth twisted in an ugly sneer. "Out of the way, old man." He thrust out an arm, giving Dr. Mercer a shove that sent him staggering to his knees. The lieutenant gripped Janine's arm tightly above the elbow and yanked her through the doorway.

"Come along, you fork-tongued baggage!"

With a sudden violent jerk Janine wrenched free from his grasp. "Take your filthy hands off me, you brigand!"

Papa got to his feet, sputtering incoherent protests. The sergeant pushed him roughly into a chair. The lieutenant drew his pistol and eyed Janine menacingly. The barrel glinted in the sunlight as he stroked it with his palm.

"You can come with us on your feet, or headfirst." His tone was deadly and she knew she'd pushed him to the limit. Her eyes blazed with fury.

"I'll go with you, if only to prove it wasn't I who was carousing with your men!"

She went to Dr. Mercer and kissed him lightly on the cheek. "Don't fret, Papa I'll be back shortly."

In the entry hall she reached for her worn brown cloak on the halltree, thought better of it, and donned the blue velvet. Quaking inside, she held to the desperate hope that when lieutenants Cooper and

Widgery saw her with her hair pinned up in a neat
coil crowning her head instead of flowing down her
back, and wearing a different cloak and gown, they'd
be unable to identify her—that their memory in their
tiddly state would be fogged, and today would play
them false.

The officers each gripped one of her arms and
yanked her through the doorway. Outside she squinted
her eyes against the sun, which was blinding against
the snow-clad street. She marched stiffly between them,
her head high, looking straight ahead, ignoring the
curious stares of neighbors and strangers who gawked
at the sight of the pale, slender girl in a blue velvet
cloak being hustled through the street by the lobsterbacks like a common criminal.

At British Headquarters the soldiers shoved her
through the door of what had in better days been
the front parlor and what now served as an office.
They bade her sit down to await Major Costigan and
left her under the protective care of a clean-shaven
young subaltern seated at a desk. Janine refused to
sit down, but stood with her back to the window,
hoping to keep her face in shadow.

Moments later the flint-eyed lieutenant returned,
accompanied by Major Costigan and her two companions from the tavern. The lieutenants' eyes flicked
over her and quickly flicked away, but not before she
had seen the glimmer of recognition in them. A cold,
desperate fear gripped her. Major Costigan, a short,
barrel-chested man whose jowls hung over his tight
collar, strutted into the room like a rooster about to
crow.

Janine continued to stand before the window, her
back to the light, gazing haughtily at her captors, who
seemed to avoid her gaze. It came to her suddenly that
there was something odd about the attitude of the
soldiers. Lieutenant Cooper stood shifting from one
foot to the other, and Lieutenant Widgery studied
his boots with intense concentration. Their flushed

countenances called to her mind the faces of naughty schoolboys caught by their teacher. An inspiration struck her. Swiftly she stepped forward and, casting a contemptuous glance at the lieutenants, she turned to Major Costigan.

"I've never seen these men before in my life."

The major's head jerked up and his face darkened in anger. "*I* will conduct this investigation, madam!"

Janine said nothing, but smiled inwardly. She had already driven home her shaft with lieutenants Cooper and Widgery.

Scowling, Major Costigan turned impatiently to his officers. "Well, is this the woman?"

Janine regarded them with an icy stare, holding her breath while they looked her over. Lieutenant Widgery's forehead was puckered in a frown, his chin sunk on his chest. Lieutenant Cooper looked at her impersonally, as though he were evaluating a horse he was about to buy. No glint of recognition shone in his bloodshot eyes.

"Plainly she's a gentlewoman," he said coolly, "a lady of quality. A far cry from the tavern wench who foisted herself upon us for a few moments at the tavern."

Major Costigan bent his sharp, questioning gaze upon Lieutenant Widgery. The man wagged his head and spoke with a trace of cockney. "She ain't be the one," he whined. "It's like we told you, Major. We was only there for a tot or two, and we ain't give away no plans," he ended on an indignant note.

Janine let out her breath slowly. As she had surmised, the men were trying to save their own skins by denying having divulged military secrets to a tavern wench.

Major Costigan crossed the room, grasped her arm, and dragged her away from the window into a beam of sunlight that revealed her features with merciless clarity. She tried to pull away from him, but his fingers held her in a viselike grip.

"Look again!" snapped the major. "Isn't this the woman?"

The scar on Lieutenant Cooper's reddening face shone white. "I told you, no, sir," he said with finality. Lieutenant Widgery continued to wag his head in denial.

Major Costigan's mouth tightened in a grim, exasperated line. After he had dismissed the officers, Janine smiled sweetly, enjoying her victory over him.

"May I go now?"

Ignoring her, Major Costigan turned to the subaltern. "Bring in the witness."

Moments later the subaltern returned with an unshaven, bleary-eyed sergeant at his heels. At the sight of him Janine's hopes drained away and her knees began to shake. Before her stood Tench Coxe, a former neighbor and member of Christ Church, now gone over to the Tories. She saw a pained expression in his gray eyes as he looked at her, then looked quickly away toward Major Costigan.

"It's Mistress Mercer, right enough," the man muttered. "It's her I seen with them lieutenants t'other night in the Golden Fleece Tavern."

The major's lips curled in satisfaction and he turned to the subaltern. "Take her to the library," he snapped. "Colonel Townsend will deal with her till General Howe returns."

Quaking, Janine's steps faltered as she walked dazedly before the subaltern down the wide entry hall to the library at the rear of the house. Her mind was numb, rejecting this dreadful thing that was happening. It couldn't be real, couldn't be happening to her!

The subaltern ushered her into a spacious room where sunlight glanced in through the windows, shining on the bright red carpet. She had a confused impression of her surroundings—the book-filled cupboards with glass doors, the wooden bust of John Locke, the low reclining couch, and huge leather-topped desk strewn with papers. Resplendent in a red tunic with gleaming gold epaulets, the colonel sat, head bent, scribbling on a document. The subaltern ordered Janine to be seated in a straight-backed chair facing the desk and left the room.

At last the colonel looked up, meeting her gaze. Janine gasped and a hand flew to her throat. She tried to speak, but no sound came forth as she stared into the piercing black eyes of the man she knew as Mark Furneaux.

He leaned back in his chair, lacing his fingers together behind his head, and regarded her with a superior mocking smile.

"So, little darling, we meet again! And once again you are in desperate straits!"

"Colonel Townsend!" shrieked Janine. "You! You traitor!"

"Ah, so you have chosen sides at last." His tone was heavy with sarcasm. "The French lily has come to the aid of her adopted country in the guise of a spy for her old friend General Washington." He shook his head in mock sorrow. "A disease that can be cured only by stretching of the neck, little darling."

"I don't know what you're talking about," said Janine, fuming. "Nor do you!"

"Don't trouble to deny it. You can save us both the embarrassment of lying."

He rose from the chair, strode around the desk, and stood looking down at her. "On December third you were given a pass to go to Frankford Mill for flour and—"

"I did go for flour!" Her voice rose in outraged indignation. "Ask the miller, he'll tell you!"

"And from the mill you continued on—"

"I was going to obtain a pass to Washington's camp at Whitemarsh to see my fiancé!" She felt her cheeks getting hot.

Scowling, Mark picked up a colored-glass paperweight from the desk and hefted it lightly in his hand, catching a beam of sunlight. "Ah, yes. The missing fiancé."

Janine's back stiffened and she gazed at him defiantly. "Would I have been so foolish as to go to the camp if I'd known an attack was planned?"

One crescent eyebrow rose and a corner of Mark's mouth turned down. "I wouldn't doubt it." He set the paperweight on the desk and turned to her. "You can, of course, produce your pass from General Washington?"

She bit her lip to still its trembling. "It wasn't ready. He—he hadn't time to arrange it."

When Mark spoke, there was suave brutality in his voice. "That I can well believe!"

Tears of anger and frustration formed in the corners of her eyes, threatening to spill down her cheeks.

"I should have known all along you were a turncoat," she burst out. "You and your ship, your mysterious voyages to heaven-knows-where. You've probably been bringing supplies to Howe right under our very noses, you—you swine!"

She jumped to her feet and whirled around, running toward the door. Before she had taken the third step, Mark lunged toward her, seized her shoulder, and spun her around to face him, his flushed and angry face inches from her own. And in his dark eyes burned an unquenchable fire.

"You're singing a much different tune than you were the day we reviewed Washington's troops!" His hands gripped her thin shoulders cruelly. "All that fine talk about law and order—all that selfless determination to remain neutral!" He shook her so hard, her head bobbed. "What of that?"

She stood rigid as a saber, consumed by a white-hot rage. "I could no longer ignore the evidence of my own eyes and ears, to quote your own treacherous words," said Janine viciously. "The British grinding us under their bootheels, the killing, maiming, raping, looting, burning"—she paused, gasping for breath and raged on. "And what of you, you summer soldier, sunshine patriot? What colossal gall you have to lecture *me* on *Common Sense*! Of all the lying, sneaking, deceitful—"

Abruptly Mark grasped her wrist and yanked her toward him, pulling her arm up sharply behind her back, drawing her body close against his own.

"Believe what you like," he said, his voice hard and cutting. "But don't chastise me for my loyalties. As I've told you before, I don't chastise you for yours!"

"No?" she spat. "Then let me go!" She took a step back and bent and twisted every way against the iron grip of his arm, trying to wrest from his grasp.

He grinned in amusement and pulled her closer. "A patriot is one thing, little darling; a spy quite another. And, may I remind you that you are my prisoner and in no position to treat me shabbily." His black eyes raked her and he was laughing softly.

"Oh, Mark, for God's sake . . ." she began desperately, her courage and control breaking.

Suddenly he caught her in his arms, crushing her to his chest, bringing his mouth savagely down on hers. Furiously she struggled against his embrace, trying to push him away. She kicked his legs, fighting him with every ounce of strength she could muster, resisting the gentle touch of his hand stroking her hair, and rebelling against his familiar warmth.

Even as she struggled against him, he made her feel loved, desired, possessed, as though they were one in mind, body, and spirit. In spite of herself she was responding to his embrace with an ardor and abandon that threatened to engulf her. She felt herself being swept away by an overpowering emotion. Then, as though clutching for a branch in a flood, a swift and stronger emotion rose to the surface: She loathed herself that she could play Jonathan so false, hated this traitor who could make her lose all control of her senses. For an instant Mark relaxed his hold about her waist and bent as if to lift her up. With a violent wrench she broke free, staggering backward until she reached the door. She braced her back against it, her breath coming in short, quick gasps.

In a low voice that shook she said, "I'm leaving now, Mark. You must let me go. Papa will be frantic."

He was leaning on the corner of the desk, his fingers gripping the edge, his eyes filled with an expression she could not fathom. Slowly she turned her back on him, grasped the doorknob, and turned it.

"Janine!" Though his voice was husky, the word was a command.

She glanced at him over her shoulder, her eyes wide and appealing. Slowly, relentlessly, he shook his head. His voice held a note of genuine regret. "I cannot let you go."

For a moment her mind could not believe his words. She managed a tremulous smile. "You can't be serious!"

His shining black eyes bored into her soul, his countenance solemn. "I was never more serious. My world doesn't revolve around you, you see. My life depends on my serving my country. You have committed an act of treason against the king. You'll be held prisoner until General Howe returns, at which time you will be tried and sentenced."

Without waiting to hear more, Janine flung open the door and bolted into the hallway. Running toward the front door, she heard Mark shout. As she flew past the parlor she saw a flash of scarlet burst through the doorway and a raised arm, and felt a blow strike behind her left ear that sent her crashing to the floor. Then darkness.

Chapter 28

She awoke to the odor of a peculiarly disgusting smell that reminded her of her days at Penn's Hospital. Bodies, urine, body waste, corruption of decaying flesh that immediately filled her with nausea. How long she had lain there unconscious she had no way of knowing, but her head throbbed and her body ached from the chill and dampness. She sat up and looked around her. The only light in the room came from a streetlamp shining through a broken pane in a small, barred window high in the wall. And the only air to relieve the fetid stench came from that pane as well. Faintly she heard barely recognizable sounds: men swearing and blaspheming; some crying, praying, raving, screaming; some groaning and dying; some dead and putrifying. With a dawning horror it came to her where they had brought her. Terrifying stories of "Bloody Bill" Cunningham—British provost marshal of Walnut Street Prison, noted for his brutality—flooded through her mind. Here they had herded the wounded after the Battle of Brandywine, had thrown them in with debtors and felons, without blankets or food, and left them to die. Surely this couldn't be happening to her!

Fighting down panic, she sprang from the cot on which she lay, stumbled across the room to a wooden door, and tugged on the latch. The door was locked and bolted from the outside. A rage the like of which she'd never known seized her, and she pounded frantically on the door till her fists were bruised and throbbing with pain, shouting, "Let me out of here! Let me out!"

Her cries echoed back at her from the stone walls, mocking her. That beast, that vile Mark Furneaux had actually allowed them to toss her into Walnut Street Prison like a common felon! Swift, scurrying sounds in the corner sent her flying back to the cot, where she drew her cloak tightly about her and huddled miserably, her arms clasped around her drawn-up knees, her head resting on her arms. Darkness came on and she closed her eyes, sinking into a lethargy of exhaustion and despair.

After what seemed like hours she was roused by a scraping sound. A panel covering a slot in the door slid open. In the gleam of light from a lantern two eyes peered in at her. She heard a muffled exclamation as the panel was pushed closed and a key grated in the lock. She raised her head, her heart thumping wildly. Surely Mark, or Colonel Townsend as he now called himself, had come to release her from this chamber of horrors.

She stared into the dim light, holding her breath as the door swung open on creaky hinges. In the light of the lantern held high above his head, a blubbery whey-faced man wearing the blue and white uniform of a Hessian soldier waddled into the cell. Petrified, Janine shrank back into the corner.

The man gave her a broad, wet-lipped smile. "Vell, vot haf ve here?" he wheezed in a thick German accent. He set a bowl of gruel on the floor. "A bird of paradise in our cage?"

Janine glared at him, stony-faced, her eyes filled with loathing. She said nothing. He slammed the door shut behind him and, raising the lantern higher, crossed the room to the cot on which she crouched and leaned over her, his pug face a mask of anticipation and lust. He was so close, she could see the red-veined whites around his pale blue eyes. She gagged at the smell of his hot breath, sour with rum, the odor of his sweat-stained jacket.

"You vill sing for your supper, little bird, yah?"

"Get away from me, you filthy lout!" shrieked Janine.

The hulking man drew back, his mouth open in mock dismay.

With all the courage she could muster, Janine said, "There's been a terrible mistake. I'm not supposed to be here. You must let me out at once."

"Ach!" said her jailer feigning indignation. "You are not nice. Dot's no vay to be. You should be grateful to Klaus. I gif you the best room in the place!" He emitted a wheezing laugh that sent a chill down her spine.

"Grateful!" cried Janine. "You're out of your mind!"

"Maybe I put you in a cell with the soldiers so you haf company. You like dat?"

Janine was well aware of the way prisoners were crammed together in tiny cells, sick, wounded, starving, left without food or water for days on end. And what her fate would be left in a cell with ten men didn't bear thinking about. Mutely she shook her head.

"You be nice to Klaus." He reached out a hand with fingers like sausages and flung back the hood of her cloak, running his hand through the silken black hair cascading over her shoulders. With a cry she jerked away from his touch.

"I von't hurt you," he wheezed through thick, moist lips. Beads of sweat stood out on his forehead and ran down his fat, flushed cheeks. "You be nice and I gif you your supper."

"Don't you dare to touch me!" shrieked Janine. "I'll report you to Colonel Townsend!"

The Hessian threw back his head and emitted a coarse bellow of laughter. "You t'ink a British colonel is going to believe a spy?"

"I'm a friend of Colonel Townsend's," said Janine, her eyes narrowing. "A very good friend."

For an instant the man hesitated, betraying the question in his mind. A crafty look came into his eyes. "I don't bother you, and I tell the colonel you refuse our good food," said Klaus, shrugging. "Dat I cannot help."

"Do you know what happens to mercenaries who take a British officer's woman?"

He stared at her, his little pig eyes calculating. "I vait. You change your mind, ya?" He picked up the bowl of watery gruel and stamped out of the cell, locking the door securely behind him.

Janine sat stiffly on the cot, her legs tucked up under her, her back braced against the corner of the cell. Thank God she'd escaped the clutches of her repulsive jailer! She bent all her efforts toward keeping awake, afraid he'd be back when he'd finished his duties and try again to charm her.

As the night wore on, her head grew heavy with weariness. She slumped against the wall and fell into a slumber tormented by nightmares of the licentious Klaus snaring her in the cell—from which there was no escape.

When she awoke, the gray light of early morning crept in through the window high in the wall. She rose from the cot and the stiff, sore muscles in her arms and legs cried out as she paced back and forth in the cell in an effort to restore circulation to her aching limbs. Hunger gnawed like a rat in her empty stomach. Suddenly she heard a key scraping in the lock on the door. She scurried back to her corner and perched on the edge of the cot, bracing herself for whatever was to come.

By now Klaus would have been relieved of night duty and another guard would appear. Any guard would be more welcome than the odious Klaus, she thought. The door swung open and she gasped in dismay. Klaus lumbered into the cell carrying her bowl of gruel.

A smile split his ruddy bulldog face and he held out the bowl as though it were laden with fresh fruit. She glanced at the gruel and her stomach turned over. The same pap he'd offered her last night, thought Janine dully.

"You change your mind, ya?"

Janine glowered at him, shaking her head, making no effort to conceal her revulsion for the man.

His smile became a leer. "I go off duty now. I tell the guard you vish to see only me, Klaus. And tonight I come back. Maybe you be nice to Klaus!"

Taking the bowl with him, he stamped from the cell, slammed the door, and locked it.

Hunger twisted and churned in Janine's stomach as she paced to and fro in the damp, evil-smelling cell. The Hessian had left her no water and her throat was parched and her tongue felt like dough in her mouth. She kept up her courage by telling herself over and over that surely Papa was trying to gain her release. Surely someone would come for her at any moment.

She pushed the cot across the stone floor below the window and climbed up on it, standing on tiptoe, stretching to see out. The sill was inches above her head. She drew in her breath and, clinging to the sill with her fingers, jumped upward, hoping for a glimpse outside. Her fingers slipped from the sill. All she saw were bare tree limbs and the spire on the State House etched against a dismal gray sky.

As the morning passed she looked forward to her midday dinner as though it were to be a ten-course banquet. But time dragged on and no one appeared. The noxious Klaus was as good as his word, thought Janine bitterly. She sank down on the cot in despair, pulling her cloak around her head, trying not to breathe in the foul air of the prison.

She finally dozed off and woke with a start at the

faint sound of scratching coming from the walls. A violent trembling seized her. A rat, she thought, stifling a scream. If I don't move, it will go away! But the sound persisted, setting her teeth on edge. With nerves strung taut as a wire, she watched the winter sun moving slowly across the sky. A brisk wind blew up, whipping about, thrashing the tree limbs. The cold seemed to close in around her. Shivering, she rubbed her arms and legs briskly in a futile effort to warm her body and to ward off a feeling of light-headedness from lack of food.

Oh, where in the devil could Papa be? Surely by now he'd had time to arrange for her release. Surely he'd not leave her here! But the sun was fast slipping down in an arc to the west and still Papa did not come, and the moment of Klaus's return drew nearer. A terrible dread overtook her as her imagination soared in wild flights of fancy. What if, after leaving orders that she was his personal prisoner, the Hessian oaf had been sent elsewhere; what if he were killed? Would anyone come to rescue her? Would she be left here to die of starvation, her flesh rotting away on her bones before she could even stand trial?

Terror closed her throat and her hands grew clammy with fear. She closed her eyes tight to shut out the oppressive darkness and again she heard the peculiar scratching above the faint cries and moans of the prisoners. She had begun to think that even Klaus was not coming when she heard the key in the lock. The door opened and the German mercenary appeared, carrying the lantern and the bowl of gruel. As before, he set the bowl on the floor and held the lantern aloft, leering at her through the gloom.

"I feed all the other prisoners first. I come to you last. Now I stay the night vit you!"

Paralyzed with fright, unable even to cry out, she gazed at him with loathing. In three lumbering strides he crossed the cell and grasped her chin in a cruel grip, tilting her face up to his. "You haf lost your tongue?"

Violently she wrenched away from him, screaming, "Get away from me, you fat ugly toad!"

Klaus lowered his head like a bull ready to charge. "You dare refuse me, you tavern doxy!" He reached out for her, his red-veined eyes bulging with rage. "You come to me or you get no food, no water, noth-ink!"

"I'd rather starve to death than submit to you!" she shrieked.

His thick, moist lips curled in a malevolent grin. "You vill not starve to death, my pigeon. Hunger makes men veak—vomen too. The day vill soon come ven you vill crawl on your hands and knees for my favor!"

"Pig!"

As though she'd struck him, the man backed away, his jaw jutting out, his lips curled in a nasty smile. "I vait. You change your mind."

Janine stared at him defiantly, her eyes blazing, her teeth clenched to keep from crying out, reviling him. In the silence she heard again the strange scratching sounds that seemed to emanate from the walls.

Klaus cocked his head, listening, "You know vas is das?" A crafty look came into his swinelike eyes.

She glowered at him without speaking, her face a mask of hate.

"You tink is rats? Ha! Here the prisoners eat the rats! Das is prisoners who don't be nice to Klaus. Dey scrape mortar and rotten wood from the valls to eat so dey don't starve to death."

"Get out!" screamed Janine wildly. "Get out and let me be!"

"Ya. I get out," said Klaus with a sly grin. "I come back tomorrow."

Janine fell back on the cot, weak and exhausted. Hunger had stopped gnawing at her insides. Her limbs felt hollow, her body empty. All hope had left her.

She could think of no way to escape her plight. Clearly Mark Furneaux, Colonel Townsend, whoever he was, had no intention of coming to her rescue, she thought dully.

The following day dragged by much as the day before. Janine disdainfully refused her morning gruel and spent much of the day lying on the cot, gazing at the dull gray sky outside the window. She tried to conserve her strength, telling herself over and over that she could hold off Klaus as long as she could convince him that she was the colonel's woman.

That evening, as before, Klaus flung open the cell door and lumbered inside, closing it behind him.

"Go away," Janine commanded, "and take that slop with you!"

Ignoring her, Klaus bent over to set the bowl on the floor and lurched forward, almost losing his balance, while the lantern waved dangerously in his other hand. He started toward her.

"Get away from me, or I'll report you to Colonel Townsend!" shouted Janine.

Klaus grinned. "You won't see Colonel Townsend, my pigeon. General Howe is back!" His speech was thick and slurred. "This night I stay vit you!"

Janine, sitting on her haunches on the cot, rose to her knees. She thought she would go crazy with terror. Her hands were damp with fright. The vile beast was drunk as a lord!

Suddenly he lurched across the cot and seized her shoulders, trying to pull her to him. She could see his eyes glittering with lust, and his wheezing, rum-ladened breath came fast. Abruptly she jerked free of him, scrabbled to the end of the cot, and gained her feet on the stone floor. Klaus lumbered after her, crooning in a voice thickened with rum.

"My pigeon, tonight ve vill feast!"

Janine, quicker and lighter on her feet than he, dodged his groping arms and darted around behind him. His voice rose to a broken shout of rage and affront. Clumsily he wheeled around, reaching out for her, his huge hands clutching at her shoulder. His fingers fastened onto the lace ruffle at the neck of her gown. She screamed and twisted away from him, and the fabric parted and ripped to her waist as she pulled from his grasp. Sobbing with terror, she leaped up onto the cot, shrinking away from him into the corner.

Slowly, relentlessly, he reeled toward her, gleaming with anticipation, his evil eyes on her breasts. He was savagely drunk and she read in his eyes determination to have her, come what may. Swiftly she gathered up her skirts and took a step forward. As he reached for her, her foot shot out, landing a violent kick in his stomach.

His breath came out in a rush as he grunted and doubled over, clutching his stomach and cursing. Then, bellowing like a wild boar, he lunged toward her in a crouch, his thick, powerful arms outstretched. His face wavered level with her knees as she stood wobbling on the cot. She tottered backward, almost losing her balance. Groping frantically behind for support, her hands found the corner walls. She braced one hand against the back wall and bunched up her skirts with the other. With every ounce of strength left in her, she kicked out her booted foot, striking Klaus a stunning blow on the face.

In the glow of the lamplight Janine saw an expression of astonishment spring to his eyes as his knees buckled under him. He crashed to the stone floor, striking his head with a thud. An unearthly silence invaded the cell as the Hessian's left arm rose weakly, then dropped to the floor and he lay still.

Chapter 29

The day advanced slowly, relentlessly, as the stars scattered outside Janine's window paled and the black sky overhead faded like a gray woolen blanket. She hadn't slept throughout the night and her mind had taken refuge in a blessed stupor. The clergyman arrived shortly before dawn, rousing her from her lethargy. She sat on the cot as though already dead, heedless of the words flowing past, as he read in calm, measured tones, passages from the Bible. At last he closed the book and bent his kindly, sympathetic gaze upon her. "The dead shall rise again." He leaned over her and patted her hand. "Did you hear me, child?" he asked softly, and murmured a few final words in her ear.

Events had moved swiftly since the night of her disastrous encounter with the Hessian. General Howe had returned to Philadelphia in a towering rage, humiliated at the failure of his surprise attack on the Continental army, only to be met by a furious Hessian officer with the news that one of his men had been the victim of a vicious and unwarranted attack by his prisoner. Eager to find a scapegoat, anyone he could hold responsible for betraying his plan to the enemy, General Howe ordered a speedy trial for the culprit also accused of treason.

Though Janine knew nothing of military procedure, she clung desperately to the hope that because she was a civilian, she'd not be sentenced to hang on the gallows. She prayed that Mark would intercede for her with the general, that she would get off with a prison sentence.

The next morning she was brought before a three-man military tribunal where she was tried for espionage. Found guilty as charged, she was sentenced to be executed at dawn by a firing squad.

At these dread words Janine lapsed into a state of shock and her mind blotted out the entire incident, as though a protective curtain had fallen, shielding her from reality. She barely remembered returning to her cell.

After a while the door creaked open and two scarlet-clad soldiers appeared to escort her outside to the yard. She felt no fear, only a numb resignation, thinking, *Dear God, let me die with dignity and composure.* The clergyman took her elbow and led her across the room to the waiting guards.

They bound her wrists behind her back and grasped her by the arms. She shook off their rough hands. Holding her head high, she walked between them, down the dark corridor, up the steps and outside, insensible to the bitter December wind whipping her cloak about her legs. They tramped across the bare, snow-crusted yard and commanded her to stand before a high brick wall. She stood as though frozen in ice, staring dazedly at six Hessians who lounged about, chatting and laughing, awaiting the order to fire.

Through the doorway of the huge brick prison strode a tall, familiar figure. Janine's heart gave a violent leap. He had come to rescue her, after all! He bawled an order, and the Hessians sprang to attention. Her blood seemed to flow from her body and she thought she would faint. Dully she regarded Mark Furneaux's crisp black hair, his thick crescent brows, his generous mouth. His face bore a cold, impassive expression, his eyes inscrutable, avoiding her gaze. Through her befogged mind drifted the thought that the man who had so often come to her rescue in the past would now order her execution.

All that was happening had a dreamlike quality. She felt like an actress watching a drama unfold in which she had no part. The rising sun bathed the yard in a rosy light. A catbird twittered on the bare branch of an elm tree overhead. Through glazed eyes she stared at Mark. In a hard, tight voice he barked the order for the Hessian soldiers to take aim and fire.

The last thing she saw was the catbird fluttering upward as the shock of the exploding rifles ripped across the yard and bounced back, echoing from the brick walls.

Swiftly Mark Furneaux strode across the yard and stood over Janine's crumpled body, looking down at her pale, smudged face framed by satin-black hair flowing from under the hood of the blue velvet cloak. He raised his pistol and with calm deliberation, administered the coup de grace. A fleeting expression of tenderness and sorrow crossed his face as the smoke rose from his gun, but before it had cleared, his face changed to a cold, efficient mask. He watched impassively while two men lifted Janine's body into a crude pine coffin and drove a few nails into the lid before they loaded it onto a horse-drawn cart.

"You are to report for duty at once, to Major Costigan," said Mark, briskly dismissing the soldiers. "I'll see to the removal of the corpse."

When the men had gone, Mark leaped lightly onto the seat of the cart and urged the recalcitrant horse into a fast trot through the gate down the cobbled street rimed with hoarfrost. Though few citizens were abroad this early in the day, passersby stared at him curiously. It was unusual to see a British colonel driving a dilapidated cart containing a coffin. Mark stared straight ahead, looking neither to the left nor the right as the cart clattered noisily down Market Street. He turned north at Second Street and reined up outside the iron fence surrounding Christ Church.

He tethered the horse to a cedar post and strode to the entrance below the towering steeple. As he entered the narthex a slight, solemn-faced man rose from a chair and extended a trembling hand in greeting. His misty, grief-stricken eyes held a question.

Mark nodded. "She's outside, Doctor Mercer."

Dr. Mercer's shoulders sagged and his voice was choked with despair. "I'll wait in the sanctuary." He turned away and walked unsteadily down the aisle of the dim, shadowy church, touching the top of each white wooden pew as if for support. He entered the door of the first pew, below the wineglass pulpit, and sat down heavily, bowing his head in his hands.

After a short while a small procession emerged from the church following a black velvet draped coffin borne by four men: Dr. Kuhn, Dr. Ransom, Eldon Lindley, and Mark Furneaux. Behind them walked Dr. Mercer, the Reverend William White, Friend Rachael Lindley, and Zoë, who sniffled loudly into a handkerchief pressed to her nose. Solemnly they made their way with slow and heavy steps up Arch Street toward Fifth and entered the burying ground where during the past fifty years members of the congregation had been laid to rest.

They proceeded down the gravel path under leafless elms that quaked in the wind, past the resting place of Deborah Franklin, and halted beside a mound of earth from a freshly dug grave. Mark's face was tight with strain and his jaw stiffened as they lowered the coffin into the cavity in the hard-packed ground. He stood with his hands behind his back, impatiently clenching and unclenching his fists while the Reverend White conducted the service. At last the clergyman murmured, "Earth to earth, ashes to ashes, dust to dust; in sure and certain hope of the Resurrection unto eternal life." Tight-lipped and moist-eyed mourners scattered handfuls of earth over the coffin.

Less than an hour later a feeble woman in a crumpled blue cloak knelt before the altar rail as a bright gleam of sunshine slanted through the tall Palladian window in the chancel of Christ Church.

Slowly she rose to her feet. On shaking legs she walked down the long aisle and through the narthex. Once outside she pulled her hood well over her head and waited in the corner in the lee of the wind, until she saw a coachman driving a closed carriage rein up before the gate. She started down the walk, swaying as the wind tore at her hood, whipping her cloak around her thin body. As she approached the carriage the door was flung open and a strong masculine hand reached out, grasping her slender, frail one, drawing her swiftly inside.

She sank down weakly on the seat, leaning into the curve of the man's arm around her shoulders and closed her eyes. With hands that were astonishingly gentle, Mark Furneaux pushed back her hood and tilted her face up to his, tenderly kissing her forehead, her eyelids. A long, shuddering sigh shook her body and she opened her eyes. She could not still the quaking inside. He held her tightly, cradling her in his arms, pressing her head against his shoulder, stroking her hair, comforting her as he would a small child. There was no mockery in his eyes now.

"It's over, little darling. You're safely dead and buried."

Janine shook her head, feeling as though she'd wakened from a terrifying nightmare, trying to fathom the miracle that she was alive.

"Was it so bad, in the pine box?" asked Mark anxiously.

She shook her head and raised her eyes to his. "I recall nothing except trying desperately to stand upright long enough for the Hessians to fire. Though the clergyman delivered your instructions, I could see no way that my life could be spared. I'd no need to feign falling to the ground," she said with a rueful laugh. "Even then I didn't truly believe I wasn't to die."

Mark smiled grimly. "Every man has his price, particularly the Hessians. Hired guns can also be paid to miss their targets. I told them I wanted to have the pleasure all to myself. And then took the precaution of removing the ball from my pistol before I fired the coup de grace. My main concern was that the sexton would pry the lid from your coffin before the air gave out, help you out, load the stones inside, and nail the lid back on before the service began."

Janine let out a long exhausted sigh. "It was done well enough."

Mark smiled wryly. "Not many can boast they've missed their own funeral!"

"My own funeral," repeated Janine, shocked. "Papa! Does he know?"

Mark shook his head. "The risk was too great. Too many eyes were watching. Your Papa, Zoë, Mister Lindley and"—he grinned sardonically—"your suitor, Doctor Ransom, unknowingly gave a most convincing performance."

"Poor Papa," sighed Janine, too tired to protest Mark's assumption that Dr. Ransom was a suitor. "He must be beside himself, thinking me gone forever."

Mark's hands caressed her tumbled hair gently, soothingly, and his voice was gentle too. "It won't be long till you're home," he said softly.

Janine closed her eyes and gave herself over to the warm comfort of Mark's arms around her. A feeling of peace and contentment swept over her. He was so tender, so infinitely comforting, she longed to stay in his arms forever.

By the time the carriage rumbled to a stop before her house on Second Street, she had regained some of her composure. The coachman alighted and opened the door, but Mark remained seated. Janine gazed at him questioningly.

"Aren't you coming in?"

Mark shook his head.

"But Papa will wish to see you—to thank you for all you've done."

"It's best I not be seen here."

"Surely you can spare a few minutes. . . ."

His voice was urgent. "I must get back to my post."

Hurt by his sudden abruptness, Janine burst out, "And to Anne Delaney, no doubt." As soon as she spoke the words, she wanted to bite them back.

Mark threw back his head and laughed heartily. "I do believe you're jealous!" He grasped her wrist tightly.

"Hold on, Janine. You may not be enamored of my charm, but you'd best listen to what I'm about to say. A word of warning—Your 'rescue' is a mixed blessing. You must take care to stay hidden away. The town is seething with Tories and one of your Loyalist friends may consider it his duty to report that the beautiful American spy is quite alive and healthy."

She hadn't thought that far ahead. He was right, and she knew she'd do well to heed his warning.

"Thank you, Colonel Townsend," said Janine somewhat stiffly. "May I go now?"

Surprise and something else flickered in his eyes and he glanced down at his hand holding her wrist in a crushing grip. He leaned forward, and for a moment Janine thought he would take her in his arms and kiss her good-bye. Instead he released her hand and sat back in the carriage. With a feeling of disappointment, as though of a promise unfulfilled, she fled across the pavement and inside the red brick house.

Janine remained sequestered inside the house like a nun in a convent, going about her ordinary business, making ointments and salves, distilling bitters, boiling syrups, spinning and weaving cloth, seeing to Papa. She read the books Papa brought her: *Joseph Andrews, Juliet Grenville, Caroline Melmoth,* as well as the newspapers and ladies' magazines.

Dead and buried, she could be of no further use to Colonel Boudinot. In fact he had written Papa a note expressing his deep sympathy at her death and commending her for invaluable service to her country. If only he had given her a safe-conduct pass to see Jonathan, she would have risked riding out to see him, even if she'd had to steal a horse. But Papa had sagely pointed out that if she were recognized and captured, she would surely be put to death and of no use to anyone, now or in the future. A live Janine, however far from Jonathan, was certainly better than a dead one.

Though Dr. Mercer had told Richard Ransom of Janine's miraculous rising from the dead, Richard had not come to call upon her. Papa said that all his time was taken up caring for the British soldiers who'd been admitted to the hospital. To her own astonishment she found she missed him more than she had thought possible. At the same time she felt relieved, for she had no wish to encourage him in any sort of romantic involvement.

Janine longed to visit Peggy Shippen, but she dared not trust her to keep secret her narrow escape from death, for Peggy had become the reigning belle of British society. Zoë, wide-eyed with wonder, had brought Janine tales of Peggy, Rebecca Franks, and Debbie Norris attending lavish parties given by General Howe and his loyalist friends. There were balls and concerts, horseraces and sleighing parties. Frequently they went to plays given by military companies at the Southwark Theatre. Peggy was often seen in the company of Captain John André, a member of "Howe's Thespians" and the idol of Peggy and her friends, the girls he called the "little society of Third and Fourth streets." Howe himself had set the pace, shocking Tories and rebels alike, squiring about his beautiful blond mistress, Mrs. Joshua Loring, wife of his Commissary of Prisoners. The town rocked with laughter at a quatrain Howe inspired in Francis Hopkinson's ballad, "The Battle of the Kegs."

Sir William he, snug as a flea,
Lay all this while a snoring,
Nor dreamed of harm as he lay warm
In bed with Mrs. Loring.

Howe had bedded down for a frolicking winter in the city, a snug, hospitable retreat enlivened by amusement and diversion and the luxury of war prosperity.

In mid-December 1777, on a cold snowy day, news was brought that Washington's army was on the march, having broken camp at Whitemarsh.

"What can General Washington be thinking of?" lamented Janine that night at the supper table.

Dr. Mercer gazed at her over the rim of his spectacles. "He may be thinking of keeping his men out of harm's way, in case Howe decides to roll out of bed and attack," said Papa, chuckling. He lifted a forkful of mutton from his plate.

"Or he may have decided that his men need to hole in for the winter. If his army is too weak to mount a winter campaign, it may be the best thing for them. They can use these months to recuperate from Brandywine and Germantown."

But all Janine could think of was Jonathan, weak and feverish, marching mile after mile in the freezing snow as it sifted down from a leaden sky. Anxiously she followed the progress of Washington's troops through reports brought by riders to the City Tavern. Day after day, starving and half naked and their clothes in shreds, many shirtless and barefoot men trudged over wretched roads with sharp frozen ridges that cut into rag-bound feet. They left a trail of blood in the snow on their way to Valley Forge. It had taken more than a week to cover thirteen miles.

They had arrived after dark, perishing from thirst, hunger, and fatigue a week before Christmas. Here on wooded slopes, twenty-one miles from Philadelphia, they were to make their winter quarters. The next morning Washington set his men to building a city

of nine hundred log huts, sleeping in a tent himself
until they could be finished.

Washington as well as Howe sent abroad foraging
parties to requisition food and clothing, desolating
the countryside. It was said that horses were dying for
want of fodder, and the overpowering stench of some
five hundred rotting carcasses fouled the whole camp.
While the troops suffered at Valley Forge, subsisting
on firecake and water, the farmers were selling their
produce to the British in Philadelphia where they
could get hard cash. Profiteers were sending hundreds
of government wagons rumbling north loaded with
flour and iron, while pork in New Jersey awaiting
shipment to the army spoiled for lack of transport.
Janine could have wept with pity and anger as tales
of their suffering continued to drift back into town.

But starvation and cold were not Janine's worst
fears. Disease ran rampant. Many soldiers were covered
with a tormenting itch, their bodies covered with
scabs. Smallpox broke out and putrid fever took an
even larger toll. Inwardly she fumed and worried,
knowing little could be done to relieve their suffering.
Much of the time she felt cross and out of sorts. Her
nerves were stretched taut as one of Papa's violin
strings, and it was with great difficulty that she hung
on to her patience. The new year looked very gloomy
indeed, thought Janine bitterly.

Chapter 30

Near the end of February 1778 a bright spot on the horizon appeared at Valley Forge in the person of a Hessian named Baron von Steuben, a lieutenant general formerly in the service of King Frederick the Great of Prussia.

With a more cheerful and optimistic air than Janine had seen in weeks, Papa told her, "Washington has appointed von Steuben acting inspector general of the army. He's drilling the men thoroughly in marching, bayonet tactics, and other arts of war. He stands before the shivering, half-starved provincials in a magnificent uniform and puts on a show worthy of paid admission! They say he came on the *Amphitrite*, one of Hortalez et Cie's ships, along with guns, powder, shoes, and blankets."

Janine's smooth brow wrinkled. "Papa, now that I think on it, I'm certain Hortalez is the name of the firm Mark Furneaux is with!" Her blue eyes widened in horror. "Do you suppose that traitor has brought this Hessian over, planting him in the midst of Washington's army to—"

Dr. Mercer shook his head, interrupting her. "He had a letter of introduction from Benjamin Franklin. Working with Colonel Boudinot has made you unduly suspicious, *ma petite*." Dr. Mercer grinned. "It's said that he speaks no English and little French, and when he can no longer curse his recruits in German and French, he calls on his French-speaking American

aide to swear for him in English! The man could be
the making of our army!"

One night during the dreary rains of early spring-
time, Dr. Mercer came home wearing a jubilant grin,
rubbing his palms together. "The Lord will provide!
Seems there's been a heavy run of shad up the Schuylkill. It's said at the tavern that the soldiers are plunging into the river armed with pitchforks, shovels,
baskets, broken branches, anything they can lay a
hand on to heave their catch onto the banks. They've
rushed up barrels and salt to store them away. There
are tons of them to eat—and to be salted down. Shad,
if nothing else, should sustain them during any lean
weeks ahead!"

She was further heartened by the news that Mistress
Washington had come up from Mount Vernon to stay
with her husband at his headquarters in the Isaac
Potts house. Janine knew she would visit the hospital
with a warm smile and words of cheer for the men.
She contented herself with the thought that Aunt
Ellen would have charged Mistress Washington to seek
out Jonathan and see that he was well cared for.

Following on the heels of von Steuben and Mistress
Washington, Major General Benedict Arnold limped
into Valley Forge seeking a new command. His "Quebec" leg had been shattered when his horse was shot
out from under him during the action against Burgoyne and he'd been incapacitated for many months.
With outraged dignity Papa reported that Arnold lay
through the long winter weeks in a fracture box, cursing the doctors as charlatans and refusing to let them
amputate. He had lost none of his arrogance and
audacity, however, and held a lavish dinner party
drawn from army stores for a select guest list of twenty,
for which he'd drawn a terse rebuke from General
Washington.

* * *

The coming of spring 1778 reinvigorated the army that had miraculously survived, better trained and disciplined than before. Although more than two thousand men had died or deserted, it was determined to fight to the death. Then, on April 30, news was brought that Washington had received word that on February 6 France had recognized the independence of the United States and would now come to her aid. The entire army celebrated with a parade and thirteen-gun salute, shouting "Huzza! Long live the King of France!"

In the wake of this report came the rumor that as long ago as last October General Howe had asked to be relieved of his command in Philadelphia. Now it seemed his request was to be granted, and General Clinton arrived to replace him.

Before Clinton took over command, word went about the town that Howe's officers proposed to stage a farewell celebration in his honor—its magnificence the like of which had never been seen before. The extravaganza, so went the gossip, was to be a pageant, feast, and ball, all organized and directed by Captain Oliver De Lancey and Captain John André. They called it the "Mischianza," an Italian word meaning medley.

Four hundred elaborate invitations were designed, engraved and sent out. And fourteen of the most beautiful and most fashionable Tory maidens in Philadelphia, Peggy Shippen and her two sisters among them, were chosen to pose as the Ladies of the Blended Rose, or Ladies of the Burning Mountain, while knights errant tilted in their honor. Captain André himself had designed their coiffures, Turkish costumes, and dazzling headdresses. The town buzzed for days on end as the promoters chased all over, searching for properties and materials for costumes, raiding enemy attics, and borrowing from lady friends for the unparalleled pageant on May 18.

Though Janine had seldom left the house since her

enforced seclusion, she could barely contain her curiosity and excitement on the day of the Mischianza.

"Oh, Papa," cried Janine, her blue eyes flashing with excitement. "It's said all the guests are gathering at Knight's Wharf at the foot of Vine Street to embark on galleys for Walnut Grove. They're all wearing magnificent costumes, and bands are playing, and there are dozens of barges floating downriver in a regatta. May I go to watch, please? Everyone will be looking at the guests. No one will be looking at me."

Papa heaved a reluctant sigh. "I dislike your taking unnecessary risks. However, I suppose in their wild carousing there's little chance that a Tory sympathizer will recognize you and report your resurrection from the dead."

"Thank you, Papa!" Smiling, Janine kissed him lightly on the forehead, then hurried to her room where she proceeded to disguise her appearance as she had done when venturing forth ever since her rescue from the British. She donned a drab brown wig Papa had bought for her and slipped into a Quaker gray gown and bonnet donated by Friend Rachel Lindley next door. Finally she tied on a linen face mask so popular with the ladies of the South, worn when riding out to protect their skin from the sun and dust.

Shortly after four o'clock Janine and Zoë hurried along the street under bright sunshine toward Knight's Wharf at the foot of Vine Street to watch the parade of colorful coaches and carriages make its way down the street toward the harbor.

Behind the coaches, heralds and trumpeters appeared. Then came a band of knights dressed in habits of pink, black, and silver, plumes waving from their hats. They were mounted on gray horses richly decked in trappings of the same colors, accompanied by attendants, all bearing silver shields and lances. Behind them rode seven knights in black and orange satin laced with gold.

Janine sighed with delight. She thought she'd never

seen anything so exciting in her entire life. As the
carriages passed by bearing the ladies in exotic Turkish
costumes, Janine strained her eyes for a glimpse of
Peggy. She stared in wonder at the elegance of their
costumes, just as André had forecast.

The women wore gauze turbans spangled and
edged with gold or silver. On the right side a veil of
the same kind hung as low as the waist, while the left
side of the turban was trimmed with pearls and tas-
sels of gold or silver and crested with a feather. The
dresses were sheer and flowing, of white silk with long
sleeves, and the sashes were tied with a large bow
on the left side, hung very low, trimmed, spangled,
and fringed according to the colors of the knight.

"I don't see Peggy," said Janine anxiously. "Do you
think she's taken ill?"

Zoë's face split in a wide grin, her black eyes dancing with devilry. "She not here 'cause the men from
the Quaker meeting go call on her papa. They say
the gowns is too flimsy and they don't want she be
sporting herself like that. And the judge, he 'grees.
Miss Peggy and her sisters has to stay home. Her papa
say she in a dancing fury!"

Janine shook her head in sympathy. Poor Peggy
would be devastated at missing the most exciting
event of her life!

Now the citizens, enthusiastic, contemptuous, or
merely curious, crowded onto the wharves to watch
General Howe, the notorious Mrs. Loring on his arm,
his brother Richard Lord Howe, and Sir Henry Clinton board a galley. A second and third galley followed,
full of officers and ladies. Twenty-seven barges, be-
flagged and lined with green cloth, accommodated the
guests.

When the entourage had embarked, Janine and Zoë
rushed back to the house and upstairs to the garret to
lean out the dormer window and watch the regatta
of festooned boats float down the river before the
city, colors flying in the breeze. Sounds of music from

bands in three barges floated across the warm May air.
The parties were to disembark at the landing place
near Gloria Dei Church and proceed to Walnut Grove,
the estate of Joseph Wharton. Suddenly there came a
great burst of cannon fire. Startled, Janine leaped back
from the window in panic until she realized that the
firing came from two anchored warships that were
saluting the generals.

At Wharton's mansion the procession would pass
under triumphant arches to an amphitheater where
the Knights of the Blended Rose and the Knights of
the Burning Mountain were to engage in a mock
tournament honoring their ladies. Then there was to
be an exhibition and procession through the triumphal
arches in honor of General Howe, after which feast-
ing and dancing inside the magnificently decorated
mansion would begin. Janine sighed with delight.
She'd never in her life seen such an extravagent show.
Why, it was better than the opera!

That same evening, shortly after ten, Janine and
Papa were reading in the parlor when she was again
startled by the sound of firing. She leaped from her
chair and ran to the window, pushing aside the curtains.

In the distance over rooftops and chimneys rose a
fountain of yellow, green, and pink stars that seemed
to hang for a moment in the air, drift downward,
and disappear from sight.

"Fireworks!" exclaimed Janine. "Papa, come and
watch. They're shooting off fireworks for the Mischianza!"

"Folly and vanity!" said Dr. Mercer angrily, not
looking up from his paper. "The whole affair is nothing but an ostentatious display—disgraceful when half
the town is starving to death—and to the everlasting
shame of the British!"

Janine said nothing. Papa was right, and she knew
that many of the citizens agreed with him. Still she
sat at the window, watching the spangles of stars,

Chinese fountains, fire pots, a flight of rockets and bursting balloons, all bathed in a strange brilliance, until at last they ended with a volley of rockets. Even though the whole town censured it, it was a sight to behold, thought Janine with a sigh of satisfaction. And undoubtedly Philadelphia would never have so elegant a celebration again.

The next morning Zoë told her that the revelry had continued until four o'clock in the morning.

Five days later Howe sailed for England. In his wake a rumor circulated about the town that filled its Tory inhabitants with fear and apprehension: Because of the French Alliance, the troops would be withdrawn. The prospect of being left at the mercy of their enemies filled many a loyal heart with indignation as well as horror, grief, and despair. And soon their worst fears were confirmed.

The king ordered the evacuation of Philadelphia and the march of the army northwards to cooperate with Sir Guy Carleton. Rather than be abandoned to the rebels, many loyal citizens prepared to evacuate the town with the troops. General Clinton ordered available shipping to be used for the Tories, sick and wounded troops, and such heavy equipage as could be crowded aboard. On June 18 at three in the morning, the last of Clinton's army of eleven thousand men began to cross the Delaware.

The next day Major General Benedict Arnold arrived to take command in Philadelphia. The thirty-seven-year-old Arnold, with jet black hair, ice-blue eyes, and strong features, expected trouble—and it was not long in coming. The town was soon split into factions: patriots who returned, Loyalists and collaborators who remained, and neutralists.

But Janine felt like a bird set free from a cage, almost like a returning patriot, for with the British gone, she felt at liberty to go about the city at will. In high spirits, she set out for a stroll in the soft June sunshine and returned dismayed and sorrowful. Philadelphia was so devastated, looked so different since the British had taken over!

"The entire city is in a shocking state of filth and disrepair," she complained to Papa. "Even the State House was left in a filthy and sordid condition!"

Dr. Mercer pushed out his lower lip in sorrowful agreement. "They used the State House as a hospital and a prison along with many other public and private buildings. You should see Old Pine Street Church! Even that was used as a hospital! They burned the pews, stripped the pulpit, and windows, and later used it for a stable. Left more than a hundred Hessians buried in the churchyard."

Dr. Mercer's eyes burned with anger. "In some of the finest genteel houses, holes have been cut in the parlor floors to serve for the disposal of horse manure!"

"And Potter's Field is piled high with fresh soil," said Janine distressed. "Lord knows how many of our Continental soldiers are buried there!"

"They say upwards of two thousand, including those executed and those who starved to death in prison."

If Jonathan were ill in the camp hospital, at least he had not been executed or imprisoned, thought Janine. And for that she was grateful.

Late in June on a stifling hot day, the town was buzzing with excitement. Washington was on the march again. Rejoined by the sunshine patriots whose plowing was done, his forces had swelled to 13,500 men and he had decided to take advantage of a heaven-sent opportunity. Clinton, on a killing march to Sandy Hook, with fifteen hundred wagons and carts stretched over twelve miles of rough, muddy roads, presented an irresistible target.

Early on June 28 the American forces caught up with Clinton near Monmouth Courthouse and Washington ordered General Charles Lee to lead an attack on Clinton's rear guard. Lee, instead of supporting the American wings and closing around the British rear, unaccountably ordered a retreat. Washington appeared on the scene like an avenging angel, took over Lee's command, and rallied his men in the swirling confusion.

The battle raged on in the sweltering heat and smoke of the swampy ravines until late afternoon, when the British retreated in good order. Darkness fell and the men lay down their arms. Near midnight the British troops took advantage of the coolness of the night to escape the fatal effects of another day's battle and resumed their march to New York.

When the news reached Philadelphia, the town was in a quandary as to the outcome.

"We've won a victory, then?" Janine asked Papa, her brow drawn in a perplexed frown.

"I don't know whether we should count it a victory or a stalemate," said Dr. Mercer judicially, sucking on his pipe. "You could say the Americans won the day, for they hold the terrain, but Sir Henry Clinton has accomplished his purpose of getting his army and baggage safely to Sandy Hook."

But for the moment all that concerned Janine was Jonathan. Had he survived? Had he ploughed through sand, swamp, and forest under Lee only to be abandoned by his commander? Was he lying wounded— or worse, on the blood- and sweat-soaked ground at Monmouth Courthouse?

Chapter 31

On a fine October afternoon in 1778, when the leaves had turned scarlet and gold and clouds hung motionless in a Wedgwood sky, Janine was sitting in the parlor, mending Papa's stockings. Suddenly she was startled by a loud rapping on the front door. She sighed, put down her mending, and went to answer.

On the threshold stood a tall, emaciated stranger wearing a patched and threadbare buff and blue uniform. His hair, the color of straw, limp and shaggy, was caught back in a piece of twine. A scraggly beard covered the lower part of his face and the sunburned skin was tight across the wide cheekbones. Even so, there was something vaguely familiar about the haunted eyes, the line of the hollow cheeks, the face, gray with weariness and fatigue. Her glance went back to his eyes, which held a dazed expression, as though he were confused. Janine's hand went to her throat.

"Jonathan!" she gasped.

The soldier's jaw fell open and he stood staring at her as though she were an apparition, shock and disbelief written on his face. Abruptly his expression changed and his faded eyes brightened with joy and astonishment.

"Janine!" he cried in a choked voice. He plunged through the door and wrapped his arms around her, hugging her to him as though he would never let her go. She clung to him, tears of happiness brimming on her eyelids, spilling down her cheeks.

"Oh, Jonathan, you're home! Safely home at last!"

"Janine, Janine," he murmured again and again.

Pressed tightly against him, her hands on his back, straining him to her, Janine was startled by the appalling leanness of his body, the bony shoulder blades protruding under his shirt, the thinness of his arms around her. But he was home, home! That was all that mattered.

At last she broke away and led him down the hall toward the parlor. Matching her step to his, she felt, rather than saw, his awkward, uneven gait, and her heart gave a painful lurch. He'd been wounded! Her mind seethed with questions: When and where had it happened? At Germantown? At Monmouth? Was he in pain? Would he recover only to go away and fight once more?

In the parlor, filled with the golden mellow light of the fall afternoon, she pushed away these unhappy thoughts as Jonathan drew her down beside him on the sofa and took her in his arms, kissing her hungrily, as if to make up for all the time they'd been apart.

At last they drew back breathless, gazing at each other in wonder, as though still unable to believe they were together even now. A sudden, self-conscious shyness with this haggard, gray-faced stranger came over her. She rose to her feet in confusion. "I must tell Papa," she said and ran from the room.

After the first joyous greeting Dr. Mercer poured glasses of brandy and settled himself in the Windsor chair. Casting a professional eye over Jonathan's emaciated frame, he said gently, "It appears to me you could stand some fattening up, my boy."

Jonathan managed a grin. "But, sir, I gorged myself on rice and vinegar at Valley Forge, and firecake in New York, with half a pumpkin for dessert!" Abruptly his expression changed to one of futility as he stared down at his long legs stretched out before him. "Even so, the army thinks I'm of little use to them now." He looked embarrassed. "Took a bullet in my right hip sometime back. It's healed well enough

—only pains me in cold, damp weather. Since I couldn't serve as a foot soldier, I volunteered for the cavalry, but they turned me down because I had no mount."

Distress shone from Janine's eyes and she shook her head in a helpless gesture. "It's beyond belief that you ever survived!"

Jonathan reached out and covered her slim hands with his own. "I'm a tough turkey, my sweet. But *you* are the miracle, Janine. Mama wrote me that you'd succumbed to pleurisy after you came home."

Dr. Mercer's brows drew together in a puzzled frown. "I did write Ellen that Janine was at death's door, but considering her youth and vigor, I'd no doubt she'd pull through."

Jonathan shrugged. "She must have misread your hand." He sighed deeply and gazed lovingly at Janine. "All those months I thought you were lost to me forever! But it makes no difference now."

Janine felt as though a shadow had passed over them. She shivered, hoping it wasn't an evil omen.

Dr. Mercer removed his spectacles and began polishing them on his sleeve. "That she survived is a miracle indeed, not from pleurisy, but a firing squad," he said dryly.

Jonathan's head jerked around in surprise.

Between them, Dr. Mercer and Janine related the story of her carrying intelligence to Colonel Boudinot and her narrow escape from death. As Jonathan listened, his face registered incredulity, astonishment, and finally awe and admiration for the role she had played in thwarting Howe's surprise attack at Whitemarsh. Jonathan shook his head, gazing at her in wonder.

"A heroine whose deeds of valor can never be told or properly honored," he said with a wry smile.

"The only misfortune was that I was never given a safe-conduct pass to come to see you, my darling."

Jonathan heaved a long sigh. "That's the truth on

it! Knowing you were alive and well would certainly have sustained me during the long dreary days and nights we were chasing the bloody Redcoats all over New Jersey!"

Over a late supper, Jonathan told Janine and Papa of his escape from the renegades and of his return to Heritage Hall, briefly touching on his campaigns with General Washington. When he finished, they returned to the warmth of the fireside in the parlor, lingering over glasses of port and brandy.

"What of Ellen and John?" asked Dr. Mercer. "The post has been less reliable than ever since the British occupation and no news of them has come through."

Jonathan sipped his wine. "I've no news from them direct, but last February Mistress Washington came up from Mount Vernon to join the General at Potts House. When she visited the hospital, she told me that though times were hard back home, those at Heritage Hall were holding on as well as any of the plantation owners. Half the slaves ran off when Dunmore offered them their freedom if they'd fight with the British. I expect Heritage Hall will be more than grateful for another hand when I return."

At his words Janine felt a cold fear squeezing her heart. A sudden silence fell between them, lengthening interminably. She bit her lip to hold back the words that rushed to her mind. Before they'd parted that fateful April night more than two years ago, they had agreed that after they were married Jonathan would stay in Philadelphia and that they would make their home here. Feverishly she wondered if he'd forgotten how violently Ellen had opposed their marriage. She longed to cry out to him in protest, but the words would not come.

At last Dr. Mercer said, "You'll be returning to Heritage Hall, then?"

Jonathan looked him squarely in the eyes. "It's my duty to go back, sir. I'm sorely needed there."

Janine stared down at the wine set swirling in the glass between her trembling fingers.

"Of course you are," agreed Dr. Mercer. "But I hope you'll remain with us for a while. Give us a chance to fatten you up."

Jonathan rose, walked haltingly to the fireplace, and stood warming his hands.

"Thank you kindly, Uncle Robert, but I must get back as quickly as possible. Not only will my family wish news of me and need me desperately, but they may be in grave danger. General Washington has received reports that the British have issued a new ruling from London that marks out the south as the main theater of war. British warships are already threatening the South Carolina and Georgia coasts. If the Redcoats march through Virginia, I'll be needed to help protect Heritage Hall."

Janine felt as though she were suffocating. She swallowed hard and took a deep breath. The months, the years of waiting for this moment when Jonathan would say, "Now we'll be married," suddenly weighed upon her like stones. Had she been waiting for a moment that would never come? Two years was a long time—and he had thought she was dead. Maybe he'd found someone else! The pulses in her temples pounded and she could not find the courage to say, "Then you no longer wish to marry me?"

Papa was gazing at Jonathan over the rims of his spectacles with something like approval in his blue eyes. She could hope for no help from that quarter. And as if to bear out her thought, Papa said, "Yes, I quite understand, Jonathan. In your position I'm sure I would do the same."

Dr. Mercer glanced expectantly at Janine, as though waiting for her to speak out. She dropped her gaze and sat staring into her wine glass, her tongue like flannel in her mouth.

Dr. Mercer turned back to Jonathan, standing before the fire, and he rose from the Windsor chair.

"Well, I must excuse myself for the present. I'll have Zoë prepare the front room for you upstairs. You're welcome to stay as long as you wish." He clapped Jonathan on the shoulder. "Good to have you home, my boy."

When the door had closed upon Papa, Jonathan turned from the fire and rested his arm on the mantel, smiling at Janine.

"I've told you my adventures after the renegades attacked us, but what of you, sweet? I take it Beauty carried you to safety?"

Janine hesitated. She wanted to tell him that was so, and be done with it. But she could not bring herself to deceive him, and in a low, calm voice she told him of her abduction by the brigands and how they had tried to misuse her. She wasn't surprised at his anger and outrage at her treatment by her abductors, but his eyes narrowed and he seemed less pleased than she'd expected when she went on to tell him of her rescue by Lieutenant Furneaux.

"You rode all the way to Philadelphia with this strange man?" asked Jonathan indignantly.

Janine nodded and decided not to worry Jonathan with how Mark had cared for her during her illness. She could feel her face flushing now, just thinking of it, and she didn't wish to tax Jonathan's understanding too far. After she told him how Beauty had disappeared, he made no effort to hide his displeasure.

"Janine, how could you have been so careless?"

"She was stolen!" cried Janine, stricken with guilt and remorse. "I'm certain I tied her securely."

Jonathan listened with a faint frown of disapproval as she rushed on, finishing the story of her journey to Philadelphia. "There was nothing to do, but to go on with Lieutenant Furneaux," said Janine vehemently.

Jonathan shrugged, but his disgruntled expression remained. "I suppose so. And at least you arrived with Brandy in hand."

"That's true, Jonathan." She paused and set her wineglass on the side table. "But I'm afraid Brandy is gone too." In a strangled voice she told him how the British officer had come door-to-door, requisitioning horses and carriages from all the citizens, making off with them without a by-your-leave!

"You didn't let them take Brandy!" exclaimed Jonathan angrily.

Janine looked up into his face, abject apology in her eyes. "I tried to stop him, Jonathan, truly I did. But it was impossible. The man flung me down on the pavement and galloped away!" She blinked back tears gathering in the corners of her eyes. "I feel as badly as you do. . . ."

Jonathan's lips thinned in an exasperated line. "A finer piece of horseflesh we've never seen at Heritage Hall, and probably never will again!" He gave a hopeless sigh. "But I guess you did the best you could."

He turned back to the fireplace and stood with his arms folded on the mantel, gazing down into the fire licking the pine knots, burning with a bright blue-green flame, apparently lost deep in his own thoughts.

She felt as if the warmth had gone out of the world. At last she could stand his shutting her out no longer. She patted the sofa beside her. "Come sit down, Jonathan," she said softly. "Let's talk about your plans for the future."

He turned and gazed at her, a puzzled expression in his light blue eyes. "I have no plans for the future, other than to return to Heritage Hall. Before I left, I promised Mother and Father I'd come home."

A swift stab of shock and disappointment went through her, but pride rose inside her like a steel rod, strengthening her resolve. She would not, could not, hold Jonathan to a vow he no longer wished to keep. She concentrated on pleating the folds of her gown.

"I thought that all soldiers in the field dreamed of

what they'd do in the future when they were done with fighting."

Jonathan walked toward her with slow steps, as though trying to make his limp appear less noticeable. He eased down beside her on the sofa and leaned forward, his elbows on his knees, staring at his hands clasped loosely between them.

"For a long time I thought I had no future"—he paused and turned to look at her—"without you."

Janine gazed deep into his eyes, searching for an answer to the question burning in her mind, but his expression was flat and bland and she could read nothing in it. At last she said, "Not hearing from you all this time, I thought perhaps you'd changed your mind—that you no longer felt the same as you did before. . . ."

"I told you," he said testily, "I thought you were dead." He turned his head and stared into the fire.

Had Jonathan's love died too? she wondered. She dared not ask, for if he said yes, she couldn't bear to hear it. He seemed so detached, so far away, as though he lived in a world that didn't include her. An over-whelming sense of abandonment swept through her and her heart ached so, that she could hardly speak. In a voice husky with emotion she said, "It's as though you're still living in another place and time—" Her voice broke.

His head jerked around, and seeing the baffled expression in his eyes, all at once it struck her that his plans for the future had, in fact, not included her. He had put their past behind him, while she had waited, not knowing whether he was dead or alive, never doubting that their love was strong enough to survive this seemingly endless separation.

"Finding you here when I thought only to pay my respects to your father, well, it's a shock that takes some getting used to." He patted her arm and spoke as one comforting a small child and smiled the easy,

familiar smile she loved so well. "I expect it won't
take long—maybe even tonight."

He pulled her to him, cradling her comfortably,
pressing her black head to his heart. Her body seemed
to melt into his, and his lips took hers, gently at first,
then ardently, as if he could never have enough. They
remained thus for a long time while the flame in the
fireplace burned low and the glowing pine knots
crackled and split and fell with a small shower of
sparks. All she heard was the swift thudding of her
heart.

At last she drew away from his embrace, acutely
aware that he was rousing feelings within her that
she had striven so long to suppress. She had learned
well that she must stay a man's ardor before her own
got out of hand. Tonight she had neither the desire
nor the willpower to resist Jonathan. Now from outside she heard the watchman crying the hour. With
an effort she forced herself to rise, and taking the
snuffer from the mantel, she put out the candles in
the wall sconces.

"Come, Jonathan, it's late and you're near exhaustion. I'll light you to your room."

Jonathan stood up and, taking the candle from
her hand, set it on the table. He clasped her in his
arms again, kissing her mouth, her throat, nuzzling
her ear. His lips, so warm and tender, made her tingle
all over. Her knees went limp and she swayed in his
arms, clinging to him. There came the creaking sound
of a door opening and closing and footsteps in the
hall.

"Do you think Uncle Robert would notice if I
shared your room?" Jonathan murmured.

Laughing, Janine gazed up into his face. "Papa
would notice an ant crawling under my door!"

"Before we're wed he'd best get used to the idea of
your room being invaded!"

"Wed!" The word rang in her ears like the chiming of bells, and the terrible depression weighing

down her mind and her heart lifted like a dark cloud blown away by a sudden gust of wind. Joy and relief flooded through her. Jonathan would settle his affairs at Heritage Hall and return to Philadelphia to marry her. They could live here. He could always go back to the plantation if need be. Weak with relief, she placed her forefinger on his chin, her eyes sparkling with happiness.

"I understand, Jonathan," she said softly. "You'll need time to put things in order at Heritage Hall."

Smiling, he held her close, his hands locked behind her waist. "True. And it will be that much easier with you at my side, my sweet. We'll be married here and return to the Hall together."

As the significance of his words penetrated her mind, she stared at him, her brow puckered in dismay and confusion. Married *here*. Return to Heritage Hall *together*! Janine took a deep breath. She wanted desperately to start off on a good footing with the Burke family and she was afraid that confronting them with a marriage would only turn them against her further. It took all her courage to say the words.

"Jonathan, Aunt Ellen and Uncle John will be terribly hurt and upset if we're married here. If you wish to wait a bit, Papa and I will come to Alexandria for our wedding and—" She wanted to say, after our wedding we'll return to Philadelphia and stay with Papa until you find work and we can settle into a home of our own.

With an impatient shake of his head, Jonathan interrupted her.

"We'll have no repeats of the scene we endured before. If I go on ahead, there may be recriminations, all manner of pleas and never-darken-my-doorstep-again threats that would be impossible to retract later on. If we arrive together as man and wife, Mother and Father may be hurt and angry for a time, but that will pass. There will be no question of whether or not. The deed will have been done, and they will have to accept you as one of the family at Heritage Hall."

Stunned, she repeated haltingly, "One of the family at Heritage Hall? You plan to live there?"

Jonathan looked surprised. "Of course. I told you I'd promised to come home." Gazing down at her flushed, bewildered face, he added, "If you think they'd be upset at our marrying here, how do you think they'd feel if I agreed to live in Philadelphia?" He grinned. "They'd blame my desertion on you, you know. No, it's far best to marry here and return to Heritage Hall together."

Janine gazed at him mutely, catching her lip between her teeth to still its trembling, pondering the wisdom of his words. There was a time when she would have impulsively gone along with whatever Jonathan suggested, heedless of the consequences. Now she thought of what the outcome might be. But she loved him desperately, and if this was the only way they could be together, then so be it. She smothered a sigh of resignation. "Whatever you say, my love." At least she was going along with her eyes wide open, and she did not deceive herself that Aunt Ellen would welcome her with open arms. She bolstered her courage with the hope that the family's joy and relief at seeing Jonathan safely home would assuage their anger and resentment over their marriage.

Early on a foggy Monday morning Janine and Jonathan were married in the front parlor of the house on Second Street by the same clergyman who had officiated at her funeral, witnessed only by Papa, Zoë and their next-door neighbors Eldon and Rachel Lindley. If it was not the wedding in Christ Church Janine had always dreamed of, the groom was her heart's desire. She wished Richard could have been there, but it seemed kinder not to ask him to witness her marriage to another. Papa had told him of her rescue, of course. And now Papa would give him the letter she had written telling him of her marriage to Jonathan.

Following their wedding Janine and Jonathan bid Dr. Mercer good-bye. Papa smiled, shook Jonathan's hand, and wished them well, but as he kissed Janine she saw that his blue eyes were filled with misgivings, which discomfited her no end. Resolutely she pushed down a sense of foreboding as she and Jonathan mounted the dappled gray gelding Papa had given them as a wedding gift and set out for Heritage Hall.

Janine thought she had never known such happiness as she experienced on their trip back to Virginia. The countryside was ablaze with color and the sky a constant Dresden blue. They gloried in the fresh, crisp air as they trotted through the damp shadowy pine forests, stopping at various inns as it grew dark. If Jonathan erupted in short outbursts of irritation at being drenched in a dismal October rainstorm, or loosed an angry tirade over a cold, shabby, bug-infested room at an inn, she was soon able to soothe his jangled nerves. Though his limp was not pronounced, she began to wonder if he had not become rather adept at concealing it and if his wound pained him more than he cared to admit.

If he wasn't as attentive as she thought he might be now that they were alone together, their lovemaking was all she'd hoped it would be; a lark, full of laughter and joy.

One night the rope supporting their mattress snapped under the strain of their tumbling.

"God's death!" Jonathan shouted, leaping up as though he'd been shot, clambering over the footrail of the bed.

Janine sat hunched on the sagging mattress, her face buried in her hands, her shoulders shaking with mirth. She looked up to see Jonathan standing naked, hands on his hips, feet astride, glaring malevolently at the mattress. Their eyes met, and his anger and embarrassment dissolved. Together they lifted the corn-husk mattress to the floor before the fireplace and took up where they had left off.

Gradually the tired lines disappeared from Jonathan's face and his war-weary eyes began to take on the sparkle and shine of their former days.

It was late afternoon when Janine and Jonathan turned up the lane to Heritage Hall. The sun, shining through the bronze leaves of the oak trees that lined the avenue, bathed the scene in a golden light. To Janine, the house waiting at the end of the lane looked proud and foreboding. Though the red bricks had mellowed, softened by the thick green ivy creeping up the walls, the once well-kept lawns, bushes, hedges, and flower beds were scraggly and unkempt, the rose gardens overgrown with weeds. She made a mental note to give them her attention, grateful for a task that would be of some help.

They reined in amid barking dogs and servants, who hurried inside to summon the family. Before they could dismount, the door flew open and Aunt Ellen, Uncle John, and Adam rushed out, calling Jonathan's name, hugging, kissing, and thumping him on the shoulder. Janine stood to one side, smiling and misty-eyed, quietly watching the joyful reunion. Suddenly there fell an appalling silence. Aunt Ellen, Uncle John, and Adam had turned from Jonathan and stood staring at her as though she were General Howe come to take over Heritage Hall.

Janine's spine stiffened, the back of her neck grew tense, and then she remembered that Aunt Ellen had thought she was dead. To them, her appearance, a ghost come to life, must indeed be a shock.

Jonathan went to her and, putting his arm around her waist, said beaming, "I've brought Janine home to stay." With the jubilant air of a victor bringing home the spoils, he added, "May I present my bride, Mistress Jonathan Burke!"

Ellen's hand flew to her throat, stifling a cry. For a fraction of a moment Janine's eyes met Ellen's. The only expression she could read, as Ellen stood white-faced and motionless as granite, was pure shock.

Quickly Uncle John strode forward, a broad smile creasing his round red face, arms outstretched, wrapping Janine in a bearlike hug. "What a marvelous surprise! Welcome to your new home, my pet. We're fortunate, indeed, aren't we, Ellen!"

Ellen, her fingers laced tightly at her waist, forced a grim smile that did not reach her eyes. "Jonathan's wife is always welcome in *our* home, of course."

Adam, though still formal, had an air of sophistication about him, and he was even more self-assured than she remembered him. He came to her, his gray eyes light with pleasure. Placing his hands on her shoulders, he kissed her solemnly on each cheek. She recalled that he was a full-fledged lawyer now.

"Jonathan has brought us a rare treasure. One which we badly need here at Heritage Hall. I wish you great happiness."

Although Janine was certain he did not intend it to be so, his tone sounded more than a little skeptical. She put it down to his brisk, nervous manner of speaking.

Supper was a joyous occasion. Ellen had ordered the shining Chippendale table laid with her best linens, silver, and china. The candlelight cast a soft glow on their faces as they dined on smoked ham, pheasant, green beans, and yams with floating island, fruits, and sweatmeats for dessert. All during the meal Ellen, John, and Adam plied Jonathan with questions about his campaigns with General Washington, expressing their horror and consternation over the wound he'd received at Monmouth and outrage at the recalcitrant General Lee's actions. Janine began to relax in the notion that the Burkes had decided to accept her marriage to Jonathan, giving in gracefully to the unalterable.

After a pleasant sojourn in the drawing room over glasses of Madeira, Jonathan rose and took Janine's hand in his, saying, "We've had a long and arduous journey. If you'll excuse us, we'll retire now."

Ellen deliberately avoided looking at Janine and said, "I've kept your old room clean and waiting for you, dear."

Jonathan hesitated, his brow lifted in question. When Ellen made no comment, he said smoothly, "Very well, Janine and I can make do in my room for the present."

Janine well knew his thoughts. He had no wish to displease his mother the very night of his return by insisting they take the more commodious guest-chamber.

Ellen's chin rose sharply. "I've had Spicy Mae put Janine's things in her old room on the third floor. There's no place for them in your room." Her tone clearly implied that there was no room for Janine either. Her black eyes, hard and unyielding, defied him to protest.

Jonathan's gaze dropped before her implacable stare. He said nothing, but took Janine's elbow and led her from the room.

Later in the darkness, after they were sated with lovemaking, Janine lay wide-eyed and sleepless, her head on Jonathan's shoulder, her body touching his. They had thrown back the covers in the heat of their passion, and his skin, damp with perspiration from their ardent lovemaking, glistened in the moonlight. Her fingertips caressed the golden mat of hair on his chest and she whispered softly, "Do you think we might move into the guestchamber? It's more spacious and much more convenient for two. . . ."

"Um," said Jonathan drowsily. "I'll ask Mother about it in the morning."

Janine bit her lip in vexation. She wanted to shout, Don't ask her, tell her! But she held her tongue. Jonathan was breathing deeply. Asleep, she thought with a slight stab of disappointment. It seemed he always fell asleep right afterward, when she was still keyed up with loving him, wanting to prolong their caresses, wanting to tell him how much she loved him. She rolled over and drifted off into a troubled sleep, hoping that Ellen's attitude was not a portent of things to come.

Though life at Heritage Hall appeared on the surface to be the same as it once had been, it was soon apparent to Janine that lack of money and the hardships of existence in the war-torn colonies had left Heritage Hall in dire straits. The abolishment of trade with England had drastically cut their income from exporting cotton and tobacco crops. And what they could sell was often paid for in Continental currency—which was worth next to nothing—or in letters of credit, individual drafts, promissory notes, or bills of exchange. To make matters worse, the crops were not what they had once been, for many of the slaves had run off to join the British forces. Worst of all, the families along the Potomac lived in constant fear that the British would creep up the river and attack.

Uncle John told them that Lund Washington had pleaded with all of the owners to contribute to a fund to fortify the Potomac. "But we had no money, and the fortifications were never built," he said worriedly.

Jonathan scoffed at their fears, telling them it would be nonsense for the British to invade northern Virginia. But the Burkes and other plantation owners still quaked at the memory of the winter of '76 when five British ships sailed up the ice-clogged Potomac and threatened to fire upon all the river mansions.

"You've no idea what it was like," said Aunt Ellen in pained outrage. "All Alexandria was frantic. Women and children fleeing the town; every wagon, cart, and horse they could scrounge moving goods out of the reach of the ships' cannon!"

It was on the tip of Janine's tongue to tell her she
very well knew what it was like, having been invaded
by the British, but she thought better of it.

"The men were determined to stay and fight to protect their property, of course. But the Lord struck
down the invaders!" A gleam of triumph shone from
her eyes. "In March the whole fleet was stricken with
smallpox. Men dropped like ticks from a dog and were
dumped into the river with the sharks!" Her sharp
jaw snapped shut with satisfaction in the belief that
justice had triumphed.

Outwardly imperturbable, Ellen managed her duties
on the plantation much as she had when Janine had
lived there two-and-a-half years ago. With the regiment of a general, she supervised the smokehouse,
icehouse, bakery, the cooking and cleaning and the
spinninghouse where cloth was made from wool as
well as flax and cotton fibers grown on the estate.

Janine spent the long, hazy October days tidying
up the gardens, routing out the choking weeds, and
cutting back plants for the winter. When she finished,
she found to her dismay that Ellen was so organized
that there was nothing left for her to do. She had
no part in life at Heritage Hall.

Jonathan, quite the reverse, plunged into the life
and business of the plantation with more zeal than
he had ever shown before, and his days were vexed
with troubles. The slaves were continually running
away. He found one of the overseers to be dishonest.
Fields of tobacco were spoiled by heavy rains. The
pigs and sheep wandered astray through rotting fences.
Fevers and illnesses spread through the slave huts,
sending Ellen into a fury at the threat to their own
health and lives. The mill dam broke and flooded the
land. And there was the constant struggle to make
ends meet. At the end of each day Jonathan fell into
bed numb with exhaustion.

Though Janine had reminded Jonathan to ask

Ellen if they might move into the guestchamber, he'd not mentioned it again. She had let the matter drop. But now the weather had turned cold and she was weary of running up to the third floor every day to fetch her clothes, and again at night to put them away.

One chilly October dawn she rose shivering with cold, eager to pull on her warm clothes. Glancing about the room, she realized she'd forgotten to bring down clothes to wear that day. Annoyed, she slipped into her flannel nightrobe and turned to Jonathan. "Won't you please ask your mother today if we can't move into the guest room? It's too cold these days to be running up and down to the third floor."

She couldn't see Jonathan's face, for his back was to her as he drew on his shirt, but his tone was sharp and impatient. "I've asked her twice, Janine. She says she likes to keep the room ready for guests. We never know when someone will come to spend the night. She prefers things as they are."

Janine bit back a sharp retort, and her jaw stiffened. When Jonathan's voice held that defensive note, she knew there was no use arguing with him.

Janine bided her time until late that afternoon when Ellen was off in the washhouse. Then, summoning two servants, she sent them upstairs to her old room and ordered them to carry down the wardrobe and the small chest of drawers and set them in Jonathan's room. After they left, she viewed the room with some misgivings.

The wardrobe was crowded into a corner, replacing a wing chair which now stood in the way of anyone entering the door. The chest, next to the window on her side of the bed, barely left room to pass. To make room for the chest she'd ordered the brightly painted rocking horse that Jonathan had used as a child to be stored in the garret. No matter how crowded it was, it would have to do, thought Janine. She was determined not to antagonize her mother-in-law.

Confronting her and demanding the more commodious guest room would certainly cause an unpleasant
scene.

She went down the broad winding staircase and
wandered through the rooms, casting about for something to do. In the dining room her eye fell upon two
branched silver candlesticks gracing the sideboard,
now stained brown with tarnish. She picked one up
and put it down with a shiver of distaste, recalling
the old days when Ellen had given her the loathsome
task of polishing them even when there had been a
full staff of servants.

Thinking to please her, Janine found a cloth and
set to work, humming over her task, rubbing the
candlesticks to a luster, taking pride in bringing the
glowing silver to life.

A short while later Janine heard voices coming
from the rear of the house. Ellen and Spicy Mae
were returning from the washhouse. Through the
dining room doorway she saw them pass through the
spacious entry hall, arms laden with freshly pressed
linens, and mount the stairs to the second floor. Moments later she heard Ellen's outraged voice raised
in a screech that sent a chill down her spine. "Who
had this furniture moved into this room?"

Janine's fingers paused over the silver candlestick.
Should she run upstairs and face Ellen's wrath or
wait for her tempest to subside? With shaking hands
Janine went on with her work. She heard Ellen's angry
tread on the stairs, her footsteps crossing the hall to
the drawing room, the sitting room, the library at the
rear of the house, and back again, stopping at the
dining room.

Janine looked up and smiled, holding out a gleaming five-branched candlestick. "I thought it would
please you to have them shining. . . ."

Ellen stood in the doorway in one of her somber
gray gowns, trembling with anger, her hands balled
into fists at her sides. "Do you think to call attention

to my poor housekeeping by showing us how well you complete your housewifely tasks? Put that down!"

The venom in her voice was such that Janine almost dropped the candlestick, and it clattered on the mahogany table as she set it down. "Aunt Ellen," said Janine, barely controlling her temper, "I've no intention of showing you up. I merely want to be of some use."

Ellen crossed the room and stood before Janine, her hands on her hips, her black eyes glittering like those of a snake about to strike. "Did you have the wardrobe and chest brought down to Jonathan's room?" Her voice, usually petulant, now conveyed a threat.

Janine rose to face her, looking her straight in the eyes. "I did."

"Where is Jonathan's rocking horse?" she demanded.

"I had it stored in the garret."

"In the garret!" shrieked Ellen. "Jonathan's had that horse since he was a child. It belongs in his room. He's always loved that horse!"

"He loves me more," said Janine, feeling an angry color rushing to her cheeks. "The horse won't be cold upstairs, but it's too cold for me to be running up and down for my clothes, not to mention the inconvenience."

"Don't be insolent as well as officious," Ellen snapped. "From now on kindly remember that *I* am mistress of Heritage Hall. Only *I* give orders to my servants. I'm ordering them to move the wardrobe and chest back to the third floor where they belong."

Janine's voice was soft as the whisper of a wave with the power of the ocean behind it. "Very well, Aunt Ellen. In that case Jonathan and I will also move to the third floor."

Ellen stood speechless. Her jaw fell open and rage glinted in her eyes.

"Please excuse me, I must write to Papa now," said

Janine. Stepping around Ellen, she crossed the floor
in long, graceful strides and swept from the room.

That night when Jonathan lighted their way up
to their room, Janine noticed that the wardrobe and
chest were standing where she had ordered them
placed. Jonathan frowned, none too pleased as he
viewed the room crammed with furniture. But when
she explained the need, he shrugged and agreed it was
the thing to do. It would keep the guest room free.
Janine thought she sensed a certain relief in his manner, now that he no longer had to push Ellen regarding their quarters.

"I'm afraid my arrangements annoyed your mother"
—she could not call Ellen "Mother" if her life de-
pended on it—"and I'm truly sorry, but it didn't seem
like such a terrible thing to do."

Jonathan yawned, flung himself on the bed, and
pulled Janine down beside him. "I've no time to
listen to female squabbles. Forget it."

In the days that followed, Janine tried to forget, but
she was distressed that she had clashed with Ellen
even though she tried to convince herself that it was
bound to happen. Papa had always said there was no
house big enough for two women. She was even more
distressed that her efforts to please Ellen by polishing
the candelabra had been mistaken as a criticism of
Ellen's housekeeping. Jonathan was right; she'd best
forget the whole thing. She thought of another of
Papa's maxims: Least said, soonest mended.

The trouble was Ellen did not forget. If there had
been little to keep Janine occupied before, now there
was less. To Janine it seemed as though Ellen were
living in a doll's house in which she would permit
no one else to play with her toys. With grim determination Janine resolved not to overstep her bounds in
Ellen's house again. Though she asked time and

again if there were anything she could do, Ellen repeatedly refused her offer of help.

In an effort to keep out of Ellen's way, Janine spent long days outside, riding the dappled gelding or strolling through the gardens. Often she would chat with Spicy Mae, a mahogany-skinned girl with the eyes of a fawn, who was about her own age. Sometimes she knelt on the rich, dark earth beside her and helped her weed the kitchen garden out of sight of the house.

One brisk, sunny afternoon early in November when Ellen was getting ready for dinner guests, Janine slipped outside, thinking to keep out of harm's way. She noticed that the dogwood was dotted with red berries and she shivered against a nip in the air. Winter was fast approaching and a killing frost threatened the roses. She found a basket and shears and made her way to the rose garden. She began cutting the last of the summer roses, heaping them in her basket until it was overflowing.

When she had finished, she sat back on her heels and brushed a strand of hair back from her damp forehead. Her back ached and her fingers were numb. Her blue muslin gown was streaked with dirt. When she pulled off her gloves, she was surprised to see drops of blood where long, sharp thorns had gone through, pricking her fingers.

"Your crown of thorns?" asked a voice behind her.

Startled, she looked up. Adam stood watching her, his lips curved in a tongue-in-cheek smile, his hands in his pockets.

"A labor of love," said Janine. It was clear to them both that her love was for the roses.

"Well done," said Adam approvingly. "I came to tell you that Jonathan will be late. One of the servants brought word that he's chasing a cow that's gone astray."

He took her arm and helped her to her feet. Then, carrying her basket, he walked with her to the house.

Once inside, she arranged the roses in lavish bouquets in three huge urns and placed them on tables in the dining room, the drawing room, and the spacious entry hall. She was standing back admiring her handiwork when she heard Ellen's firm footsteps approaching. She spun around, gesturing to the roses.

"Aren't they lovely, Aunt Ellen?"

The brief flicker of admiration Janine had seen in Ellen's eyes died, replaced by sparkling anger.

"Who told you you could cut the roses?" she demanded.

"Why, no one," said Janine, taken aback. "I thought with guests coming, you'd like—"

"*You* thought?" Ellen's lips curled in annoyance. "May I remind you that our flowers are not yours to cut?" Her voice was heavy with sarcasm. "And may I remind you again that I make the decisions at Heritage Hall!" She turned away and marched up the stairs.

Nonplussed and completely deflated, Janice gazed hopelessly at the roses, feeling as though thorns had pricked her spirit as well as her fingers. Slowly she turned and climbed the stairs to dress for dinner. *I won't allow that pecksniff to get the better of me,* thought Janine fuming. *I won't let her spoil the evening!* She dressed carefully in a new pink gown Jonathan had bought her and reached in her jewelry box for her medallion. The pearl-edge miniature of her mother was gone. Frantically she dumped the box on the bed and scanned the contents. It wasn't there. She searched the wardrobe and chest without success. She couldn't look further for it now, or she'd be late for dinner. Composing her face, she hurried from her room and started down the stairs just as the last of the guests were arriving. The Carlyles stood chatting in the entrance hall with Aunt Ellen and Adam.

"Roses in November!" exclaimed Sarah Carlyle. "How exquisite!" She bent over the lavish bouquet, breathing in the sweet fragrance. "Did you arrange these, Ellen?"

"Janine brought them in," Ellen replied, waving a negligent hand. "What I really prefer in that urn this time of year is an arrangement of cattails and eucalyptus. . . . Something that will last out the winter." Her voice trailed off as she led the Carlyles into the drawing room.

Adam glanced up the stairs and saw Janine poised for flight. She saw his eyes travel admiringly over her shining black hair, her white shoulders, down her pale pink gown. He held out his hand as though to draw her toward him.

"You are more beautiful than all the roses in the world."

It was quite a gallant speech, thought Janine, for a man who was usually so self-contained. Smiling into his eyes, she lifted her head and descended the stairs. Adam tucked her hand in the crook of his arm.

"Allow me to escort you into the lioness's den."

Chapter 32

Winter of 1778 brought a succession of raw, cold days that forced Janine to remain inside. Thinking to keep out of trouble, she spent many hours at the spinet, playing her favorite tunes and practicing new and difficult pieces by Haydn that she was eager to learn to play well. Uncle John particularly enjoyed her music and would often ask her to play for the family in the long winter evenings. He would listen as long as she'd play, tapping his foot, nodding his head, and smiling.

One evening when Uncle John and Aunt Ellen were out calling, Jonathan spoke to her about the spinet. "Your practicing gets on Mother's nerves. The continual noise sorely tries her patience. She is under a constant strain, you know, trying to manage . . ."

With a start, it came to Janine that Jonathan's handsome face suddenly looked stern and forbidding. She forced her mind back to what he was saying.

". . . and perhaps it would be best if you found some other pursuits."

"Yes, Jonathan," said Janine meekly, although she inwardly seethed. She had no quarrel with him, but she did wish that Ellen would speak directly to her when she had a complaint instead of going behind her back to Jonathan. It was almost as though Ellen thought to provoke a quarrel between them. Did Ellen envision Janine in the awkward position of trying to defend herself to Jonathan, annoying him by speaking out against his mother? Immediately Janine dismissed the idea as uncharitable and unworthy of Ellen, ashamed of herself for entertaining such thoughts.

One day in her search for a quiet pursuit Janine asked Uncle John if she might use his library.

"Indeed, yes. We've more books than you can read in a lifetime, my pet."

She was fascinated by the room's contents—shelves of leatherbound books reaching to the ceiling, Adam's law books and papers spread over the gleaming walnut library table, the wing chair done in crewel, and the great terrestrial globe. It amused her to set it spinning on its stand and watch the dull green, gold, and rust-colored countries flowing past. On the shelves she found Mr. Samuel Johnson's Dictionary that had once caused such a furor. In addition were all of her old friends: *Tristram Shandy*, *The Vicar of Wakefield*, and *Robinson Crusoe*; Benjamin Franklin's *Poor Richard's Almanack*, and, she frowned, Thomas Paine's *Common Sense*. What was Mark Furneaux doing now? she wondered. Even thinking of him brought a hot flush of excitement to her cheeks and her heart beat faster. What nonsense, thought Janine, angry with herself. She must dismiss this arrogant, mocking scoundrel from her mind at once! She found the complete works of Shakespeare and took down *The Tempest* from the shelf. Reading her way through Shakespeare should keep her busy all winter long. And it would be quiet enough not to disturb Aunt Ellen, thought Janine in annoyance.

One cold snowy afternoon in that same month of December, Jonathan stalked into the library and flung himself into a chair, a disgruntled expression on his face. Janine marked her place in the book she was reading and glanced up at him curiously.

"With all the work there is to be done around here, I'm surprised to see you idling away your time so," he said irritably.

Janine drew in a deep breath. She didn't need to

be told that Ellen had been complaining to Jonathan again.

"Jonathan," she began, holding on to her patience by a thread, "I've asked Aunt Ellen time and again if I could be of help and she always says no!"

"I'd think you'd see tasks that need doing without having to ask," said Jonathan tersely. "Mother runs herself ragged, but she can't do everything. Don't you realize how short-handed we are?"

Janine felt the rage growing inside her. "Jonathan, I've tried. Truly I have."

Seeing her anger, Jonathan took a kinder, more gentle tone. "I'm sure you have, sweetheart, but try a bit harder, won't you? I don't want Mother to think you're lazy."

"Lazy, am I?" She snapped the book shut and jumped to her feet. Jonathan had never thought she was lazy before, and he wouldn't think so now, unless his mother had put the thought in his head. She crossed the room and stood before him, trembling with emotion.

"You didn't think me lazy in your own mind, Jonathan, nor a lot of other things, either. Do you think I don't know how your long-suffering mother has tactfully pointed out all my shortcomings to you, real or imagined, since the day I first set foot in Heritage Hall? Talking against me behind my back, giving me no chance to defend myself against her accusations? Do you think I don't notice when she carts you off to the sitting room for one of her 'private' chats?"

Jonathan's eyes kindled with resentment and anger. "Janine, you know very well I pay no heed to her nitpicking."

"Nonetheless, her little drops of poison are like dripping water wearing away a rock," said Janine breathlessly. "And you do listen to her, or you wouldn't have come in here now accusing me of idling away my time!"

Jonathan stood up, his face cold and hard. "Forget

it. I'm sorry I mentioned it." He turned toward the
door, but Janine reached out and grasped his forearm.

"Hold on, Jonathan, please!" Her anger had dissi-
pated and her voice was pleading. "We can't go on
like this, with Ellen undermining me behind my
back. Don't you see, she's trying to destroy our marriage and you're letting her succeed!"

"*I'm* letting her succeed!" he erupted. "You're the
one who has blown this up out of all proportion."

Janine's gaze challenged him. "I'll wager that today's complaint is only one of countless times she's
pointed out my failings!"

The guilty, uncomfortable expression that flashed
across Jonathan's face told her she had struck a vein
of truth.

"Jonathan"—her throat went dry and her voice
quavered—"you must do something about her."

He turned on her, his face livid, eyes glistening
with anger. "What do you expect me to do, for God's
sake. Shoot her?"

In the face of his rage a sudden, cold calm came
over her. Her voice was low and urgent. "You can tell
her you refuse to listen to her complaints and accusations, that if she has anything further to say, she can
say it to me, to my face. You can take my part for a
change, instead of standing silent while she faults me.
Do you think I'm deaf or insensitive to her subtle
criticisms?"

He threw up his hands in disgust. "I don't know
what you're talking about!"

"Oh, yes you do!" said Janine sharply. "I can hear
her now: 'You know how Janine is, she's so frail, I
can't ask her to do this or that.' Or her sad plaint:
'Jonathan, we have so little time together, now that
Janine has come.' You say you love me, Jonathan.
Don't you believe in standing up for those you love?
You're willing and eager to defend your home, your
country. Why aren't you willing to defend me?"

Jonathan's jaw tightened, and glared at her belligerently. "I love Mother too, Janine."

"And well you should. I'm not asking you to abandon your mother. But for God's sake, don't let her
keep on disparaging me."

He shook his head as if to clear it. "I cannot manage a plantation and become involved in petty female
squabbles too. I wish to hear no more about it. Let
this be the end of it!" He turned and strode from
the room, slamming the door behind him.

Janine sank wearily into the chair, spent with trying to make Jonathan see what his mother was doing
to their marriage. If Ellen wanted to cause friction
between them, she was succeeding, thought Janine
bitterly. Her love for Jonathan was as strong as it had
always been, but her respect for him was slowly ebbing
away. A man who could deny the woman he loved,
sidestepping the issue for his own ease, had the backbone of a jellyfish. That Jonathan lacked the courage
to take her part, to handle the situation with his
mother, threw her into despair. Clearly he had no
qualms about telling *her* how he stood. Why, then,
could he not tell Ellen? To sacrifice her to his mother's
consuming jealousy could mean only one thing. He
did not truly love her at all.

Heretofore she had never told Jonathan when his
mother had taken her to task, venting her spleen over
some trivial incident. She had no wish to lower Ellen
in his estimation. Maybe she, too, should voice her
complaints, fight fire with fire. But in her heart she
knew she would not. She could not bring herself so
low as to denigrate her mother-in-law, to tattle on her
like a child. Janine let out a long sigh. She had one
ally. Time. Perhaps after enough time had passed
and Ellen saw that her barbs were failing to destroy
their marriage, she would weary of the game.

Quietly the library door opened and Adam strolled
into the room. With a studied calm he went to the
library table and began to search through his papers.

She thought he'd not seen her, sunk deep in the wing chair. Then, without looking up, he said in his crisp, nervous voice, "I thought I might interest you in a game of piquet."

Janine gazed at him in surprise as he went on sorting his papers. At last he looked up, his pale straight brows raised in question.

Had he heard the violent argument between Jonathan and her that had taken place here moments ago? If so, he made no reference to it. She smiled, nodding assent. Concentrating on the game would give some measure of relief from the thoughts tormenting her mind. Adam pulled out the card table and dealt the cards. By suppertime he'd won three games out of four.

By mutual consent, neither Janine nor Jonathan mentioned their argument again. Even so, a certain constraint developed between them. Though Jonathan's duties had fallen off during December and he had more free time to spend with her, he had taken to visiting neighboring plantations. Before long the gossip whispered among the servants reached her ears: that Jonathan was indulging in diversions of cockfighting and gambling at dice or card tables. With great difficulty Janine controlled her impulse to take him to task, and bided her time.

Christmas of that year passed quietly and uneventfully. The only news they heard as 1779 came in was that British troops under Lieutenant Colonel Archibald Campbell from New York and General Augustine Provost, sailing up from the coast of Florida, had captured Savannah. Eighty-three Americans had died and four hundred fifty-three were captured. The shattered American survivors had fled to join General Benjamin Lincoln across the Savannah River in South Carolina. Janine had a letter from Papa saying that the northern American army was hutted in canton-

ments from Danbury, Connecticut, to Elizabethtown,
New Jersey; Dr. Franklin had been sent to Paris as the
first American minister to France; and they were still
caring for a number of convalescent soldiers admitted
last September to the wards of Penn's Hospital. To
Janine it seemed the whole world was out of joint.
The clouds of doom hung over Heritage Hall.

Spring came on overnight. Forsythia burst into yellow popcorn blossoms. Dogwood and redbud flourished. And with the reawakening of the world outside,
Janine pulled herself from the doldrums. When Jonathan began riding out again, she rode with him on
the dapple-gray gelding, hoping to recapture the joyous, carefree days they had known so long ago. But
Jonathan was preoccupied with wheat and corn and
tobacco and cows and sheep, and seemed not to notice
whether she was with him or not. At last, feeling she
was only in the way, she sent him off alone. Though
she enjoyed visiting with Uncle John, she seldom saw
him these days. He was either buried in his ledgers
and accounts or in the town on business. And Ellen
was turning the house inside out in a frenzy of housecleaning.

It was near the end of April when another letter
came from Papa bearing news that set Janine's head
spinning from shock and surprise. It seemed that
Major General Arnold, the cocky, arrogant military
commander in Philadelphia had a knack for causing
nerve-rasping discord and had alienated many of the
citizens by ostentatious living, far beyond his known
means of income. Ugly rumors spread that Arnold was
selling army provisions to unscrupulous merchants at
great profit to himself. To make matters worse, he
had courted and won the beautiful Peggy Shippen.
They were married on April 8 in the parlor of her
father's house with only the family and a few friends
present. It was said that Arnold was supported by an
aide during the ceremony and sat with his leg propped

on a cushion during the reception. As a wedding gift
he had purchased Mount Pleasant, heavily mortgaged,
and at present, rented so they could not live there.
Janine folded the letter away, smiling to herself.
Mount Pleasant was the most elegant mansion in all
of Pennsylvania. It was easy to imagine her merry,
luxury-loving friend in such a setting.

As spring turned into summer and then fall wore
on, Janine grew bored and restless. She began to look
forward each day to the time Adam would return
from Colonel Simms's law office in Alexandria and
entertain her with stories and incidents that had occurred in the town. Sometimes he spoke of his ambitions for the future—in the Virginia Assembly and in
time, if things went the way he hoped in the colonies,
a post in the new government of the United States.
Janine began to perceive that Adam was a man who
always viewed others in relation to himself and that
beneath his controlled detachment, a great deal was
going on.

Frequently he played cards with her to amuse her,
and serious though he was, occasionally he would
surprise her with his quick wit and sensitivity. Often
she would look up from the card table to find him
watching her with an attentive, speculative gaze.

The passing of time had not changed Ellen's attitude as she had hoped. In fact Ellen had recently
renewed her efforts with a vengeance. It seemed to
Janine that her mother-in-law constantly found new
ways in which to bedevil her. Her response was to
avoid Ellen as much as possible. To this end she spent
as much time as she could outdoors.

By the time October rolled around, Janine was
ready to divulge the secret that had occupied her
mind and heart since late August. One warm Indian
summer night when the stars hung low in a darken-
ing sky and she and Jonathan was strolling in the

garden before going to bed, she told him she was pregnant. His joy at the news that she was to produce an heir was all she could have desired. He swung her up off the ground and whirled her around in delight. Immediately he began making plans for the boy. Laughing, Janine said, "And if *he's* a girl?"

"If he's a girl, it will be all the same," said Jonathan with a jubilant grin. "She'll be beautiful and tall and slender and ride with me over the plantation, just like her mother!"

Jonathan's happiness over the coming heir was matched by Uncle John's, who made much over it. Aunt Ellen accepted the news impassively, her face a mask of indifference. Janine had hoped that Ellen would be happy. She fully expected her to be either very happy or very put out, but her apparent disregard of the coming event was baffling. The fact was Ellen simply ignored Janine's pregnancy.

Shortly thereafter Janine began to perceive a change in Jonathan's attitude toward her, a hostility and withdrawal that disturbed her greatly. The days passed quietly, but once again he was absent from home for long afternoons and evenings, taking his pleasure at the gaming tables and cockfights. Though he came home every night, more often than not it would be almost dawn before he staggered to bed, reeking of rum. Once, behind the closed door of the library, she heard Jonathan's and Uncle John's voices raised in argument over gambling debts.

As before, Adam often played cards with her to amuse her, or he would accompany her on the daily afternoon walks she felt were good for her health. Afterward they would take a glass of brandy in the library, talking of current events. He brought the latest news from town, though word that the French and the Americans under General Lincoln had failed in an attack on Savannah in the bloodiest battle since Bunker Hill hardly cheered her. Adam also followed closely the workings of Congress and when he talked of the Articles of Confederation and other political activities, she listened intently, watching the fires of ambition gleaming in his gray eyes.

Jonathan grew increasingly restive and quarrelsome. On several occasions she asked if something was troubling him. Each time he would brush her off, saying there was nothing. Miserably she suffered under his cold looks and bitter tongue, her heart aching with hurt and despair. She stood his silence as long as she could, then one night in their room she sat on the bed, her knees drawn up under her, watching Jonathan poke at the fire. She swallowed hard and said, "Jonathan, I can't continue this way any longer. I know you're unhappy, and I must know why. You may not wish to upset me by admitting that these are lean times at Heritage Hall, or divulging your losses at cards and dice, or admitting that your hip injury pains you. But I'd far rather know the reason for your long, dour silences, your shutting me out than to be left wondering. . . ." She let her words trail off.

He stood silent for a moment, gazing out the window into the blackness. When he turned to face her, his expression was hard and tight. "Janine, I've tried hard to forget the past, to put it behind me. I thought as time wore on it would recede, but now that you are to be the mother of our child . . ."

Janine's mouth fell open in astonishment. "I haven't the vaguest notion what you're talking about."

Jonathan's eyes narrowed and he gazed at her intently. "Come now, Janine. Surely *you* haven't forgotten your lurid past."

"Lurid past!" cried Janine, appalled. She did not have to be told who put those words in his mouth. "Jonathan, you're mad!"

He strode to the foot of the bed and gripped the footrail, his knuckles white. "Mad, am I? Surely you've not forgotten your arduous journey to Philadelphia, spending the nights at inns and taverns with your cavalier, Lieutenant Furneaux!"

She felt color creep into her neck, up into her face.

"And your friend Doctor Ransom who taught you so much at Penn's Hospital. . . ."

"Jonathan," she said heatedly, "Doctor Ransom is a friend and nothing more. I swear to it!"

He went on as if she had not spoken. ". . . not to mention your devoted Redcoat patients. I'd say you were suffering from Scarlet Fever!"

"Scarlet Fever!" sputtered Janine, aghast. It was a term Aunt Ellen and others used for those who were enamored of the British soldiers. "There were Continental soldiers at Penn's Hospital as well as British. Illness and pain know no sides!"

But now that his tongue was loosened, Jonathan's pent-up resentment and anger poured forth in a torrent. "Consorting with the British like a common whore!" he said furiously.

Janine rose to her knees, clutching the bedpost for support. "Jonathan, this isn't true! Please, I can explain—"

"You have explained—how you sat in a tavern and wooed information from the Redcoats for Colonel Boudinot—"

"I did nothing wrong. Nothing!"

"Do you deny that a certain Colonel Townsend saved your life at the risk of his own neck? Why would a high-ranking British officer commit such folly unless you were having an affair with him?"

Stunned, Janine rocked back on her heels. He was so consumed with jealousy and rage, she knew there was no use trying to make him listen to reason. Now she saw Ellen's design. Ellen had collected a store of ammunition and placed it in Jonathan's hands to fire! With a face like stone, she said, "If you wish to believe that of me, there's nothing I can say to change your opinion."

He turned and paced the floor, running his hand

over his hair in agitation. "I don't wish to believe it of you. I've tried my best not to believe it! But thinking of the mother of my child as a common—"

"Oh, oh!" cried Janine, beside herself with rage, knowing full well who put such concern in his mind. "Believe what you want to believe, then. Or what your mother tells you to believe!" Tears stung her eyelids. She whirled away from him and lay on her side, rigid, facing the wall. She heard his uneven gait as he stamped across the room, heard the door slam behind him as he left.

For the next three days Jonathan was absent from the house all day; he did not appear for supper, nor did he return to their bedroom at night. Outwardly Janine preserved a calm, unruffled demeanor. Inside, her mind was a turmoil. One night at supper when Uncle John asked where Jonathan was, Aunt Ellen replied, "He has business to attend to in town." She glanced at Janine, her eyes gleaming with secret knowledge.

Janine shivered, fighting down fear and apprehension that the seeds of suspicion planted by Ellen, tended and nurtured more carefully than her garden, had taken root and grown.

On Friday, late in the afternoon, a gale blew up and rain lashed the house, bending the pines, swaying the oaks, pelting the windows. Janine and Adam had just finished a game of piquet before a cozy fire in the library and she was laughing as she had not laughed in a long time at one of Adam's stories. Suddenly the flames in the fireplace leaped high and she felt a chill draft blow across the room. At the same time Janine and Adam turned to see who had opened the door. Jonathan stood in the doorway, gripping the frame, a dark, ugly expression on his face.

Janine jumped up and ran to him, arms outstretched. "Jonathan! I've been so worried about you!"

He glared at her as though she were a cur about to leap upon him and soil his clothes, and his voice lashed out like a whip. "I can see you've been frantic with worry."

Swiftly Adam rose and strode to face his brother. "Hold on, Jonathan," he said sharply, "there's no need to—"

Jonathan's jaw hardened as he scowled at Adam. "Naturally you'd defend her," he said sarcastically. "Clearly she's been working her wiles on you!"

Adam's gray eyes turned to granite and an angry flush spread over his face. "Jonathan, I'll not stand by and let you accuse us of anything. . . ."

"Then get out!" shouted Jonathan. "This is between Janine and me. It's none of your affair. . . ."

Before he could finish speaking, Adam stalked from the room, shutting the door firmly behind him. Janine was pale and shaken, staring at Jonathan with wide incredulous eyes. His brow furrowed with rage and his voice was harsh and accusing.

"Do you think I don't know what's been going on behind my back for God knows how long?" he shouted.

"It's not true, what you're thinking," cried Janine. "I swear before God, it's not true!"

"And how am I to know that? Tell me how I'm to know that the child you're carrying isn't Adam's?"

"Adam's!" she shrieked. It was unthinkable!

"Adam's," he said with finality.

Janine felt the blood drain from her face, and something inside her seemed to explode. "It's my word against Ellen's, isn't it?" she asked venomously. "That's what it comes down to, doesn't it, Jonathan?"

He stood over her, breathing heavily, consumed with such anger, she thought he might strangle her in the next moment.

"For less than a shilling I'd go back to the army," he shouted. "Fighting the British is one hell of a lot easier and more pleasant than fighting with you and my mother!"

Janine's eyes blazed, her fury matching his own. "Why don't you, then? If that's what you want, go!"

He pushed her from him with a shove that sent her reeling backward across the room. Wildly she grasped at the air, trying to regain her balance. She collided with the waist-high globe on its stand, and at the same instant she heard the door slam shut. She clutched the globe; it spun under her hands, and together they crashed to the floor. She lay panting, facedown, pain stabbing through her until she became aware that the iron foot of the stand was jabbing into her distended stomach.

She rolled on her back and lay still, gasping for breath. A dull pain coursed through her body. She struggled to her feet and flung herself into the wing chair, gripping the arms, arching her back, tensing and relaxing her body. Finally the pain subsided. She went to the window and parted the curtains. Gazing out through the heavy, slashing rain, she saw a gray figure mounted on a horse, galloping pell-mell down the lane leading away from Heritage Hall.

Chapter 33

At first Janine had quieted the fear clutching at her heart by telling herself that Jonathan had merely ridden off to town and that when the tempest raging inside him had blown itself out, he would return. But as the days lengthened into a week and he had not come home, dread and apprehension mounted inside her.

At midday on Friday Adam rushed home from town and broke the news to them at the dinner table. Someone he'd run into at City Tavern recalled that a week ago Jonathan, having quaffed enough ale to float a frigate, had announced to all and sundry that there was more peace to be found on the battlefield than at Heritage Hall and he was off to join General Benjamin Lincoln's troops.

For a moment everyone was stunned speechless. Adam's accusing eyes rested briefly on his mother, but he said nothing. Uncle John, after an outburst of astonishment, appeared vexed and saddened at the same time. Aunt Ellen slammed her fork down on the table and turned angry and outraged eyes upon Janine.

"You knew he'd left to join the army and you didn't tell us!"

"I—I wasn't certain what he had done. He's gone off before and returned after several days," said Janine, falteringly.

"Nonsense!" Ellen snapped. "Don't tell *me* you didn't know. You quarreled, didn't you!"

Janine could have cursed the telltale redness that suffused her face and neck. Before she could answer, Adam broke in.

"A misunderstanding is hardly sufficient cause to desert one's home and family."

Ellen's head swiveled toward Adam. "That's correct, Adam," she said sharply. "A misunderstanding is not sufficient. Therefore it's plain there must have been a much more serious reason." She turned to Janine, her eyes fixing her with a piercing stare. "You drove him to it!" Her strident voice grew louder. "You, you vixen! You drove him from his own home —his family! Ever since the day you first set foot in this house, you've—"

Janine waited to hear no more. She leaped up from the table and pushed her chair back, knocking it to the floor. Blindly she rushed from the dining room, through the entrance hall, and out the back door. She fled across the frozen grounds to the stable, panting, blinking back tears.

"Noah!" she shouted at the startled stableboy. "Bring out the dapple-gray!"

The old stableboy stared at her through milky-brown eyes and shook his head. "Mister Jonathan, he ride off on the dapple-gray."

"Bring me a horse!" cried Janine frantically. "Any horse!"

"There's only Judas, Miss Janine. You don't want for to ride—"

"I don't care!" yelled Janine. "Saddle him up!" She leaned weakly against the stable door, furious with herself, and at the same time, overwhelmed with feelings of guilt and remorse, all the more painful because what Ellen had said was true. She *had* driven Jonathan from his home—not because she was the wanton Ellen liked to think her, but because of her own runaway tongue!

Noah led out the snorting, prancing black stallion. "He not been ridden for awhile, Miss Janine." His worried milk-clouded eyes flicked momentarily to her slightly rounded stomach and back to her face. "He got the bit in his teeth, an' like to fly!"

She didn't care if he did fly; she wished he could! She had to get away from this house that spawned evil. Had to be by herself to gain some perspective on her plight. She felt that she couldn't have a thought of her own at Heritage Hall.

"Give me a leg up," she said, bunching up the skirt of her blue muslin gown.

Noah shook his dark, woolly head in disapproval and bent to do her will.

Spurring her mount into a canter, she dashed down the narrow rutted track past withered cornstalks in the dead garden, ducking leafless branches that suddenly seemed to reach out for her. She raced across the stubble of the meadow, heedless of the flying hooves striking smooth stones, the holes that pockmarked the field, blindly giving Judas his head. At breakneck speed they plunged down a long, sloping ravine and up the other side, slipping and sliding on sodden leaves, and on into the woodland.

Steam rose from the horse's nostrils and his lathered flanks. Still he raced on. They bolted from the woodland, circling the tobacco fields, then down to the river's edge, cantering along the marshy ground, past swaying cattails and quacking ducks. Clouds hid the sun and a pall lay over the land as the horse charged up the hill on the far side of Heritage Hall.

Janine's forehead was beaded with perspiration and a feeling of exhilaration swept through her. The breathtaking ride had exorcised her worries and anxieties and given her a heady sense of power and strength. With startling clarity it came to her what she would do. She would leave Heritage Hall and return to Philadelphia to wait for Jonathan. Uncle John and Aunt Ellen might be scandalized, but it seemed the sensible thing to do. And she must do it quickly before she lost her nerve.

Both she and Judas were tiring, but she dug in her heels, urging the great stallion on. They cantered through the apple orchard and came up on the east side of the house, bordered by a waist-high stone wall. Her momentum was such that she knew the animal could easily clear it. She gathered the horse in, feeling his powerful muscles bunch under her knees, and urged him forward.

The stallion, whose feisty mood matched her own, flattened his ears. An instant before leaping the wall, he jerked his head and veered abruptly to the left. The momentum of the great beast carried Janine forward and the wall came up to meet her.

Through layers of darkness came a harsh and strident whispering. Aunt Ellen's voice rasped from behind the hall doorway. "I told you so! I told you long ago that she was wild and willful, and now it's come to this—driving our son from his home, risking the life of our grandchild!" Uncle John's pained voice. "Hush now, Ellen." A tap on the door and Spicy Mae's voice. "She in here. . . ." She heard a door open and close. Her head throbbed as though someone had buried a hatchet in her skull. She reached up to touch it and felt the soft folds of linen binding her head. She opened her eyes and her heart skipped a beat. Her blue muslin gown lay over a chair, and crimson blotches marred the skirt. Someone moved and stood before her, blocking her view. A tall man with stooped shoulders and grave, kind eyes was bending over her, his pulse watch in his hand.

"I'm Doctor Craik, come down from Alexandria."

After a moment he put away his pulse watch, and rolling back each of her eyelids with his thumb, he gazed earnestly into her eyes. Spicy Mae stood at the foot of the bed clutching a brass bleeding basin, her bright eyes white-rimmed with fear. The candlelight glinting off the bleeding basin hurt Janine's eyes, and she closed them.

Dr. Craik finished his examination, then opened the bedroom door to admit Ellen and John Burke. As they entered the room Janine's eyes met Ellen's, gleaming with hate. She felt a shock go through her body. Lines of worry and concern creased Uncle John's round face.

Dr. Craik snapped shut his leather case and smiled at Janine. "You're a very fortunate young lady." He turned to Ellen and John. "Other than a head wound, she's suffered no more than a slight concussion."

Janine let out her breath slowly. It was only blood dripping from the gash on her head that had stained her skirt.

Ellen stood stiff-backed, her face paper-white, her white-knuckled hands clenched at her waist. "What of our grandchild?"

Dr. Craig shook his head. "Except for a monstrous headache, she's in no pain, no birth pangs or sign of premature labor. Everything will be fine. In a day or two she'll be up and about."

The next afternoon Janine was feeling much better. She sat up in bed, propped against the pillows, in a white cambric nightshift trimmed with lace. Occasionally sounds drifted up from below, but no one had come to see her except Spicy Mae, who brought her a bowl of broth and gave her a draught of medicine, which Dr. Craik had left for her. Spicy Mae had told her that when Judas had come galloping back to the stable alone, Noah had summoned Mr. Burke. They had found her lying beside the wall, bleeding profusely from a gash on her head.

Her head still hammered despite the draught but she forced her mind to think. She could understand the family's anger at her for driving Jonathan away and for taking off on Judas, jeopardizing her child's life. But surely they felt no worse over the matter than she, herself.

There was a soft tapping on the door, and Adam entered, bearing a tea tray, which he set down beside her bed. "Good to see you looking so chipper," he said amiably. He tossed a few pine-knots on the fire in the hearth and pulled a chair close beside the bed to sit down. He gave her a swift glance of appraisal. "No worse for the wear, eh?"

Janine shook her head. "No, thank the Lord."

He poured her a cup of tea and steadied her hand while she sipped it, savoring the hot brew. She gazed at him over the rim of the cup, smiling ruefully.

"Am I to take it that one of the Burkes is still speaking to me?"

"Life in the Burke family is not always as it seems." He crossed his legs and allowed himself a tongue-in-cheek smile. "Perhaps I enjoy playing the she-devil's advocate."

"I'm afraid even you will lose your case this time," said Janine wryly.

"Have no fear, Janine. I'll let my devoted mother take her pound of flesh, but not one drop of blood!"

Janine set her cup down on the tray. "It's no use, Adam. I've tried twice, and twice I've failed."

His voice held a challenge. "Surely you're not giving up so easily. The game is not yet played out."

"But *I* am played out." He started to speak and she raised a hand to silence him. "I've made up my mind, Adam. I'd made it up yesterday and was in a rush to get back here to carry it out. I'm leaving Heritage Hall. This time for good."

Alarm sprang to his gray eyes. "Surely you jest."

Janine turned her head to face him directly. "I'm as distressed as Aunt Ellen and Uncle John over Jonathan's going. . . ." She threw up her hands in a hopeless gesture. "Well, surely you can see that staying on would be impossible, with the whole family hating me."

He reached over and covered her slender hand with his long, capable one. "*I* don't hate you, Janine. You must know that. You're the best thing that ever happened to Heritage Hall."

She could not be sure whether it was a trick of the firelight reflected in his eyes, or her imagination, but she thought she saw a glint of desire, a gleam of anticipation there that sent a tremor of fear and caution down her spine. She withdrew her hand from under his and pushed her mass of black hair over her shoulder.

Adam leaned forward and touched her cheek, turning her head to face him. "You must be aware of the problem. . . ." He let his voice trail off.

"Jonathan's jealousy," said Janine wrathfully, "inherited from his mother!"

Adam shook his head. "It's quite apparent, my dear. You are more of a woman than Jonathan can manage—as is his own mother." Adam's cool gray eyes seemed to bore into her soul. "I can manage you, and Ellen as well! With Jonathan gone, things will be different, I'll see to that. Everything will be just fine, I promise. If only you'll stay." His voice was urgent, pursuasive. "Please say you'll stay."

His free hand came up, resting on her other cheek. Holding her face firmly between his hands, he looked directly into her eyes.

The intensity of his gaze frightened her and she tossed her head, escaping his light embrace. She picked up her cup and sipped the tea, thinking, pondering Adam's words. She still felt weak and her head ached horribly. She knew she was in no condition to bolt and run—now or the next day.

"All right, Adam. I'll stay—for a little while. We'll see how things work out."

He sat back in his chair, his mouth curved in a small triumphant smile. "You won't be sorry."

She smiled uncertainly and her heart was heavy with foreboding.

The following Sunday Janine felt well enough to come downstairs. Ellen had not been to see her since the day of her accident. And though Uncle John stopped in her room briefly each evening, he was fidgety and ill at ease, and she had the feeling he had come without Ellen's knowledge or consent. There was an awkwardness between them, and Janine felt his silent censure of her wild ride even though he tried to conceal it. Long silences fell between them and he sat on the edge of his chair, tapping the arms, staring into the fire. There seemed to be nothing to say.

The life of the house went on around her as though she were not there. If Ellen had been distant before, now she was unapproachable. She treated Janine as though she were invisible, not speaking to her, looking through her if they happened to pass in the hall. At mealtimes Ellen addressed her remarks directly to Uncle John and Adam. If Adam spoke to Janine or Janine ventured a comment, Aunt Ellen swiftly interrupted, changing the subject. Janine's impulse was to burst into tears and run from the room, but she had been treated so much as a child by Ellen that she would not now, on any account, act like one. She resolved to have it out with Ellen, for she would not be treated like an outcast.

The next morning, when Janine passed the sitting room, she saw Ellen in her drab brown bengaline dress, her hair pulled straight back in a knot, going over her accounts at her writing desk. When she was certain Ellen had finished, she went in and closed the door behind her. She crossed the room and sat in a straight-backed chair facing Ellen.

"Aunt Ellen, may I have a word with you?"

Ellen opened the account book she had just closed, and frowned at a column of figures. "I'm busy."

"I'll wait till you're done," said Janine quietly.

Ellen regarded her with a cold, forbidding stare. "We've nothing to talk about, you and I." She turned back to her ledger.

Janine drew a deep breath. "I agree. You've made that quite clear. I've come to tell you something."

Ellen snapped the book closed, straightened up,

and turned to consider Janine. "If you've come to apologize for your outrageous behavior, you have come too late."

She had resolved to keep her own voice detached, the conversation on a cool unemotional level. Now she was hard put to hold on to her temper.

"I've not come to apologize, Aunt Ellen."

Ellen's thin arched brows rose in surprise and disbelief.

"Come now, Aunt Ellen," said Janine, impatience creeping into her voice, "if you were to be honest with yourself, you'd admit that my behavior is the result of your own actions."

A red flush of anger suffused Ellen's face. "How dare you say such a thing to me?"

Janine plunged on, encouraged that she *had* dared, thankful that at last their feud was out in the open. "Since the day I came, you've done nothing but find fault, point out my failings to everyone behind my back. And if your accusations were not true, you invented them, starting with your letter to Jonathan telling him I had died of pleurisy!"

Ellen's head jerked up and her face took on a darker hue. "I thought you had died," she said indignantly.

"That is not what Papa told you, Aunt Ellen. And when that failed, you incited Jonathan to believe I was a—a wanton with a lurid past; and if that were not enough, you planted seeds of suspicion as to who fathered our child. . . ."

Ellen jumped up from her chair and faced Janine, her hands on her hips, her pinched face contorted with fury.

"And since the day you set foot in Heritage Hall, you have not fit into our family. You are a thorn in the flesh! You came here determined to take over, and so you would have done, had I not been much the stronger. And to this day you have not learned your place in this household!"

Janine folded her hands tightly in her lap to still

their trembling. With a strangling pain in her throat, she forced herself to speak out. Her voice was louder and sharper than she'd intended.

"I have no place in this household, Aunt Ellen. That's what I came to tell you. I cannot remain in a home where everyone hates me. Today I am leaving Heritage Hall."

Ellen gripped the carved back of her chair. Her mouth fell open and closed again. Janine saw an expression of astonishment flash across her face, quickly followed by a shrewd, calculating stare through narrowed lids. Ellen drew herself up to her full height and looked haughtily down at Janine. Her tone was challenging and filled with scorn.

"That's your solution to every situation, isn't it? Running away."

Janine sprang up to face her, meeting Ellen's stare, her eyes sparking as flint striking steel. "It must be obvious that I cannot remain here," she said sharply. "I should think my leaving would make you happy. It's what you've wanted all along!"

Ellen bit off her words, tight and hard. "What *I* want is of no consequence. You have a duty to your husband and child. You will not run away, but wait here for Jonathan, and have your child here, where it is his right to be born!"

Janine's chin rose with a proud tilt. "I'll consider staying on, Aunt Ellen, but only if I'm *accepted*"— she stressed the word—"as a member of the family."

Their eyes locked, each recognizing they had reached a stalemate. "We shall do our best," said Ellen loftily. "I hope it will be good enough."

Janine gave her a long, level gaze. "So do I, Aunt Ellen. So do I."

During the evening meal Janine was relieved to find that a more relaxed atmosphere prevailed. Although she was far from gracious, Ellen unbent sufficiently to include Janine in the conversation. They spoke of the crops that had been destroyed by the torrential rains, the counterfeit Continental paper money circulating throughout the colonies, and the news and gossip in the town. When the talk turned to the war, as it always did, Uncle John's usually cheerful and optimistic countenance turned grave. "If the British didn't know before, they most assuredly know now how weak our defenses are in the South." No one voiced the thought that was uppermost in all their minds. Jonathan was with Lincoln's defeated, decimated army. And, ironically, thought Janine, their concern for Jonathan was the common bond that held them together.

That evening John and Ellen retired early and Adam asked Janine to join him in the sitting room for a game of piquet. After he had won three games hands-down, he gathered up the cards and put them away. With a teasing smile he said, "It's no fun to win if your partner can't remember what is trumps."

Janine smiled apologetically. "I'm sorry, Adam. I can't keep my mind on the cards; I'm distracted."

Adam rose from the table, poured them both a glass of brandy, and sat down across from her, fixing his bright, intelligent gaze on her face. "Why so distracted? I noticed at supper tonight that Mother is coming round, just as I said she would. And in his heart Papa has always been fond of you, but he dare not show it, lest Mama fly at him like a chicken hawk —just as I've not dared because of—"

Quickly she interrupted him, afraid of what he might say. "As you once said, life in the Burke household is not always as it seems. This morning Aunt Ellen and I had a discussion, and my mind is alive with doubts."

Adam leaned back in his chair and stretched out his legs, staring at the toe of his boot. "And why is your mind so uneasy?"

Janine related the gist of their conversation, ending

with her decision to consider remaining at Heritage Hall.

Adam leaned across the table and took her hand in his. Color had come into his cheeks and his expression was smiling and confident. "But, my dear, you should have no doubts whatsoever."

She gazed at him, perplexed. "No?"

With an exultant air, as though he had delivered the winning argument in a case he was pleading, he said, "Don't you see? You have my dear mother over a barrel."

Janine frowned, uncomprehending, and shook her head.

"If Jonathan returns and finds that our mother has driven away his wife and child, he'll never forgive her."

Janine withdrew her hand from his and sipped her brandy. "Adam, you know as well as I that Ellen will convince him I've deserted him, that I no longer love him, that I'm indeed the wanton she's always said." She gave a hopeless sigh.

Adam leaned toward her, and when he spoke, his tone was slightly reproving. "My dear, you've forgotten your loyal barrister. Your devoted brother-in-law will see to it that Jonathan knows the truth of the matter."

A cold and ruthless determination she had never seen before sprang to his eyes and mouth, convincing her that he would do just that. It came to her then that Jonathan had gone through life reacting to others rather than taking the initiative. Yes, he would believe Adam.

"So you see," he went on smoothly, "if Mother wants to keep her son and have her grandchild born at Heritage Hall, she must pull in her horns. Don't think for a moment she isn't aware of that!"

Janine was silent, thinking over what Adam had said. Now she understood the reason for Ellen's sudden about-face, wanting her to stay. Suddenly she

perceived what Ellen must have seen and feared: If
Janine were gone, Jonathan would leave to follow
his wife and child.

"There's no question about it," Adam continued in
an authoritative voice. "You must remain here . . .
for many reasons."

Still she was in torment. All she wanted to do was
escape this house that imprisoned her like a cage. Yet
she felt duty-bound to stay for Jonathan's sake and
for the sake of the child whose right it was to be born
here. She nodded, smiling at the irony of her situation. That she would not allow herself to leave
Heritage Hall was a measure of how much she had
changed in the past three years.

The Christmas season of 1779 was brightened by
the arrival of two letters. The first from Jonathan.
Tears of joy and relief trickled down Janine's cheeks
as she read the large untidy scrawl.

> *My dearest wife,*
>
> *I'm serving under General Isaac Huger in the
> Continental cavalry in General Benjamin Lin-
> coln's army. We are stationed at Monck's Corner,
> some thirty miles distant from Charles Town.
> Though General Lincoln urged the French Ad-
> miral d'Estaing to renew the assault on Savannah,
> he has sailed off for Martinique, and our army is
> wintering in Charles Town.*
>
> *There is death all about us, Janine, which has
> a way of bringing home to us a new sense of
> what is important. I know now that you and our
> child are the most important things in the world
> to me, my sweet. Being gone from you all this
> time has only served to make me prize what I had
> so nearly thrown away. Every night I dream of
> the moment when I can once again hold you in
> my arms, and most of all I want to be with you*

when our child is born. I hope to return to Heritage Hall in time to see the lilacs, the dogwood, and the redbud bloom. As soon as this bloody battle ends, I'll come for you and we'll start our lives over together in Philadelphia.

Your loving husband,
Jonathan

Janine wiped the tears from her eyes with the back of her hand and tucked the letter in her bodice, close to her heart. Time and again she would take it out and read it, until the creases were frayed and torn. Her heart ached with a longing for Jonathan such as she had never known, and during the long, cold winter nights, she would hug his pillow to her breast, seeking comfort, wishing it were Jonathan she held in her arms.

Her second letter was from Papa. He, too, missed her and planned to come to Heritage Hall for her confinement in May. General Washington had settled a command this winter with the main army in the neighborhood of Morristown, New Jersey. A familiar name leaped up at her from the page.

Your friend Peggy Shippen has been leading her husband a merry dance. The Arnolds entertain lavishly—though they have yet to move into Mount Pleasant—seeming to seek out wealthy Tories who have not gone with Clinton. It's an open secret that Arnold has fallen deeply in debt trying to satisfy his wife's extravagant tastes. Congress has called him to account for his expenditures, but to no avail.

Continental soldiers are still accommodated in some of the hospital's beds, conditions are tolerable. The managers have at last raised money to purchase new beds and bedding. The hospital is clean and in good order. We've twenty-eight resi-

dent patients, sixteen of whom are insane and from families of some means who can afford to pay for their safekeeping, which means that we have been under the sad necessity of refusing many proper objects of our charity, the industrious poor. However, our number of out-patients has increased greatly, forty-eight to fifty each month.

He closed with news of the weather—the severest winter in years—and wished her continued good health.

Chapter 34

The long gray winter days wore on in a tense truce. Ellen brought out lengths of muslin she'd put aside for making bed linens and gave them grudgingly to Janine to make baby clothes. Janine refused to allow Ellen's dour mood to affect her. She was happy and hummed to herself as she sewed the small garments, laying them away in Jonathan's chest of drawers.

Early in February Janine asked Ellen's permission to turn the small sewing room into a nursery. Though she could see that Ellen was torn between providing a room for her grandchild and giving in to Janine, she reluctantly gave her consent. Janine had the small room painted a pale sunlight yellow and fashioned white fringed muslin curtains for the windows. A crib with caned sides, a walnut rocking chair, and a small chest of drawers were brought down from the attic and placed in the room, along with Jonathan's rocking horse, which stood in one corner. When the room was finished, she called Ellen in to see it.

Ellen stood in the doorway, her face expressionless as her eyes traveled over the room. Finally she said, "It will do nicely." And then her gaze fell on Jonathan's painted rocking horse standing in the corner. In spite of herself, Ellen's eyes softened, her lips curved in a smile, and her sallow face took on a rosy flush. "Jonathan will be well pleased."

After Ellen left the room, Janine permitted herself a congratulatory grin. She thought she saw a crack in Ellen's granite soul. She stood before the mirror, smoothing her gown over her swollen abdomen. If she had been the cause of Ellen's ill nature in the past, soon she would be the cause of her change for the better, thought Janine happily. May could not come too soon!

March brought with it bitter cold winds that buffeted the house and whistled around the corners, rattling the window frames, as it crept down the chimneys, and swept through the mansion. On the second Thursday a fine snow began sifting down from gray skies, blanketing the white and yellow and lavender crocuses pushing up through the dark earth. All day long Janine felt restive, turning from one task to another, dusting her room and the nursery, mending a skirt that had split at the seam. Finally she sat down at the library table to write a letter to Papa. Leaning over the table made her back ache, and she shortened the letter somewhat. She sank down into the wing chair by the fireplace and opened a book she'd been reading. She shifted uncomfortably in the big, soft chair, changing her position frequently, but the dull ache in the small of her back persisted.

After reading the same page over several times without making sense of it, she went upstairs to her room and stretched out on the four-poster bed. She supposed her muscles were strained, carrying their unaccustomed burden. She must have dozed off, for she awoke to find Spicy Mae leaning over her, holding a candle, shaking her gently by the shoulder. The windowpanes were black, their sills furred with snow. The fire had burned low in the grate and she shook with a sudden chill.

"Miss Janine, you come down for supper now?"

She gazed dumbly at Spicy Mae without answering. Despite her rest, she felt heavy and terribly weary; her back still ached. Two great bands squeezed her like a girth cinching her belly. Janine gasped and her eyes widened in pain.

Spicy Mae's round black eyes rolled in alarm. "Miss Janine, you all right?"

Her belly relaxed, and Janine let out her breath slowly. "I'm fine." The thought of sitting erect in the high, straight-backed Chippendale chairs made her groan inwardly. "But I don't feel like coming down to supper."

Spicy Mae's eyes narrowed. "I bring you supper on a tray." Before she left, she took a blue wool blanket from the chest and tucked it around Janine, then turned to the wood box and threw several pine-knots on the fire in the hearth.

When Spicy Mae returned with the tray, Janine lay as she had left her, her eyes closed. Spicy Mae set the tray down and placed her sturdy dark hand on Janine's belly. Janine opened her eyes and just then the bands encircling her back tightened again. She stiffened, drawing in her breath sharply.

Spicy Mae's dark brow furrowed and she shook her head, forcing a smile. "It's your time, Miss Janine."

Janine's jaw stiffened. A fine mist of perspiration formed on her brow and her upper lip. "Not till May. We have to wait for Jonathan. This will soon pass."

Spicy Mae said nothing, but helped Janine sit up, tucking the pillows behind her, pulling the night-stand closer so she could reach the tray. She handed Janine a fork. "You eat your supper, Miss Janine. I be back soon."

When the door closed behind her, Janine set the fork down on the tray and picked up a glass of wine, sipped it, and put it back. She leaned against the pillows, willing the ache in her back to go away.

After a while she heard the door open and footsteps crossing the room, stopping at her bedside. She opened her eyes. Ellen stood gazing down at her, an inscrut-

able expression on her face. Janine felt herself shrinking inside. In the circle of light from the candle
Ellen held in her hand, her face looked like a death's-
head.

"Spicy Mae says you're having pains."

"It's nothing. They'll go away."

Ellen nodded. "False labor, no doubt, brought on
by the cold. Do you think you've taken a chill?"

Janine nodded and tried to suppress a shudder that
coursed through her body as the cinch tightened
again.

Ellen's eyes bored into her. "If you're not better
by morning, we'll have Carrie take a look at you."

"Thank you," said Janine through stiff lips. "I'm
sure that won't be necessary."

She closed her eyes, shutting out Ellen's death's-
head image. Carrie had birthed all the babies born to
the slaves on the plantation and no doubt she knew
what had to be done. Janine had nothing to worry
about.

She heard Ellen's footsteps march across the room,
the door close behind her. She raised up on her elbow
and took another sip of wine, then lay back and
dozed again. The sharp, tangy wine made her feel
warm and relaxed until the pain came again. She
sipped and dozed off and on until the sounds of the
house grew quiet and the only sound she heard was
the snow, tiny icy flakes tapping against the window-
pane, and the pine sap hissing in the grate.

She didn't hear the door open or the sound of
footsteps padding across the floor, but the touch of a
soft, cold palm on her forehead roused her. The
blanket was pulled back, her bodice and skirt loosened,
drawn down, her shift pulled up, and firm hands
pressed against her belly. Numbed with wine, Janine
opened her eyes and saw Carrie, her head and shoulders muffled in a scarf glittering with snow, and
worried eyes in her round brown face peering into

her own. Over Carrie's shoulder Spicy Mae gazed at her, her face tense with anxiety.

"I bring Carrie, Miss Janine. She make you feel better."

"Aunt Ellen will be furious, Spicy Mae. You'd best be gone before—" She arched her back against the pain that clutched at her insides.

"Ever'body's sleeping. Don't pay no never mind."

"I don't need anything," said Janine weakly. "Go away." Her voice lacked conviction, and even as she spoke the words, she wished Carrie would do something, anything, to relieve the ache in her back. "It's cold," she said, her teeth chattering. The chill in the room made gooseflesh rise on her pale skin. Spicy Mae pulled the draperies and heaped more wood on the fire.

Ignoring Janine's protests, Carrie finished her examination, poking, pressing with firm, sure hands, and drew back shaking her head, her lips sucked in between her teeth.

"Um-hum!" she said emphatically, drawing the blanket up over Janine. She threw off the scarf covering her head and shoulders and draped it over a chair. Turning to Spicy Mae, she said, "This chile ain't waiting for nobody. We's got work to do!"

"No!" cried Janine, raising up on her elbows, glaring at them. "Go away. It's not time."

Carrie pulled a chair up beside the bed and sat down heavily. "I can wait. I gots all the time in the world."

In the first light of dawn there came a sharp rapping on the door, and Spicy Mae opened it a crack.

"Oh, Master Adam, you give me a fright!"

"Spicy Mae!" exclaimed Adam in a harsh whisper. "I heard all sorts of doors banging and thumping on the stairs. What in the name of God is going on here?"

"Miss Janine. It's her time. I got to help Carrie," she said breathlessly.

Adam let out an incredulous gasp. "You mean the child's coming? Now?"

Spicy Mae shook her head. "It's time, but he don't want to come. Poor Miss Janine!"

Thunderstruck, he stood for several seconds without speaking. Then he said, "What can I do? There must be something!"

"You can't come in here, Master Adam. Miss Janine, she busy. Carrie and me, we doing all we can. Miss Janine is plumb wore out. This baby be stubborn. Ain't nothing you can do!" The door closed in his face.

He hurried down the hall and rapped smartly on John and Ellen's door. He heard his father's voice fogged with sleep. "Who's there?"

Adam burst into the room. "Janine!" he said excitedly. "The child's coming."

Ellen sat up in bed, frowning, drawing the bedclothes around her neck. "What do you mean? It will come when it's ready and not before."

"It's ready!" Adam's cheeks were flushed and his eyes flashed with impatience. "Carrie says it's coming and Spicy Mae is down there helping."

Ellen shrugged and sighed with irritation. "I'll go down and see what's happening, but sometimes this takes hours, Adam. There's nothing we can do."

"Don't you understand? There's some problem. Spicy Mae says all is not right. . . ."

Ellen's mouth turned down in exasperation. She got up and clutched her nightrobe about her. "Men don't understand these things." She swept out the door and padded down the hall.

Adam strode to the window and gazed out over the gray dawn, marbled with pink. He plunged his hands deep in his pockets, barely controlling his impatience, waiting for his mother to return.

In a few minutes she was back. "Carrie and Spicy Mae are doing all that can be done." She sighed heavily and climbed back into bed.

"Aren't you concerned for the safety of your own grandchild?" he asked angrily. "Jonathan's child?"

Ellen's ebony eyes flew open. "Of course I'm concerned. Didn't I just go down there? If there were anything I could do, I would!"

Adam turned away, pacing the floor, his hands clasped behind his back. "I think Doctor Craik must know more about this than two slaves."

"I doubt that!" Ellen snapped. "Carrie has delivered hundreds of babies. She's an excellent midwife."

"I think we should send for Doctor Craik."

Ellen yawned widely. "Good night, Adam."

Adam stalked from the room, slamming the door after him. He went to his room, flung on his clothes, and dashed outside through the feathering snow into the barn. Shortly after he emerged astride Judas. Puffs of steam rose from the black stallion's nostrils as Adam urged him into a canter, flying down the long white lane between the oaks.

The sun crept slowly up the sky, slanting through the oaks and pines, shedding golden light on the crusted snow, not yet reaching the purple shadows in the hollows. Somewhere a catbird called. A cardinal flashed red against the white landscape.

Adam stared out the window in the sitting room, his thumbs hooked in his pockets, his back stiff and tense with anxiety. His father sat clutching his pipe, tapping it, sucking at the stem to set it drawing. Ellen sat in the armchair by the fireside, sipping tea, calm and composed.

"How can you sit there as though nothing were happening," asked Adam irritably, "knowing what must be going on upstairs?"

It seemed they'd been waiting for hours, until at last they heard Dr. Craik's footsteps thumping down the stairs to the sitting room. Adam spun to face him. He could read nothing in the drawn expression on Dr. Craik's face. The man sank down on the settee and leaned forward, elbows on his knees, fingers laced together.

"We delivered Janine of a son, half an hour ago." He paused and stared down at his hands. "Stillborn."

For a second the only sound in the room was the loud ticking of the clock on the mantel.

"God's death!" exclaimed Adam. "It can't be!"

The color drained from Ellen's face and the teacup rattled in the saucer as she set it down on the table. John appeared stricken and set down his pipe, bowing his head as if to hide the tears that sprang to his eyes.

"And Janine?" Adam asked, drawing in his breath sharply.

"Sleeping. She doesn't know . . . I felt it best to wait until she's rested . . . a little stronger. I've never known a young woman to go through so much with equal fortitude and patience."

"Jonathan's son," Ellen murmured dazedly. "She as good as killed him with her own hand. She brought this on herself, she has no one to blame but herself, a hellion, riding off like that. . . ."

Dr. Craik raised his head to look at Ellen. "It was not her fall from Judas that caused this. The child was fully developed." A pained expression crossed his face. "The cord was wrapped around the infant's neck. We turned him, right enough, but—" Sighing, he placed his hands on his knees and straightened up. "The child was dead before—"

He got up and went over to Ellen and put a hand on her shoulder. She sat stony-faced with glazed eyes. "Don't despair, Ellen. There will be others."

Ellen made no reply, but continued to stare into

space. John pulled a handkerchief from his pocket and dabbed at his eyes.

"It's Janine we must think of now," said Dr. Craik.

Adam said, in his crisp, quick way, "We'll make it up to her, somehow."

Chapter 35

At first Janine was inconsolable. It seemed to her that her own life had ended with that of her son. The next time Dr. Craik came, he explained to her again that these things happen, that it was not her wild flight that caused the death of the infant. Still the doubt remained, and Ellen did nothing to alleviate it. Accusing Janine with her eyes, she maintained a tight-lipped silence as cold and unforgiving as before, all the more devastating in her self-righteous justification.

The one advantage Janine had gained was that Ellen no longer had the power to hurt her. She no longer cared what Ellen thought or said or did.

When not under Ellen's watchful gaze, Uncle John would pat her on the shoulder in an effort to comfort her, but the bleak expression in his eyes told her the pain their loss had caused him.

As spring came on, Janine regained her strength, but she passed through the days like a sleepwalker. And during the long, lonely nights she twisted and turned, unable to sleep, weighed down with grief and despair. Adam alone seemed to understand her feelings of sorrow, guilt, and remorse. He tried in every way he knew to reason with her, but all his lawyer's skill and logic could not penetrate the wall she'd built around herself.

"I understand what you're telling me, Adam," said Janine, distraught. "I understand that it was not the fall; that there will be other children; that one cannot stop living, but reason is of little comfort—it does not touch the region of the heart." She placed her hand on his arm to soften her words. "And I'm indeed grateful for your company and appreciate your efforts to help."

Adam stopped trying to reason with her. He coaxed her to accompany him on leisurely walks through the garden, and often she felt his eyes upon her as she paused to admire the flowers. He brought her books to read from Alexandria, and during the long, soft twilight evenings they took up playing their games of piquet. Gradually her zest for life began to return.

There was no word from Jonathan and she was afraid he may never have received her letter, for the siege of Charleston had begun the end of March and the Americans were still resisting Sir Henry Clinton and Lord Cornwallis. Papa wrote frequently, telling her bits of news from Philadelphia he thought would interest her. At first he, too, was distraught at the loss of his grandchild, but he tried to mask his sorrow. A long sigh escaped her and she longed for the day, surely not too far off now, when Jonathan would return and they could take up their lives together.

One warm, lilac-scented Sunday near the end of April Janine heard the dogs barking furiously outside the house. She rushed to the window and, peering out, saw a blond, bearded stranger slumped in the saddle astride a chestnut horse, the dogs nipping and yapping at his heels, riding up the lane to the house. A tattered sleeve flapped at his side where his right arm should have been. Her heart leaped to her throat and she ran downstairs and out the door to greet him. As she watched him draw near, her joy quickly faded. The man was not Jonathan.

He reined in his horse and stared down at her for a moment from deep-socketed, empty eyes.

"Lieutenant Ross, Continental Cavalry," said the

man swinging down from the saddle. "I've word for Mistress Burke of Heritage Hall."

"She's inside, sir."

Janine showed him into the parlor and summoned Aunt Ellen and Uncle John. Then, suddenly aware that she, too, was Mistress Burke, eased down on the slipper chair. Her heart began to race. He must bring word from Jonathan, else why would he have come?

As soon as he began to speak, Janine was filled with foreboding. Now she was afraid, more afraid than she had ever been in her life. There was something in his eyes, the set of his mouth, the drawn expression on his face. She braced herself, listening to his slow, deep drawl, trying to make sense of what he was saying.

He told them that before he was wounded he had served with Jonathan at Monck's Corner. There they were holding open a line of communication with Charleston, sending supplies of men, arms, ammunition to the garrison—holding the way open for General Lincoln and his men as an escape route in the event their defenses were destroyed. The cavalry had been posted in front of the Cooper River."

Oh, would he never get on with it? thought Janine in a frenzy of impatience.

"Jonathan was with the militia in a meetinghouse that commanded Biggin Bridge, and some of the militia were on the opposite bank. About two weeks past, April fourteenth it was, at three o'clock in the morning the British, Lieutenant Colonel Tarleton, along with Ferguson's marksmen, took us in a surprise attack."

Lieutenant Ross cleared his throat and went on. "There was fierce skirmishing, and Major Vernier and some other officers and men who attempted to defend themselves were killed or wounded. General Huger, along with many other officers and I, fled on foot to the swamps close to our encampment and escaped through the darkness."

Janine let out a long breath of relief. Jonathan had escaped!

As though reading her thoughts, Lieutenant Ross said, "Jonathan was not among those who escaped into the swamp."

Janine stiffened against the chill that ran down her spine. The weary soldier paused, smoothing his hat on his knee.

"The British took four hundred horses belonging to officers and dragoons, with their arms and appointments; about one hundred officers, dragoons, and hussars, together with fifty wagons loaded with arms, clothing, and ammunition."

She wanted to shout at him to stop beating about the bush and get to the point. Why didn't he simply say that Jonathan had been taken prisoner?

The lieutenant's voice grew husky. He cleared his throat again and swallowed as though it pained him to relate the events of that day.

"Tarleton ordered his men to force the bridge and the meetinghouse with the infantry of the British legion. He charged our militia, took possession of the pass, and dispersed everything that opposed him. Only a handful of us survived. I promised Jonathan I'd come to see you, should he not survive the attack—" His voice broke, and the significance of his words fell upon them like a cannon shot.

With an anguished scream Ellen jumped up and fled from the room. Uncle John, his face ashen, eyes blurred with tears, stumbled from the room after her. Numb with shock, Janine could only stare at Lieutenant Ross.

"Your husband fought well and died honorably. He wanted you to know."

"Yes," she whispered. She caught her lip between her teeth and sat rigid, staring expectantly at him as though waiting for him to tell her this was not really true, that there had been a terrible mistake in identity, that Jonathan's wound had not been fatal after all. . . .

As though sensing her need, the man said quietly, "Jonathan thought it would be of some help to you and his family if someone were to tell you the circumstances. . . ."

Janine nodded, her head bent, her fingers twisting her wedding ring around and around. She could not speak over the strangled feeling in her throat. She understood what Jonathan had done for them, sending Lieutenant Ross, establishing the certainty, the reality of his death, so that they would not go on hoping, expecting him to return someday. So that they could get on with their grief, she thought bitterly. Tears glistened in her eyes and rolled down her cheeks.

Life at Heritage Hall went on as though they were on a treadmill regulated by the clock. They rose in the morning because they had always done so; they ate their meals because it was time to eat; and went to bed at night because it was their habit. It seemed as though the heart and soul had gone from the house, leaving only a shell in which they moved like ghosts. As though fearful of the pain it would cause, by tacit agreement Jonathan's name was never mentioned. Ellen withdrew from the world around her, wrapping herself in a cocoon of inexpressible grief. Uncle John threw himself into the running of the plantation and was seldom home. Janine moved through the days like a disembodied spirit, out of time, out of place. Adam was the lone survivor. The qualities in him which she had once thought cold and ruthless, she now looked upon as a backbone of steel, which would not be bowed down. She did not doubt his devotion to Jonathan, but he was cool and logical, concerned with the living, with the future, and he was able to put the past behind him in a way that she could not.

It was Adam who brought the news that on May 12 General Lincoln was forced into an unconditional surrender that turned his five thousand odd Continentals and militia into prisoners of war. Huge quantities of supplies were lost, and nearly all the patriot leaders of South Carolina, political and military, were seized, leaving the entire Charleston Revolutionary movement headless. Only Governor John Rutledge and one or two others had managed to slip out of the city, and British rule now seemed to be tightly restored in the two southernmost American states. The American cause had suffered the severest disaster of the entire conflict.

One sultry Sunday afternoon in early August Janine wandered into the library and found Adam working, his papers spread out on the walnut table.

"Excuse me, Adam. I didn't realize you were working. I'll not disturb you." She turned to leave.

"Hold on, Janine." He smiled and shuffled his papers together. "You'll not disturb me. Come in." He motioned toward the wing chair. "Sit down." He rose from the table, pulled up a leather armchair, and sat facing her.

"Care for a game of piquet?"

Janine sighed and shook her head, fanning herself against the heat. Though the windows were wide open, the air was still and heavy and the sound of churring cicadas announced the continuation of the oppressive heat. Absently she watched two blue jays screeching at a passing cat.

They chatted aimlessly about trivial matters, and gradually Janine became aware that there was something on Adam's mind. He seemed to be circling whatever it was, as though waiting for an opening.

Finally he said, "I think it's time we spoke of Jonathan."

The mention of Jonathan's name went through her

like a knife blade. Tears stung her eyelids. "There's nothing to say of Jonathan."

"It's foolish and unhealthy for us to pretend he never existed. It would lessen the strain if we spoke of him—shared our memories of our lives together— it would ease the pain. To blot him from our lives forever is wrong, Janine."

She gazed at him accusingly. "You are a fine one to talk—you who so easily put the past behind you, as I can never do. . . ."

Adam leaned forward, gazing at her intently. "In a sense I put the past behind me, but I don't erase it from my mind, my life. All our past is woven into the fabric of our lives—you will never forget Jonathan, nor will I. But you cannot live in the past. You, and my mother and father are shutting out the present . . . the future . . . spending all your days—"

"There is no future without Jonathan," said Janine dully.

"Not if you don't let go of the past. You're hanging on to it like a life raft!"

She hated Adam then, hated his cool, rational mind, his calm practical assessment of the situation, but in her heart she knew he was right. She'd been clinging to Heritage Hall, afraid to let go of her last tie to someone she had loved, the last vestige of Jonathan. Tears of anger and frustration glistened in her eyes.

"What you are really saying is that I've no future here. Well, you're quite right!" And though she had not been thinking of it, she thought of it now. Until now she had lacked the courage to do what she knew she must do, but his words stiffened her resolve. "I sought you out today to tell you good-bye. I'm leaving Heritage Hall."

Adam's head snapped back, his pale eyes widened in astonishment. His voice was sharp with shock. "Janine! Never for one instant did I mean to say you've no future here. On the contrary, I was trying to point out that one must go on living, that one must let go of the past to make room for the future, and your future is here. You are a Burke. This is your home now. You mustn't, you cannot leave!"

Startled at the vehemence of his denial, the ardor of his insistence that she stay, words stuck in her throat. She met his gaze, shaking her head slowly, implacably.

A distant boom of thunder, like cannon fire, shattered the silence. Adam rose to his feet and stood before her, his hands folded behind his back.

He looked as though he were pleading a case in court, thought Janine, stifling a mad impulse to laugh.

"Janine, you must stay. We need you here." He paused as though choosing his words carefully, looking down on her bowed head, her hands in her lap, her fingers twisting her wedding ring. "This is not the time to speak of it, but you force the issue, force me to a declaration I'd planned to make some time in the future."

Janine raised her head to look at him. His face was flushed, his eyes burned with an intensity she'd seldom seen.

"I've come to admire you greatly, Janine. You have possibilities—I can help you, mold you into a magnificent mistress of Heritage Hall. . . ." At Janine's gasp he added hastily, "As my wife. You know my ambitions. I'd like to share my future with you. You could be a great asset. . . ."

Janine opened her mouth to speak. Adam raised his hand as if to silence her.

"No, don't speak. I know what you're going to say. Well, Mother, God bless her, won't live forever, and you will find that I'll quickly put an end to her persecutions, her petty accusations. . . ."

A clap of thunder drowned out his words. The sky darkened as clouds gathered overhead. He went on, but she did not hear what he was saying. She gripped the arms of the chair, afraid she was going to dissolve into hysteria. Adam's declaration was so incredible, she could hardly believe her own ears.

That he would speak so, with Jonathan barely cold in his grave; his lofty, condescending admission that she had "possibilities"; his readiness, yes, his eagerness to use her as he would some chattel he had decided to acquire; not to mention the glaring omission of one word of love, devotion or affection! He was so outrageous, so secure in his plan for his and for her future. Now with his usual ability to turn a setback to good account, he was so confident that he was bestowing upon her the favor of a lifetime. He was a fool—worse than a fool! She clung to the arms of the chair not knowing whether she would laugh or cry.

Arrows of lightning pierced the heavy black sky and the clouds broke open, spilling a torrent of rain. Adam strode to the window on the far side of the fireplace and slammed down the sash. Janine hurried to close the other window, thinking frantically what she would say to Adam. There was, after all, only one answer, no matter how she chose to say it.

He met her halfway across the room, before the fireplace. His arms went around her waist in a hard, demanding grasp, pulling her to him. She put her hands on his shoulders, pushing him away, leaning back, looking up into his face.

"No, Adam," she said emphatically. "I'm sorry."

His arms gripped her more tightly, squeezing the breath from her body, and his eyes burned with a determined light.

"You feel that way now, but after some time has passed, you'll feel differently."   ,

"No, Adam, I—"

Her protest was cut off by his lips coming down on hers, bruising her mouth. His fingers entwined in her hair, pulling her head back, hurting her scalp. She clenched her jaw and tossed her head free. A crack of lightning bathed the room in a brilliant white light, and at the same instant the door was thrown open. Over Adam's shoulder Janine saw Ellen framed in the doorway, her unbound hair streaming over her shoulders, her white nightrobe flapping around her body. Ellen let out a shriek, whirling upon them like an avenging fury. Her eyes were bright with a fanatical gleam the like of which Janine had never seen.

Ellen thrust out her arm like a bayonet, pointing a long bony finger at Janine, screeching, "Get away from my son, you harlot! Isn't it enough that you've taken Jonathan from us? It's God's judgment upon you!" she cried. "Jonathan's death! God is wreaking his vengeance upon you. You are the cause of Jonathan's death. *You!*" She darted across the room to the fireside and wrenched the long iron poker from its hook.

"Mother!" shouted Adam, lunging toward her. "Control yourself!"

Janine picked up her skirts and ran from the library, through the entrance hall, up the stairs and into her old room. She slammed the door and shoved a wooden chair under the knob. Shaking all over, she pulled her leather traveling case from the bottom of the wardrobe and stuffed her few possessions inside it. She snatched up her cloak, shoved the chair aside, and fled down the stairs. As she sped across the entrance hall she heard Ellen's high-pitched voice raised in malediction, and above it Adam's sharp, commanding tones.

She flew out the door in the slanting rain, across the lawns, into the stable. Noah loomed up before her in the doorway, his clouded eyes wide, staring at her hair straggling down her back, water running down her face, her cloak dripping.

"Judas," she gasped. "Saddle Judas for me quickly."

He shook his head. "Miss Janine, you can't go—"

"Never mind," she snapped. "I'll do without!" She brushed past Noah, yanked the reins from a peg on the wall overhead and bolted into Judas's stall. Mo-

ments later she emerged astride the stallion. Kicking
him into a fast trot, she urged him out into the
driving storm. Tears of anger and hurt mingled with
the rain coursing down her cheeks as Judas galloped
down the lane away from Heritage Hall.

She reined up before City Tavern shortly after
dark, exhausted, drenched, and spattered with mud.
She entered the tap room as if she were dressed in
all her finery and demanded a ticket on the stage to
Philadelphia.

The tavern keeper, who had a face like raw meat
and a bulbous nose, stared at her curiously. "Stage
don't leave till tomorrow morning at five. Sorry,
miss."

"Then I must have a room for the night."

His eyes narrowed and he scratched his head.
"Traveling alone, are you?"

"Yes," said Janine imperiously. "and I've no wish
to share my room."

His eyes took in her fine features, the rich fabric
of her cloak. " 'Tisn't proper for a woman to be traveling alone."

Janine tried to keep her teeth from chattering. "I
must take the stage to Philadelphia. There's been a
death in the family." She fished a coin from her purse
and tossed it on the counter.

The innkeeper pocketed the coin and gave her a
room to herself.

The next morning in the gray light of dawn before
Janine boarded the stage, she left a note with the innkeeper instructing him that Judas was to be returned
to Heritage Hall. That done, she went outside and
settled herself in the carriage. It had begun to rain
again and the driver was letting down the curtains
and buttoning them on the outside. Over the shoulder
of the old gentleman seated on the bench ahead of
her, she gazed at the paper he was reading. It was
dated August 16, 1780, and bore the headline: CORN-

WALLIS CRUSHES AMERICANS AT CAMDEN, SOUTH CARO-
LINA—GATES DEFEATED!

Surely the South was lost, she thought in despair.
Yet a curious sense of lightness, of freedom pervaded
her now that she had finally hardened her heart
against all that bound her to the old days and Heritage
Hall. A bell rang, announcing the departure of the
stage. The driver shouted to the horses and they moved
off down the street, swaying and jolting, axles squeak-
ing. Janine sat stiff-backed and dry-eyed on the hard,
uncomfortable seat in the rear of the carriage. With
a little shock of surprise she remembered that today
was her twenty-first birthday.

Chapter 36

It was late on a steamy August afternoon when the stage rumbled into the town. With a sinking heart Janine saw that the steeple atop the State House was dangerously aslant, that the wood had rotted and the bell had been taken down. In the State House yard stood a new octagonal watch house from which the watchmen could fan out to alert the neighborhood in case of danger.

She recalled that Papa had written that government officials continued to harass people they considered dangerous. Elizabeth Shoemaker, for one, was continually giving refuge to her nieces Anna and Peggy, and when the two girls were packing to leave, the militia had broken into the house, searching in closets, drawers and trunks for arms.

Now she saw that many of the homes that had belonged to Loyalists who had fled with the British were still deserted and many of the shops were closed. The gutters ran with filth, and starving cats and dogs scrabbled in the rubbish that was everywhere piled waist high. A feeling of desolation swept over her and it came to her that the war, which had seemed so remote in the South, had left such scars upon Philadelphia that she feared the town would never be the same again.

After the first excitement of her homecoming was over, she saw with a slight sense of shock that Papa, too, had suffered the ravages of time and the occupation by the British. His face had taken on a gray pallor, and new creases furrowed his brow. His shoulders were more stooped than they had been when she had ridden off with Jonathan almost two years ago. Though he seemed cheered at having her home again, Janine noticed that he could not conceal his sadness and distress caused by the events that led to her return. If he had written to Aunt Ellen and Uncle John, or they to him, he made no mention of it.

"Have you heard that General Washington has given Peggy Shippen's husband command of the American installation at West Point?" Papa asked.

Janine shook her head. "How Peggy must love holding sway with her General at an army post!"

Papa then suggested that she call upon her other friends, but she found she had no wish to take up old ties.

"It seems as though they've all turned Tory anyway," said Janine with a hopeless sigh.

"Surely not Peggy Arnold," he protested. "After all, she's married to an American general."

"Peggy, most of all," said Janine. "She was a close friend of Major André."

Dr. Mercer nodded. "I'd forgotten." He paused, as though searching for the right words. "Doctor Ransom has inquired after you. He hoped he might call, after a decent interval of mourning has passed, of course."

"I would have thought Doctor Ransom would have long since married, Papa."

Dr. Mercer bent his bright gaze upon her over the rims of his spectacles. "It's not for want of a willing female," he said archly. "He's been seen everywhere with one after another beautiful lady on his arm. But toss the noose around his neck they have not."

Janine sighed wearily. "I've no desire to see him, Papa."

"Surely you can do him the courtesy of allowing him to offer his condolences."

Janine smiled and shrugged. "Maybe later, Papa. . . ."

On a sunny afternoon late in September Janine was returning home from a visit to the bookseller's when halfway down the block she saw Peggy Arnold alight from a carriage before her father's house, carrying her infant son in her arms. With a surge of joy Janine waved wildly and called out, hastening her steps. But before she reached the house, Peggy stepped swiftly inside and closed the door firmly after her.

Baffled, Janine gazed up at the imposing brick mansion. The curtains were drawn and there was no sign of life. Perhaps Peggy hadn't recognized her after all this time, thought Janine. But she had certainly recognized Peggy. Perhaps Peggy had heard of her death at the hands of the British, but surely she'd also heard of her subsequent rescue and marriage to Jonathan. That was it, thought Janine, relieved. Peggy knew she'd gone to Virginia to live and had no thought of seeing her here. She would give Peggy time to settle in, and then call upon her.

But that evening Papa told her news that stunned her so, that she could only stare at him, and yet, as she listened to the incredible tale she knew it was not beyond belief.

In a voice distraught with shock and concern, Papa, pacing the parlor, spilled out the incredible tale that spread through the town like fire.

"On September twenty-third, four days past, a man named John Anderson was captured near Tarrytown in the Westchester no-man's land. The militiamen who took him had found concealed in the feet of his stocking detailed plans of fortifications of West Point, data on ordnance, and digests of confidential orders issued by Washington, some apparently in General Arnold's hand. Anderson was revealed to be none other than Major John André, Adjutant General to Sir Henry Clinton."

Janine's hand flew to her throat. "It can't be!"

"At the time," Papa continued, "General Washington had been conferring with Rochambeau at Hartford. On his way back, Washington, accompanied by General Lafayette and his aide Alexander Hamilton, decided to inspect fortifications at West Point.

"On that same morning Arnold was having breakfast at his headquarters when word was brought of André's capture. He told Peggy he must fly to save his life and had no time to explain. He dashed outside, sprang onto his horse, and plunged off, down the slope to the Hudson where he boarded his official barge. He ordered the crew to row him downstream to the H.M.S. *Vulture*, riding at anchor, waiting for the return of the passenger it had brought north— Major John André. Arnold sailed for New York. When General Washington arrived at West Point, he found Peggy hysterical, screaming and weeping in her room."

"That I can well believe," said Janine with a catch in her throat. "It's always been Peggy's way, whenever crossed. . . ."

"Washington was still there waiting for Arnold to return when the damning papers, captured from André, or Anderson as he'd called himself, caught up with him. Washington sent an armed vessel after Arnold, but he escaped, and they say he arrived in New York yesterday."

"Oh, Papa!" cried Janine. "That's why Peggy has come home, then! I saw her today, but she didn't see me, or pretended not to see me."

Dr. Mercer shook his head sadly. "I can well understand why she'd no wish to face you or anyone else. Her husband had disclosed Washington's plan for an attack on New York and he had offered to hand over the American fort at West Point for the sum of six thousand three hundred and fifteen pounds sterling. It seems that André had been corresponding with

Arnold for months. Some say it was Peggy who suggested André as an intermediary."

"Peggy!" cried Janine astonished. "I cannot believe it! Nor that General Arnold would—"

Dr. Mercer ceased his agitated pacing to regard Janine with a solemn stare. "Neither can his comrades in arms, but it's true, right enough. It's said that General Green called his act 'Treason of the blackest dye.' They are all asking, 'Whom can we trust now?' and each peeping at his next neighbor to see if any treason was hanging about him. There are those who attribute Arnold's treason to the pernicious influence of his wife—the Tory Hellcat they call her! Well, we can take comfort from the thought that happily the scheme to wreck the American army was discovered in time to prevent the final misfortune."

Sick at heart and miserable, knowing the unbelievable had to be true, Janine shook her head helplessly. "But why, Papa? Why would Arnold do such a thing, after capturing Ticonderoga . . . the hero of the march to Quebec . . . Saratoga . . ."

Dr. Mercer shrugged and lifted his brows. "His excuse is that he disapproved of the French Alliance, but no one believes it. Some say he'd grown resentful of imagined slights. He had been passed over in promotion—others were made generals ahead of him. And, of course, when he was military commander of the town, he'd been court-martialed and censured for aiding the escape of Tory sympathizers and accused of using army wagons and supplies for private purposes. The man was convinced of his own superiority and he probably *was* influenced by Peggy. As you have pointed out, it's well-known she was a close friend of André's long before Arnold appeared on the scene."

"And what of André?" asked Janine, distressed. "What's to become of him?"

Dr. Mercer shrugged. "All manner of people are imploring General Washington to treat him as a prisoner of war. Even Hamilton is urging the exchange of André for Arnold."

With a stab of sadness, Janine recalled the days of the dashing André in the town. Handsome, brilliant, charming, and so talented. She sighed, thinking of poems and dramas he'd penned, plays he'd staged, paintings he'd dashed off for the ladies. "Even his enemies admired him, Papa."

Dr. Mercer nodded. "Some compassionate minds are ready to wish for his pardon. Washington may be persuaded to spare his life."

"Oh, I hope so, Papa," said Janine fervently. "I do hope so!"

Several days later the news came, shocking all who heard it. No matter what General Washington felt personally, he had performed his duty to his country. On September 29 André was tried by a military board and convicted as a spy.

The next evening about dusk, a Saturday on the last day of the month in 1780, Janine was reading in the parlor when she heard a great commotion outside in the street. She threw down her book and ran to look out the window. Her hand flew to her mouth, stifling a cry. At the center of a laughing, jeering crowd, mounted on a horse-drawn two-wheeled cart, was a ridiculous figure of General Arnold with two faces, one looking ahead, one looking back. Over him towered a figure of the devil, jabbing him with a pitchfork. At the front of the cart swung a huge square lantern of green paper on which were inscribed his crimes. Her horrified eyes beheld several hundred men and boys with candles in their hands, all in ranks, officers and infantry, men with guns and bayonets, parading down the street toward Peggy's house.

Angrily she jerked the curtains closed and went back to trying to read her book. It wasn't until the next day, still seething with anger and indignation, that Janine heard the mob had burned the effigy somewhere near the coffee house.

On the following Monday at Washington's Headquarters at Tappan, Captain André went to the gallows with sun-shrinking courage and unshakable nerve. Janine's eyes dimmed as she read the account in the paper:

> 'Twas a melancholy scene . . . he died universally esteemed and universally regretted. Lafayette wept openly. Even the hardy Wayne was deeply affected. Washington remained within his house, the shutters closed tight, unable to endure the scene. Arnold, of course, was safe in the arms of Clinton.

"The Americans are well rid of him," said Papa emphatically. "Arnold was not to be borne! Not to be borne!"

Gradually Janine eased back into the life she had known before her marriage to Jonathan. Still it was not the same. Papa told her more than once that she was a much different person than she had been, that her blue eyes were more sober, her lips less prone to laughter, nor did she sing about the house in the same lighthearted fashion of her girlhood.

Janine would smile at him and pat his arm, saying, "I'm no longer a girl, Papa. I must grow up sometime." She again took up gathering herbs and preparing medicines for his apothecary chest, stocking the drawers with calomel and tartar emetics and ointments and salves. And so the months went swiftly by, with her household tasks taking up all her time.

It was not until the spring of 1781, when Jonathan had been dead almost a year, that Richard came to call on Janine. When she went down to the parlor to greet him, he was standing by the window, looking out at the street, as though preoccupied with his own thoughts.

"Doctor Ransom?" she said softly from the doorway.

He went to her with a pleasant smile on his face and put his hands on her shoulders, studying her face carefully. For a moment she thought he would kiss her, but he did not. He was as she remembered him, straight and slender, his auburn hair drawn back in a queue, his russet eyes grave, and yet his face had changed. The line of his jaw had hardened and there was a firm set to his mouth. His bearing conveyed a new assurance. Gone was the awkward, embarrassed youth she had first met.

"You're looking uncommon well, Janine."

"Yes." She stood motionless, waiting, her eyes searching his for some clue to his feeling for her since they had parted three years ago.

He let his hands drop from her shoulders, but in his eyes she saw approval and interested concern. "I wished to call long since," he said pleasantly, "to offer my condolences, but your father said you weren't prepared to receive callers."

"Yes, he told me you wished to call." She turned from him and sat down in the Windsor chair. "I appreciate your concern and I am happy to see you now. Do sit down, Richard."

He eased into the chair across from her and began telling her of his work and the news of the hospital— the passing of all the old guard and other Quaker leaders who were responsible for the founding and early success of the hospital.

"Israel Pemberton, King of the Quakers," said Richard grinning, "died of a fever in mid-April in 1779. . . ." On and on he went, and Janine made appropriate comments and listened politely until finally Richard said, "We've only forty-one patients now, and twenty of those are paying lunatics."

Janine nodded and said nothing. A long silence fell between them, as though they were strangers meeting for the first time.

Finally Richard said, "I've sorely missed you, Janine."

Wary of the serious tone of his voice, she said lightly, " 'Tis said you're not wanting for female companionship." Her lips curved in a smile and there was a glint of mischief in her eyes.

"I don't deny it," said Richard, his level gaze meeting her own. "And yet, among all the charming young ladies in Philadelphia, not one could I truly love. They're all pink and pretty butterfly maidens or solemn, staid widows with a passel of offspring."

She could see that he was in no mood for levity, and her heart went out to him. "I'm truly sorry, Richard. Your single blessedness is surely a great loss to some deserving young woman seeking a husband."

"And what of you, Janine? Are you not wasting away in single blessedness?"

She stiffened like a wounded animal held at bay. He'd gone too far, intruding on her private life. "I prefer it that way," she said coldly, thinking if he started to lecture her, to tell her to put the past behind, she would scream.

As though aware of her sudden withdrawal, he leaned back in his chair and crossed his legs, regarding her impersonally. "That's your privilege, of course," he said easily. "But shutting yourself away from the world is foolish and unhealthy. We've observed that a limb lying still will soon atrophy and die, so with a person—as will the spirit. Do you agree?"

Janine nodded without speaking. She could not deny the truth of it.

"There's no reason why we can't enjoy each other's company, is there?"

She dropped her gaze to her wedding ring, twisting

it on her finger, thinking. It had been almost a year since Jonathan's death. Dr. Ransom was not casting himself upon her with doglike devotion, eyes spilling over with love as he once had. Rather more, he was treating her as he would a patient, with a professional reserve, keeping his distance. It was pleasant sitting here quietly, talking with him. The afternoon had brought home to her how lonely her life had been during the past year since she'd come home. If he were willing to see her occasionally, it would assuage her loneliness.

"No," she said softly. "No reason."

Richard smiled and stood up. "Well, I'll call again then, when I'm in the neighborhood," he said casually. He wished her a pleasant evening and left.

When the door closed behind him, Janine's lips curved in silent amusement, laughing at herself. She had thought he'd immediately set a time to call again. Apparently he felt no burning desire to see her at the earliest opportunity. Now it dawned on her that he had acted upon impulse or a sense of obligation to see an old friend through a difficult time. Well, she told herself, that was all right with her.

On a warm afternoon late in May, when Janine had long since decided that Richard's promise to call again was a polite gesture and nothing more, he called again and Dr. Mercer invited him to take supper with them. They lingered at the table over glasses of brandy, and as always the talk turned to the hospital and the war and the news of Cornwallis joining the infamous Benedict Arnold at Petersburg, and the demise of Continental currency. "It is entirely over," said Dr. Mercer, throwing up his hands in a hopeless gesture. "At least, it's good for nothing but taxes. Some ill-applied remedies from council, no doubt, has occasioned its hasty exit. They say the sailors are dressing up dogs with it and sending them about the streets. But it is not so merry an incident with many people; they are provoked instead of being diverted at it!"

Janine sighed and stopped listening. It seemed to her that the war had been going on all her life and that it would never end.

As summer wore on, Richard became a frequent visitor at the house on Second Street and Janine began looking forward to his visits. Sometimes he called twice within the week and then would not appear for as long as two or three weeks, but she was content. Their relationship had become one of easy camaraderie and she felt relaxed and happy whenever she was with him. Sometimes she would play the spinet for him and they would sing the new songs Francis Hopkinson and Trumbull had penned. Often they would ride out on a picnic in the woodland grove beyond the hospital where she had gone picnicking with Peggy.

One afternoon early in October, when the summer had waned and the golden haze of autumn had settled upon them, they had returned from a particularly enjoyable afternoon strolling on the common and were admiring the last of the delphinium, silver penny, and roses in the side garden.

Suddenly, and without preamble, as though he'd just thought of it, Richard asked, "Are you happy, Janine?"

"Yes," she agreed, without thinking, and then realized she was. But she had no wish to start a serious discussion with Richard. "Though I'm always sorry to see the garden come to an end," she said lightly.

Richard grasped her hand gently and smiled down at her. "Sometimes it's not so bad to see things end. My residency at the hospital has also long since come to an end and I've decided to leave."

She started to speak, and he rushed on, smiling, eager. "I'm going to move into town and devote all my time to my practice. In fact I've rented a small house in Elfreth's Alley. It's quite cozy—has a stable and a garden in back. Would you like to see it?"

Janine smiled up into his face. "Indeed, yes!"

"It needs a woman's hand." Suddenly Richard's expression turned serious and he looked directly into her eyes. "I'd be most happy if you'd share my home with me, Janine."

"Share it!" murmured Janine, nonplussed.

"As Mistress Ransom."

Quickly she turned away from him and plucked a yellow rose, breathing deeply of its delicate fragrance to give herself time to think.

Finally she said, "I'm extraordinarily fond of you, Richard, but I've no wish to marry again. I'm happy as things are now."

He drew her down beside him on the seat in the white latticed arbor, and in the stubborn, determined voice she recalled from days gone by he said, "But I am not."

Her face clouded over. "I thought we were getting on uncommon well."

"And so we are. That's the rub." He gazed deeply into her eyes with the old look of longing that made her heart turn over. "I want to be with you always. And I thought you felt the same."

"I am happiest when I'm with you, Richard," said Janine softly. "You know that, but—"

"Then why should we not marry?"

Once again she was at a loss for a reason. She said nothing and the warm twilight seemed to close in about them. Somewhere a whippoorwill called, as though demanding a reply.

"Is there someone else?" he asked huskily.

"No. No one else." In truth there was no one else whose company she enjoyed more than his . . . and yet. . . . "Why must things change because you've finished at the hospital, because you're moving into town? Why can't we go on as we are?" Her heart began to race and she could feel the blood pumping in her ears. Why did she feel so trapped when Richard spoke this way?

He put one arm around her shoulders and held her hands with his. "Because I'm not content to go on as we are. I've always loved you, Janine—never stopped loving you. I want you to be my wife."

Troubled and utterly miserable, she dropped her gaze, unable to endure the yearning she saw in his eyes. "Let me think about it, Richard. Give me time to—"

Richard shook his head. "No, Janine. Enough time has passed. By now you must know in your heart whether or not you wish to spend the rest of your life with me. I've come to a decision, if you have not. It must be marriage or nothing between us."

Her head lifted and tears glistened in the corners of her eyes.

"Are you telling me if I don't marry you, we'll no longer be friends?"

His nod was heavy with regret. "I can't pretend, Janine. Friendship isn't what I'm looking for. I want more than that. I don't want you merely as a friend. I need a wife. You. I can't settle for less. Ours would be a good and lasting marriage based on mutual respect and admiration—and love on my part, if not on yours. If you feel for me no more than a deep and abiding affection"—he shrugged—"well that is more than many wives feel for their husbands."

Without answering she gazed thoughtfully at the strong, lean hand holding her own in a firm, gentle clasp. She knew it would be a good marriage, if not one of grand passion and excitement. And it was true, there was admiration and respect on her part as well as his. Happy marriages were made on less. And she felt a deep affection for him, if not a heart-throbbing love. Frantically she examined her heart and her conscience to be sure that she wasn't marrying him only because she wished so much to be kind to him, that she didn't accept his proposal merely because it pained her to disappoint him. She'd no right to tie him to her, to keep him from finding a wife who would give him the love he deserved. And yet, he'd had time to find such a woman, and had not. The thought of losing him, of his going out of her life forever was unendurable. At last she looked up into his face.

"Richard, I care very deeply for you. . . ."

As though he understood the torment she was going through, he said, "Janine, sometimes we have to make choices whether we want to or not. Sometimes doing nothing becomes a choice in itself."

She took a deep breath and at last she said, "If you still feel the same about me at the war's end, I'll be honored to marry you." At the same time she wondered how much of the choice would be hers and how much the result of events she could not control.

Richard smiled ruefully and patted her hand. "It is not the answer I had hoped for, but it is, after all, an acceptance of my proposal." He left her there in the garden with a quickly murmured good-bye, and without touching her, and a wave of disappointment swept through her, as of a promise unfulfilled.

The evening of Betsy Warren's ball in that same month of October, 1781, was sharp and crisp with a tangy scent of hickory in the air and the moon hung like an orange disc in a star-studded sky. Janine sat before the mirror in her room, her eyes glowing with excitement while Zoë dressed her hair. In years past, when she was growing up, Philadelphia's brilliant society had rivaled that of New York, laying claim to even more charm and vastly more exclusive social functions. Long before the coming of General Howe the wealthier families had given balls that delighted and astonished foreign visitors. Tonight, at last, she would be a part of the lavish entertainment, along with the dazzling Mrs. Bingham and her beautiful sister, the Allens, the Chews. She thought she would burst with joy. Betsy's party was to be a masked ball, for which Janine was grateful, thinking that her mother's wedding gown that she had worn so long ago would do nicely as a costume.

Entering into the spirit of the party, Zoë was combing and curling her hair in the high coiffed style of the ladies of the French court. Janine laughed delightedly at her reflection in the mirror, and her face suffused with color. Carefully she applied a beauty patch high on her left cheek. Richard would appear as Thomas Jefferson, to whom Janine insisted he bore an uncanny resemblance. And Papa, after no little coaxing, had agreed to don a plain brown suit of clothes to impersonate Benjamin Franklin.

Papa and Richard awaited her now in the parlor. When she appeared in the doorway, Richard stood mesmerized, gazing at her as though he could not get his fill.

"You are surely the most exquisite creature in all the world," he said, smiling fatuously.

Papa, peering at her over his spectacles in astonishment, as though he had never seen her before, extended his hand. "Marie Antoinette, I believe!"

Smiling, Janine pirouetted before them, flicked her fan flirtatiously and made a deep curtsy, thinking that tonight would be one that she would remember all her lifetime.

The glittering assemblage in the Warren's elegant mansion on Third Street was all that Janine hoped it would be. Extravagantly dressed men and women wearing all manner of sequined, jeweled masks moved among the rooms. The furniture and carpets had been taken from the large drawing room to make room for dancing. The tiered crystal chandelier was ablaze with candlelight. Colorful autumn flowers graced the mantels and side tables, and musicians at the far end of the room played softly, waiting for the dancing to begin.

The room buzzed with gaiety and excitement as the guests engaged in the sport of playing their roles, guessing who the others might be.

"There's no doubt that the lady in black velvet is Sally Bingham," Janine whispered to Richard, fluttering her fan. "And I'm certain that Sarah Wister is hiding behind that outrageous costume of the notorious Mrs. Loring!"

She had danced two gavottes with Richard and a minuet with Papa, which had just ended when a tall masked stranger wearing the fringed buckskins and a beaver hat of a backwoodsman claimed the next dance. The wide brim of his hat shaded his forehead and a luxuriant black beard hid the lower half of his face. The tall stranger held her lightly in his arms, yet possessively. He spoke not a word, but his eyes never left her face.

At last, feeling uneasy under his intense scrutiny, she smiled and said, "Surely Daniel Boone has not come to take Philadelphia!"

The man bent his head close to hers, his beard tickling her cheek, and whispered in her ear, "Only to stake his claim on territory already explored."

Something about the timbre of his voice made her spine tingle. She shivered and tried to draw back from him, but he drew her closer to his chest. A current seemed to flow between them as his eyes clung to hers. A bell rang an alarm in her head and her heart beat rapidly. She felt a familiar awareness, a heightening of her senses with this man, a feeling that stirred her as no one had ever stirred her before—except for that wretched turncoat, Mark Furneaux.

She glanced up sharply at her partner, studying the curve of his mouth, the dark eyes burning behind the mask. No, it could not be. His eyes were almost black, his wide mouth curved in a broad smile that she had never seen on the face of Mark Furneaux. Nor did he have the lean grace of the red-coated Colonel Town-

send. This man appeared thicker of body, broader of
shoulder. Quickly she averted her gaze.

When the dance ended, Richard appeared at her
elbow to claim her and the tall backwoodsman bowed
briefly and left. He did not dance with her again,
and her attention wandered from Richard as her
eyes searched the room for another glimpse of her
mysterious partner.

"You seem distracted, my love," said Richard solicitously. "Is something the matter?"

Janine blushed, suddenly aware that she had been
neglecting Richard shamefully, and tried to make it
up to him by being especially attentive during the
rest of the evening. Shortly before midnight the
musicians struck up the lively tunes of the country
dance and again she caught sight of the backwoodsman, a head taller than most of the men in the room.
Suddenly the great grandfather clock in the entry hall
struck twelve, and amid loud chatter and laughter
the guests removed their masks. Turning her back to
Richard so that he could undo the ties of her mask
from the cluster of curls at the back of her head, she
saw the black velvet clad Miss Bingham dancing with
Daniel Boone. At that instant he doffed his hat and
she reached up and slipped the mask up over his head.

Janine felt as though her blood were draining from
her body. It could not be! At that moment the stranger's eyes met hers across the room, challenging and
mocking at the same time, his insolent grin scarcely
hidden behind his beard. Shock, indignation, and
anger passed through her in quick succession. It was
outrageous, beyond belief that Mark Furneaux would
appear at such an occasion posing as a patriot!

She flicked open her fan and fanned herself rapidly,
staring at him in outrage. She racked her dazed mind
to recall what Papa had said at supper a few nights
ago, about a siege at Yorktown. Washington and
Count Rochambeau were said to be at Williamsburg

opposing Cornwallis. Could Mark be running a ship-load of supplies to Cornwallis? Could he be on some mission for the British here in this very room?

She knew what she should do. There stood William Will, Colonel of the Third Battalion of the city militia, not ten feet away. She should report Mark Furneaux immediately. Colonel Will would put him under arrest as a Tory spy. Exactly like Major André, she thought venomously, he was a British officer wearing civilian clothes in enemy territory. But recalling the fate of Major André, she stood as though rooted to the floor, her gaze locked with Mark's. Her legs seemed paralyzed and she could not force herself to move. He turned then and tucking Sally Bingham's hand in the crook of his arm, strode into the dining room where a lavish buffet was being served. She should denounce him at once! Hastily she glanced across the room, searching for Colonel Will, but he had disappeared, lost among the guests milling about.

Richard placed her hand on his arm and led her through the crowded room. "They're serving supper, my love. Shall we go in?"

"Yes," said Janine abstractedly, thinking perhaps she would find someone in the dining room who could take action. Swiftly her eyes roamed the room and in the corner she caught sight of Colonel Will holding a plate heaped with food, chatting with guests. Mark Furneaux was at the table, helping himself to cold mutton, asparagus, and meat pie as though he had all the right in the world to be there. She raked him with her eyes and at that moment he looked up. His brows lifted in perplexed surprise, as though questioning her stabbing glance.

Other guests swept in around them, blocking her view of Mark and Colonel Will. Richard found an opening in the crowd and steered her through the press of people to a window seat on the far side of the dining room.

"Sit here, Janine, I'll bring you a plate," Richard said and moved away.

Janine sat on the cushioned window seat, her anger at herself mounting by the minute. She told herself that she didn't have to turn in Mark to Colonel Will. She could simply stand up and point her finger and denounce him for what he was. Why wasn't she doing just that? She caught her lip between her teeth as if to keep from shouting out, thinking feverishly, *He once saved my life. I owe him a chance to escape, that's why. He knows I've seen him, recognized him, surely he'll leave. But suppose he hasn't completed his mission? Will he stay to carry out whatever evil intent he's come for?*

Her mind was distracted by a commotion that seemed to come from the entry way. Gruff voices barking orders rose above a flurry of loud protests and exclamations from the guests. Suddenly the crowd parted, and a major wearing the blue coat and buff breeches of the Continental Army strode into the room followed by two young subalterns. Accompanying them was the dark-haired lieutenant, with a thin, drooping mustache and white powdered hair, Janine had danced with earlier. He was wearing the white and rose colored uniform of a French officer of the Soissonais and had told her his name was Lieutenant Farquhar.

The lieutenant motioned toward the corner where Mark stood. "There he is, sir! Follow me."

They strode swiftly across the room, and a sudden hush fell upon the spectators. Janine heard the words, "You are under arrest," and startled exclamations erupted from the guests. What's going on? What's happened?

Janine jumped up and stood on the window seat, peering over their heads. Lieutenant Farquhar stood to one side. The subalterns grasped Mark roughly by the arms and, marching him between them, followed the major across the dining room, and the guests fell back, making way. As they passed Janine Mark's head jerked up and his gaze locked with hers as she stood aghast, watching him being led from the room. His dark accusing eyes were so filled with loathing and hate that she flinched under his gaze as though he had struck her. The crowd closed in behind them and they disappeared into the entryway.

Chapter 37

Janine's knees went limp, her hands were damp, and her stomach felt queasy. Weakly she sank down on the window seat and tried to compose herself. Not only had Mark been captured, but he clearly thought she had betrayed him!

When Richard returned with a plate of food, he found her flushed, fanning her face agitatedly. He held out the plate and the sight of the rich sweetmeats and pastries heaped upon it turned her stomach. She shook her head. "I'm sorry, Richard, I—I'm feeling a bit faint. I can eat nothing."

He set down their plates on a side table and touched his hand to her forehead. "You may be slightly feverish, though it is uncommon warm in here. Perhaps if we go in the drawing room. . . ."

She gazed up at him imploringly, her eyes unnaturally bright.

"Please, Richard, I'd like to go home. . . ."

He looked at her, a puzzled expression in his fine russet eyes. "Surely the arrest of that—that Tory spy hasn't upset you!"

Guiltily she wondered if her face reflected the truth. She shook her head. "Truly, I feel unwell."

Richard held out his hand and drew her up from the window seat. "Come, I'll find your father and have the servant bring our cloaks."

Once home in bed with the curtains drawn, Janine lay on her back, wide-eyed and distraught over Mark's arrest. Carefully she went over the brief words she'd exchanged with the French officer during the quadrille. They had spoken jokingly of his De Soissonais regiment, she going along with the pretense that he was a French army officer. True, they had speculated as to the identity of the other guests, but she was certain that she had said nothing to arouse his suspicions. When he'd asked if she were acquainted with the rough-clad, bearded pioneer, she had merely laughed and said, "I believe he is Daniel Boone." And there the matter rested.

At the ball she had convinced herself thoroughly that she indeed owed Mark a chance to escape with his life. Now she was still more convinced of it. Maybe it wasn't too late. A plan formed in her mind that was so preposterous it might work! She rolled over on her side and fell into a dreamless sleep.

Early the next morning she walked into the headquarters of the Continental Army holding her head high, assuming an assurance she was far from feeling, and asked to see Colonel Boudinot. A scrawny young sergeant with an Adam's apple that bobbed when he spoke informed her that Colonel Boudinot was not in the city, but if she'd care to leave a message, he'd be pleased to deliver it.

"No," said Janine imperiously, "I'll see Major—" She halted abruptly, realizing she didn't know his name. She described him as nearly as she could recall, ending with, ". . . the major who arrested the spy last evening."

The scrawny sergeant rearranged some papers on his desk. "The major is questioning the prisoner at this moment. He'll be back shortly if you wish to wait."

"Oh! Is the major here at headquarters?" She held her breath, waiting for his reply.

He looked up annoyed. "Naturally, not, madam. We keep our prisoners in the Walnut Street Prison."

"I'll return later, then. Thank you." She smiled sweetly at the sergeant and left.

She forced herself to walk slowly out the door and down the steps to the street. She wanted to run, but it would never do to arrive at the jail before the major had left. A light fog had settled over the town, and wet brown slippery leaves covered the pavement. A shiver went down her spine, whether from the cold, the raw day, or the fear of what she was about to do, she didn't know. She turned onto Walnut Street and walked slowly, occasionally stopping to peer into a shop window. When she came abreast of the jail, she glanced at the doorway and walked on, watching the entrance from the corner of her eye. At the end of the square she turned about and strolled past the building, down the block. Back and forth she ambled, her nerves stretched taut. At last her vigil was rewarded. The major emerged from the building and set off at a brisk stride down the street.

Swiftly Janine crossed the yard, mounted the steps to the entrance, and stopped short. A burly guard inside barred her way with a huge hairy hand.

She drew herself up to her full height and addressed him with an air of authority. "I wish to see Colonel Townsend. Take me to him."

The burly guard gazed at her appreciatively from rheumy eyes, shaking his massive head. "Ain't no Colonel Townsend here, ma'am."

She leveled a stern, direct gaze upon him. "He was brought here last night. . . ."

The man grinned. "Who wasn't brought here last night? We're cleaning out all them Loyalists and Quakers, too, pretending they ain't for the crown, playing both ends against the middle. They won't get away with it!"

With great effort she restrained herself from screaming at him. "This man was dressed like a patriot . . . fringed shirt and breeches, he was brought in by Major. . . ." She let her voice trail away.

The guard's rheumy eyes lit up. "Oh, the Tory

spy!" He stopped picking his teeth long enough to wave a hand in the air. "No way you can see that one. The major left orders. He ain't to see nobody but the major. Nobody in there but him and the rats. He's not going to talk to nobody for so long, he'll be begging to talk to the major."

Janine's mind raced. "If he's in a cell alone, then no one will know if you let me see him."

The guard switched his toothpick to another tooth. "Can't do it, ma'am."

"But I must see him," said Janine frantically. "It's of the greatest importance." She dropped her gaze demurely. "It's a family matter of great urgency."

"A family matter, eh?" His lips curved in a leer and his gaze slid to her waist. "He ain't be marrying anyone now. You ought to be more careful the sort of company you keep. . . ."

Janine reached out and grasped his arm, her blue eyes raised imploringly. "Please! You do understand!" Her voice rose on a note of hysteria. "I'll make it worth your while." She took out her purse and rummaged in it for a coin, but she didn't miss the glint of greed that sprang to his rheumy eyes.

His gaze fastened on her purse. "Hard specie?"

"Hard specie." Her fingers found the golden sovereign that Papa had given her on her twelfth birthday.

The man inclined his head, squinting at her. "What's it worth to you to see him, eh?"

"Worth all I have," said Janine desperately. She held the shining coin out to him.

He reached out a hairy hand and she snatched her arm back, clutching the coin tightly in her fist. "First let me in his cell. Then the money."

He glared at her, as though considering whether to wrest the money from her then and there. Then, apparently thinking better of it, he took up a lantern and jerked his head toward a doorway that opened onto a flight of stone steps. As she followed him down, the dampness seemed to cling to her skin and the odor of human filth, sickness, and urine almost choked her. Their footsteps echoed on the stone floor, and as they passed the crowded cells the prisoners beat on the doors, crying out piteously for food and water. Again a chill shook her and she tried to overcome her horror of the frightful shrieks and groans issuing from the cells.

At the end of a long dark narrow passage the jailer paused before a door, took a key from the ring at his waist, and unlocked the heavy door. It grated on rusty hinges as he swung it open just wide enough for her to slip inside. The door clanged shut and locked behind her.

A pale light filtered through a small grate high on one wall of the dungeonlike cubicles. She shivered, drawing her cloak more closely around her, and as her eyes became accustomed to the semidarkness she saw Mark sprawled facedown on a narrow cot against the stone wall. The room could have been the same in which she herself had once languished.

"I've told you everything I know!" Mark's voice was a hoarse rasp. It came again, a raven croak. "Get out!"

"Mark?" Janine's soft voice carried clearly across the cell. He rolled over, rose to his feet, staring into her face, his eyes filled with anger and hate. His black hair in wild disarray, his arched brows and heavy beard, gave him the sinister appearance of the devil in hell. But it was the look in his eyes that shattered her.

"You!" he rasped. "Have you come to gloat over your prisoner? Isn't it enough that you've done your duty, turning in a spy?" His voice was scathing and it seemed to go on and on, searing her soul. "Or have they sent you to question me, thinking you can wrangle answers from me that their less subtle methods failed to produce?"

She ran to him, putting her hands on his shoulders, her eyes wide and pleading. "Mark, I didn't betray you! Truly, I did not!"

He seized her hands, pulling them from his shoulders, and thrust her roughly away from him. "Get out! I never want to see you again!" He turned his back to her, as though waiting for her to leave.

She staggered backward, pressing her hands against the door for support. "Mark," she cried in a strangled voice, "you must believe me! It wasn't I who turned you over to—"

He swung around to face her and bore down on her, his hands balled into fists, as though to keep from choking her.

"You expect me to believe that?" he shouted. "You, a convicted spy? You don't deceive me for one moment with your gentle manner and innocent smile!" His voice was heavy with sarcasm. "The French lily is wrought of iron and no one has better reason than I to know it!"

"Mark!" shrieked Janine, quaking with fear and desperation, "please listen to me!"

"Listen to you!" he thundered. "All I've ever done is listen to you!"

Terrified, she shrank away from him, her back sliding down the door.

"I never thought I'd rue the day I saved you from the firing squad," he shouted, his face white with fury. "Get out! Get out before I—" He moved toward her, and something inside her erupted.

"Go on, strangle me! Add murder to your list of crimes."

He grabbed her by the shoulders and shook her till her head wobbled on her neck, then flung her onto the cot. She lay still, panting, gasping for breath, her wide and terrified eyes watching him pacing up and down the cell, his hands clenched at his sides, his brows drawn in a furious scowl.

Shakily she sat up and pushed the hair from her face with the back of her hand. "All right," she said in a hard, tight voice. "Believe what you will. I came here to tell you the truth—that I had not betrayed you. I didn't want you to think I'd used you ill!"

Mark snorted derisively.

". . . and to bring you some food."

At the mention of food she saw his step falter in his wild pacing to and fro in the cell. From a pocket inside her cloak she brought forth a meat pie wrapped in a napkin and set it on the end of the cot. She unfolded the napkin, and the faint aroma of meat wafted upward. Just then she heard a swift scurrying sound coming from a dark corner. She cringed at the sound and quickly drew her knees up under her on the cot. "You don't have to eat it, since you distrust me so—"

"Thank you," Mark snapped. "How kind of you to bring the condemned man his last meal. Now get out!"

His words wounded her like a stab in her heart. She blinked back tears stinging her eyelids and lifted her chin haughtily. In an icy voice she said, "I'll be happy to get out—as soon as your jailer comes and unlocks the door!"

Her attention was distracted by a quick movement at the corner of the cot. Two glittering beady eyes and a nose appeared over the edge. She let out a scream that echoed and reechoed, bounding off the stone walls of the small cell. At the same instant Mark's booted foot shot out in a kick that sent the rodent smashing against the wall across the room. He picked up the meat pie, glowering at Janine.

"Since this is doing nothing but drawing all the rats in the prison to my cell, I'd best get rid of it." His voice held an amused mockery that seemed to scorn her offering at the same time he accepted it. He resumed pacing the floor, devouring the meat pie as though he'd not eaten in months.

Janine, tense with fear and excitement, hunched on the cot watching him. She felt greatly heartened. Everything seemed to be going smoothly, if not just as she'd planned it. Confidence and courage rekindled within her as Mark's steps slowed and he shook his head as if to clear it.

"My mind is dulled," he remarked, sinking down on the end of the cot. He leaned back on his elbows, bracing his broad shoulders and head against the wall. His lids drooped. His eyes closed.

She studied him intently through narrowed lids until at last his breathing was deep and even. With a quick graceful movement she slid off the cot and walked slowly and deliberately around him, observing him as her father would a patient. Purposefully she moved closer and placed a cool slender hand on his forehead. It was hot and moist to her touch. She smiled in satisfaction and shook him by the shoulder, gently at first, then roughly.

"Mark?" she whispered. He made no reply. "Mark!" she said sharply. He slumped over on his side like a broken sack of grain. She slid her hand inside his open shirt. The mat of curly black hair on his chest was damp with sweat. She withdrew her hand and, holding his arm, pushed back the fringed sleeve and pinched the thin skin on his wrist. He lay still. His breathing slowed and his face was mottled and flushed. With a pleased smile she sat down on the cot, drawing her knees up under her chin, and braced herself for what was to come.

In a short while she heard the heavy footsteps of the jailer clumping down the passageway, the turn of the key in the lock. The creaky door opened and the guard stepped inside, slamming the door behind him. "You got to go now." He glanced at Mark slumped on the cot and his rheumy eyes bulged in surprise. In the same moment Janine leaped from the cot, flew across the room and began tugging at the door, shrieking, "Let me out of here, quickly!"

"Here, here! What's amiss?" bellowed the jailer. He shook Mark roughly by the shoulder. Mark lay like a bundle of rags on the cot.

"Don't touch him!" cried Janine.

The jailer straightened, up staring at Janine. "The bloody bloke's out like a light!"

"Of course he is!" exclaimed Janine. "He's got the ague! Look at his face! And we'll have it too, if we don't get out of here. Hurry!"

The man yanked open the door and bolted into the passageway, Janine hard on his heels. As he slammed the door and locked it, Janine said, "I hope you've not been too close to him, you'll surely contract it!"

The burly man shook his head. "I only takes his food in and out." He turned and started hastily down the dim passageway.

"Oh, a pity!" cried Janine over his shoulder. " 'Tis all you need—to touch his bowl—a bit of spit on your fingers, then picking a bit of beef from the teeth. . . ."

"He couldn't have the ague. . . ." The man's voice shook with fear.

"Oh, I do hope not," said Janine worriedly. "He's been at sea, you know, the Indies—the sailors brought it back with them. Now it will sweep through the jail —but then that will mean fewer men for you to look after—if you're still here."

They had reached the top of the stone stairs, and in the bright glow of the lantern Janine saw beads of sweat on the man's forehead, and his hand shook as he set the lantern down on a table near the door. He sank onto a wooden bench, breathing heavily. Janine smiled at him.

"You could be right," she said in a voice filled with doubt. "Maybe he doesn't have the ague. Look here, you've done me a great favor. My papa is a doctor. I'll ask him to come and look at your prisoner."

The man shook his head. "Nobody is to see the prisoner."

Janine bit her lip in vexation. "Under ordinary circumstances, yes. But this is the only way you'll know if the Tory has the ague—and if he has, Papa can give you something to keep you from getting it—like they do the pox."

She could see conflicting emotions flitting across the man's face, torn between duty and desire.

"No one need know," she said softly. "And it would be worth the risk to know if the man hasn't the ague, to know that you haven't taken it yourself. And if he has, you'll want to get him out of here!"

The burly guard ran his tongue nervously over his lips. "Let the doctor come," he growled.

Persuading Papa to accompany her to the jail to examine Mark Furneaux was not an easy task, but she won out, prevailing upon his sense of obligation to the man for saving her life. And finally, with great reluctance, he agreed to do as she asked.

Little more than an hour later she and Papa followed the jailer down the stone steps in the damp, putrid dungeon. The lamp cast eerie flickering shadows about them and Janine held her breath against the fetid stench that emanated from every crack and corner of the place.

When the guard swung open the door, Janine saw that Mark lay exactly as she had left him. The jailer stepped back to let Dr. Mercer enter, and Janine plucked at his sleeve. "We'd best wait here, best not to be too close, what with the humors in the air."

Dr. Mercer crossed the room and grasped Mark's wrist, his fingers feeling for a pulse. He let his arm fall limply on the cot and rolled the man over on his back, pushing up his eyelids, gazing intently into his eyes. He rolled down the lids and regarded Mark hopelessly. Heaving a sigh, he turned to Janine and the guard standing in the doorway.

"This man is dead!"

Janine let out an anguished cry and covered her face with her hands.

The jailer muttered an oath. "The dirty bastard! Should've had his neck stretched on the gibbet!"

"I'd say you were well rid of him," said Dr. Mercer, brushing his hands together with an air of finality.

"What done him in?" asked the jailer fearfully.

Dr. Mercer studied the ceiling, as though the answer were written there. "It appears to be the ague. But I can't be certain unless we do a postmortem."

The jailer frowned. "A what?"

"A postmortem, to determine the cause of death."

"Then hurry up and do it now."

"It's not possible to do that here. We'll have to cart him down the street to the medical college."

Janine exchanged a quick glance with Papa, knowing the moment was at hand when she would either see her plan succeed or go down in failure.

The guard eyed Dr. Mercer suspiciously. "You'll bring him back after?"

Dr. Mercer shook his head violently. "Out of the question. You'll not be wanting him back when we've finished. Aside from that, they've desperate need for cadavers at the college. They'll not permit me to bring him back." Dr. Mercer strode to the doorway. "I wash my hands of the matter, sir. If you wish me to leave you with a rotting, infected corpse, riddled with disease, it's your funeral. . . ."

The man stood blocking the doorway, his brow furrowed with indecision. "You'll sign a paper saying he's dead? This here Colonel Townsend's a bloody spy. I can't just leave go of him. . . ."

Dr. Mercer nodded. "I'll sign a death certificate for Colonel Townsend, yes."

"Take him away with you, then, but do it quick!"

Dr. Mercer turned back into the room. "I'll need some help."

"I'm not touching the corpse," said the jailer, backing into the passageway.

Janine darted into the room and grasped Mark's ankles. Dr. Mercer seized his shoulders and together they dragged him across the floor, into the dark corridor. Holding the lantern high, the quaking guard stepped smartly, as though a pack of dogs were snapping at his heels. Between them, Janine and Dr. Mercer hauled Mark up the narrow staircase and lowered him to the floor beside the guard's wooden table. While Dr. Mercer signed the necessary papers, Janine hurried outside and hailed a passing carriage.

It was well after eleven the next morning when Janine entered the spare room and pulled the curtains, wincing at the sound of rings scraping across the rod. She went to Mark's bedside and, bending over him, placed her hand on his brow. Thank God, it felt cool under her hand.

Mark opened his eyes, then shaded them with his hand against the bright sunlight streaming in the window.

"Is Lazarus waking from the dead?" asked Janine, smiling.

Mark shook his head as if to clear it. "My brain is fogged." An amused glint came into his dark eyes. "By what miracle have you managed to save me from the Walnut Street Prison, a fate worse than death, I'm sure."

Janine felt her cheeks grow hot. "A bit of a drug is all it was."

"Oh?" he asked in the jeering tone that always irritated her. "I thought I'd flown from hell to heaven."

Janine straightened up and looked at him, her hands on her hips, her mouth pursed in a wry grimace. "It's not likely you'll ever see heaven, Mark Furneaux. But while you're waiting to be called, Papa has instructed me to look after you. You're to stay in bed a day or two. . . ."

His face broke into an insolent grin. "No place I'd rather be with you, little darling."

She knew he was teasing her and she was determined
not to let him see how unnerved she was. Ignoring
his remark, she went on, assuming a composure she
was far from feeling.

"The drug I mixed in your meat pie drains the
water from the body. You'll need time to—"

He interrupted her, his dark brows arched in amusement. "So you decided to poison me rather than give
me to the gallows. I should have known there was
method to your madness. You wish me to endure a
long, lingering death. You saved my life in order
to torment me!"

In spite of her resolve Janine felt anger boiling up
inside her. She drew herself up and stared at him
with cold contempt. "Don't flatter yourself, sir."
Haughtily she added, "I was simply paying off a debt
of honor. I've no relish for being indebted to a
traitor!"

Mark's bearded jaw dropped for barely an instant,
then with swift, easy grace, he raised up on his elbows,
reached out an arm, curved it around Janine's waist,
and drew her to him, pulling her down beside him
on the bed.

"Take your hands off me, you wretched turncoat,"
she said in a low, furious voice.

He laughed softly and, gripping both her wrists in
one hand, flung her over his own body lengthwise on
the bed. She choked and sputtered, gasping for breath,
her eyes flashing fire. He flung her arms wide, pinion-
ing them to the bed, crushing her slender body under
his. Her scream died on her lips as Mark's mouth came
down on hers in the familiar, demanding, loving caress
that melted her resistance like tallow. She was conscious of the wild beating of a heart, not knowing
whether it was his or her own. Nothing existed for
her but the rapture of this moment. They stayed in
each other's arms for some while, and when at last
she opened her eyes, she saw over Mark's shoulder a

robin perched on a branch of the elm tree, peering in the window. Brought to her senses, Janine jerked her head back, raising her eyes to meet Mark's. She read in their dark depths an ardor that she knew could lead only to the ultimate embrace. The words she intended as a command came forth in a husky whisper.

"Mark, let me go!"

He covered her mouth with his hand. She struggled to rise to her knees. He sat up and with his free hand he held her clasped tightly to his chest.

"Mark! Let me go!"

He kissed her again and she pounded his back, her fists flailing harmlessly on his well-muscled shoulders. He laughed derisively, jeering at her. "Now I'll tell you the real reason you saved my life. You wished to relieve your conscience for having betrayed me. Admit it!"

Maddened beyond endurance, she shrieked at him. "I did not betray you! It was someone dressed like a French officer, someone who knew you'd gone over to the British! Now let me go!" Frantically she tried to wrench from his grasp, her hair tumbling in her face. As she wrestled with him her gown slipped from her shoulder and she was hampered by her full skirts. In a quick movement Mark grasped both her arms and drew them behind her back, imprisoning her wrists in one strong hand.

Panting furiously, she flung the stinging words at him, "And the minute you can walk, you'd best be gone." Breathless, she paused, twisting on her knees in an effort to escape him. Mark laughed softly and leaned toward her. There came the sound of footsteps pounding up the stairs. Mark relaxed his hold and Janine flung herself from the bed and stood up, feverishly pushing her hair back into place with her hands. The door burst open and Zoë appeared in the doorway. She stopped short, her dark eyes wide and frightened, staring first at Janine, then Mark.

"I thought I heard you call out, Miss Janine."

Mark had stretched out on his back, his arms folded behind his head, his eyes closed in an attitude of complete relaxation. As though he had every right to be here, thought Janine wrathfully. Watching him, Janine thought she saw a slight quirk at the corners of his mouth. She gazed at him with loathing, despising him for his bold, arrogant assumption that she would fall into his arms like a ripe plum. Her lips clamped together in a thin line.

Zoë asked in a puzzled voice, "Why you call out, Miss Janine?"

In a scathing voice she said, "I saw a rat!"

She turned from the bed and swept from the room, slamming the door behind her.

That noon Janine asked Zoë to carry a dinner tray upstairs to Mark. But in the evening, against her better judgment, Janine carried up his supper tray. She found him sitting up in bed reading the *Pennsylvania Gazette,* apparently feeling none the worse for his ordeal. Thinking to keep a safe distance from the bed, she sat in the chair by the window, where a mockingbird called from the branch of the elm tree. If Mark noticed her cool reserve, he made no mention of it, but instead inquired with the polite interest of an old friend as to her life during the past two years.

In a low, quiet voice she told him of her marriage, the loss of her child, Jonathan's death, her flight from Heritage Hall, and how she spent her days keeping Papa's apothecary stocked and managing the house.

Mark told her of his voyages at sea, taking on cargoes of indigo and rice in Charleston, trips to Jamaica and the Indies. It wasn't until after Janine had retired for the night, just before she drifted off to sleep, that she realized that Mark hadn't really told her anything at all about his own life.

Early the next afternoon Janine was in the study

with Papa, going over his accounts when they heard
a knocking at the front door. Moments later Zoë
announced Colonel Boudinot.

Janine's heart leaped to her throat. With trembling
fingers she set down her pen and blew sand across
the figures she had just entered in the ledger. "I don't
wish to see him today, Zoë. Tell him I'm not at home."

Dr. Mercer gazed at her in astonishment. "Janine,
what's possessed you? Why should you refuse to see
him?"

"He must be inquiring about Mark—Colonel Townsend, Papa. It's a delicate matter." The fear and guilt
sweeping through her gave way to alarm.

Dr. Mercer removed his spectacles and gazed directly
at her. "You'll surely arouse his suspicions by not re-
ceiving him. We'd best hear him out."

Janine sighed deeply and tried to pull herself together, though inside she was quaking with fright.
"Very well, Papa."

They joined Colonel Boudinot in the parlor and
exchanged pleasantries. He appeared calm, composed,
not about to accuse her of helping a spy escape. Relieved, Janine sat down on the sofa, still wary of the
reason for his call.

Now he was saying affably, "I've been away much of
the time and have not been at liberty to call upon
my old friends as I'd like to have done."

Dr. Mercer waved a hand in airy dismissal. "Think
nothing of it, Elias. We understand."

Colonel Boudinot smiled and turned to Janine.
"I'm happy to be able to tell you personally how
much we appreciate your loyal assistance to our cause
—even to the point of death!"

Janine blushed furiously. "It was a narrow escape,
but as Papa says, all's well that ends well. I'm sorry I
couldn't continue to help, but after my untimely
demise. . . ."

"That's what I wished to speak with you about,"

said Colonel Boudinot easily. "Actually there's no need for you to protect Colonel Townsend."

"Indeed there is not!" said Janine quickly, knowing she'd spoken too eagerly. "He certainly deserves no protection, deserting the rebel cause, turning traitor—another Benedict Arnold!" Her breath caught and she thought she would strangle over the choking feeling in her throat. She knew that she could not turn Mark Furneaux over to Colonel Boudinot, for they were bound by ties even she did not understand. And now there was no limit to her patience, determination, or guile.

Colonel Boudinot leaned forward in his chair and his eyes were grave in his oak-leaf-lined face, as he regarded Janine.

"Upon my return to Philadelphia I learned that Colonel Townsend was taken prisoner and subsequently died. You and your father were in attendance."

Janine felt the blood drain from her face. She said nothing.

"The—uh—body of Colonel Townsend seems to have disappeared from the medical college—that is, of course, assuming the corpse arrived there as the jailer was told it would."

Janine's brows rose in feigned surprise. "Indeed!"

Colonel Boudinot's keen dark eyes bored into hers. "Would you know where I might find Colonel Townsend?"

Janine stared vaguely over Colonel Boudinot's shoulder at Papa's French landscape hanging on the wall over the mantel. "No, Colonel Boudinot, I really can't say where you could find him."

In a voice that sounded somewhat strained he said, "Janine, you test me sorely. The man was last seen in your presence. We must have him at all costs. He's imperative to our cause. We can afford him much greater protection than you are capable of, please believe me."

Janine's startled gaze returned to Colonel Boudinot's worried face. "Protection?"

"My dear, I've told you how much we valued your aid in the past, and yesterday too, helping the man escape. But now you must permit us to take over."

Janine's brows puckered in a frown. "I'm afraid I don't understand. Are you *thanking* me for helping this traitor to escape from prison?"

Colonel Boudinot nodded grimly. "If you'd not been a step ahead of us . . ." he sighed, shaking his head, ". . . we'd arranged for his escape in another manner." At Janine's startled gasp, he said, "Come now, Janine. Surely you can't believe it's common practice to allow visitors to drug our prisoners and cart them away unmolested?"

"You knew!"

"The instant you left, the jailer reported a possible case of the ague and the removal of the body. The man was terrified. In point of fact, we had taken great pains to arrange for the French lieutenant to denounce Colonel Townsend at Betsy Warren's ball so that we could arrest him."

Baffled, Janine exclaimed, "You *knew* the man was a turncoat!"

Colonel Boudinot nodded. "A most cunning and convincing turncoat, concealing a rebel soul. From the start Lieutenant Furneaux has brought French arms and ammunition to us by way of the Indies. And he helped to establish a French firm, Hortalez et Cie, to bring in supplies for our army, sending back rice and indigo in return. But his most outstanding achievement, of course, was joining the British forces in Philadelphia."

"It's beyond belief!" said Janine appalled.

Colonel Boudinot's sharp eyes glittered with pleasure as he nodded assent. "Our intelligence had conceived the plan to expose him as a traitor and a spy for the purpose of imprisoning him in order to convey

further instructions and collect information. When
we'd finished our business, his escape would have been
arranged so that he could continue to work for us.
But before we could carry out our purpose"—he
smiled wryly—"our iron butterly set him free."

Janine's mouth fell open in stunned surprise as
Colonel Boudinot went on.

"Colonel Townsend, or if you prefer, Mark Furneaux, was entirely unaware that his arrest and
escape had been arranged. Our ruse had to be convincing, you see. Eyes are always watching. Now we
need him desperately to obtain information regarding
the whereabouts of the French fleet." Colonel Boudinot smiled again. "However, I strongly suspect that
Colonel Townsend is being held prisoner in your
home—is he not?" He bent his piercing gaze on her.

Janine, white with shock, felt color flooding her
face, her throat and neck. Shakily she rose from the
sofa. "I'll see if he's about," she said in a hoarse
whisper and ran from the room. She dashed down
the hallway and, picking up her skirts, hurried up
the stairs. Breathless, she paused outside Mark's room.
The door was ajar. She pushed it open, stepped inside
the room, and stopped short, stifling a cry. His bed
was empty.

Her eyes traveled swiftly around the room, stopping
at the open window where a stiff breeze billowed the
curtains and a branch of the elm tree scraped the
side of the house. Mark's fringed shirt and breeches
were gone from the peg behind the door. Suddenly
a feeling of desolation such as she had never known
swept over her—she felt lost and alone and a vibrant
feeling inside her slowly died.

Weeks later it was reported that on a bright sunny
autumn morning a French flotilla under Admiral
Comte de Grasse had driven a British naval force
from Chesapeake Bay. Had Mark played a part in the

victory? If so, had he survived? It came to Janine then that she would probably never know. And why she should feel so forlorn and desolate was beyond all understanding.

Chapter 38

In October of 1781 the city was tense with rumors of victory. One dark, frosty morning of that same month Janine was awakened by the sound of watchmen's rattles in the streets, alerting the citizens of danger. The alarm grew louder as it was passed from watchman to watchman. She leaped from her warm bed, threw open the window, and leaned out. Someone was running up the street, banging on all the doors. The hoarse cry of German Charlie echoed clearly through the cold air.

"Basht—dree o'glock, und Gorn-val-lis isht da-ken!"

It was beyond belief! The words rang in Janine's ears. *Cornwallis is taken! Cornwallis is taken!*

With trembling fingers she lighted a candle and rushed to Papa's room, shaking him roughly awake, shouting wildly, "Papa! Cornwallis is taken! Listen!"

Dr. Mercer rose up and looked at his daughter as though she'd gone soft in the head. Again came the cry from the streets, "Gorn-val-lis isht da-ken!"

They ran downstairs and, throwing their cloaks over their nightclothes, dashed out into the streets along with their neighbors, hysterical with joy, shouting questions. After the first excitement was over, Papa built up their fire in the parlor and planned to keep open house all night. They invited German Charlie in for food and drink and made a great fuss over him.

They made him tell his story over and over. How he had seen Washington's exhausted aide-de-camp pull up before the quarters of the president of Congress, slide from his horse, and rouse the house to hand over the long awaited dispatches—how he had overheard enough to take up his cry of victory and had hurried from door to door with the news.

It wasn't until later the next day they learned that American troops under Washington, and French regiments commanded by Lieutenant General Rochambeau, pushed closer and closer to the British lines, bottling up Cornwallis. Cornwallis, suffering short rations, dwindling ammunition, and decreasing supplies, scanned the sea day after day for sight of the Royal Fleet he knew was on the way to him from New York. But the once friendly sea behind him swarmed with French ships and the land routes were blocked by hostile troops; for Cornwallis there was no escape from Yorktown.

Washington and Rochambeau had brought heavy artillery to bear on the British position. They pounded the Redcoats at pointblank range with almost one hundred guns firing an incessant barrage. The pounding continued for two days until on October 14 Cornwallis delivered a note to Washington under a flag of truce requesting a cessation of hostilities for twenty-four hours to settle the terms for surrender. Two days later the surrender document was signed.

That afternoon, with a band playing "The World Turned Upside Down," color bearers surrendered the British and Hessian flags to the victors. The Redcoats paraded out of Yorktown between drawn ranks of Americans and Frenchmen and stacked their arms in accordance with capitulation terms. Lord North, when he heard the news exclaimed, "Oh, God! It is all over."

Several days later, on a dismal foggy afternoon, Janine went to answer a bold knocking on the door. On the threshold, grinning like the devil himself, stood Mark Furneaux. Tall and handsome in his fringed hunting shirt and breeches, his eyes danced and his teeth gleamed whitely in his olive-tinted face. Janine stood stunned speechless, thinking surely her heart would stop beating. Her anger at him for having left them with not a word battled with her joy at the sight of him. With an iron force of will she kept from flinging herself into his arms. Her face betrayed her.

His mocking, challenging gaze swept her from head to toe. And, as always, there was something hot and vital and exciting about him.

"May I come in?"

She showed him into the parlor and poured them both a glass of brandy, not knowing which of them needed it more. Mark stretched out on the sofa, his long legs sprawled before him, as though he were welcome as spring.

Janine perched stiffly on the edge of the Windsor chair. At all costs she must not wear her heart on her sleeve, must not let him see how vulnerable she was to his easy charm. She defended herself in the only way she knew, withdrawing into a cool reserve. In a slightly ironic tone she said, "Do you mind telling me what you're doing here, after fleeing from our home like a thief in the night?"

His brows rose in amusement at her display of aloofness and she had the annoying feeling that she wasn't fooling him at all. He always seemed to read her mind. His eyes roamed over her, noting the quick rise and fall of the rose point lace ruffle at her breast, her hands clasped tightly in her lap, the rosy glow suffusing her cheeks.

A lazy smile spread across his face and lights danced in the depth of his black eyes. He sipped his brandy slowly.

"That's why I'm here, little darling."

She wished he wouldn't call her that. She wasn't his little darling, and the familiar term of endearment was like a knife turning inside her.

"I wanted to apologize for sneaking off, as you say,

like a thief in the night without a good-bye or a thank you. You see, I heard Colonel Boudinot come in and I'd no wish to see him at the moment."

Though she'd certainly no reason to find excuses for this rogue's actions, now she recalled that Colonel Boudinot had said that Colonel Townsend was not to know his arrest was planned. She couldn't fault Mark for escaping him.

"And I wanted to thank you for saving my life—making off with my body under the very noses of the prison guards." His gaze sought her lips and lingered there a moment.

She blushed furiously and dropped her gaze, studying her hands folded in her lap. Surely he knew as well as she that her desperate effort to rescue him was not only unnecessary but had thrown Colonel Boudinot's carefully laid plans into a cocked hat. Now, though he was saying all the polite phrases expected of him, they didn't sound as they should. He was laughing at her. She should be angry, but her anger was long since spent and she didn't know what to say. She raised her eyes to his.

"And I wanted to tell you," he continued smoothly, "how much I appreciate your hospitality and thank you for taking such good care of me during my illness. . . ." He paused, smiling wickedly.

Remembering that her meat pie was the cause of his illness, a stab of guilt went through her. Was he truly grateful that she had fed him, bathed him, washed his clothes . . . or was he mocking her as always. She smothered a sigh. The fight had gone out of her and she'd no wish to argue. She would give him the benefit of the doubt.

"I was happy to care for you—" She halted abruptly, thinking she'd made an unfortunate choice of words, and quickly added, "I'd do the same for any ill and exhausted patriot."

"At the time I was not the patriot you once thought me to be. I was a Tory traitor."

She knew he was deliberately taunting her, putting her on the defensive, and she could feel swift anger stir, even now. But she would no longer rise to his bait. She set her brandy glass down carefully on the table. "I owed you a favor," she said pleasantly.

"Since then, I gather, I've been vindicated. You know me for what I am. . . ."

She nodded and smiled inwardly, thinking she well knew him for what he was. "Indeed. And have I too been vindicated? Are you convinced it wasn't I who turned you over to the rebels?"

Mark had the grace to blush. "Colonel Boudinot enlightened me. That's another reason I felt duty bound to return."

Duty bound! she thought, nettled. She should have known he'd come only from a sense of duty.

"To apologize for having misjudged you and to bid you a proper good-bye."

"Good-bye!" she blurted. "But you've only just come!" She bit her lip, realizing too late the implication he would draw from her protest at his leaving. She should have known he'd be eager to leave, eager to fall into the arms of that woman Anne Delaney. To cover her confusion she asked, "What will you do, now that the war has ended?"

He rose and strode to the fireside, warming his hands. "The war's not over and done, despite Cornwallis's surrender. True, it was a great victory, but the British must give up Charleston and Savannah—their main army is still in the Manhattan area. We've yet to win the peace.

"As for the future," he smiled into her eyes, "my ship has so far survived the hazards of the seas. I'll continue to import and export goods, God willing. . . ."

"You'll take to the sea again, then?"

He left the warmth of the fireside and crossed the room to stand before her, feet spread, smiling down at her. "I've had more than enough of life on the sea.

I'm done roaming. I wish to marry, and if the lady will have me, I'll hire a captain to man the *Adventure*."

Janine felt her knees go limp, the blood drain from her face. A sense of desolation such as she had never known swept over her, threatening to overwhelm her. She had never thought of Mark Furneaux marrying anyone. *I love him,* she thought, wondering at herself. *I don't know how long I've loved him, but it's true. And if it hadn't been for Jonathan, I'd have realized it long ago. I've never been able to see anyone but Jonathan.* And now that Mark had spoken of a commitment to someone else, she knew she loved him desperately, unprincipled rogue that he was, with all his arrogance and fine conceit she loved him—and she hated him for returning, stirring up emotions she thought she'd put away forever.

"I'm to be married too," said Janine through quivering lips.

"Married!" exclaimed Mark. His face showed shocked surprise and his voice took on the mocking, superior tone of the days when they'd first met. "To whom?"

"Doctor Ransom—Richard Ransom. You met him at the assembly some time back." She could not look at him. Again her eyes fell to her hands, smoothing the folds of her dress. From under lowered lids she saw him watching her closely, his dark brow drawn in a perplexed frown, as though wondering how anyone who was speaking of the man she was to marry could appear so miserably unhappy.

"And when is this to be?"

Janine bit her lips to still their trembling. "At the war's end."

He turned away and strode to the window, pulling back the curtain, staring out as though there were something to see other than the gray mist swirling about the brick houses across the street.

She sat silent and miserable on the sofa, trying to

compose herself. Why should she feel so desolate, so devastated? Mark had never said he loved her. Yet now she perceived that from the start they had been bound by bonds not of their own making—ones he could apparently throw off with no thought. She had known all along he was mad about the Delaney woman. And now she had to accept that he was lost to her forever. She wished he would go. She could hardly bear to be in the same room with him, knowing he loved someone else.

At last he turned back to her. He took something from his pocket. "I believe this belongs to you." He opened his hand and on his palm lay her medallion, the ivory painted miniature, the image of herself. She raised her blue eyes to his olive-tinted face. His expression was cold and impassive. "Go on, take it."

She longed to tell him to keep it, a talisman to remember her by, but clearly he had no wish for a keepsake. With shaking fingers she took the medallion from his hand.

"Where did you find this?"

Again he smiled the old mocking, insolent smile that wrenched her heart. "You left it in my cabin on the *Adventure*. If you remember, you left in somewhat of a hurry."

Her heart raced at the memory of that day. Why had she run from him, denied her feelings? If only she hadn't, things might be different now. She pressed her lips into a firm line. She must pull herself together or in a moment she would burst into tears. She tossed her head and lifted her chin in a haughty pose.

"I'd forgotten," said Janine coldly. "Thank you for returning it."

He made her an exaggerated bow. "I believe our business is finished, Mistress Burke. I wish you every happiness with your Doctor Ransom. Good day."

He strode from the room and she could hear his

footsteps receding down the hall, the door open and close behind him. She put her head in her hands and burst into tears, giving way to uncontrollable sobs that shook her whole body.

"Oh, God! It is all over. He's gone. Gone forever."

Chapter 39

The following morning Janine was in the kitchen taking freshly baked loaves of bread from the oven when Zoë rushed in with a broadside that had been left at the door. Now she stood curiously at Janine's elbow, waiting while she read it.

"What that say, Miss Janine?"

She read it aloud.

> "ILLUMINATION: Colonel Tilghman, Aide-de-Camp to his Excellency General Washington, having brought official accounts of the Surrender of Lord Cornwallis, and the garrisons of York and Gloucester, those citizens who choose to illuminate on the Glorious occasion, will do it this evening at Six, and extinguish their lights at nine o'clock.
>
> Decorum and harmony are earnestly recommended to every citizen, and a general discountenance to the least appearance of riot. October twenty-fourth, seventeen eighty-one. Committee of Safety handbill."

"We'll set the candles in the windows now, Zoë. And if I forget to light them, be sure to remind me. The whole town will be celebrating the Yorktown victory."

Candles illuminating the windows in the town had become a sign that one supported the Revolution. Janine smiled ironically, thinking that in years past they had illuminated their windows in celebration of the king's birthday.

That same evening shortly before six Janine lighted the candles in the windows in the parlor and those in her bedroom facing the street. Sounds of merry-making and rejoicing came faintly to her ears. A mob was forming, carousing through the streets, making certain everyone had candles in their windows.

Just before suppertime Dr. Mercer burst into the house, red-faced, babbling in a fine fury.

"I've just come from the Drinkers. The mob has broken every pane of glass in the house, the sash lights, and two panels of the front parlor. The door cracked and burst open and the rowdies threw stones into the house. John Drinker has lost half the goods out of his shop and been beat by them. I admire the Drinkers, that they cling to their Quaker beliefs, but, Lord, the price they pay!"

Agitatedly Dr. Mercer swept his hands through his hair. "The suffering of those they please to style Tories would fill a volume. It's beyond belief! Some are faring better, some worse. Some houses, after breaking the door, they entered and destroyed the furniture. Many women and children were frightened into fits. It's a mercy no lives were lost!"

Janine felt a chill of alarm pass through her. "Are they molesting *all* the Quakers, Papa?"

Dr. Mercer sank wearily into a chair. "All who've not set candles in their windows. They went on to the Rawles and took up their attack, surrounded the house, broke the shutters and the glass of the win-dows and were coming in. But Coburn and Bob Shewell fixed lights up at the windows, which paci-fied the mob, and they moved on. Had it not been for Coburn and Shewell, I really believe the house would have been torn down. Waln's pickles were thrown about the street and barrels of sugar stolen. They'll go on like this until it is one general illumination

throughout the town. Just now, as I came in, they
were working their way down Second Street."

Janine ran to the window, and through the autumn
darkness she saw a band of men brandishing lights,
shouting, pausing to pick up stones, as they made
their way down the cobbled street. Her flesh crawled
and her heart pounded wildly.

"What of the Darraghs, and Eldon and Rachael
Lindley next door, Papa? Have they illuminated?"

Dr. Mercer shook his head. "I didn't notice, *ma
petite*. I was in such haste to get home to make certain
we'd lighted our own windows."

Janine cocked her head, listening as the sounds of
the mob grew more violent—wild, drunken, borne
on as though they let loose all the pent-up feelings of
hate and deprivation they'd endured throughout the
war. Shaking with rage and fright, she rushed to the
front door, flung it open, and ran down the steps to
the pavement to peer at the house next door. The
window panes shone black against the yellow glow of
the streetlamp.

Two men running ahead of the large body of men
advancing down the street shouted to their comrades
as they reached the house. They came on the run,
wielding pickaxes and iron bars, yelling insults and
obscenities to the Tory sympathizers.

Janine ran inside and slammed the door, shouting,
"Papa, Papa, they're at the Lindleys' next door!"

The sound of glass shattering came clearly to their
ears, followed by a terrible banging heard above the
tumultuous voices of a large body of men.

"What shall we do?" cried Janine frantically.

Dr. Mercer threw up his hands in a helpless gesture. "It would be in vain to oppose them. The
Lindleys will light their candles to make peace with
the mob, or the mob will do it for them."

Janine ran to the door and opened it a crack. At
that moment one of the mob hurled a brick at her
neighbors' door. The door cracked and burst open.

Another of the men held a pistol at the ready and they rushed inside. Paralyzed with fright, Janine gripped the doorjamb, her mind refusing to believe what she was seeing. She heard sounds of furniture being broken up. A woman screamed. Raging, cursing, the men beat about inside.

Suddenly a flicker of light shone from one of the windows, brightened, glowed. At the same time someone in the street threw a rock, which shattered the glass. Janine's mind spun dizzily. It would be impossible to fight through the crowd of angry men to try to help her neighbors. She shut the door and raced through the hallway to the back of the house, out into the yard. Perhaps she could go in the back way. If she could help them to escape, she could at least offer them refuge.

No sooner had she gained the yard than the Lindleys' back door was flung open. With a wailing babe in her arms and a small boy clinging to her skirts, Rachel rushed out screaming, "Fire! The vandals have set the place on fire!"

"Rachel," shouted Janine wildly. "Over here! Hurry!"

Rachel whirled about. Blood streaked down her panic-stricken face. Again Janine shouted at her, and the woman ran toward the picket fence between their yards. Blood from her nose dripped onto the infant's blanket. Janine snatched the crying baby from her arms. Rachel hoisted the boy over the fence, then lifted her skirts and scrambled over after him. She turned, looking back over her shoulder at the house. In the doorway stood a lanky man clinging dazedly to the frame, peering into the darkness, and behind him rose a faint red glow.

"Rachel!" came a hoarse broken cry. "Rachel! David!"

"Eldon!" Rachel screamed. "We're here—at Doctor Mercer's!"

The man staggered across the yard and clambered

over the fence. Panting, gasping for breath, he followed Janine and his family inside the house. Blood flowed from a wide gash over his left eye. Sweat rolled down his smudged face, and his shirt-sleeve was ripped from one shoulder.

"The curtains in the parlor caught fire," he gasped. "It's sweeping into the hallway and I fear it's going up the stairs . . . they've cut up the furniture and heaped it onto the flames . . . our pictures are broken . . . the parlor's full of men . . . I tried to stop them. . . ." Exhausted, he sank down on a chair at the table and bowed his head in his arms.

Rachel dabbed at her eyes and nose with the hem of her skirt. The baby in Janine's arms began to scream, and the boy David erupted into violent crying, clinging to his mother's skirts.

"Papa, Papa!" shrieked Janine down the hallway. "Come quickly!"

Zoë ran into the room. "Your papa's gone to give the alarm to the fire brigade!"

The acrid odor of smoke and a terrifying crackling sound came to her then and fear flooded through her. She ordered Zoë to fetch water and clean cloths, while she searched for ointments from among her supplies in the hutch. Then she began to clean Eldon Lindley's wound. He slumped back in the chair, his eyes closed while she worked over him. In an effort to soothe her squalling infant, Rachel paced agitatedly to and fro.

Moments later, to Janine's intense relief, Dr. Mercer burst into the room and set about bandaging Eldon's head. Rachel continued to pace the floor, ranting and raving, "If thee's not for them, thee's against them! They are wild beasts! I tried to stop them, till they pointed a pistol at my breast while I was endeavoring to shield David from the rage of one of the men. . . ."

"They struck her a violent blow in the face, which made her nose bleed," Janine told Papa indignantly.

Rachel ranted on. "These rowdies wish not to be oppressed and yet they oppress those who wish only peace!"

Eldon shook his bandaged head hopelessly. "Perhaps it is as necessary for our Society to ask for terms as it was for Cornwallis!"

Suddenly there came the sound of bells ringing in the State House, in Christ Church, and other churches about the town, summoning the volunteers of the fire companies.

Janine ran through the house, snatched up the heavy leather fire bucket hanging by the front door, and rushed outside, Eldon Lindley and Dr. Mercer hard on her heels. Giving her infant and David over to Zoë, with orders to take them upstairs for safekeeping, Rachel followed. The mob of celebrators had gone on, but figures were flying through the night, converging on the burning house. Swirls of black smoke poured out through the front door and the broken windows and hung in the clouds overhead.

Horses came clanging down the street, dragging an engine behind them from Benjamin Franklin's Union Fire Company. Minutes later came the Hand-in-Hand fire fighters, along with a rival brigade. Thank God the companies no longer carried their rivalries to the point where they refused to help put out a fire at a house displaying a rival emblem over the doorway, thought Janine.

Quickly a double line of men and boys formed from the blazing house to a pond nearby, passing a steady relay of leather buckets filled with water hand-to-hand to the fire engine. As soon as the contents were dumped into the pumper, the empty buckets went back down the other line. Janine and Ellen took their places in the "dry" line.

Relays of men at both handles worked the clumsy pump. Two of the men held the hose, playing a steady stream on the Lindleys' roof. Two more set up hooks and ladders against Janine's house and began spray-

ing the roof lest the fire spread. Flames were licking
out the Lindleys' upper windows, creeping onto the
roof. Sick and shaking, Janine turned her head away.
She could not bear to watch.

From the corner of her eye Janine saw another
engine draw up, taking a stand the length of a hose
apart, between the last engine and the pond, pumping
water from one engine to the next, until the last hose
reached the flames. By pumping furiously the men of
one company could sometimes "wash" the next engine, pumping the water in so fast that the men
pumping on the next engine could not empty it out
before the tank overflowed. The men pumped themselves breathless, defending the honor of their engine.
If it was washed, the exhausted men would weep with
shame. Janine watched them, white with rage. This
battle of the engines was providing better sport for
the spectators than was the fire itself!

In spite of the uproar and excitement the more
courageous men rushed inside the house, braving the
smoke and the scorching heat to splash bucket after
bucket on the leaping flames. Suddenly there came
excited shouts and yells and men pointing to the roof.

Janine looked up from the line and froze in horror.
The flames, fanned by the wind, had jumped to the
roof of her own house and were devouring it like dry
leaves. Someone shouted orders and the men changed
the hose, aiming the stream at the flames consuming
the roof. Men carrying long poles with swabs on the
end climbed the shaky ladders set up against the
front of the house and began drenching the roof.
Others carrying canvas bags ran inside to salvage what
they could from the burning house.

A shattering scream jolted Janine from her paraly-
sis. Rachel Lindley threw down her bucket, shrieking,
"My children!" and raced toward the house. At the
doorway two men seized her arms, holding her back,
shouting, "You can't go in there!" Rachel struggled

with the men, trying to wrench from their grasp, twisting and shrieking, "My babies, upstairs!"

Janine rushed to Rachel's side and put her arms around the hysterical woman, cradling her in her arms. Dr. Mercer came running toward them and, seeing the half-crazed woman pointing and screaming, realized the cause.

"Which room?" he shouted.

Sobbing, Rachel shook her head. "We don't know," cried Janine. Dr. Mercer pushed past the fire fighters in the doorway and disappeared inside the house.

"Papa has gone to get them," she told Rachel with more confidence than she felt. "There, there," she said soothingly, "He'll find them. They'll be all right."

Just then one of the fire fighters put his arms around them both and dragged them down the steps onto the pavement. "Keep out of the way," he yelled. "You're blocking the doorway! The men can't get through!"

Janine stood on the pavement, her eyes riveted on the house, her arms about the hysterical, sobbing Rachel, frantic with worry over Papa. Through the smoke clouding the window of her bedroom she thought she saw a flicker of light. Was it Papa with a candle, or . . . "Dear God," she prayed, "help him find them!"

Before her terrified eyes a fountain of sparks shot toward the sky and descended slowly, lazily through blood-colored clouds of smoke, and fear licked through her veins as swiftly as the flames she saw.

"Get out!" someone yelled. "Everybody out! The roof has caved in!"

Three men, red-faced, sweat pouring down their smoke-streaked faces, emerged from the house carrying canvas bags spilling over with whatever possessions they thought should be saved. Dimly Janine's mind registered the French clock, a porcelain punch bowl, the hall mirror, brass candlesticks, pewter plates,

Papa's Watteau painting— *Where, oh, where was Papa?*

"Where's Doctor Mercer?" she shouted at the men, nearly out of her mind with fear. She clutched the sleeve of a man who had been one of Papa's patients, shaking his arm.

"Doctor Mercer," she gasped. "He went inside. Where is he? Have you seen him?"

"We all had to come out. Nobody's inside, miss. 'Tis hotter than the hinges of hell—"

"But he's in there, I tell you!" shrieked Janine over the panic that clutched her insides. "He's gone to find two children and the servant upstairs."

A gleam of pity shone from the man's red-rimmed eyes. "Maybe so—the smoke was so thick, you couldn't see the sunrise in there. . . ."

A shriek from Rachel distracted her. Whirling around, she saw Zoë, her face a peculiar ashen color, standing at the edge of the crowd. She was holding the blanketed infant in her arms and clutching the crying David by the hand. Janine's breath left her in a rush of relief. Rachel tore from the shelter of her arms and plunged through the crowded street toward Zoë. Thank God Zoë had the sense to get out, thought Janine. She must have fled down the stairs and out the back door before Papa found them. But where was Papa?

Her mind rushed incoherently here and there. Papa, too, must have left by the back door. Janine pushed and shoved her way through the throng toward Zoë.

"Papa!" she shouted. "Have you seen Papa?"

Zoë shook her head, her mouth a thin line of despair.

The fire fighters had dragged the hose up the front steps and inside the smoke-filled house. There was no way she could get past them. Her heart beat wildly and her breath was coming in short quick gasps. She raced around to the side of the house, around the corner to the yard, and through the garden. The back of the house was bathed in an eerie red glow, and a fog of smoke swirled through the door. The smell of water hissing on charred wood, the odor of burning choked her. Smoke stung her eyes. She took a deep breath and, clapping her hand across her nose, plunged through the doorway. Crouching down low where the smoke seemed less dense, she groped her way through the kitchen, shouting frantically, "Papa! Papa!"

She had left the back door open and the draft sucked out some of the smoke in the hallway. A pool of water shone on the oak floor halfway down the hall. The fire fighters' hose hadn't reached the stairway to the second story.

She gained the foot of the stairs and started up, choking, gasping, seeing only dimly through the thick gray haze. Halfway up the stairway she stumbled and fell to her knees. Reaching out, groping for the next step, she touched an arm, a shoulder, the head of a figure sprawled facedown on the landing.

"Papa! Papa!" she screamed, shaking him violently by the shoulder. He lay still. She could not rouse him. The smoke has overcome him, she thought dully. Seizing both his shoulders, she tried to lift him, to drag him down the stairs, but his unconscious form resisted her.

Fighting down panic, she gripped his ankles, easing him down the steps one at a time, pulling, tugging. Her eyes were streaming and the smoke seared her throat. If only she could reach the last step, it would be easier to drag Papa through the hall. Desperately she tugged Papa down the next step, and the next. Through the roiling smoke and heat she heard a voice shouting, "Janine! Janine!" She tried to call out, but no sound came from her parched throat.

With a final wrench she gained the hallway and Papa tumbled off the bottom step, rolling onto his back. In the pale light filtering through the front door and down the hallway from the lanterns in the street, she looked at his face. Papa's blue eyes, wide and alarmed, stared sightlessly up at her.

"Papa!" A long keening cry issued from the depths of her soul. She collapsed over his still figure, burying her face in his chest. Footsteps pounded down the hall and someone shouted her name.

"Papa! Papa!" she sobbed, clutching his shoulders in a viselike grip.

Someone was trying to pull her away from Papa. She clung to him with all the strength left in her. Strong hands grasped her waist, lifted her upward, bearing her away down the hall, out into the darkness tinged with smoky red clouds. Powerful arms cradled her snugly against a rough-clad shoulder. Dimly she heard the sound of horses' hooves clattering down the cobbled street. Darkness closed in around her.

Chapter 40

Janine opened her eyes, squinting against the brilliant sunlight flooding the room, and quickly closed them. Her eyelids stung. Her throat felt scratchy. Slowly she opened her eyes again. She had a confused impression of a beamed ceiling, whitewashed walls, and a carved mahogany post at the foot of the bed on which she lay. Her gaze swept over the room, touching on a tall wardrobe, a carved teakwood chest, and a desk piled high with books and papers. Before the window stood a captain's chair and a table holding a brass candlestick and a spyglass.

She sat up and the chill air struck her shoulders, raising gooseflesh on her skin. With a gasp of surprise she perceived she was naked as a blue jay. Hastily she looked around for her clothes. They were nowhere to be seen. A soft hissing came from the bright orange and red flames licking at the grate in a fireplace across the room. On the mantel stood a pair of pewter candlesticks, a pipe stand, a candle snuffer. Janine shivered. The warmth of the fire failed to reach the bed and she sank down, burrowing deep into the feather tick.

Every bone in her body cried out with fatigue. She wanted to exist only here and now, looking neither ahead, nor into the past. She had closed a door, shutting out the past. It would not bear thinking about. Closing her eyes, she tried to sink into the pleasant release of sleep. Sounds from the street outside invaded the room: gulls mewling, pigs squealing, men shouting, carts clattering over cobblestones. The scent of pitch assailed her nostrils, mingled with the familiar odor of rotting fish. Sounds and smells of the waterfront, she thought dully.

She heard a door opening and closing softly, footsteps striding across the bare wood floor. Someone was standing beside the bed, watching her, waiting. . . .

She opened her eyes and she thought her heart would surely stop beating. Mark Furneaux stood over her, his thick brows furrowed, his mouth drawn down in lines of worry and anxiety. Looking up into his dark eyes, she saw sparks of light kindle and brighten as he gazed down at her.

"Little darling?" he said softly.

She could only stare at him in stunned silence.

He sat down on the side of the bed and smoothed her hair back from her face in a tender caress. Unbidden tears sprang to her eyes. She could cope with anything but his sympathy. Impatiently she brushed the tears away with the back of her hand. Mark took her hand and held it in his large warm ones. She tried to summon the courage to ask him the question tormenting her mind. She knew from his gentleness, his concern for her, what his answer would be, but she had to ask—to establish the reality, the truth of what she knew.

She ran her tongue over dry lips. "Papa?"

"Your Papa is dead, Janine. He lies in Christ Church burying ground."

Choking back the sob that rose in her throat, she dropped her gaze from his face and studied the black hairs on the back of his hand.

"Zoë and the children," she murmured. "Three lives saved for one given . . . that's the way Papa would count it . . . but his effort was to no purpose." Her voice quavered and she caught her lip between her teeth to still its trembling.

Mark took her chin in his hand and tilted her face

up to look at him. "Your father's death was not a futile sacrifice. He suffered a seizure of the heart."

Miserably Janine shook her head. "Papa didn't want to give up living. . . ."

"It was his time to go," said Mark softly. "Let him go gently. . . ."

Janine swallowed over the lump in her throat. "The house?"

Mark shook his head. "The brigade couldn't hose down all the roof. It caved in over the garret. There was little saved upstairs. Downstairs the smoke and the water took their toll. They saved what they could." He drew his finger lightly down the curve of her cheek to her chin. "We saved you, little darling."

Janine sighed deeply and turned her head away, staring out the window at the tattered clouds sailing across a vivid blue sky. "You must be weary unto death of saving me, Mark."

"God's death, but that's the truth of it!"

Stung by the vehemence in his voice, she jerked her head around to face him. The old amused, arrogant smile was there, mocking her.

With an effort she held her temper in check. "Then why in God's name do you continue to come to my rescue?"

Mark shrugged helplessly, and merriment sparkled in his dark eyes. "It's become something of a habit. . . ."

"Oh!" said Janine coldly. "And how did you manage it this time?"

"When I heard the church bells ringing out the fire alarm, I came on the run to help. I was sore distressed to see it was your neighbor's house afire. I looked for you." He grinned. "I owed you one, you see. I couldn't find you." His expression turned somber and he sighed heavily. "I did find Zoë. She had seen you flying down the alley around the back of your house, searching for your father. By then the brigade had evacuated the house, and I went in to bring you out."

Janine's voice was soft and incredulous. "You went in after me, after the fire fighters had fled for their lives like scared rabbits?"

Mark's brows rose and his mouth turned down at the corners in a rueful smile. "It was hard enough to lose you to another man, Janine. And that I've had to accept, however ungraciously. But I could not endure losing you to the flames. . . ."

"To *lose* me, Mark?" asked Janine wonderingly.

"Oh, well, I know I've never had you," he paused, grinning at her wickedly. "But I had the lunatic hope that things would work out so that someday—"

"Someday?" she asked softly.

"There's never been a time I've rescued you that I've not wished to claim the prize for my own."

Her heart raced wildly and she gazed at him speechless.

His face was quiet, almost somber, and there was no mockery in his eyes. "I truly love you, Janine."

Surely he couldn't mean what he was saying! Swift images swept through her mind of Mark laughing lovingly down at Anne Delaney in the State House yard, tucking her arm in his at the assembly ball, rushing away to meet her. Always, Anne Delaney. They had shared a life in which she had no part, and he had certainly made it plain enough that he sought out Anne Delaney's company and even preferred the woman's company to her own.

It came to her then that Mark was the sort of man who made the woman he was with feel that she was the only woman in the world. Only later would the lady discover to her great chagrin that she was but one star in his galaxy. Such actions hardly served to make her feel that he cared for her a whit more than the others, that she was the one true love of his life. And yet, here he was, confessing that he couldn't stand to lose her.

Janine gazed at him coolly. "I'm deeply flattered, but I daresay you are a man of easy emotions, heels-over-cock-a-hoop over the lady you happen to be attending at the moment."

An angry flush spread over his face, and in a hard, tight voice he said, "Didn't it ever occur to you that I loved you as much as a man can love a woman? Loved you for years! During the war I'd sail away to France, to the Indies, and try to forget you, but I didn't, and I always had to come back. Why do you think I risked my neck to save you from the firing squad—from a burning house? Oh, yes, I loved you, but I couldn't let you know it, you were so loyal to your Jonathan!"

Janine looked up to meet his dark eyes, full of pain and anger. She forced herself to speak through quivering lips.

"That's a strange thing for a man to be saying when he's betrothed to someone else, Mark."

He appeared thunderstruck. "Betrothed! *I'm* not the one who is betrothed to someone else!" His voice was harsh and his mouth turned down in a wry grimace.

Her blue eyes wide and incredulous, Janine burst out, "But, Mark, you told me not more than a month ago that you were planning to marry—that you had come to bid me a proper good-bye—and then you rushed away to the arms of your Anne Delaney!"

Mark threw back his head and laughed. "So that's it! Well, I cannot tell you the entire story now, but let it suffice to say that my association with Anne Delaney was connected with my work—feeding her false information concocted by General Washington to pass on to the British. If I'm not misinformed, the lady fled to New York immediately after Cornwallis surrendered and is now on the seas headed for the safety of England. Thank God we're rid of her!"

He sighed deeply and rose from the bed, turning his back as though he could not bear to look at her. "No, Janine, it was you I wished to marry—once again too late." There was a bitter note to his voice she'd never heard before.

He loves me! thought Janine ecstatically. Her heart sang and a feeling of such joy and happiness swept through her, she thought she would burst.

"I've sent your clothes to be laundered," he went on. "When they're ready, I'll escort you to your Doctor Ransom."

"I've no need for medical attention, Mark."

He spun around, staring at her in astonishment.

Janine sat up in bed, drawing the patchwork quilt high around her shoulders and looked him square in the eyes, her heart thudding so loud, she was sure he could hear it.

"I told Doctor Ransom that if he still wished to marry me after the war's end, I'd marry him." She felt herself blushing furiously. "I doubt he'd wish to marry a woman who loves someone else." A deep pang of regret for the pain she would cause this man who had shown her nothing but love and devotion swept through her. Still, much as she hated to hurt him, she knew it was best for both of them. And in time she hoped he would agree. Time—and marriage to a woman who could love him as he deserved to be loved —would heal Richard's wounded pride.

"Mark?" She held out her arms toward him.

Mark strode across the room and gathered her in his arms. Burying his face in the soft luxuriance of her hair, he murmured all the loving words she longed to hear.

8 MONTHS A NATIONAL BESTSELLER!

EVERGREEN

by

BELVA PLAIN

From shtetl to mansion—Evergreen is the wonderfully rich epic of Anna Friedman, who emigrates from Poland to New York, in search of a better life. Swirling from New York sweatshops to Viennese ballrooms, from suburban mansions to Nazi death camps, from riot-torn campuses to Israeli Kibbutzim, Evergreen evokes the dramatic life of one woman, a family's fortune and a century's hopes and tragedies.

A Dell Book $2.75   (13294-0)

Dell Bestsellers

☐ TO LOVE AGAIN by Danielle Steel $2.50 (18631-5)
☐ SECOND GENERATION by Howard Fast $2.75 (17892-4)
☐ EVERGREEN by Belva Plain $2.75 (13294-0)
☐ AMERICAN CAESAR by William Manchester . . . $3.50 (10413-0)
☐ THERE SHOULD HAVE BEEN CASTLES
   by Herman Raucher $2.75 (18500-9)
☐ THE FAR ARENA by Richard Ben Sapir $2.75 (12671-1)
☐ THE SAVIOR by Marvin Werlin and Mark Werlin . $2.75 (17748-0)
☐ SUMMER'S END by Danielle Steel $2.50 (18418-5)
☐ SHARKY'S MACHINE by William Diehl $2.50 (18292-1)
☐ DOWNRIVER by Peter Collier $2.75 (11830-1)
☐ CRY FOR THE STRANGERS by John Saul $2.50 (11869-7)
☐ BITTER EDEN by Sharon Salvato $2.75 (10771-7)
☐ WILD TIMES by Brian Garfield $2.50 (19457-1)
☐ 1407 BROADWAY by Joel Gross $2.50 (12819-6)
☐ A SPARROW FALLS by Wilbur Smith $2.75 (17707-3)
☐ FOR LOVE AND HONOR by Antonia Van-Loon . . $2.50 (12574-X)
☐ COLD IS THE SEA by Edward L. Beach $2.50 (11045-9)
☐ TROCADERO by Leslie Waller $2.50 (18613-7)
☐ THE BURNING LAND by Emma Drummond $2.50 (10274-X)
☐ HOUSE OF GOD by Samuel Shem, M.D. $2.50 (13371-8)
☐ SMALL TOWN by Sloan Wilson $2.50 (17474-0)

At your local bookstore or use this handy coupon for ordering:

Dell DELL BOOKS
P.O. BOX 1000, PINEBROOK, N.J. 07058

Please send me the books I have checked above. I am enclosing $ _____
(please add 75¢ per copy to cover postage and handling). Send check or money
order—no cash or C.O.D.'s. Please allow up to 8 weeks for shipment.

Mr/Mrs/Miss _____

Address _____

City _____ State/Zip _____